D1522368

1

TABLE OF CONTENTS

DEDICATION

To Cece Younger, former member of the U.S. Equestrian Team, and her family, for their help in researching this book. And to the riders and horses of the USET who bring honor and glory to our country.

PROLOGUE

XVII Olympiad
Rome, Italy
Summer 1960

The crackling hum of the buzzer sounded a sixty second warning. In the stadium arena, the Swedish rider, a slender, fine-boned man, shoulders squared, back straight, cantered his sleek gray gelding in circles, preparing to begin the jumps. Only the competitors waiting nervously along the fence knew the tension the man was feeling.

The rider didn't acknowledge the cheering crowds applauding his entry. His concentration remained on the gray horse prancing beneath him and the gold medal round of show jumping he was about to begin. As the noise in the stadium subsided, the man urged the gelding into a faster gait, heading down the path that led to the first fence, a red and white vertical, five feet high.

Behind the fence, mounted and waiting for the seconds to tick past and his own turn at the jumps, Janus Straka watched the Swede only a moment, taking in the precision of man and animal as they cleared the last fence with the soft thud of hoof against rail. A potted white chrysanthemum shook on its perch atop the uprights but didn't result in a fault. The Swede was a talented rider and a tough competitor—but so was Janus Straka.

Since his arrival in Rome, Janus had ridden like the skilled rider he was. At nineteen, black-haired and blue-eyed, a Hungarian Soviet from the southern slopes of the Carpathian Mountains, he had trained with his father since childhood, trained without pause for fifteen years— all for these next few crucial moments. Everything he'd ever done, everything he'd ever wanted, depended on this round.

Though he was the youngest rider in the competition, he had

trained with Stefan Straka, one of the finest horsemen in the world.

Settling himself against the familiar smooth surface of his saddle, Janus took the forward seat his father had taught him fifteen years ago, comfortable in the subtle indentations of the leather. In seconds he would be entering the ring to compete in the final round of the competition. Time and accuracy over the jumps would decide the winner of the Olympic gold medal.

Janus took a steadying breath and forced himself to relax. As he'd done a thousand times, he adjusted the iron stirrups beneath his black knee-high boots until they rested securely against the balls of his feet. He stood up, testing their length in proportion to his long legs. From years of repetition, he made the same exact movements without conscious thought.

Janus glanced around the Stadio Olympico, the magnificent hundred thousand seat stadium filled to capacity for the individual equestrian show jumping competition. He could feel the tension in the crowd, the nervous silence as all eyes focused on the rider straining for victory in the middle of the ring.

Janus blotted the perspiration from his brow with the back of a leather-gloved hand. The Rome sun beat down without mercy on his black-billed cap, seared his shoulders beneath his dark serge coat. Olympic programs in ten different languages waved an urgent breeze against faces glowing with perspiration and the excitement of the event.

"You must not try too hard, Janus." A gnarled hand patted his thigh. The familiar, lined face of Eugeny Radchenko, the show jumping coach, lit with a grin. "The gold is yours, my friend, I can feel it. Filov has won our first medal, now it is your turn."

Janus forced a smile. Sergei Filov had taken the gold medal in the dressage event held in the Piazza del Siena inside the Villa Borghese. It was a first for the Soviets in any Olympic equestrian event.

"Even Cossack can feel it," Eugeny said, running his thick-fingered hand along the sleek neck of the blood bay stallion tossing its head in nervous anticipation, ears twitching beside the dark strands of his topknot that fluttered in the breeze. "He will soar over the jumps. He wants the medal as much as you do."

The Swedish rider finished the round with eight faults in forty-three point two seconds, his horse lathered with sweat and pulling at the bit with unspent energy, but the time wouldn't win him the gold today.

The crowd applauded loudly, showing their appreciation, then settled into a restless hum.

Janus could hear their shuffling feet, the drone of distant conversation. A vendor passed, his cart loaded with warm roasted peanuts, but Janus knew the aroma of food wasn't the cause of his roiling stomach or the brittle, parched texture of his tongue. He swallowed against the dryness, then the voice on the microphone, the words spoken in Italian, English, and French, echoed on the stadium walls, and the crowd fell silent.

"From the Union of Soviet Socialist Republic—the horse, Cossack. The rider, Janus Straka."

A burst of applause rising from the grandstand blotted the rest of the announcer's words. Cheers, stomping feet, and clapping hands spoke their approval and mirrored the friendly Italian welcome that had marked the games of the XVII Olympiad.

Janus carefully slotted the reins between his tightly gloved fingers and tried to ignore the dampness of his hands inside the leather. Only one rider still waited to complete the jump-off round, Raimonde d'Inzeo of Italy, the favorite. So far, the time to beat was forty-two point twelve seconds with four faults. The course was difficult, the time to beat, fast.

But if he pushed hard, set the pace and encouraged Cossack to the greatness the stallion possessed, Janus believed he had a chance to win the gold. It was a chance for honor and glory. A chance to be remembered along with other men of greatness—the chance of a lifetime.

But Janus Straka would not claim that chance. There was something he wanted more.

"Good luck, Comrade." Eugeny gave him a final nod as Janus straightened in the saddle. He took a last long look at the aged face of the man who had been his friend, the man who had, along with his father, schooled him, prodded him, and led him to this moment, this test of greatness.

"Thank you for all you've done," Janus said. "I will never forget you." Without waiting for a reply, he whirled the big bay stallion and rode toward the ring.

As he cantered through the gates, a look around the stadium bolstered his courage. Nikolai Popov in his serviceable brown suit, white shirt, and non-descript tie, stood watching from behind the arena fence, speaking in quiet conversation with some of his KGB security men. A few moments from now, Popov would be his chief concern, but for the present his concentration had to remain on the jumps.

Janus rode around the arena, cantering between the rear fences to give Cossack a look at the course. The jumps were huge and lavishly decorated with flowers, shrubs, and banners. In the first round, Cossack had snorted at the newness, then willingly accepted the challenge. Now he seemed almost eager.

The buzzer sounded and Janus passed through the beam of the timer, beginning the round that would decide the course of his life.

With a last glance at the audience and a long steadying breath, he let instinct take over and increased the pace. Cossack cleared the first fence with ease. The footing was solid, the horse's landing perfect. Janus pressed him, knowing him capable, riding against the clock, trying to discern the fine line between completing the course without knocking over a rail and beating the time of the first-place competitor. No matter the outcome, he would compete as the champion he had trained to be.

The second fence was more difficult, a parallel jump set at an angle. A row of box hedges along the bottom made it a little deceptive. Another vertical lay ahead, then an in-and-out combination that taxed both horse and rider with its demand for perfect timing. A six-foot brick wall loomed four strides farther. Janus urged Cossack forward, leaning above his neck at precisely the right moment, urging the big bay over the jump. The audience applauded wildly, then hushed.

Another vertical fence, then a parallel jump. He could feel Cossack's stride, the tremendous power of the animal beneath him and knew the horse's speed was holding up. The click of a hoof as it cleared the bar brought the crowd to its feet. The final obstacle was a water jump painted red and white and lined with small greenish-gray cypress. The jump sat at an angle, four short strides in front of the seven-foot arena fence that closed off the back-alley entrance.

Janus pressed Cossack forward, setting him up for the water jump—*and the fence leading to the streets behind the arena.* Giving up precious speed for the difficult combination ahead and the huge height of the outside fence, he slowed the animal's pace.

Janus held his breath. If Cossack failed him now, the result would be injury and defeat for them both.

The crowd roared as they cleared the water jump, making it look almost easy. Then he did the unthinkable. Janus missed the final turn toward the timer, kept up the pace he had set—and urged the big stallion over the outside fence. A hoof ticked the top, and for an instant time seemed frozen.

Then Cossack's hooves clattered against the pavement as he landed, the sound muffled by the shrieks of the astonished crowd.

Janus didn't look back. He could hear men shouting his name, hear their pounding feet as they tried to catch up with him, feel the rapid thudding of his heart. He raced Cossack down the alley between the towering rows of spectator seats, dodging contestants, vendors, media people, news cameras, and the blinding strobe of flash bulbs.

Two men jumped in front of him and grabbed for the reins. At first, he thought they were KGB and his hands tensed on the leather. Cossack knocked them reeling, just helpful spectators, thinking the horse had bolted. Pounding on, he finally broke free, but he didn't stop until he'd left the stadium far behind.

Reining up some distance away, out of sight of all but a few prying eyes, he hurriedly dismounted and tied the horse behind the ruins of an ancient Roman wall. There he stripped off his cap and perspiration-drenched wool jacket.

Cossack nickered softly.

"They will take you home," Janus said as if the horse could understand. He ran a hand along the animal's neck, now damp with sweat from his exertion. "I shall miss you, my friend." With a last glance at the proud animal that had carried him so far, Janus stepped away, melding into the surging humanity leaving the Olympic grounds.

He was on his way to the American Embassy. On his way, he prayed to a new life. On his way to freedom.

For as far back as Janus could remember, his father had dreamed of being free, as he had been before the war. It was a dream he had passed on to his son. Now Janus was making that dream come true. He didn't know what to expect or where his journey would lead. He knew only that it was a journey he must make.

Janus hailed a cab, folded his tall frame into the backseat, and spoke to the driver in heavily accented Italian the single phrase he had practiced over and over—"*Ambasciata degli Stati Unita, Via Vittorio*

Veneto 119, Palazzo Margherita." The address of the U.S. Embassy.

The little yellow taxi pulled away from the curb and into the bustling Rome traffic. Horns honked and people cursed but Janus barely heard them. He kept his head down and hoped he had enough of a start to reach the consulate before Nikolai Popov and his men could intercept him. He'd left the stadium and his teammates in chaos. Popov and his KGB security people would be looking for him everywhere.

He wondered how long the KGB man would keep up his search. As Chief of Security for the Soviet Team, Popov wasn't a man who easily accepted defeat.

Janus shuddered at the thought. He knew the man would suffer a tremendous embarrassment, that the incident would be a detriment to his ambitious political career.

Janus Straka also knew, till the day he died, he would wonder if he could have won the gold.

CIA Headquarters
Langley, West Virginia
1960

"Sit down, Mr. Straka, make yourself comfortable. I'm Daniel Gage." Leaning over a stack of manila files that sat in rows along the front of his desk, Gage extended a wide-palmed hand, engulfing Janus's more slender, darker one in a firm, self-assured grip.

Janus sat down in a straight-backed wooden chair and carefully positioned one arm on the armrest, trying to appear nonchalant, which was far from how he felt.

"I trust your trip from Europe was not unpleasant," Gage said. With his round face, hazel eyes, and warm smile, Daniel Gage seemed a common man, a man of the people, and then again, he did not. Barrel-chested, Gage's slightly crooked nose looked as though it had been broken. Janus suspected he was younger than the years his lightly freckled face betrayed. Younger and tougher.

"Your people were very competent," Janus said. "They saw to everything. I thank you." He shifted nervously in his chair.

The CIA headquarters building near Washington, D.C. was much as he'd expected: long corridors, doors leading to small, confined offices occupied by dark-suited figures who all looked much the same. At home, KGB headquarters probably appeared very similar. But there the similarity ended.

The United States of America was nothing like Janus expected, nothing like he'd imagined even after all the hours he and his father had spent talking about it.

"There are some questions I'd like to ask you," Gage said. "We might as well get started."

"Of course." Janus found himself liking the American's no-nonsense attitude, liking the candid way the man looked him straight in the eye.

"You lived in Moscow, is that correct?"

"Since I was nine. I was born in Beregovo, Ruthenia. I am Hungarian, not Russian."

"I see." Daniel scanned the manila folder that lay open on his burn-scarred walnut desk. Picking up the cigarette smoldering in the ashtray, he took a deep, soothing draw and watched the young Soviet rider across from him.

Straka carefully worked to hide his nervousness and was doing a damned good job. Only an occasional sideways glance from his astonishing blue eyes hinted at how ill-at-ease the young man actually was.

Tall and spare, with angular features that made him look more man than boy, Straka rested an elbow on his armrest while one long leg stretched a little in front of the other. Blue-black hair, so thick and shiny it reflected the fluorescent light overhead, curled just above his collar.

Daniel admired Straka's fortitude but with Khrushchev in power, Soviet relations were strained at best. Daniel needed to know exactly why Janus Straka had come to the United States and had already taken the steps necessary to determine exactly that.

In the weeks since Straka's defection, Daniel's men had put together a dossier that covered every aspect of the young man's life. Daniel had read the file more than once.

He glanced down at the page. Janus Straka, only son of Stefan Straka, an international celebrity in the horse world in the nineteen twenties and thirties. At the turn of the century, Stefan's father, Vaclav Straka, a wealthy landowner, had accepted a political appointment in Ruthenia, then controlled by the Austria-Hungary Hapsburg Dynasty. In 1920, Czechoslovakia took over the government, but the Strakas decided to stay.

At twenty, Stefan Straka joined the Czechoslovakian cavalry, a career that gave him the chance to work with the horses he loved. As a lieutenant, Stefan participated in the IX Olympics in Amsterdam, winning the silver medal in the individual show jumping event.

Daniel rolled a yellow pencil between his thumb and forefinger, his thick hands the result of too many fistfights in too many unnamed Korean bars during his Army years. He'd been recruited by the agency when it was time to re-up four years ago. Since then, he'd traveled extensively and already become a senior case officer. He loved the work, the excitement, and especially the danger.

"Tell me about your father," Daniel prodded.

For the first time, Straka smiled, softening his features and betraying his youth. "He was one of the finest horsemen in the world," Straka said in his heavily accented English. "He rode in three Olympics. He won a silver medal at Amsterdam."

"Your father once visited this country," Daniel said, encouraging Straka to continue.

"Yes. In nineteen thirty-two. He loved the people and the opportunity he saw all around him. He believed that in America a man could achieve whatever he was willing to work for. All his life he wanted to come here. Listening to him made me want to come, too."

"Enough to defect, even after his death?"

The piercing blue eyes dimmed for an instant. "We planned for years in secret. He came up with the idea for Rome. By then I wanted to leave as much as he did. When he died...it was a great loss to us all."

"What about your family? Won't you miss them? Who will take care of them?"

"I will send whatever I can. My mother and I were never close. My sister, Dana, is eleven years older. They knew I would go if I ever got the chance."

"Why didn't your father come to the States before the war? He was a wealthy man. He could have afforded to make the move."

"He had responsibilities, family to think about. After the Soviets took over, he regretted not leaving. He never got used to the repression, the constant mistrust. He was Hungarian. He never accepted Soviet domination."

Daniel glanced back at the file. In 1950, Stefan Straka moved to Moscow to lend his skills to the Soviet Team. Janus was nine and already a horseman. He learned to speak Russian and improve his English, graduated from the University of Moscow and became a member of the team the following year. His record was impressive, the man even more so.

"What will you do in this country?"

"It is my dream to become an American. I wish to go to school to perfect my English. I want to become a citizen."

"You're a fine rider, Janus. One of the best in the world. After what happened in Rome, you're a celebrity—"

"That is not what I want," Janus interrupted. "I want to change my name, make my way on my own. I am a private person, Mr. Gage. I do not enjoy...how do you say? No-tor-it-y?"

"Notoriety."

"Yes, notor-i-ety. I want to be as you are. I want to live my own life, my own way."

"I won't lie to you, Janus. Your father may have had a somewhat romantic picture of life in the States. If you use your celebrity, things could be a whole lot easier for you."

"That is a decision I made years ago. I have not changed by mind. I am just grateful for the chance."

"What about Popov?" Daniel asked.

"You know him?"

"Only by reputation. Will he give you any trouble?"

"I do not think so. I know no military secrets. I am just an ordinary man."

Not so ordinary, Daniel thought, then he smiled. "The arrangements have already been made. I just wanted to be certain."

Daniel shoved back his chair. Straka stood up as Daniel rounded the desk and extended a hand, which Janus shook.

Daniel was eight years older than the tall man in front of him. But there was something in his eyes, a look of determination and gratitude. Daniel felt the power and believed Janus Straka would succeed in whatever he attempted.

Daniel leaned across his desk and picked up a piece of paper. "There's a man in Florida named Thurston Brock. He knows who you are, but I've explained your desire for privacy, and he has agreed to help you."

He handed the paper to Straka. "He'll give you a job while you're going to language school here in Washington. Then later if things work out and you want to join him at his stable in South Carolina, he'll give you a job there, working with his horses. Brock owns one of the finest strings of jumpers in the country."

"I am very grateful."

"From now on you'll be Jake Sullivan. Sound American enough for you?"

"Jake," he repeated with the hint of a smile. "It pleases me. You have been more than kind, Mr. Gage. I will never forget all that you and your people have done for me."

"I won't be far away if you need me."

Janus prayed the United States government would not be

19

watching over this shoulder with secret cameras and listening devices as the Soviets had done in Moscow. His father had said it was not so. But Janus would live unobtrusively, watch, and wait. Soon he would know the truth about America.

In the meantime, he had the opportunity to build the life he had dreamed. He owed a great debt to the man with the face of a youthful Ukrainian farmer. With his confident manner, Daniel Gage inspired trust in a man.

Instinctively, Janus felt he had made a friend. Still, he wondered if his instincts would prove correct.

"Come on," Daniel offered, "it's about time for lunch. Why don't we grab a bite, then I'll take you over to the Berlitz language school. They can help you get rid of that accent if anyone can."

Janus nodded. Daniel held open the heavy door and Janus moved past him into a corridor bustling with dark-suited men.

"Smoke?" Daniel offered, pulling a pack of Camels from his inside coat pocket.

"Thank you." Janus lifted one from the pack, waited while Daniel took one, then they shared a match to light up. Janus inhaled deeply, exhaling a trailing blue plume. The smooth American tobacco tasted mild in comparison to the harsh Soviet brand he'd smoked at home.

I *am* home, he corrected, and felt the same exhilaration he had been feeling since he'd first arrived.

Janus exhaled the smoke and took a long deep breath. Even the air in America smelled free.

CHAPTER ONE
Los Angeles, California
April 1988

Maggie Delaine tried to conceal her nerves as she walked along the narrow, white-fenced lane that led into the Los Angeles Equestrian Center. She was on her way to the judging stand and the final day of competition in the Grand Prix Classic.

Riders in breeches and hunt caps passed those in cowboy hats and chaps, but none seemed to notice her, each feeling the tension of a world-class competition. Even with her nerves on edge, it felt good to be a member of the elite society of horsemen at last.

She wondered what Les would say if he could see her—the newly appointed Assistant Director of the United States Equestrian Team. Her late husband would never have thought she'd be capable of handling the job, but a lot had changed in the past four years.

"Hello, Maggie." Shep Singleton, one of the riders, waved as she walked by.

Maggie waved and smiled as Shep rode on. The day was blustery, whipping strands of blond hair around her face. The wind had blown most of the usual L.A. smog away, exposing the mountains in the distance. The equestrian center nestled at the base of the hills.

Nearing the stands, Maggie passed several more familiar faces, but their attention was fixed on the ominous-looking fences dominating the center of the arena or on the animals they were riding. As the day progressed, horse and rider would be tested to the limits of their endurance and knew what was at stake.

Walking next to the wind-tousled, umbrella-topped tables surrounding the grassy arena, Maggie headed for the staging area. There the competitors were warming up over practice fences. Maggie watched the graceful movements of horses and riders taking the jumps, low

21

fences in comparison to those they would face in the Grand Prix.

She felt a pang of regret that her nine-year-old daughter, Sarah, couldn't be there with her. Just as her late husband had, his daughter loved horses. But Maggie hadn't wanted her to miss school, and the trip was long and tiring, and strange hotel rooms weren't conducive to a good night's rest.

"Hello, Maggie. Didn't expect to see you here."

A gust of wind fluttered the pant legs of William Fletcher's beige gabardine slacks and the sleeves of his blue oxford shirt."

"Hello, Will." The same breeze ruffled Maggie's white silk pantsuit. "You heard about my appointment?"

"Of course." Will smiled. "Congratulations. No one deserves the position more than you do."

"They didn't really expect me to be here for the judging since I only accepted last week, but something came up that needed my attention, so I decided to head west a day early."

Will laid a protective hand on the petite young woman beside him. "You remember my daughter, Ellie?"

"Of course." *How could she forget?* Though Maggie had seen Ellen Fletcher at only a few East Coast competitions, they had met the day before the car accident that had killed Maggie's husband.

The Fletchers had been in Tampa Bay for the horse show. Afterward, both couples and their children had gone out to dinner. During the evening, Maryann Fletcher, Ellie's mother, had quietly explained that because of Ellie's partial blindness their daughter rarely accompanied them on the show jumping circuit, but they'd turned the trip into a vacation of sorts and convinced Ellie and her brother, Tommy, to come along.

That had been a little over four years ago. Ellie had been twenty, a petite yet curvy young lady much shorter than Maggie's tall, slender frame, with a pretty face, and thick dark auburn hair.

Four years ago, huge horned-rimmed glasses with Coke-bottle thick lenses distorted her eyes, giving them the appearance of great green trout in a fishbowl. Through surgery, today the glasses were gone, the nightmare of Ellie's seeing disorder a well-guarded secret.

"I assume you'll be competing today." Maggie noticed Ellie kept glancing over her shoulder at the horses taking the fences in the practice ring.

She nodded. "I drew number eighteen. That should give me a chance to watch some of the others ride before I take the course."

Her hand trembled as she tucked a strand of red-brown hair up under her riding cap. "I'm a little nervous, but Jubilee has been working well. He's more than willing, as always."

"From what I've read, he's been performing like a champion." In the past twelve months, Jubilee and Ellen Fletcher had become top contenders. Her performance at the Olympic selection trials had only been average, but she still had a chance, albeit a slim one. Today's competition would weigh heavily as to whether she would make the Olympic team and be competing this summer in Europe, then go on to Seoul.

"I need to start warming up." Ellie made a weak attempt at a smile. "It was nice to see you again, Mrs. Delaine."

Her father gave her a hug. "You'll do fine, honey."

Ellie managed another un-smile and headed off toward the stables. Maggie noticed several appreciative glances cast the girl's way as she walked past in her tight beige riding breeches. She had a full-busted figure many women would envy, though she seemed unaware of her charms.

Maggie smiled. "I'd better get going. I'll be crossing my fingers for Ellie." She waved to Will and started walking, then noticed a man in conversation with one of the riders. For an instant, the ground seemed to tilt beneath her feet.

She should have been prepared for this. She thought she had been.

"Are you alright?" Will asked, catching up with her.

Maggie forced a calm she didn't feel. "I'm fine. I just...I should have eaten breakfast, I guess."

Unwillingly, Maggie's eyes fixed on Jake Sullivan, the taller of the men in conversation. His wavy black hair, touched with silver at the temples, curled above the collar of his shirt. Maggie remembered the way it felt between her fingers. Tiny lines radiated out from the corners of his eyes, a brilliant, mesmerizing blue.

"I've got to go," Will said. "I need to talk to Ellie's coach before her round begins. I'll see you later."

Maggie barely heard him. Will moved off across the hoof-torn grass and Maggie looked at Jake. She wondered if he was there with a woman. The fact she cared stirred a self-directed shot of disgust. How could Jake still affect her after nearly a year?

She had known she would run into him sooner or later. He was *Chef d 'Equipe,* head coach of the U.S. Olympic show jumping team. She'd taken that fact into consideration before she'd accepted the job as assistant director. She'd just been caught off guard.

With a calming breath, Maggie headed for her place in judging stand. After her husband's death four years ago, she had immersed herself in the horse world he had loved, reading every journal, determined to know as much about what was happening as she possibly could. Eventually, she'd accepted the job as Assistant Director of the U.S. Equestrian Team.

Now that she was in L.A, fully immersed in her role, Maggie wondered if Les would have been proud of her.

Climbing into the booth, she greeted the judges, took her seat and began making pleasant conversation. But as she waited for the show to start, her thoughts drifted from the colorful sights and sounds, back to a time in the not-so distant past.

It was the day of Les' funeral. She and Sarah were sitting in front of the casket beneath a dark green canopy. The Florida air smelled musky though the mound of damp earth from the grave was covered with a canvas tarp.

Maggie held onto the five-year-old's small hand, as moist and clammy as the air around them. Her own felt cold and dry. It seemed like an eternity since the funeral had begun in the grassy cemetery on the hill, but finally, mercifully, even the graveside portion of the service was over.

There was nothing to do now but accept the condolences of the throng of people around her. Dozens of horsemen were in attendance, people Les had competed with as a rider or been involved with in his work as director of the three-day eventing team. Someone handed her an Olympic flag.

She remembered seeing the Fletchers, more emotional than some of the others since they'd all been together the night before the accident. Through her thick horn-rimmed glasses, Ellie must have seen her as a faceless blur.

Then Jake Sullivan had spoken in his deep masculine voice. "My condolences, Mrs. Delaine." Jake was an assistant coach then, a rider and an accomplished horse breeder who lived in Charleston, South Carolina. Les had known him well, but until that day, Maggie had never met him.

"Thank you." In her numbed and disoriented state, she hadn't thought of him again until later when she had remembered his reputation as a loner, a man obsessed with privacy, and wondered what made him that way.

Footsteps sounded, snapping her out of the past. "You seem a little lost, Maggie. Don't let all this tension rub off on you."

She glanced up to see Clayton Whitfield grinning down at her, a broad smile dimpling his cheeks. Muscular and handsome with dark brown hair and warm brown eyes, Clay looked at the whole world as his private amusement park.

He was the top rider in the country, certain to make the team even if he made a poor showing today—which was highly unlikely since Clay rarely put in a less than shining performance.

"I guess I am a little nervous. Everything's so new to me and I want to do a good job. Besides, there seems to be something in the air. Everyone's a little tense."

"Not a damned thing in my air," Clay said. "Max and Warrior are both more than ready, and so am I." Max was Maximum Effort, a huge blood bay stallion, the best show jumper in the nation. Warrior was the second horse Clay had entered in the event.

"The only thing I'm nervous about," Clay said, "is whether that cute little blonde across the way is going out with me tonight." He tipped his head toward a woman near the entry gate and Maggie couldn't help but smile.

"Are you sure you mean *out?* The way I hear it, the only place you take a date is up to your room."

Clay flashed another grin. "Don't go prudish on me, Maggie." He's smile slowly faded. "You know it wouldn't hurt you to try it— dating someone, I mean."

It wasn't meant to be one of Clay's come-on remarks. He knew her affair with Jake had ended badly and he was showing his concern. Unlike most of the women he considered his playthings, Clay had always treated her with respect. Initially because of Les, then later because of her involvement with Jake.

At thirty-one, Clay was seven years younger than Maggie, but they were friends of a sort. Maggie knew he carried some deeply buried childhood scars and a loneliness he glossed over with his give-a-damn attitude and cavalier ways. He antagonized most of the riders, the rest were jealous of his unequaled talent. Though she often found him exasperating, Maggie liked Clay.

She just wished he liked himself.

Clay left the booth and Maggie glanced across the arena to find Ellie Fletcher in conversation with Jake. Unconsciously her fingers tightened in her lap.

Surely Ellie wasn't the object of Jake's affections? Maggie shook her head. No, if Jake was involved with someone, it wouldn't be Ellie. She was pretty enough, but at forty-seven, Jake's tastes ran to older, more sophisticated women—and he never mixed business with pleasure.

Ellie Fletcher fidgeted with the riding crop dangling from her wrist.

"Where's your coach?" Jake asked.

"I can't find him and it's almost time for my round. I need all the help I can get, Jake. Is there anything you can tell me that will help?"

Like everyone else today, Jake seemed a little restless, his gaze darting back and forth over the crowd. Ellie wondered if he had seen Maggie, if that was the reason he seemed so on edge. But Jake had been nervous and jumpy the last few times she'd seen him, more withdrawn than usual. They were friends and had been for years, but Jake was an extremely private person who rarely confided his thoughts to anyone.

"I walked the course a while ago," he said. "It's tough, all right. The first jump looks worse than it is, the second is worse than it looks. There's a big oxer like the one I took at Montreal in '76. The damned thing nearly got me killed. Watch the way it spreads out beneath you, the way part of it falls in shadow."

Ellie nodded and they both looked back out at the jumps. She'd met Jake Sullivan through her father four years ago, right after her eye surgery. He was one of the few people in the show jumping world who knew her secret, since he had coached her for a while after she was first able to see.

Though she looked perfectly normal, she'd been born with a seeing defect, her eyes misshapen, more elongated than round, causing an astigmatism. She was also myopic—nearsighted.

By itself, the myopia could have been corrected with prescription lenses, but the combination of the two, and the unusual degree of severity, made normal vision impossible. Even wearing glasses, she had lived in a world of blurred shapes and fuzzy colors, light and shadow without form, all tilted at disturbing angles.

Fortunately, if she held the books close enough, she was able to read and get an education.

Then a little over four years ago, her father brought Dr. Albert Halstein to see her. She'd been out in the barn at first light, feeding, watering, and grooming, followed by her daily two-hour riding practice.

The arena had been set up especially for her, with low practice fences carefully positioned to school Gentle Lady, her sorrel mare. Ellie knew the height of the jumps, and though she couldn't see them clearly, their bright red color allowed her to gage the distance between them.

Once Lady was warmed up, Ellie took the three-foot fences with ease, using her senses and the feel of the horse beneath her instead of her eyes. Sometimes she wondered if her inability to focus wasn't an asset instead of a liability.

Except that she was limited to riding in the practice arena, and taking higher fences was out of the question. It was just too dangerous.

"There you are!" her father said. "You can finish working Lady later. There's someone I'd like you to meet."

Ellie dismounted, handed the reins to a groom, and took her father's hand to lead her out of the arena. The family owned five acres in the middle of Hope Ranch, an exclusive development on the Santa Barbara coast. From the house and grounds, Ellie could see the blue color that distinguished the ocean, though some days it was difficult to tell where sky left off and water began.

"Dr. Halstein, this is my daughter, Ellie."

The doctor, a thin, stoop-shouldered man, extended a fine-boned hand. Ellie caught the movement and extended her own. The doctor adjusted his reach in order to connect.

"Dr. Halstein is here to talk to us about a new surgical procedure that might be able to help you," her father said.

Ellie felt the familiar knot in the pit of her stomach. How many times had she been through this same routine?

"How new is it?" she asked, an unwanted edge to her voice.

The doctor just smiled. "Myopia surgery was introduced here five years ago. By then, doctors in Russia had been using the procedure for some time. It's still considered experimental in this country, though I and dozens of others are convinced of its safety."

"Surely my father told you I have astigmatism as well," she said.

"I was coming to that." Patiently he explained the procedure, a radial keratotomy. "If, after testing," he finished, "we decide you're a candidate, it's possible for you to achieve completely normal vision."

Shock ran through her. No promise so big had ever been made. If she agreed, she'd be setting herself up for another disappointment. But if it worked?

"I've seen the results myself," her father said. "You've got to let him test you, honey."

Ellie swallowed hard and nodded. "Yes," was all she said.

CHAPTER TWO

"You've got plenty of time to watch the riders." Jake's voice pulled Ellie out of the past and back to the moment. "Pay close attention to Whitfield. These spread jumps are his meat and potatoes. Unless I miss my guess, he'll make that oxer look easy."

Whitfield. Always it was Clayton Whitfield. "Thanks, Jake. I know how busy you are." She'd watch Clay Whitfield, all right. There was nobody better. But God, what a conceited, self-centered ass! She'd once had a crush on him—when she was younger and dumber. She was a whole lot smarter now. Besides, Whitfield barely knew she existed.

She flicked a last glance at Jake. "Keep your fingers crossed for me, will you?"

He smiled. "Good luck, Ellie."

She watched Jake's retreating figure as he headed toward a group of riders near the edge of the staging area. For the past few days, he'd seemed distracted. But Ellie's own nerves were stretched to the breaking point.

Everything she'd trained for, everything she'd dreamed of, rested on this competition. She'd done so poorly in the last set of trials she'd have no chance at all if she made a bad showing today. On the other hand, she'd put in an outstanding performance at Phoenix and again at Rancho Murrieta. Maybe that would help.

Clamping down on her anxiety, Ellie listened as the speaker announced the start of the event. Denny Beeson, a top competitor, had drawn the number one slot.

The rules were simple: horse and rider had to complete the course in the time allotted or receive time faults. For every fence knocked down, two points were lost. If the horse refused a jump, three points were lost. Three refusals were a disqualification. Riders who went clear in the time allotted went into a second-round jump-off over a revised course, shorter, but often more difficult.

This being an Olympic selection event, the fences had been set for the highest degree of difficulty. To Ellie it looked insurmountable.

Denny must have been having similar thoughts. He clipped the first fence, a tall red and white vertical, knocking the rail from its cup. The second fence went no better. Then his horse, Windsong, seemed to settle down—until the gelding reached the triple combination in the middle of the course. Three refusals and Denny and Windsong left the arena in head-hanging defeat.

Ellie's heart hammered. How in God's name would she and Jubil get through it?

The next four riders made an equally poor showing, and Ellie began to worry the course was insurmountable. It didn't happen often and wasn't the objective of the course designer, who wanted to challenge.

The fifth rider to enter the arena was Clay Whitfield—more appropriately, Clayton Whitfield III. She'd been watching him ride since she'd first been able to see, been reading about him since long before that. Her father had spoken of him often, his skill with the horses, his rowdy escapades, and when he thought she wasn't within earshot, Clay's expertise with women.

The latter, Ellie could easily understand.

Riding his second entry of the day, Whitfield cantered around the arena on a big black stallion named Warrior, looking like the hero in every girl's fantasy. Tanned and handsome, he had thick dark brown hair, a powerful build with a vee-shaped torso, and long, muscular legs. A pair of dimples flashed whenever he smiled, making the women drool.

"He's entered two horses," her father said as he walked up beside her. "This one's green as it gets—it's Warrior's first Grand Prix. The stallion's got good blood, but he's too hot. Not much chance Whitfield can hold him down enough for a win."

"If anyone can, he can," Ellie said grudgingly. "He certainly isn't worried about impressing the judges."

"He's bound to be selected."

"You'd think he could at least pretend a little humility."

Her father chuckled. "Clay may be a lot of things, but humble

30

isn't one of them."

She watched as Whitfield touched the bill of his cap to signal the start of his round. At first it appeared her father's prediction would prove true. The stallion pranced and pulled at the bit and began to lather even before the tone signaled the start. But Whitfield held him easily, controlling him with seemingly little effort, soothing him with a gentle pat or an undistinguishable word.

As the horse broke into a canter, it strained with bottled-up energy. The stallion rushed the first fence, over-jumping it, using more power than needed. The second was almost a disaster, the animal cutting the curve too close, then landing wrong. It seemed they were bound to err, but at the middle of the course, Clay's ride remained faultless.

The difficult triple combination, a five-foot-wide double oxer, followed by a Liverpool water jump, and ending with another tough oxer, waited two fences ahead. The triple was painted brown, difficult for the horses to see, the fences close together, allowing the animal only two short strides in between.

Clay took the eighth and ninth fences, setting himself up for the triple. The stallion had settled into a graceful, second-eating gate while still clearing the jumps with inches to spare. By now the pair moved with such precision it seemed as if each knew what the other wanted and was determined to achieve it.

Though Whitfield was taller than most of the riders and more powerfully built, his height and weight were no disadvantage to the big black horse. With perfect timing, Clay used his size in precisely the right manner to help the animal, not hinder him, guiding him and rewarding his trust.

Clay cleared the triple, leaving the crowd gasping and cheering. The round went faultless.

Ellie released a rush of air and realized she had been holding her breath. God, he was magnificent. Then the thought occurred—now she would have to go clear just to face Whitfield in the jump off.

As her round drew near, Ellie walked back toward the staging area to begin final preparations and take a few practice fences. Passing Clay Whitfield, still mounted, along the way, it was impossible not to admire the easy grace with which he sat his horse.

Ellie glanced up at him, but two female riders vying for his attention stepped in front of her and she couldn't see if the look was returned. The brunette asked for his autograph. The other girl said something and smiled up at him. Clay chuckled and winked at her.

Ellie kept on walking, but the sound of his voice and the look he'd flashed the girl stayed with her the rest of the day.

By the end of the afternoon, only six of the thirty-six competitors had earned a chance at the jump off. Amazingly Ellie was one of them. The course was shortened, but the fences were even higher. Whitfield was number four, clearing the jumps without disturbing a single rail. Ellie made the round in the time allotted but took down two fences.

When the meet was finished, Clay had won the twenty-five-thousand-dollar purse and Ellie had finished third. Considering the caliber of the competition, she still felt proud. She'd done her best, *almost* all she expected of herself. She just wished it had been enough to make the team.

Jake Sullivan stepped off the plane at the Newark Airport at two o'clock Monday afternoon. Walking briskly, he headed for the baggage claim. He'd have to hurry to make it from the airport to Gladstone, headquarters of the U.S. Equestrian team and his four o'clock meeting with members of the Olympic selection committee.

Though it wasn't more than an hour's drive, he needed time to stop at the house he had leased in Peapack, a few miles from the training grounds. He wanted to make some phone calls and change out of his flight-wrinkled clothes. Rounding a corner as he hurried along, he reached the baggage claim to find a fair-haired man in a dark blue suit holding a sign with his name on it. As usual, he was thankful for the efficiency of the Gladstone secretarial staff.

"I'm Jake Sullivan," he told the limo driver as he approached.

"Just point out your bags, Mr. Sullivan, I'll do the rest."

Jake grabbed his suitcase and pointed to the hanging bag on the conveyor belt beside it. Together he and the driver made their way through the crowded room, out through the wide glass doors that led onto the busy street in front of the terminal. The New Jersey sky was clear, but the air was cool, with just the hint of a breeze.

A black Ford sedan waited at the curb. The driver loaded Jake's bags into the trunk. As the car pulled into the bustling airport traffic, he made himself comfortable in the back seat for the forty-five-minute ride home.

Home. He ran the word over his tongue. Gladstone didn't feel any more like home than it had when he'd moved there two years ago to coach the team.

Pleasant Hills was his home and always would be. The first call he'd make when he reached his destination would be to the man who ran his breeding stables. Then he'd check with his housekeeper, though he was certain to find everything in order.

Still, he missed being there. Sometimes he wished he'd never accepted the job as coach. If he hadn't, maybe things wouldn't have gotten so screwed up.

Thinking about it, Jake glanced out the rear window of the town car. It took a minute to spot the plain beige Chevrolet following a few leagues distant. But as the town car weaved in and out of traffic, a pattern began to develop and there was no mistaking that the car was being followed.

Damn them! Jake clenched his fists in frustration. He ought to be used to it by now. They hadn't let him out of their sight for the past eight months. Not since that first phone call—the reason he'd been forced to end his relationship with Maggie Delaine.

Maggie. At one time the words *home* and *Maggie* had seemed destined to go together. But now?

Yesterday, when he'd found out she was on the show grounds, his stomach had balled into a hard tight knot. By the end of the show, when he'd finally worked up the courage to face her, he discovered she was already gone.

He could still recall the profound relief he'd felt. Thinking about Maggie and seeing her again were two far different things, though her position as assistant director insured it would happen sooner or later.

Jake glanced back out the window. The beige Chevy remained some distance behind, but the man at the wheel didn't really care if Jake spotted him. In fact, they *wanted* him to know they were there. For eight months they'd kept him on edge, giving him no explanations, only veiled threats and vague innuendos.

But Jake was no stranger to the kind of pressure these men were using. He'd been raised on it.

He'd just been foolish enough to believe that in this country he'd be safe.

Leaning back against the deep leather seat, he forced himself to relax. On his plane ride home, he'd come to a decision. Whatever these men had planned, he would be told when they were ready for him to know.

They had successfully destroyed his relationship with Maggie, but his job as head coach was another matter entirely. He had obligations to fulfill, duties, responsibilities. He couldn't simply resign.

That much had been made clear.

In the meantime, the only option he had was to do the best job he could, and that meant helping select the finest team of show jumpers the United States of America could produce.

With that goal in mind, Jake pushed his thoughts away from his troubles and mulled over the competition he'd seen in Los Angeles and the other selection trials he'd attended across the country.

Clayton Whitfield was the nation's top rider. But his personal life was in shambles. He'd be chosen, Jake had no doubt. Clay would be his usual pain in the ass, but he'd give the American team their best shot at the gold.

Jake ran through the list of other possible contenders: Denny Beeson had made a poor showing in L.A. but done well at other shows. Shep Singleton and Prissy Knowles would be high on the list as well as Peter Grayson, Flex McGrath, and Jack Dillon.

Then there was Ellen Fletcher.

Though she'd taken only a third in Los Angeles, her performance had been outstanding. Considering the short time she had actively been competing, her progress was incredible. She was definitely Olympic caliber—if the others on the selection committee were willing to give her the chance.

Jake had coached her for a while right after her eye surgery. She'd been a gem to work with, willing to tackle any task, fearless in the extreme, always finding joy in the sport and in her accomplishments.

Ellie's years of partial blindness had caused her to live inside herself more than most of the people he knew, a feeling of isolation Jake could relate to. Neither of them seemed to have the courage to reach out and grasp the intimacy others offered.

Ellie's mother and father had both been nationally acclaimed riders. Jake guessed being a winner in the sport was Ellie's way of dealing with the insecurity she felt in other areas. She had little experience with people and often felt out of place. The truth was, even after her vision problems were corrected, Ellen Fletcher had never come out of her shell.

"Should I take you to Gladstone or your house in Peapack?" the driver asked, breaking into Jake's thoughts.

He checked his watch. "Looks like we've got plenty of time. You can let me off at the house. I'll drive on over from there."

"Whatever you say, sir."

Whatever you say. Jake wished the members of the selection committee would be as easy to convince.

CHAPTER THREE
Gladstone, New Jersey
May 1988

Clayton Whitfield drove his shiny red Ferrari faster than he should have along the lane leading to the Gladstone training compound.

Verdant and rolling, the New Jersey countryside blossomed with bright spring flowers though the air remained brisk. Tiny white snowdrops lined white-washed fences, and apricot and peach trees rained pink and white blossoms on the ground.

Clay rode with the top down. He loved the feel of the sun and wind on his face, the stereo vibrating with a new Tchaikovsky compact disc. Turning through the gates, he roared up in front of the two-story wood-frame building that housed the main offices and stepped on the brake. The Ferrari skidded to a halt, stirring up dust and gravel and turning several hunt-capped heads in his direction.

Yesterday Clay had received his official notification of selection as an Olympic team member, but the letter made no mention of the other four riders, one of whom would serve as an alternate. Clay had come to Gladstone to find out who else would be making the trip to Europe for the summer competitions, then going on to Seoul for the Olympic games.

Still wearing his riding clothes after the morning's exercises, Clay opened the Ferrari door and swung his boots to the ground. He rounded the car, took the steps to the porch two at a time and walked in, taking the place by storm, as he always did.

"Hey, pretty Patty." Leaning across the counter, he smiled at the girl behind the desk. "Jake around?"

The leggy blonde blushed and toyed self-consciously with her spiky bangs. "He's out at the training ring."

Clay winked and grinned, flashing his dimples and eliciting a smile in return. "You'd better start eating again. You're getting too skinny."

Patty's smile widened and a slash of pink touched her cheeks. She was always on a diet, always looked exactly the same, and always wished she were thinner. Clay had slept with her years ago, though on which occasions he couldn't quite recall. She was married now, which made things easier on both of them.

"I'll track him down. Thanks, Patty." He could feel her eyes on his back as he headed out the door and knew she'd sleep with him again if he made the slightest effort. He wouldn't. He knew he'd hurt her the first time, though it hadn't been his intention. Patty had wanted a serious relationship. Clay just wanted to have some fun.

Spotting Jake near the door to the stable, Clay strode across the compound in that direction. Jake was busy with one of the grooms, a thin-faced youth who jumped at his every command. Handing the boy a bridle, he gave firm instructions to saddle soap the leather more carefully this time, then turned as Clay approached.

"I thought you were in Palm Beach," Jake said, surprised to see him there.

"Got back the first of the week. I just dropped by to find out the results of the selection trials."

"You didn't get your letter?"

"Oh, I got it, but I wanted to know who else would be riding."

"I think we've got one helluva team. Besides you, there's Flex McGrath, Shep Singleton, and Prissy Knowles. Ellie Fletcher is the alternate."

Clay smiled until the last name was read. "Fletcher. You can't be serious. Fletcher's been chosen over Peter Grayson?"

"Look, Clay, there were a lot of good riders to choose from. It was a tough decision by a lot of hardworking people, and one I'll stand behind all the way."

Clay regarded him closely. Both tall men, they stood nearly eye to eye. Jake had come into his own in the two years since he'd been named head coach. He'd always been confident in his abilities as a rider. Now he displayed an authority in dealing with people he hadn't revealed before.

"Damn it, Jake, the girl's only been competing for the last few years. She hasn't got the experience Pete has, or even Jack Dillon for that matter."

"I've been watching Jack and Peter closely. They're both good riders, but they don't show the potential Ellie does. She's come farther in the short time she's been competing than most people do in a lifetime. Besides, that horse of hers is one of the best show jumpers in the country."

Footsteps sounded behind them as one of the grooms walked past, and Jake glanced over his shoulder to see who it was. After he'd met Maggie Delaine, he'd lost some of the guardedness that kept him so aloof, but once their affair had ended, his wariness had returned full force.

"I won't argue about the horse," Clay said. "Jubilee's one of the best. But what makes you think the girl will hold up under Olympic competition? You know the kind of strain she could face in Seoul."

"Because beating the odds isn't new to her. Because she's got balls—and she's got heart. And because I'm going to coach her myself. What have you got against her? It couldn't have anything to do with her beating you at Madison Square Garden?"

Clay clenched his jaw. "I won't deny she rode brilliantly that day. I won't deny I hated losing to her. But Peter has experience. That's worth a lot more than potential. The committee should have asked her to loan the horse to the team."

"Look, I know you and Peter have been friends for years, but that's beside the point."

Clay grunted. He'd been looking forward to the tour with Peter along, one of the few riders who could keep up Clay's demanding, over-indulgent, after-hour's pace. Hell, Peter could drink until dawn then ride all day with no more to show for it than a smudge or two beneath his eyes.

"I realize Peter's consistent while Ellie is a little sporadic," Jake continued. "But you don't win gold medals by being mediocre, or even just good. The girl's a worker. She's got a chance for greatness, and I intend to see she gets it."

"Christ," Clay grumbled, "a month in Europe with that Pollyanna is more than I can stand."

"You always were a chauvinist, Clay. I'm surprised you aren't complaining about Prissy, too."

"Prissy's one of the best. There's no denying that. The Fletcher girl, well, she's—"

"She's what, Mr. Whitfield?"

Clay stiffened. He cut his eyes to Jake, whose mouth edged up in one corner. With a silent curse, Clay turned to face the female voice touched with anger. Ellie Fletcher glared up at him, green eyes snapping, her riding crop gripped against her thigh.

"Ellie," Jake said, "I believe you know Clayton Whitfield."

"So you think Peter Grayson would have been a better choice," she said.

"Peter has more experience. Even Jake said that."

"By the time we reach Seoul, *I'll* have more experience."

Clay felt the pull of a smile. "Yes, you will, Ms. Fletcher." Since she rode the West Coast circuit and he the East, he'd seen her only a few times over the years. He hadn't really noticed her until she won the twenty-five-thousand-dollar purse in the Mercedes Grand Prix last year at Madison Square Gardens. He'd chalked it up to bad luck for him and good luck for her.

After that, he'd seen her in Amsterdam, and in Aachen, Germany, where he'd gotten drunk and lewdly asked her to screw. She had a reputation as the most untouchable woman in the show world.

"I didn't know you were in Gladstone, Ms. Fletcher. Now that I do, I'll be sure to mind my manners." He caught Jake's look of amusement but addressed his words to Ellie. "Will you be competing in North Salem, Ms. Fletcher?"

"I think it's time for *Ellie and Clay,*" Jake said. "We're all on the same team, remember?"

Ellie smiled tightly. "As to the Empire State show, yes, *Clay,* I'm competing."

He almost smiled. "Then I guess I'll see you there. Thanks, Jake. Believe it or not, I appreciate the explanation. I know you didn't owe it to me." Whitfield started walking, dust rising to cover the toes of his black knee-high boots.

For no reason he could explain, he stopped and turned. "There's a party at a friend's after the show on Friday night. I'll see you both get invitations."

Don't bother, Ellie thought with a pang of dislike. *Clayton Whitfield.* The man wore his Florida tan as majestically as he did his riding clothes and his too-cocky attitude. Sunlight sparkled on his thick brown hair, streaking it with gold. He was wearing light beige riding breeches, the material stretching over his muscular buttocks and thighs.

Ellie found her eyes locked on their rhythmical movement as he took the last several paces to his car.

"I've read he lives in Far Hills," she said to Jake. "Is that nearby?"

"Just down the road a few miles. He's got a riding stable full of horses and house as big as a hotel, but he does most of his training right here."

Ellie couldn't hide her surprise.

"I take it you two don't get along," Jake said.

"The man's an arrogant jerk." As if in emphasis, she slapped her crop against the side of her boot, then felt instantly guilty. After all, as Jake said, they were on the same team.

"To tell you the truth," she amended, "I hardly even know him. I've watched him ride, of course. He's magnificent. The best I've ever seen."

Jake smiled. "Clay's a total pain in the neck, but you're right, he's the best in the country, one of the best in the world. I'm sure he didn't take losing to you kindly. He thinks you've only been riding a few years. Maybe you should tell him the truth."

"It's none of his business. And I'd appreciate it if you didn't tell him, either."

Jake shrugged. "Far be it from me." He turned toward the stable. "Let's get back to work."

They'd been at it off and on since daybreak, working six different horses. Over the past three weeks, Ellie's respect for Jake had grown stronger than ever. He was brilliant, disciplined, and a worker, just as she was. Determined that she would succeed, Jake didn't know the meaning of *can't* or *tired* or *afraid.*

The routine with each horse had been the same: they started with lunging—working the animal in a circle at the end of a rope. Then elementary schooling, Cavalletti and gymnastics, followed by jumping.

"The program improves the horse's physique and confidence," Jake had told her. "And the rider's overall ability."

Walking into the dark, musky, two-level stable, he untied Cookie's Delight, a dappled gray Dutch warm blood mare, standing in front of the stall, saddled and waiting. Slipping the bridle over the horse's ears, he straightened her coarse gray topknot, and led her toward the outdoor practice ring.

"The more varied the horses you ride," Jake said to her, "the better your seat and the more confident you'll become."

Several riders walked past, laughing and talking, the women waving a Jake, who gave Ellie a leg up onto the mare's back. "Your biggest problem is still the position of your head and shoulders. You've got to look forward, use those precious eyes of yours. Your balance is perfect, leg position good, but your head goes down and you wind up a little in front of your horse."

Ellie nodded. Coming from a rider as good as Jake, every word was a pearl of wisdom. He'd stuck his neck out with the committee to get her on the team. She was determined he wouldn't regret his decision. Ellie liked him more every day. He didn't say much, but when he did, his words were succinct, his criticism well thought-out and always poignant. He gave little praise, which only made his few rare compliments more meaningful.

He looked handsome in his riding clothes, with his swarthy complexion and incredible blue eyes. Compared to Clay Whitfield, Jake was leaner, more sinewy than muscular, and probably fifteen years older. But Jake stayed in shape.

She knew he ran for an hour every morning before he started giving lessons. He was solid as a rock, as physically fit as any man she'd ever seen. Women fawned over him. Jake gave them an appreciative glance or a word of flattery, but he never asked them out. One of the newer female grooms had asked her if he was gay.

Ellie just laughed. "Not a chance."

The groom chuckled. "Well, there's certainly nothing missing in the look he gives a woman—he just never seems to follow through."

Ellie knew exactly what was wrong with Jake. He still wasn't over Maggie. She wondered what had gone wrong between them, but Jake's personal life wasn't a subject open for discussion. Which was fine with Ellie, since the same rule applied to her.

As the afternoon wore on and her riding continued, her mind returned to Clayton Whitfield. Every time she thought of him, her adrenaline began to pump. How dare he have the gall to judge her abilities! Who the hell did he think he was?

He was just as arrogant as he'd been in Aachen—and just as rakishly handsome. She'd never forget that evening after the show. She'd been exhausted as she'd led Jubilee back to his stall. The afternoon had been excessively warm with only a few sparse clouds to block the sun. She'd been hot and tired and dusty. All she wanted was a bath and a good night's sleep. Instead, as she neared her assigned stall, she heard laughter and women's voices, the clink of glasses coming together in a bawdy toast.

Beneath the yellow-striped canopy shading his entourage from the sun, Whitfield's Fox Hollow Farm's stalls were overflowing with expensively dressed celebrants. Bright green Astroturf covered the dirt, protecting the women's high heels.

Ribbons and plaques decorated the rough wooden walls along with pictures of Clayton Whitfield soaring over dozens of jumps in competitions all over the world.

Ellie's grip tightened on the Jubilee's reins, and she started walking faster. Her stalls were right next door. She could have used a little peace. Obviously, she wasn't going to get it.

Her groom, Gerry Winslow, walked up beside her. "You look beat," Gerry said, always solicitous. Tall and lanky, with a thatch of brown hair, Gerry had worked for the Fletchers for the past five years.

"I'm exhausted." She glanced toward the man lounging nonchalantly against a stall, knee bent, one booted foot propped against the wood. A slinky blonde in a green silk dress arched against him, her arms wrapped possessively around his waist.

He laughed at something she whispered in his ear, his voice husky. The look he gave the blonde steamed with sexual heat.

"*He* certainly doesn't look any the worse for wear," Ellie said, tipping her head toward Clay.

"He always looks like that. Disgusting, isn't it?" Gerry took Jubilee's reins and led the stallion away to begin his grooming ritual.

As she draped her dusty red hunt jacket over the back of a dark green canvas director's chair, Ellie glanced up and was surprised to see Whitfield untangle himself from the blonde and make his was over to her.

"Nice ride," he said, referring to the last event of the day in which she'd placed fourth. He, of course, had won. She caught a whiff of liquor on his breath and a hint of his cologne. He was still dressed in his riding breeches, smelling of horses and leather. The combination was masculine and sexy, and butterflies rose in her stomach.

"I misjudged the oxer on the jump off," she said, determined to make conversation. "I'd been over it once, I should have known better."

"Are you always so hard on yourself?"

Ellie felt his eyes on her face and heat rushed into her cheeks. "I expect a lot of myself. I won't settle for less."

"I've already learned you're a tough competitor."

She wondered if that was meant as a compliment and found herself hoping it was. His eyes moved down her body, judging the size of her breasts beneath her white cotton shirt.

"Nice," he said, returning his gaze to her face.

Ellie flushed even more and realized how drunk he really was. "I think your lady friend is missing you." She hoped he'd go back to his friends, but she couldn't deny the soft thudding of her heart as he moved closer instead.

"Why don't we leave her to Flex and the boys and find someplace of our own?"

"I don't think so, Mr. Whitfield."

"Clay," he said. The soft way he said the word moved fine strands of auburn hair beside her ear. Self-consciously, she tucked the loose strands under her riding cap. "You'd really better be going. You have guests."

"To hell with my *guests*. I'm in the mood for a little diversion. We'll go out to dinner at the Heidelberg, dance awhile, then go screw. How does that sound?"

Shock rolled through her. Ellie stared at him in dismay. As hard as she tried, no words came out of her mouth. For an instant she'd been flattered. She'd actually believed Clay was leaving the beautiful blonde, asking her out on a date.

"How does it sound? It sounds like you're a conceited, arrogant ass." She tried to brush past him, but he caught her arm and pulled her up close.

"No sense of humor, I see." He chuckled. "No sense of adventure, either. Or are you just frigid, like everyone says?"

"Let go of me."

"If you don't want to fuck, at least give me a kiss." Before she could stop him, his mouth swooped down over hers. When she gasped and tried to jerk free, he slid his tongue inside and Ellie felt the warmth clear to her toes. For an instant, the delicious sensations held her immobile.

Then her senses returned, and she pressed her hands against his chest until she broke free. Embarrassed and angry, she slapped him hard across the face. The ringing crack brought Gerry Winslow from his place around the corner but was lost in the noise and laughter of the crowd next door.

Whitfield rubbed his cheek, his brown eyes dark.

"Are you alright?" Gerry asked.

"I'm fine. Mr. Whitfield was just about to leave...weren't you, Clay?"

He bristled.

Gerry grinned. "Holler if you need me." He ducked back out of sight.

"Well, at least my curiosity is satisfied," Clay said.

"What's that supposed to mean?"

"It means you're just as cold as they say." Turning, he strode back to his friends, taking his place beside the blonde as if he'd never left. Within seconds he was laughing and talking, the incident already forgotten.

But Ellie didn't forget. She's spent half the night tossing and turning, remembering that kiss. Maybe Clayton Whitfield thought she was cold, but Ellie knew better. It had been all she could do to tear herself away.

That was in the past, she reminded herself. But now she and Clay would be working together. They would be traveling across Europe on the same team. Clay was conceited, jaded, and selfish, a philanderer of the very worst sort. The kind of man she despised. But, God, she was attracted to him. Heaven forbid he ever found out.

Clayton Whitfield took the Far Hills Road turnoff even faster than he usually did. The Ferrari merely hummed a little lower as it shifted down and rounded the corner with all the grace that made the car worth the hundred-and-fifty-thousand he'd paid for it.

Clay loved that car. Probably more than just about anything he could think of—except of course his father, and his stallion, Maximum Effort. He smiled to himself. Max was special, all right.

Clay had never known an animal who thought exactly the way he did. When they competed, it was if Max read his mind, or he read Max's. Either way, they worked in unison. They were a team. Clay felt closer to Max than he did most human beings.

Slowing the car to a powerful purr, he turned into the long, hedge-lined driveway that led past the guest house to the main house and stables beyond. Clay had spent most of his life in Far Hills, though his family owned homes in Palm Beach and Beverly Hills, a farm in Greenwich, Connecticut, and a brownstone in Manhattan. The Far Hills house was as much a home as Clay had ever known.

Occasionally, his father was in residence, but for the last few weeks Avery had been soaking up the California sun.

Clay smiled as he thought of the spicy little California girl, Ellie Fletcher, he had tangled with that afternoon. He'd been surprised to see her. He could have strangled Sullivan for not warning him she was in earshot, but then, that was Jake. He liked to stand back and let other people's antics amuse him.

The Fletcher girl had looked just as pretty as she had at the selection trials in Los Angeles. He hadn't had a chance to talk to her there, but he felt he owed her an apology for the way he'd acted in Aachen. And he wanted to take a closer look at her, see if she was as appetizing as he remembered.

Today had confirmed his assessment, but he'd made an equally bad impression. Not that he cared, he assured himself. He wouldn't mind taking her to bed, but he doubted the effort would be worth it.

Then again.... All that guff he'd given her about being cold had been just that. He hadn't missed the little growl of pleasure he'd heard in her throat when he'd kissed her in Aachen, or the way she'd swayed against him. It would take more than a kiss to find out for sure. Maybe he'd expend the energy, maybe not.

Hell, he'd never even seen her with her hair down, or wearing a dress for that matter. He hoped she'd come to the party Friday night. Maybe he'd get lucky.

"Hey, Clay!" Denise Leander leaned against the fence near the stables. Wearing faded skin-tight jeans, her hair swept up in a long black ponytail, she looked younger than her twenty-four years.

Clay inwardly groaned. He'd forgotten his promise to give her riding lessons, the lure he'd used to get her into bed three days ago. She'd been an enthusiastic lover, but her responses seemed rote, and Clay wondered how many times she'd gone through the same motions with somebody else.

"Hello, Denise," he called to her as he turned off the ignition and opened the car door.

"Bobby has the horses all saddled and ready. I told him you promised to take me riding, and he said you'd be back pretty soon." Her plump red lips turned pouty. "That was an hour ago. You didn't forget me, did you?"

He leaned over and kissed her full on the mouth. "Don't be silly. Come on. Let's get going." *Let's get this over with,* was what he meant. Damn, why did bedmates have to be so costly? If women weren't after his wealth and social position, they were after his time. It was the latter he valued the most.

Taking her arm, he smiled down at her. Denise flashed a bright smile in return, the scent of her perfume drifting up. Obsession, a little too heavy for his taste, but not unpleasant.

He checked the time on his Patek Phillippe, a gift from his father. Twelve-thirty. He could give her a lesson on the horse, one in the bedroom, and be back schooling Max by mid-afternoon. What the hell, he had plenty of time.

CHAPTER FOUR

The Empire State Grand Prix, held in North Salem, New York, began on Tuesday and wound up with the Grand Prix competition at two o'clock Sunday afternoon.

Jake had been at the show grounds all week, watching the events and giving Ellie Fletcher as much of his attention as he dared. His *shadow* as he had come to call the unknown man who followed him, appeared occasionally, but since Jake had made the decision to focus on his job, he found himself more and more successful at ignoring him.

Maggie Delaine was still on business in Los Angeles, for which he was grateful. One problem at a time. At the moment, that problem was getting Ellie Fletcher ready for the competition in Europe.

Every day, she'd been competing in three or four events, riding three different horses. She'd ridden several times against Flex McGrath and Shep Singleton, two of her team members, and held her own, but nothing seemed to challenge her efforts more than a round against Clay.

Each time they'd competed, Whitfield had placed ahead of her.

"Competition brings out the best in a person, Ellie," Jake told her as she worked in her stall on Friday afternoon, "but it isn't supposed to eat you up. Or is there more to beating Whitfield than just winning?"

"I just want to be the best. If Whitfield's number one, then he's the man I have to beat." Ellie didn't add that as usual Jake's perception wasn't far off. There was a whole lot more to beating Clay than just the fact he was the top rider in the country.

"You rode well in the open," Jake told her. "But you misjudged the strides between the fourth and fifth jump in the modified and pushed your mare too hard."

"I know." She'd done well enough, but she needed to do better.

"You going to the party?"

"No."

"Well, if you change your mind and go, remember I expect you to be working that Dutch warm blood, Cookie's Delight, by six a.m. tomorrow morning."

"I haven't forgotten."

Later that afternoon, she was surprised when Clay showed up at her tack room. Sitting on a bale of straw, she was cleaning alfalfa from the bit of Jube's show bridal when he walked up.

"Did you get the invitation I left with your groom?" Standing in the doorway, he filled the room with his booming voice as well as his imposing presence.

"I got it." Her fingers tightened around the metal bit. "I won't be going. I'm working a couple of different horses tomorrow and I want to get plenty of rest."

"How old did you say you were?" Clay teased.

"I didn't, but I'm twenty-four."

"Surely you've still got enough stamina to spend a few short hours with friends. Flex and Shep will be there. You'll know several others."

"Flex and Shep have more experience than I do, as you so helpfully pointed out. I have to make up for it by working harder."

"All work and no play make Ellen a dull girl," he teased.

"What makes you so concerned with my private life? Or did you intend to get me drunk and make the same lewd proposition you made in Aachen?"

A muscle twitched in Clay's cheek. "Actually, the invitation tonight was my way of apologizing, but right now, I don't think I regret my actions at all. Good luck on Sunday," he said coldly. Turning his broad back to her, he stalked out the door.

Ellie felt like a fool. Clayton Whitfield had been trying to apologize, and she had insulted him. She rubbed the snaffle so hard her fingers ached. Damn it! *Damn him!*

Ellie worked on her equipment till well after dark, then flicked off the lights and left the tack room. Driving a rented Toyota, she drove to the Cross River Motel where she was staying, unlocked the door, checked the closet for intruders as was her habit, and stripped out of her grimy, sweat-stained riding clothes.

It wasn't till after a long soak in the tub that the idea of attending the party began to take root.

She could apologize to Clay, she rationalized. Tell him she appreciated his invitation and try to encourage his friendship, since they'd be traveling together through Europe. She'd also have a chance to get to know Flex McGrath and Shep Singleton a little better. She'd just have a quick glass of wine and come home.

She blow-dried her hair, leaving it in loose curls down her back, then stepped into a yellow cotton sundress and a pair of white high-heeled sandals that went with everything in the minimal wardrobe she had packed for the trip to North Salem.

With a white knit sweater draped over her shoulders, she grabbed her car keys and a white clutch purse and headed out the door.

The directions to the party, written on the back of the invitation, were a cinch to follow, just a few miles out of town on State Route 124 then turn onto Deveau Rd. The driveway was a quarter mile past the Hammond Museum and Gardens on a hill overlooking the lake.

As she pulled up in front, yellow lights glowed through the windows while laughter and the music of classical guitar drifted across the manicured lawns.

A bit hesitantly, Ellie climbed the steps to the double mahogany front doors. Having paid little attention to the invitation, she assumed this would just be a casual lawn party. It appeared she was wrong.

"Your wrap, madam?" A tuxedo-clad attendant stood in the entry. Ellie removed the sweater and handed it over. Through the opening to her left beneath crystal chandeliers, she could see men in black suits and women in silk cocktail dresses. Some wore sequins.

Horrified to be there ridiculously underdressed, she caught the attendant just as he handed her sweater to the uniformed girl in the cloak room.

"I'm afraid I've changed my mind." Hastily grabbing the sweater, she started for the door. Clay Whitfield's voice froze her where she stood.

"Not so old after all," he teased.

"I didn't...I mean I'm not dressed appropriately. I just...I came to apologize for what happened this afternoon." Why couldn't she stop rambling? He was doing it to her again. He looked magnificent in his black evening clothes. She looked like a surf bunny.

"Don't be silly. You look lovely." He slipped an arm around her waist. "Come on. I'll introduce you to Virginia and her husband, our host and hostess."

Ellie hung back. "Please, Clay. I wouldn't feel comfortable." Silently, she pleaded with him to understand and surprisingly, he seemed to.

"All right. We'll go for a drink someplace else."

She managed to nod. The man was so imposing she'd have followed him into the party if he'd pressed her, knowing she'd be making a fool of herself.

He tugged her down the steps and gave instructions to one of the youths parking cars to retrieve his Ferrari.

"I'm not sure this is a good idea," Ellie said. "I have to be up at five-thirty."

"You do keep the most god-awful hours."

Her head came up. "How do you know what hours I keep?"

Clay chuckled. "My spies are everywhere."

"I almost believe you."

Clay stopped at the edge of the driveway. "I know because I've returned to the show grounds at dawn a few times and seen you working one of your horses. Jake says you do that every day."

Ellie made no reply. If she wanted to be as good as Clay, she had no choice.

The car arrived and the valet opened the passenger door. As Ellie climbed in, Clay's gaze roamed over her legs. Rounding the car, he slid in behind the wheel, leaned over and reached in the glove box. "Here, put this on."

She eyed the white silk scarf, a distinctly feminine article of apparel. "Always prepared, I see."

Clay didn't miss the barb. "Jealous already?"

"Hardly." She sat up a little straighter, tied the scarf around her head. "We barely know each other."

"The night is young." Clay grinned at her worried expression as the engine roared to life. He tore off down the driveway, stirring up dust and the dogs in the kennel, and turned onto the road. Driving like a speed demon, he seemed surprised to find Ellie smiling instead of objecting.

"So you have some adventure in your blood after all."

"What?"

"The speed. You don't seem to mind."

"I love it. I like the rush, just like taking the fences."

He tossed her a glance. "What about men? Most women find men the most exciting sport of all."

"I don't have time for men."

Clay arched a brow. "No lovers, not even a boyfriend?"

"Now you're getting personal. But no, no boyfriends."

"Or lovers?" Clay pressed.

She turned wary. "Don't you ever think of anything but sex?"

Clay grinned. "Actually, I think about show jumping a lot more than sex, but when I'm sitting beside a beautiful woman, the latter seems to spring to the front of my mind."

Ellie flushed at the compliment. Clayton Whitfield had called her beautiful. She'd discovered she was attractive four years when she'd looked at herself in the mirror. Without her thick glasses and wearing a little make-up, she was someone pretty.

Clay pulled the Ferrari into the parking lot of a small roadside tavern. A neon sign above the door flashed Willow Creek Inn in big red letters.

"I've enjoyed the ride Clay, really I have. But I think I'd better Shep the drink and be getting back."

"One drink," he cajoled. "Then I'll take you to your car."

One look in those warm brown eyes, one quick flash of his dimpled grin was all it took. "All right. But we'd better make it quick. Five-thirty comes early."

They went into the bar, a softly lit room with a juke box playing Sinatra. The patrons were locals, some watching the television behind the bar, others waiting for a table in the dining room.

Clay chose a quiet spot in the corner. When the barmaid arrived, he ordered Ellie a glass of white wine and himself a Dewars and soda.

Clay leaned back in his chair. "All right, I know you're twenty-four, you love to ride jumpers, and you're a speed freak. You don't have a boyfriend, but you may have a lover. What else should I know?"

Ellie fought a grin. "You should know I'm not in the market for a one-night stand. You should also know I have every intention of beating you on Sunday."

Clay grinned. "Now I also know you're a dreamer."

"I've beaten you before," Ellie reminded him.

"A fluke," he declared.

They bantered back and forth, Ellie feeling a little more relaxed with every sip of wine. True to his word, when they finished, Clay pulled out her chair, helped her up, and escorted her out to the car. When she fumbled with the seat belt, he leaned across to help her, snapping it easily across her lap. He didn't move away.

Instead, his head came down and he covered her lips in a leisurely kiss that made her stomach drop out and warmth spear through her body. His lips were soft and teasingly insistent. Ellie prayed he hadn't heard her tiny purr.

Another brief kiss and he eased away and started the engine. Ellie leaned back against the head rest, enjoying the memory of his mouth moving hotly over hers.

She shouldn't have done it. She knew what he wanted. But God, his kiss felt good and dammit, she wasn't a saint. Why shouldn't she kiss him?

She found out the answer when he turned the car south instead of north—opposite the party and her rented Toyota.

"Where are you going?" Nervously, she glanced around. "I've got to get back to the motel."

Clay's white teeth flashed in a wicked grin. "That's exactly where I'm taking you, love."

"But I need to pick up my car."

"We'll pick it up in the morning."

We'll pick it up in the morning? The words rang a warning bell in her head. "Stop the car, Clay." The words came out so high and strained, he pulled to the side of the road.

"What's the matter, love, are you sick?"

Ellie didn't answer. She popped her seat belt, opened the car door, and stepped out onto the roadside. The lights of a passing truck flashed by, closer than she would have liked. Without a glance at Clay, she slammed the door and began walking back toward her car.

"Where the hell do you think you're going?" Clay's voice was no longer warm. Jamming the car in reverse, he backed along beside her as she marched down the sandy road, high heels sinking into the dirt.

"Home," she said through clenched teeth. "Alone!"

"Dammit, get back in the car before you get us both run over!"

"Not a chance."

Clay slammed the car into park and opened the door. In a few long strides he'd caught up with her. "Look, I'll take you back to your car."

"No." She kept on walking. Clay stepped in front of her, and she collided with his chest.

"All right." He tried for a smile. "So now I know something else about you. You're easily insulted, and you don't want to make love—at least not tonight."

Ellie wanted to kill him. She ground her teeth and tried to brush past him. "Leave me alone. I don't trust you. I don't believe you—and I don't like you."

Clay held her immobile. "You kissed me like you liked me."

"Damn you!" She drew back her hand to slap him, but he caught her arm.

"Not this time. I let you get away with before because I deserved it. Don't try it again. I said I'll take you back and I will. I just forgot for a moment how *untouchable* you really are."

Ellie watched him closely, trying to read his expression. The lines of his face were set, his jaw clamped tight. With a sigh of resignation, she relaxed in his grip. "I guess for a moment, I forgot that, too."

Clay released her arm and together they walked back to the car. They rode along in silence. The wind on her face cooled her temper but did nothing for the nerves in her stomach. When they reached the house party, Clay parked the Ferrari beside her Toyota, helped her out, and waited while she unlocked her car door.

"Thanks for an interesting evening," he said dryly as he settled her inside the car. She could tell he was still angry. Not trusting her voice and the knot that lodged in her throat, she only nodded.

Clay left his car where it was parked and headed for the house. She watched him till he disappeared inside, then started the engine and drove away.

She hated that she suddenly felt so alone.

CHAPTER FIVE

"Where have you been, you naughty boy?" Virginia Burbage, the hostess, walked toward him, a full-hipped woman who looked ten years younger than her fifty something years. "Don't you know it isn't nice for the guest of honor to abandon the party?"

"Have I ever led you to believe I was nice?" Clay teased.

Virginia smiled up at him. "I'll tell you what. It'll just be our little secret. I wouldn't want to spoil your image."

Clay returned the smile. He admired Virginia Burbage. She'd been smart enough to marry Cecil Burbage, a wealthy steel magnate, keep him happy, sexually sated, and on a very short leash. She was also chairwoman of the Children's Home Society, Clay's favorite charity, and a very good friend.

"I just stepped out for a little fresh air." Clay kissed her unlined cheek. "Lead me to the bar—I could use another drink." *God could I,* he thought.

Another round lost to the fiery little redhead. Her riding breeches showed off her figure far better than the yellow sundress, but he had never seen her hair down, a rich, glorious auburn, hadn't expected her to look so deliciously feminine.

He shook his head. The lady was really something. He hadn't been turned down by a woman in years, at least not one who returned his kisses the way she did. Ellie was a challenge—and there was nothing Clay loved more.

Skirting the ornate living room, Virginia led him to the crowded library. A black-haired woman laughed at something her escort said and leaned over the billiard table to complete her shot, giving Clay a magnificent view of her gold-lame backside. He smiled and kept on walking.

"What'd you do, slip off for a quickie?" The voice belonged to Felix McGrath, "Flex" to his friends, a member of the team. Standing in front of the bar, Flex sipped his usual Bacardi and Coke.

"Clay just went for a little fresh air." Virginia winked and patted his arm, still entwined with hers. Clay's mind flashed to a pair of shapely legs and the feel of soft breasts against his chest.

"Not a quickie?" Flex prodded.

"Not even close," Clay said with a scowl. He accepted a scotch and soda, took a welcome drink. "You riding Sebastian tomorrow?"

"Sure am. He's really in top form."

"I'll say. He's been consistently in the money for the last four months."

Virginia took a sip of champagne. "Before I forget, Clay, I got your check for the Society. The board of directors loved the idea of a party for children on the fourth of July."

Clay frowned. "I told you I wanted my involvement kept anonymous."

Virginia rolled her eyes. "If I live to be a hundred, Clay Whitfield, I swear I'll never understand you."

Flex sipped his drink. "What's the matter, Clay? Afraid someone'll discover your secret stash of illegitimate children?"

"Very funny."

"Excuse me, darlings." Virginia went up her toes to look over his shoulder. "I think I see my devastatingly handsome husband." She kissed Clay's cheek. "Thanks again, dearest." Turning, she blended into the throng of well-dressed partygoers.

"So where did you slip off to with Ms. Untouchable?" Flex asked, the freckles on his nose standing out after his day in the sun. "Or maybe she isn't so untouchable after all."

At five-foot-ten, spare to the point of thin, Flex was an attractive man in a G.Q. sort of way. He was two years younger than Clay, but they'd known each other as long as either could recall.

"Little Ms. Fletcher and I went for a ride."

Flex arched a burnished eyebrow, his flame-red hair cut in a long-on-the-top buzz-cut, a Californian all the way. His favorite restaurant was Spago, he loved Bruce Springsteen, and drove a yellow Sting Ray. "A ride, huh?"

"Not that kind of ride, though I think I would have enjoyed it."

"That's the first time I've seen her in a dress," Flex said, parroting Clay's earlier thoughts. "She could be one sexy lady if she learned to relax and enjoy life a little."

Clay grinned. "I've tried to convince her of that very thing on several occasions."

Just then Shep Singleton walked up. "You must be talking about women. You have the unmistakable signs of lust written across your boyishly handsome faces."

Shep was a half out-of-the-closet gay. Since his father was Gordon Singleton, the former U.S. Equestrian Team coach, he maintained a low profile when it came to his sexual preferences.

Clay and Shep had come to blows years ago, when Clay had knocked him over a coffee table for a furtive squeeze on the inside of Clay's thigh. Since Clay had never told anyone the real reason for the argument, the two of them had eventually become friends.

Flex took a sip of his drink. "We were discussing our new teammate, Ellie Fletcher. It seems the mighty Clayton has struck out."

"I may have been at bat three times," Clay drawled, "but it's only the top of the inning."

Shep rolled his grey eyes, a close match to his platinum hair. He'd turned silver-headed by the time he was thirty. Now at forty-one, he was the oldest member of the team.

"I can't wait to see the score at the bottom of the fifth," Shep said. "I'd bet my last hunt cap our beloved Clay will have scored a home run."

All three men laughed.

Flex took another sip of his drink. "Maybe you ought to give the girl a break, Clay. She's a hell of a rider, and Jake says being on the team means everything to her. She's got all she can handle without you trying to screw her every five minutes."

"What's life..." Shep said dramatically, "without a little diversion?"

Clay felt a twinge of conscience. "Maybe you're right. I'll give it some thought." In fact, he'd thought of little besides Ellie Fletcher since he let her out of his car. Still, what Flex said made sense. He wanted what was best for the team.

For himself, he wanted to win the gold.

The party was in full swing when Jake approached the group of riders in the game room. Shep was just leaving, returning to the bar for fresh drinks while Clay and Flex continued talking about the Grand Prix on Sunday.

Overhearing part of the conversation, Jake walked up to join them. "Think Zodiak will be ready for Paris?" he asked Clay. Clay's alternate mount had been diagnosed with an ulcer, ironically, just like his master. But neither horse nor rider would be kept from the competition by the annoying illness.

"He'll be ready," Clay said. "Personally, I'm more than ready— there's no place I'd rather be than Paris."

"French women are so beautiful they can make a grown man weep," Flex said.

Jake smiled. "For once, will you two try to think of four-legged beauties instead of the two-legged kind?"

Flex grinned. "Now you're asking the impossible."

Jake shook his head, took a sip of his whiskey, and drifted away from the men. Though the house was crowded, he noticed little of what went on around him. His mind was on coming events and the threats he'd been receiving. Somewhere outside, one of the men who'd been following him watched the house. For the ten thousandth time, he wondered what they wanted.

Passing the classical guitar player strumming the chords of *Malagena,* he glanced around the room, noting a few late arrivals. Knowing he had a long day tomorrow, he decided to finish his drink and slip away.

Turning toward the patio and the cooler air outside, he stumbled as someone bumped into him from behind, spilling some of his drink on the front of his black suit while some splashed on the white silk skirt of the woman walking past.

"I'm sorry," he said. "I didn't mean to..." The words died in his throat as he stared into the gentle blue eyes he remembered every night in his dreams.

"Hello, Jake," Maggie said softly, making his chest clamp down.

"Hello, Maggie." She looked lovely. He couldn't stop staring, trying to absorb every detail, aching to touch her and knowing he couldn't.

"I heard about your appointment," he said hoarsely, finally finding his voice. "Congratulations."

"Thank you." In her newly acquired position as Assistant Director, Maggie would be traveling to Europe with Evelyn Rothwell, the director, meeting the team in different countries, then traveling with them to the Olympics.

It was the director's job to keep things running smoothly, arrange every aspect of the tour, and handle the problems that came up every day. As the director's assistant, Maggie Delaine would have more than her share of work to do. Jake knew they'd be thrown together. This brief encounter showed him how difficult being near her was going to be.

"I didn't know you'd be here," she told him almost apologetically.

"It was a last-minute whim. I guess I was feeling a little lonely." The instant he said the words he regretted them. The flash of hurt in her eyes was unmistakable. He wanted to pull her into his arms and never let her go. He couldn't do that, but he couldn't deny the thrill he felt at that one small sign she still cared.

"You look beautiful," he said and never meant it more. In the last eight months he'd forgotten how pretty her eyes were, the way the light reflected on her honey-gold hair.

"Thank you. You're looking as fit as ever." Now that she'd recovered from the shock of seeing him, a biting tone crept into her voice.

"How's Sarah?"

Maggie's chin came up. "Sarah's fine. She misses you. For the first few weeks she kept asking me if you were mad at us. Now she understands that you had more important things to do. Excuse me, I'd like to say hello to Virginia." She tried to brush past him, but Jake caught her arm.

"Maggie, I...." He swallowed. "It's good to see you. Tell Sarah I think of her often."

Maggie nodded brusquely and walked away. He watched her hips sway gently in the elegant silk dress and remembered the silken feel of the body beneath. Downing his whiskey in one long gulp, he set the glass down on a crystal coaster and headed for the door.

On the way back, he'd buy a bottle of Johnny Walker to take

back to his motel room. Three or four stiff shots and maybe he could get some sleep.

Maggie walked across the patio, rounding the side of the house just in time to see Jake climb into his shiny black Mercedes. She hadn't wanted to see him and thankfully had missed him in L.A. But when she'd accepted the job as Assistant Director, she'd known their paths would cross sooner or later and more often than she would like.

It had been the single negative factor in accepting the job.

But she'd talked it over with Sarah and she and her daughter had agreed that taking the job was the right thing to do. It was what Les would have wanted.

Four years ago, the Olympic committee had asked Les Delaine to be the Manager of the 1984 Olympic Equestrian Teams. It was an honor he'd coveted for years. That night they'd gone out to dinner at the yacht club to celebrate.

Maggie had hoped they'd take Sarah along. Excited, she had already bathed and combed her hair.

"Some other time," Les had said. "I've got too much on my mind to worry about a kid." Tall and slim, with sandy hair and hazel eyes, Les was an attractive man. He kept in shape playing handball and still did a little riding on the weekends.

"Besides," he added with a smile, "this way I'll have more time for my favorite girl." In a rare display of affection, he leaned over and kissed her cheek.

That evening, he drank more heavily than usual, and Maggie didn't blame him. For years, Les had worked hard for the U.S. Equestrian Team, had coveted the position of team manager, and finally achieved it.

"You'd better let me drive," she told him as they left the club and reached Les' Jaguar in the parking lot.

"Don't be silly. I'm perfectly fine."

"Please, Les. Just this once?"

"All right, all right." Grumbling something about paranoid females and the rigors of being married, he handed her to keys.

Maggie was so relieved she didn't care. By the time they were headed east on the expressway, he was slumped against the headrest, snoring softly. That was the last thing she remembered when she woke up in the Tampa Bay hospital three hours later.

The police said she had swerved to avoid a car and ended up in the path of an oncoming truck. Maggie had survived with only a concussion and a few minor bruises, but the Jaguar had been totaled and Les had been killed.

For years afterward, Maggie had blamed herself. She'd done penance in the only way she knew how, involving herself in the horseshow world Les had loved, reading every journal available, learning as much as she possibly could. Through Les, she had connections, knew the right people to get the job.

She was here now more for her dead husband than for herself.

Maggie glanced toward the driveway in front of the house. She could barely make out Jake's tall figure behind the wheel of his Mercedes, but she didn't need to see him to remember their time together. Les had been dead three years the night she had attended the Olympic fund-raising dinner at the Helmsley Palace in New York.

Slightly bored, she had spotted Jake across the crowded room. All evening, she had found herself watching him off and on. *Those eyes,* she remembered thinking. She even remembered the way his evening clothes fit so perfectly across his broad shoulders, the way he carried himself.

Afterward, she'd felt guilty. In all the years she'd been married, she'd never once looked at Les the way she'd looked at Jake.

Now, as he drove off down the tree-covered lane, Maggie wrapped her arms around herself, suddenly feeling chilled. For the first time, she wondered if she'd done the right thing in accepting her new job.

For the hundredth time she wondered if she'd ever stop loving Jake.

CHAPTER SIX

Ellie awoke with a headache and feeling generally out of sorts. She hadn't slept well after her confrontation with Clay.

She was thankful she had a fairly easy schedule today, only competing in two events: the modified and the opening jumping competitions. She'd be done by noon.

After an extra-long, extra-hot shower that revived her lagging spirits, she dressed in beige breeches, a white shirt, and a navy-blue pin-striped riding coat. Braiding her heavy hair, she wound it into a knot at the nape of her neck and added a little make-up to hide the smudges beneath her eyes.

As she drove to the show grounds, she thought of Clay and got mad all over again. Last night was absolutely the last time the man would make a fool of her. She'd be pleasant to him but stay well out of his way. Which should be easy. Now that he knew she had no intentions of sleeping with him, Clay would have little interest in her.

The morning slipped past, the events going off without a hitch. She took a blue ribbon in the modified, riding Cookie's Delight, took a red ribbon in the open on Rose of Killarny, her alternate horse. By noon she was finished for the day.

It wasn't like her to leave the grounds till the final event, but the bright sunshine felt warm, clear skies beckoned, and Ellie gave in to a sudden urge to escape.

Why shouldn't she? She'd ridden well all week and so had the horses. She deserved a little break.

Stopping by her motel room long enough to slip into faded jeans and a clean white blouse, she headed up State Route 124 to the Hammond Museum and Gardens, the exhibit she'd passed the night before. She parked the Toyota and walked inside, pleased to find the gardens even lovelier than she had hoped.

Done in the manner of a 17th century Japanese Edo Garden, there were Zen, autumn, and dry landscape gardens, a reflecting pool, and a lake among the fourteen loosely connected sections. Ellie strolled the grounds, surprised to feel her tension draining away and peace settle over her. She'd been walking for half an hour when she spotted a familiar tall figure lounging on a bench in the shade beneath a red maple tree.

Ellie's heart began to pound. What on earth would a man like Clay Whitfield be doing in a Japanese garden? He was still wearing his riding breeches, his white shirt open at the throat. In the vee at the front, she could see curly brown chest hair and suntanned skin. Holding a yellow pad in his lap, he stared off toward the lake, then wrote something down on the pad.

If she came up the path on his left side, she could slip around behind him without being seen and find out what he was doing. Immersed in his task, Clay continued to concentrate on his writing. With his broad back angled in her direction, she was able to get close enough to look over his shoulder.

Her eyes widened as she read the words on the pad. *Good Lord, the man was writing poetry!*

At her quick intake of breath, Clay whirled in her direction. Instead of being angry and berating her as she expected, his face flushed, and he glanced away. Wordlessly, he closed the notebook and laid it on the bench beside him.

"Hi..." Ellie fought to suppress a bubble of laughter.

"Hi," Clay said, but he wouldn't meet her eyes.

It was the first time she'd seen him at a loss for words. With his cheeks pink and a lock of hair falling over his forehead, he looked vulnerable in a way she had never seen him. Any thought of teasing him faded away.

"I like poetry, too," she said softly. "But I was never any good at writing it."

Relief swept over him. He didn't even try to hide it. His eyes found hers and his easy grin returned. "You do?"

"*Uh-huh.* I like Keats and Elizabeth Barrett Browning and Shelley, but Shakespeare's sonnets are my favorite."

"I'm a Shakespeare lover myself. How did you find this place?"

"I passed it last night. What about you?"

"Saw it from the back of the Burbage house." He moved over to make room for her on the low stone bench. "Here, why don't you sit down?"

She glanced away, suddenly uncertain. "Thanks, but I ought to be going."

He nodded. "It really isn't a place to share, is it?"

"Only with someone you feel close to. Then it would be lovely."

Clay looked up, the words drifting over him, touching a place inside. For an instant, he wondered what it might be like to share the gardens with Ellie. He'd been dumbstruck when he'd turned and found her looking over his shoulder—dumbstruck and embarrassed. Nobody in the world knew he wrote poetry. He'd been certain she'd make fun of him, but she hadn't.

"Keep my secret?" he said to her with a smile. He wondered if she could hear the tension in his voice he tried to hide.

She returned his smile. "Cross my heart." She drew the sign of a pledge and Clay could see she meant it.

"How about dinner?" For the life of him, he couldn't believe he'd said the words. "We could just go someplace close."

Ellie's smile slid away. "Thank you, but no. You and I are oil and water. I appreciate the invitation, but I'm afraid I've learned my lesson."

"I give you my word I'll behave like a gentleman."

Ellie shook her head. "You gave me your word last night."

Clay shrugged. "Nobody's perfect."

"Why don't we just work at being friends?"

He didn't have women friends. Hell, he didn't have that many people in his life he could actually call a friend and almost no one he could really count on. "Now that you know my darkest secret, I guess I have no choice."

Her smile returned. Through the branches of the tree, he noticed the different colors in her hair. Warm brown with rich red highlights. Mahogany, he decided. The wind whipped several loose strands across her cheek, and she tucked them primly into the braided knot at the back of her head.

"I like it better loose, the way you wore it last night."

63

Her cheeks grew pink, making him smile. "I think I'd better be getting back."

"I'll walk you to your car."

She didn't argue as he rose and they strolled the gardens in companionable silence, Clay wishing she had accepted his invitation and grudgingly admitting he might even enjoy her company without the prospect of sex.

Then his eyes slid down her body as she walked a few steps in front of him and came to rest on her perfect little ass.

He sighed.

They reached her car and he held open the driver's side door. "Sure you won't change your mind?"

She only shook her head. He caught a whiff of orange blossoms as she slid into the seat.

"White Shoulders," he said. "One of my favorites."

She slanted the seat belt between the points of her breasts, which were full and high and intriguing. She snapped the latch and rolled down her window.

"Your poetry," she said, her pretty green eyes full of sincerity and a hint of kindness. "It was lovely. You should be proud of it."

Clay felt the warmth returning to his face. It crossed his mind that he hadn't blushed since he was a boy. "Thank you," he said softly.

He watched her Toyota speed along the lane until it disappeared. Oddly depressed, he returned to his Ferrari.

Where he carefully tucked his poetry-filled pages down deep between the seats.

Since William Fletcher had business in New York, he rented a car and drove up to North Salem to see his daughter ride in the Grand Prix on Sunday. Ellie and Clayton Whitfield both went clear in the first round, but Clay took first place by completing the jump-off with a slightly faster time.

Will was pleased by his daughter's near-win and the progress she'd made in the short time she'd been working with Jake Sullivan. Every time he watched her, he marveled at how far she had come since her eye surgery and thanked God for the gift of her vision.

Will and his wife, Maryann, had both been riders. He'd been six years old when he'd sat his first horse out on Grandpa Fletcher's farm.

His family had very little money, so Will mucked out stalls to earn riding privileges from a nearby stable and eventually got good enough to ride the grand prix circuit for them.

Now it appeared his daughter would carry on the tradition he and Maryann had established twenty years ago.

He found Ellie in the stables and engulfed her in a warm hug. "Keep riding like that, honey, you'll be ready to compete in Seoul for sure."

In Europe she'd be riding individually in dozens of equestrian events, but as an alternate would only represent the American team if one of the members couldn't perform. The same held true for Seoul. But the rule was flexible, and the other riders knew it. The coach retained the right to make any last-minute substitutions that would be in the best interest of the team.

"Wasn't Jube wonderful?" Ellie stroked Jubilee's velvet nose and held up the second-place ribbon. The horse nickered and nipped at the bright red streamers as if he understood how well he'd done. The big sorrel stallion, a thoroughbred and quarter horse mix, stood sixteen-two hands tall, a difficult mount for Ellie's small stature. Still the pair had worked miracles together.

"Your mom sends her love."

"I talked to her a few minutes this morning." Being an extremely close family, Ellie made regular phone calls home, and either her dad or mom usually called her every few days.

Will knew she'd been trying to become more independent, but he and Maryann had worried about Ellie all her life. That hadn't changed.

Her groom, Gerry Winslow, took Jubilee's reins. "Hello, Mr. Fletcher."

"Hi, Gerry. How do you like the East Coast?"

Gerry grinned. "It ain't sunny California, but it's all right, I guess."

"Gerry likes Gladstone just fine, Dad. The female grooms flirt with him all day. I think he's going out with one of them, but he won't admit it."

Gerry blushed, made a soft clucking sound, and led Jube away. "Wouldn't hurt *you* to go out with someone once in a while," Gerry called good-naturedly over his shoulder.

Ellie just smiled. Gerry was head groom. When she was younger, partially blind and more dependent on him, he'd had a crush on her. Now...well, he seemed happy to have her friendship, and she was more than grateful for his.

She'd never been much for dating, not even after her surgery. Teddy Wilson, a college basketball star, had captured her attention for a while. She'd almost gone to bed with Teddy, had waited because she'd wanted it to be right. Her father and mother loved each other so much. It was hard for her to settle for anything less.

Someday, she told herself. After the Olympics, she'd take some time off, maybe try dating again.

In her mind's eye, Clayton Whitfield's tall, powerful image flashed through her head. Ellie clenched her teeth at the unwelcome flutter in her stomach.

Her father tipped her chin up and looked into her eyes beneath the bill cap. "Gerry's right, you know. Met anyone new and exciting?"

Ellie managed not to look away. "Nobody new." Unfortunately, she had never met a man who excited her more than Clay. Along with his good looks, there was his dedication to the horses. She admired his expertise and uncanny ability to communicate his skills to the animals he rode. And there was something deeper, something she read in his eyes. Some part of him even he couldn't seem to reach.

Speak of the devil and he'll appear. As if she had conjured him, Clay came roaring toward the stables in his red Ferrari, the top down, stereo blasting, stirring up clouds of dust, getting the finger from one of the grooms.

A handsome, gray-haired man sat in the passenger seat. The two looked so much alike Ellie knew it had to be Clay's father. Two beautiful blondes sat in the backseat behind them, their breasts practically spilling out of their low-cut tops. They laughed as they passed a bottle of champagne back and forth between them.

"Celebrating already?" her father said to Clay with a brittle smile. The car purred for a moment, then Clay turned off the engine and the dust began to settle.

"Winner's privilege." Though he spoke to her dad, his eyes were fixed on her. They traveled down her body so intimately, she was instantly reminded of the Clayton Whitfield she'd known in Aachen.

Clay climbed out of the car and his father did the same. "Stay,"

Clay said to the girls, purposely treating them like lap dogs.

Ellie's temper swelled.

"I'd like you to meet my father," Clay said. It was obvious he'd been drinking, though he didn't really seem that drunk. "Ellie, meet Avery."

"Hello, Mr. Whitfield," she said.

"Hi, honey. Nice to meet you." His eyes ran over her body just as Clay's had, but he made no comment.

Her dad said nothing, but his jaw clenched, and he folded his arms across his chest. He'd been a rider once, had known Clay and Avery for years. Ellie knew they were not his favorite people.

"Why don't I buy you two a drink?" Clay returned to the convertible and lifted the lid off a small ice chest on the passenger-side floorboards beneath the blonde's feet. He hoisted an unopened bottle of Dom Perignon.

"No, thank you," her father said tightly.

Ellie just shook her head. Clay popped the cork, took a long draw, passed the bottle to his father, who repeated the performance, then Clay rounded the car to the driver's side to climb back in. The blonde on his side of the car giggled and hugged his neck.

Avery Whitfield grinned as if to say, "That's my boy!" and got back in the car. Ignoring his seat belt, Clay turned the key and the powerful engine roared to life.

"See you in Paris!" he called out as he shifted the Ferrari into gear and roared away, throwing up another cloud of dust.

"What was that all about?" Jake walked up as the convertible rounded the corner out of sight.

Her father's gaze swung in Jake's direction. "Just Clay's usual obnoxious show of victory for his father."

"What do you mean?" Ellie asked.

"I hate to say it," her dad replied, "but Avery Whitfield is probably the biggest horse's ass who ever lived. He was the world's worst parent. He drove poor Elizabeth, Clay's mother, to an early grave with his whoring and drinking. Now he's doing his best to ruin Clay."

"Clay never really had a family," Jake added. "His mother died when he was five years old. Clay was raised by a string of nannies, moved from one estate to another while his father traveled the world, cavorting with glamorous women. I think Clay's love for riding was all that kept him sane."

"I think Clay is basically a decent sort," her dad said, surprising her. "But he wants Avery's approval and he'll do anything to get it. He's thirty-one years old, and half the time he acts like a schoolboy— but then Avery is in his fifties, and he acts just the same."

"I think they're both jerks," Ellie said.

The words snagged Jake's attention. He hadn't missed Ellie's expression when she'd watched Clay with the blonde.

Sonofabitch! On top of everything else, the last thing Jake needed was for naïve Ellie to get involved with Clay.

She kicked a clod with the toe of her riding boot and watched it sail off in the distance. Her father was watching her with an odd expression and Jake wondered if Will's thoughts mirrored his own.

"I'm starving," Ellie said, trying for a smile that looked a little too bright. "Come on, Dad. I bet Jake's hungry, too. Be a sport and buy us some dinner."

"I'm afraid I'll have to pass," Jake said. "I've got a couple of errands to run."

"Next time." Will turned to his daughter. "Come on, honey. I know a place that has the best steak in North Salem."

Jake waved at them as they walked away. In the arena, workmen were tearing down fences, loading the potted shrubs onto a trailer, getting ready for the next show, which would be starting in another town on Tuesday.

The tough regimen never let up. The riders traveled on Sunday night and Monday. The show began on Tuesday and ran through the weekend. Then the contestants packed up their horses and equipment and headed off for another grueling week.

Jake spotted Flex McGrath, who was loading up his gear, and stopped to give him a few last-minute instructions about the flight to Paris scheduled for Thursday. He spoke to Shep Singleton about Sebastian's performance, then headed for the parking lot.

Firing up his Mercedes, Jake drove off down the road, grateful for a few minutes to himself. Little by little, the ride through the countryside toward his rental house in Peapack began to relax him. He loved the rolling green hills, the hundreds of small lakes and ponds that reminded him of his home in the Charleston. Pleasant Oaks.

He had loved the farm from the moment he'd laid eyes on it

twenty years ago. He'd been riding for Thurston Brock, the man who had given him his first job in 1960 after he'd arrived in the States. By then, he had graduated from language school, where he'd studied English and gotten rid of his accent, then gone to Charleston to work as a trainer and rider for Brock at his equestrian center.

He'd never forgotten the feeling of driving through the impressive, white-washed gates of Pleasant Oaks that first day. Bright pink azaleas draped majestically over the fences along the lane leading up to the mansion, a big white plantation style house, high-ceilinged and elegant, with balconies around both floors.

He'd arrived wearing denims and boots. Brock had come out to greet him in an expensive suit and tie, and Jake had been embarrassed. He'd vowed one day he'd make enough money to dress as he pleased and feel comfortable in any man's presence.

By the time he was twenty-five, he spoke like a native and was competing on the American circuit. Brock provided the horses. Jake provided the wins. He'd saved his money and rarely gone out, so the dollars began to stack up. On a whim, he invested in a machine that turned culled carrots into dried pellets, feed for horses. The company grew, went public, and Jake had made a small fortune. Years later, when the property had come on the market, Jake had bought it.

He glanced up, saw his Peapack rented colonial ahead. Pulling into the garage, he stepped out of the car and started for the back door. The telephone rang as he walked into the kitchen. Hurrying across the room, he grabbed the receiver and pressed it against his ear.

"Sullivan."

"Ah, so you are home at last, *Tovarich*."

The once familiar voice calling him *comrade* sent an icy chill down his spine. "I just got in. But you must know that."

"How was North Salem?" Nikolai Popov's voice came through in heavily accented Russian. When the man had phoned eight months ago, Jake had tried to speak the language, but twenty-eight years was a long time. Popov was forced to speak English, which only made him angry.

"The show was fine," Jake said. *What the hell do you want?* But he knew the Russian would come to the point in his own good time. The KGB man had always enjoyed toying with his prey, keeping them guessing. Apparently, that hadn't changed.

"Your mother and sister are fine, also," Popov said.

Jake's pulse shot up. "Have you seen them?"

"I see them quite often. I am sure they miss you."

Jake's insides tightened. When he made no reply, the Russian's voice turned hard.

"We must meet before you leave the country."

Jake's fingers tightened around the receiver. "When?"

"There is a diner near the junction of 287 and Washington Valley Road. Do you know it?"

"Yes."

"Be there at ten o'clock Tuesday morning."

"I'll be there."

Popov chuckled, the sound grating. "I have no doubt you will. Do nothing you will be sorry for, *Tovarich*."

Jake's answer lodged in his throat. "I told you before, I'll do whatever you say."

Popov grunted. "Just like your father. Always a sensible man. Too bad you and he were both fools. I will see you at ten."

Only a slight click marked the Russian's departure. Jake set the phone back in its cradle and let out a long slow breath. Pushing open the swinging kitchen door into the dining room, he made his way wearily down the hall to the bar in the den where he poured himself a double shot of Napoleon brandy. His hand shook as he set the crystal decanter back on the mirrored shelf.

With an exhausted sigh, he sank down on the leather sofa in front of the rock fireplace, his pulse beginning to slow. The showdown he'd been expecting for the last eight months was finally at hand. Until the day he'd heard Popov's voice on a gusty, chilly day last October, Jake had all but forgotten his past. He was an American in every way. He thought like an American, he spoke like an American, he looked like an American.

In the last five years, he'd even begun to dream like an American, the words spoken in English, not Russian, or the Hungarian he'd been raised with.

In America, just as his father had said, opportunity had beckoned, and he'd been able to make a life for himself. Popov, a man dedicated to the Marxist philosophy, would never understand.

Jake swirled the brandy in his glass. Thank God he'd been

honest with the selection committee when they'd asked him to accept the job as head coach. He'd told them his real name was Janus Straka, told them how he'd escaped to this country from the Soviet Union, and how much he had come to love it.

"I don't see why that should make any difference," one of the committee members had said. "Baryshnikov and dozens of other Soviet exiles have made great contributions to America. Besides, you're not Russian, you're Hungarian. Bertalan de Nemethy was Hungarian, for God's sake."

De Nemethy was considered the father of American show jumping. He had coached the U.S. Equestrian Team for twenty-five years, had brought it to the greatness it still maintained today.

"We'd be honored if you would accept the position, Jake," the head of the committee had said.

It had been the proudest moment of his life.

Jake downed the last of the brandy and set the crystal snifter on the coffee table. *I owe this country,* he thought. He owed its people a debt so great it could never be repaid.

But he owed his mother and sister, too. They were family, and though he hadn't seen them in twenty-eight years, he loved them. He couldn't let them come to harm.

There was no easy answer.

But then there never had been.

Not for Janus Straka or for Jake Sullivan.

CHAPTER SEVEN

Clayton Whitfield tossed and turned on the king-sized bed, thrashing the covers off his naked body while he dreamed of making love to Ellie Fletcher.

His lips grazed the smooth white skin at the base of her throat where a tiny pulse throbbed in anticipation. His hands moved down her body, stopping to cup each breast then teasing the peak until it hardened into a small dark bud. She softly called his name.

Shrill laughter down the hall awakened him. Clay jerked upright, only to find he had a pounding headache and a raging hard on. With a groan, he rolled to his side.

A woman with sleepy blue eyes stared back at him, her gaze traveling down his body, all the way to his groin.

"Angela," he said, surprised he remembered her name.

"Good morning, Clay." Her fingers slipped through the dark hair curling on his chest, down to his navel, then moved lower. A surge of heat went through him, and he hardened even more.

Unfortunately, it wasn't Angela he wanted.

"Why don't we shower first?" he suggested hoping he could summon a little more enthusiasm. After all, Angela was sexy and obliging, with long blond hair and a repertoire of sexual tricks.

Instead, he thought of Ellie's sweet smile, the warm look she'd given him in the Japanese garden.

Angela was persistent and, in the end, he gave in to her skillful machinations. Clay told himself not to think of Ellie Fletcher. She was probably frigid anyway, just like people said. The notion distracted him enough to immerse himself in the moment. It wasn't until he finished that he saw Ellie's smiling face again.

An hour later, Clay sent Angela on her way and climbed into the limousine waiting in front of the Plaza Athenee in mid-town Manhattan where, after a night of celebrating his North Salem win, he and his father had taken a suite. Avery was already seated in the back for the ride to the La Guardia Airport. Clay climbed in beside him.

"I can't wait to get a look at the castle," Avery said as the limo pulled away. "You sure you can't leave the team for a couple of days and join me for the hunt?"

His father was headed to Scotland. He and a dozen others had been invited to attend a stag hunt.

"This month in Europe is pretty important," Clay said. "It gives the team a chance to get to know each other, feel out one another's strengths and weaknesses. If we work well together, it'll mean a better chance for the team gold in Seoul."

Avery nodded. He leaned back in the deep leather seat and grinned. "How about that Angela? Didn't I tell you she was something? Mouth like a warm silk purse."

Clay had never liked the idea of bedding one of his father's paid-for women. But he'd never said so. And he wouldn't now.

He managed a half-hearted smile. "She was something." His head still ached and the knot in his stomach had returned.

Damned ulcer. He'd been fighting it off and on for years. He pulled a bottle of Maalox from his inside coat pocket and took a long swallow. In a couple of minutes, he'd be fine.

After dropping his father at the airport, the limo hauled Clay all the way back to his Ferrari, parked where he'd left it in the lot of a small roadside bar not far from the North Salem show grounds.

At least he hadn't driven drunk. He'd learned that lesson years ago when he'd been picked up and jailed in Palm Beach for drunk driving. At his home in Far Hills, he kept a chauffeur on staff and a Bentley in the garage, but unless he was going into the city, he preferred to drive the Ferrari.

In the bar parking lot, Clay climbed into the car, fired up the big V-12 engine, and pulled out onto the winding, tree-lined road, heading for his Georgian mansion in the quiet New Jersey countryside. There he could change into fresh clothes, check to see that Max and the other horses had been cared for properly, then head out to Gladstone to get any final instructions from Jake.

He brushed aside the voice that said he might also get a chance to talk to Ellie Fletcher.

His senses flared when he spotted her walking toward her rental car, apparently finished grooming and checking on her horses. Thursday, they would be leaving for Paris. The three days in between gave the horses a chance to rest and get ready for the show the following week.

Clay drove up beside her. "Morning, Ellie." He smiled and kept his voice friendly.

"Hello, Clay." She just kept on walking, sparing him not even a sideways glance.

"I guess congratulations are in order," he said, thinking of her second-place win.

Ellie's jaw tightened.

"Of course, I did beat you, so I guess you should really be congratulating me."

Ellie turned, her small hands balling into fists. "Congratulations, Clay, for winning the Grand Prix—and for making your usual horse's ass of yourself. Now, if you'll excuse me, I've got to get going."

Clay slammed on the brakes, shoved the car into park, and threw open the door. So what if he'd been a little drunk and slightly obnoxious. He was celebrating, that's all.

He caught up with her in three angry strides. "What the hell business is it of yours how I behave?"

"It's none of my business."

"Then stop acting like a bitch." He was breathing hard, fighting to control his temper.

"If you can act like an ass, then I can act like a bitch."

"Damn you!" He took a steadying breath as she stomped off to her car. She had the cutest little ass, he thought as she marched along, and felt a tug of amusement.

"How about dinner?" he called after her, knowing she wouldn't go and enjoying the rigid posture that meant he'd gotten to her again.

"I wouldn't go out with you if you were the last man on earth!" She unlocked the Toyota and climbed inside. Clay walked over and opened her door, stared down at her over the top of the rolled-up window.

"Do you really dislike me that much? Or is it men in general? You never go out. You never have any fun. Maybe you really are frigid."

"When it comes to you, Clay, I'm definitely frigid. There are, however, men who affect me differently. They think I'm plenty warm enough."

The barb smarted more than it should have. Clay clamped his jaw shut, fighting his temper again. What the hell was he doing wrong? He could charm most people as easily as he did the pretty little jump-bunnies who hung around his stalls.

With Ellie he felt constantly on the defensive, often at a loss for words, and furious half the time.

The other half, he wanted to carry her off over his shoulder, take her to bed and find out the truth once and for all. Was she frigid, as the rest of the riders believed? Or as warm and passionate as Clay suspected?

"Would you mind closing my door so I can leave?" she asked tartly.

"I'll let you go if you agree to go out with me."

One of her reddish eyebrows went up. "Haven't you figured out I have no intention of sleeping with you? That's all you want from me, so why don't you find someone else?"

"I admit I'd like to take you to bed. Why wouldn't I? You're pretty, you've got a great figure, and I'm intrigued. But for some strange reason, I actually think we might get along." He had used the same line a dozen times, usually with success. It surprised him to realize this time he meant it.

"Are you kidding? You and I get along? That has to be the biggest joke of the year."

"Hey, Ellie, congratulations!" Flex McGrath walked toward them, red hair gleaming in the sun. "You, too, Clay."

As usual, Clay thought, Flex's timing was rotten. At Ellie's furious expression, a slow smile bloomed on Flex's freckled face.

"Hope I'm not interrupting anything."

"You are," Clay said.

"You're not," said Ellie.

Flex's smile widened. "Jake saw you drive in, Clay. He's over behind the barn. He wants to talk to you." When Clay made no move to leave, Flex added, "He's edgy as hell this morning. I wouldn't keep him waiting."

Clay clenched his jaw, nodded and started walking. Dammit, enough was enough. He'd be drawn and quartered before he'd ever ask that woman out again.

Ellie followed Clay's retreating figure, furious and wishing she could keep her anger in check.

"He still trying to put the make on you?" Flex asked.

Ellie's head came up. "How did you know?"

"That's easy. Nobody's been able to score with you, and Clay can't pass up a challenge."

The words stung. Some insane part of her wanted to accept Clay's invitation. Her common sense reminded her what a dumb idea that was.

"You're right, I know, but..."

"But what? But he's handsome, one of the world's best riders, and you've secretly got the hots for him?"

"Of course not!"

"Don't worry about it. Half the women on the circuit feel the same way. The other half have already been to bed with him."

"He's really a conceited jerk."

"Clay's all right, once you get to know him. Believe it or not, deep down he's got a heart of gold. He'd do damned near anything for somebody he cares about." Flex lifted her chin with his fingers. "Just don't sleep with him unless you can do it without getting involved. Somehow I don't think you're that liberated."

Feeling as if she were on her way to making a friend, Ellie smiled. "Thanks for the advice, Flex. Believe me, I couldn't agree with you more."

"Looking forward to Europe?"

"I'm nervous, but yes, I really am. I think Rose is mostly ready and Jubilee is always ready."

There were five riders on the team, but only eight horses. Rose and Jubilee had both been chosen.

"Jube's one hell of a horse."

"Thank you."

"You've done a great job training him. Jake's told me how hard you work."

"Being on the team is the most important thing in the world. I've dreamed of going to the Olympics since I was five years old. I still can't believe I'm really going, even if it's as an alternate."

"Keep riding the way you have been, and Jake may substitute you in."

"I'd hate to wish anyone else bad luck, but I can't say I wouldn't love the chance."

"By the way, Prissy Knowles is arriving tomorrow. Have you met her?" Prissy was the other female rider on the team.

"A couple of times. I really admire her riding. I hope we can be friends."

"Prissy's easy to like. I know she'll like you."

"I hope so." Thinking how easy it was to like Flex, Ellie's good mood returned. "I'd better get going. I've got a couple of things to do, and Jake will be expecting me for my afternoon workout. And you're right—he is edgy as hell. What do you think is wrong with him?"

"Probably just worried about leaving for Paris. There's a shit load of last-minute details to handle."

"That's probably it." With all his responsibilities, Jake was bound to be worried. She hoped there was nothing else wrong. "Thanks for the talk, Flex. I really appreciate it."

"No problem. Just remember what I said and keep Clay as a friend. He can be a really good one."

Flex closed her car door and Ellie started the engine, a little surprised by Flex's last words. She couldn't imagine Clay Whitfield being a good friend to anyone but himself.

Then she remembered the poetry he'd been writing that day in the garden. Beautiful words about love and caring about others. Maybe her suspicions were right and there was more to Clay than it seemed.

The thought made her nervous. She'd need all her defenses to stay out of Whitfield's clutches. She was attracted to him, and every time she saw him, she remembered the way he'd kissed her. Worst of all, she wanted him to do it again.

Ellie sighed. Six weeks with Clayton Whitfield was going to seem like a year.

"Anything else I should know?" Clay asked, his gaze following the little Toyota down the road. Jake had filled him in on the final details of their departure.

"There's nothing I can think of right now," Jake said, but his glance followed Clay's, his expression nothing short of grim.

"She's a grown woman, Jake," Clay reminded him.

"She isn't in your league."

"Don't play the outraged parent," Clay said, beginning to get angry. "It doesn't suit you. Besides, she's made it clear she wants nothing to do with me."

"Fine. I'd appreciate it if you'd keep it that way."

Clay didn't answer. What happened between him and Ellie was none of Jake's business.

Clay frowned. Jake never interfered in matters that didn't concern him. The fact he'd said anything at all spoke of his regard for Ellen Fletcher.

Clay knew Jake had coached her before, and of course he was working with her now. Jake felt protective of her, that much was clear.

Or was there something more? Jake was a handsome, virile man. As far as Clay knew, he'd had no serious involvement with a woman since his break-up with Maggie Delaine. Maybe it wasn't Ellie's virtue he was protecting, but his own self-interest. Maybe Jake had plans for her of his own.

When Clay glanced back at him, he noticed Jake's attention was fixed once more on the road, where a beige Chevrolet sat parked some distance away.

"I've seen that car before," Clay said.

"What?"

"That car. I've seen it before. Last week at the horse show."

"There are lots of beige cars," Jake said evasively.

"It wasn't so much the car. The guy in it sat there all afternoon. I wonder what he's doing out there."

Jake shrugged. "Probably just a fan."

"Probably." There were some real zealots in the show world. "I'll see you Thursday." As he headed to his car, Clay wondered about Jake Sullivan. Though few people knew Jake well, Clay believed he was an honorable man—far more honorable than Clay.

Now, as he thought about Ellie, and Jake's possible intentions, Clay began to have his doubts.

CHAPTER EIGHT

Ten o'clock Tuesday morning, Jake walked into the Washington Diner. At the back of the busy café, Nikolai Popov stood beside a quiet booth in the corner. He tipped his head as Jake arrived, indicating he should take the seat on the opposite side of the table.

"You're looking fit," Popov said. Though Jake hadn't seen the man in twenty-eight years, he would have known that grating, smoker's voice anywhere. "Your pictures do not do you justice."

Jake's pulse quickened but he didn't reply, just slid onto the worn red Naugahyde bench.

"The Moscow winters have been far less kind to me," Popov said.

So true, Jake thought. On that final day of competition in 1960 beneath a hot Rome sun, Popov had been thinner, with a thatch of sandy-brown hair where now just a few gray strands had been combed over to disguise his baldness. But it was his eyes that had changed the most, narrow and hard, far more cunning now than they had been back then.

"What do you want with me?" Jake asked bluntly.

"Relax, Comrade. All in good time. You were always impatient. I see that has not changed."

The waitress arrived to take their orders, black coffee, not regular, the Jersey version that came with a liberal dose of milk. When the broad-hipped woman returned with two steaming cups, Popov made a grand show of stirring in heaping spoonfuls of sugar, the lengthy display designed to rattle Jake's nerves.

"Smoke?" Popov pulled a pack of cigarettes from the inside pocket of his navy blue suit. Even in America, the man smoked the harsh Soviet brand.

"I quit years ago. It isn't healthy. Or haven't you heard."

"A troublesome attitude may not be healthy either," Popov warned with a thin-lipped smile. "But I am certain your curiosity has been piqued quite enough. It is time we come to the point of our meeting." The Russian took a small sip of the scalding coffee then settled the cup back in its saucer with a soft china clink.

"It has come to our attention that you are in a very convenient place to help the country that birthed, housed, and fed you for the first nineteen years of your life. The State has cared for your family even longer. You owe us a great debt and now you will repay it."

Popov blew a smoke ring across the Formica-topped table. The odor of the Russian tobacco Jake had once enjoyed now seemed heavy and cloying.

"And if I don't?" Jake asked.

"If you do not do as you are told—as you were told before—it is your mother and sister who will bear the consequences. They are old women, *Tovarich,* and life has not been kind to them. They have you to thank for that, just as I do."

"You? You're obviously in a position of power and authority. Surely what happened twenty-eight years ago had little effect on you."

Popov's dry, liver-spotted skin reddened, veins popping out on his forehead.

"No effect, Comrade? It took me twenty years to achieve the goals I set for myself. Twenty years to move into the position I should have attained in three or four. My career was blossoming until Rome. I had high expectations. There was no limit to what I might have accomplished."

Jake said nothing.

"Instead of garnering great respect, my wife and I were assigned a dismal Moscow apartment. My children were forced to attend schools well below their level of abilities. Today my son, Aksandr, holds a mediocre job as a People's Inspector, and my daughter, Irina, and her husband work on a collective near Kiev. They eat boiled potatoes and sausages, while you, *Tovarich,* dine on imported Beluga Caviar from your own mother country and live here like a king."

"I'm Hungarian, not Russian, and I've worked hard for everything I have. In this country, hard work is rewarded. But then you wouldn't understand that, would you?"

"I understand, Comrade Straka, that you are going to repay the debt you owe your country. If you do not, your mother and sister will face the full wrath of the Soviet Government. They will pay for your disloyalty. They will be relocated, assigned new duties. To put it bluntly, Comrade, it is doubtful your mother and sister will live out the remainder of their years."

Jake gripped his coffee cup, fighting to control his temper. His mother was seventy-eight years old, his sister fifty-eight. They had already suffered enough by his leaving. The Soviets had allowed no communication between them for twenty-eight years. Letters he had written had been returned unopened, the money he'd sent them still inside.

In a way, he'd believed it was better. Time had a way of easing the loss. The letters would have been a constant reminder for all of them.

"What is it you want me to do?"

"When the time is right, you will be told. For now, it is enough for you to know that you will be called upon soon. Enough to know the consequences, should you fail to do as you are asked. Your family will be kept under surveillance until such time as you have completed the tasks we assign."

"And when will that be?"

"Not long, my impatient friend. After twenty-eight years of waiting, for me it will seem only minutes." The Russian downed the last of his coffee. "It would be best if you stayed a while before leaving." With a parched smile, Popov slid the check across to Jake and headed for the door.

Jake left the diner fifteen minutes behind the Russian and drove down highway 78 to Black River Road, taking the long way home. He needed time to sort out his thoughts, time to decide what to do.

Whatever Popov and his associates planned had something to do with the upcoming Olympics, of that Jake was certain. And it was bound to be detrimental to the American team.

It had been years since Jake had dealt with the Soviets. In his youth in the late nineteen fifties, the government under Khrushchev had been rife with suspicion. Things were better than they had been under Stalin, but still, constant arrests of dissenters, anyone who disagreed with the State, affected everyone's lives.

He and his father had often talked politics when they felt certain no one would overhear. Just before Jake had left in 1960, Article 70 of the Criminal Code had been adopted, making slander of the Soviet political system punishable by imprisonment for up to seven years.

The KGB was adept at planting subversive material, falsifying documents, then bringing charges against individuals under Article 70. It was an easy way of ridding themselves of anyone who happened to disagree with them.

Because Janus Straka had fled to the West, it would have been easy to use those same tactics against his mother and sister.

Though Jake hadn't been able to correspond with them, Daniel Gage had kept him informed. Jake's sister, Dana, had married a tradesman and delivered two sons. Now the boys were grown and married, with children of their own. When her husband had died five years ago, Dana had moved back in with their mother. The women now lived in a small flat in Moscow.

At least that was the last Jake had heard. He hadn't spoken to Daniel in almost three years.

Jake cruised the Mercedes along the winding, two lane road leading back to Gladstone. With his once-close ties to the Soviet Union, he remained a dedicated follower of world events. Over the past few years, newspaper accounts told stories of greater personal freedoms enjoyed by the Soviet people, of a country that desired to live in peaceful co-existence with its neighbors.

The Reagan-Gorbachev Summit had recently ended, with both sides receiving plaudits for the advancement each had made toward peace.

Was the Soviet government behind Popov's threats? Or was Popov acting on his own?

"After twenty-eight years of waiting...," the Russian had said.

Had Popov risen high enough in the hierarchy of the KGB to work without the knowledge of his superiors? Was he willing to jeopardize his career to gain revenge on the man he believed had destroyed his life and that of his family?

They were questions Jake pondered as he drove through the lush New Jersey countryside. Recalling the threats the KGB man had made, one thing was clear—Jake had done the right thing in breaking off his relationship with Maggie Delaine. He couldn't afford to endanger

Maggie and her daughter's lives.

He couldn't afford to give Nikolai Popov another club to hold over his head.

Jake spent a sleepless Tuesday night and a restless Wednesday running over his options.

The team had been briefed and were meeting at the La Guardia Airport tomorrow for their five-p.m. flight to Paris. Since he had first been contacted by Popov eight months ago, Jake had been waiting to meet with him. Waiting for an answer to the puzzle of what the Russian wanted. Now that the meeting had occurred, he knew little more than he had before.

Time was running out. If he was going to take action, it had to be soon.

Wednesday night, after a frozen TV dinner Jake only picked at, he made a decision. Certain his phone lines were tapped, he drove to the Peapack Village Inn to use a pay phone.

In the coffee shop, he ordered a hamburger, just to make his trip believable, then used the phone while he waited for his order to arrive. The number he carried in his wallet was three years old. He hadn't spoken to Daniel Gage since 1985 when the brawny Irishman had called him in Charleston, just a friendly call at the time. By then, Daniel had been retired from the CIA for five years.

The phone rang several times before Jake reached the disconnect recording. He cursed beneath his breath. Daniel Gage was the only man alive he could trust with his problem. He and Daniel had been friends since Jake had arrived in the States, remained friends even after the FBI took over the duties of the CIA inside U.S. boundaries.

Jake dropped another quarter into the slot, the pay phone chimed, and he heard a new dial tone. His tiny address book had another number listed, an old night number that rang through to Daniel's inner office at the CIA. Maybe someone there could put him in touch.

Three short rings, and a business-like female voice came on the line.

"My name is Jake Sullivan. I know it's after hours, but I was wondering if you might be able to help me."

"How did you get this number?"

"It used to belong to Daniel Gage. He's a friend of mine. His other number has been disconnected. I was wondering if you might have a number where I could reach him."

"Give me your number and I'll see what I can do."

Jake read the numbers on the faded information card above the phone and prayed he was making out them out correctly. Then he hung up the phone and waited impatiently for the woman's call.

"Your order's up, fella," the waitress called to him over her shoulder as she walked past the hall where Jake stood next to the phone. "Don't blame me if it gets cold."

"Would you mind wrapping it up? I think I'll take it with me."

She grunted. "Shoulda' ordered it to go, if that's what you wanted."

The phone rang as the woman walked away. Jake lifted the receiver on the first ring. "Sullivan."

"Jake? That you?"

He released a slow, relieved breath at the sound of Daniel's voice. "That was fast. Thank God you were home."

"I'm not home. I'm in my office. Two doors down from where you called."

"You're back at the agency?" Jake's pulse began to hammer. Daniel's involvement with the bureau was a circumstance he hadn't expected. Maybe he was doing the wrong thing.

"I've been back almost three years. Started right after Marie died. Only way I could handle it."

"Damn, I'm sorry, Dan. I hadn't heard."

"I'm used to it now, at least for the most part. But enough about me. You don't sound good. What's going on?"

For a moment Jake didn't answer. He'd have to be cautious, but it was too late to back out now. "I got a phone call from an old acquaintance. First one eight months ago. One lasts Sunday. Nikolai Popov." Jake let the words sink in.

"I knew he was in the country. He's on staff with the Russian Embassy, Chief of Security."

"It may be a front for something more. I'd like to meet you in person, but I'm being watched."

"What does he want with you?" Daniel asked, the timbre of his voice changing, betraying his concern, and the old authority and confidence Jake recalled.

"He hasn't told me what he wants, but he's threatened my family in Moscow."

"Christ," Daniel growled. "That puts you in a helluva position. You'll have to play along until we can find out what he's up to. If the Soviets are behind the move, we've got big trouble."

"He may be acting alone. It seems my leaving the country caused him no small amount of trouble. He may be after some sort of revenge."

"We'd better hope so. If the government's behind him, there's not a whole lot we can do to protect your family."

"I know."

"You should have called me sooner," Daniel said.

"Probably. But I wanted to know exactly what was going on." *And I didn't want to get my family killed.*

"I'll get on this thing, Jake. Where can I reach you?"

"You can't. In the morning I'm leaving with the team for Paris. I'll have to find you."

Daniel gave him a number. "Keep me posted. I'll need to know everything as it happens. We'll have men in Paris, but you won't know who they are."

"Dan? This is my mother and sister we're talking about."

"Trust me, Jake."

"I always have, haven't I?"

Daniel rang off and Jake felt somewhat better. No matter what happened, he was no longer alone.

CHAPTER NINE

Just before two p.m. on Thursday, Ellie loaded her bags and left the small apartment she had rented above the garage of a two-story house in Gladstone while she was training.

Her rooms in Santa Barbara, luxurious by comparison, were above her family's four-car garage at their exclusive residence in Hope Ranch. Her apartment there had a fireplace, kitchen and dining room, and a jumbo-sized bedroom. She'd decorated the place herself in a Southwest motif, using soft mauves and beiges with a trace of mint green.

In New Jersey, her tiny rented apartment overflowed with Duncan Fife mahogany and white lace doilies. Not her style, but it reminded her of her grandmother's house, and she would miss the place over the coming weeks.

Ellie returned her rented Toyota to the Avis drop off at the airport. She'd rent another when she returned for the horses' twenty-one-day quarantine before the Olympics. With the recent outbreak of Pyroplasmosis, the quarantine was imperative.

In the meantime, there were four European competitions ahead: Paris, Rotterdam, Hickstead, and Dublin.

At the terminal, a kindly dark-haired woman checked Ellie's tickets and sent her along the corridor to gate thirty-seven, a chartered Lufthansa flight that would arrive in Paris at eight forty-five in the morning.

The horses had already been loaded. Ellie entered the front of the plane to find a dozen members of the dressage, three-day eventing, and show jumping teams. Numerous grooms and handlers were already seated. Once they reached Paris, the teams would split up, each attending shows in different cities. They'd return on different planes at the end of the tour.

The big 747 had been sectioned in half: the horses quartered in the rear, the riders and lay members of the team in the front. Jake Sullivan wasn't on board.

"Have you seen Jake?" Ellie asked Prissy Knowles. Four inches taller than Ellie, Prissy weighed twenty-five pounds more, but she was far from fat. She was attractive, with light brown hair and hazel eyes.

Though they had only recently met, Ellie knew a little about her. Raised in Massachusetts, Prissy had been riding the Eastern circuit since she was ten years old. Since her family wasn't wealthy like those of most world-class riders, she'd worked in the stables to earn her keep. By the time she'd reached eighteen, she'd been good enough that several stables were willing to provide her with horses.

At twenty-eight, a gold medalist at the Pan American Games, Prissy could pick and choose. Julius Caesar and Deuteronomy, owned by the Greenbriar Stables just outside of Boston, were the horses she would be riding in Seoul. As Flex had predicted, she and Ellie were becoming fast friends.

"Jake's in the back, making a final check of the horses." Prissy eyed the quilted down jacket Ellie carried beneath her arm. "Don't tell me you're planning to ride back there?"

"Jake said I could since Jube isn't used to flying. I want to be near in case he gets nervous."

"Why don't you send Gerry back? Surely he can handle him."

"I'd just feel better being there myself."

"Well, you brought the right clothes. It's twenty degrees colder back there. The horses don't mind, but you will."

"I'll be fine." Ellie flashed a smile and headed back out through the open cabin door. She couldn't resist a last glance around the interior for Clay. Probably chartered his own private jet, she thought waspishly, and realized she was still mad at him.

She had no right to be. If the man wanted to get drunk and make a fool of himself that was his business. It just seemed such a waste.

Hurrying along the tarmac, Ellie made her way into the back of the plane, her boots ringing against the metal stairs. It already held the musky, alfalfa-horse scent of the stables, and Ellie was immediately glad to be there.

Glancing at her surroundings, she found Jake checking the horses, Gerry cooing to Jube, and several grooms feeding their animals handfuls of oats in an effort to keep them calm in their unfamiliar surroundings.

"This has got to be scary for them," Ellie said to Gerry. "Flying's always scary for me."

"Jube will be fine." Gerry patted the horse's nose. "And Rose is a veteran. She won't move a muscle." He glanced at Ellie's heavy jacket. "Sure you don't want me to ride back here?"

She shook her head. "Thanks anyway, Gerry."

"I'd better get going. We're about ready for takeoff. Find yourself a seat and strap yourself in."

Gerry and all but two of the other grooms left for their seats in the front of the plane, and Jake followed them out the door.

Ellie checked her watch. If the plane left on schedule, it would be backing away from the loading dock any minute. Folding down a narrow jump seat, she buckled herself in and settle back to prepare for takeoff. Across the way, two of the grooms did the same. She noticed one reading the June issue of *Playboy Magazine*.

Outside the plane, crewmen were closing the heavy cabin door. It was almost shut when the sound of boots ringing on the stairs caught her attention. Ellie's mouth dropped open when Clayton Whitfield stepped into the converted cargo bay.

"Sorry I'm late," he said to no one in particular, then cocked an eyebrow and flashed Ellie a charming, cheek-dimpling grin. "I should have known you'd be back here."

Ellie decided the remark was meant as a compliment and the last of her pique slipped away.

To her surprise, Clay took a seat beside her and strapped in his muscular frame. He draped the Navy issue trench coat he carried across his long legs, which looked uncomfortably cramped.

Ellie glanced at the coat. There was no way Clayton Whitfield had been in the military.

"It belonged to my half-brother," Clay said as if reading her thoughts. "He was a Navy pilot." He examined an invisible speck on the sleeve of the jacket. "He was killed in Nam in '68."

Surprise trickled through her. "I didn't know you had a brother."

"I don't talk about him often. It still bothers me after all these years. He was ten years older, but we were close just the same." A sad smile touched his lips. "John was a really great guy. In his preflight training in Pensacola, he got the highest score ever received. He was so proud of being a pilot." Clay glanced away. "I was lost when he died."

Every time Ellie talked to Clay, she had the feeling there was something more to him than people believed, something he kept bottled up inside. "I'm sorry."

"It was a long time ago." He smiled and changed the subject. "How's Jubilee taking all this?"

"He's okay so far. Rose is content. Your Max could care less."

"He's done this so many times he's used to it, but on such a long flight, I like to keep an eye on him." Just then the powerful jet engines roared to life and Ellie glanced worriedly at the horses. Inside their wooden pallets, they nickered and stamped their feet, but seemed okay.

The plane taxied down the tarmac, lined up on the runway, and revved its engines, the noise vibrating her less-than-padded chair and sending a shiver of dread up her spine. She gripped the armrests hard enough to make her knuckles ache. The scenery outside her window passed by in a colorful blur, reminding her of the world she'd lived in before her eye surgery.

Several horses whinnied as the plane angled upward on takeoff, but the pilot seemed concerned for his precious cargo, settled into a smooth steady climb, then leveled off.

"Are you alright?" Clay asked, frowning.

Ellie swallowed. "I usually have a couple of glasses of wine before I fly."

"This time you're out of luck."

Ellie just nodded, her heartbeat beginning to slow. "More people were killed in train accidents last year than in airline crashes, but still..."

"But, still, it scares the hell out of you."

Her lips edge up. "Now you know my deepest, darkest secret."

Clay looked at her and grinned. "You mean we're finally even?"

"You've got to be kidding."

Clay looked contrite, but his brown eyes flashed with mischief. "I guess you're right."

At forty-two thousand feet, the plane's cruising altitude, they all put on their coats. It was cold and uncomfortable, but bearable. The horses seemed resigned, all but Julius Caesar, Prissy's chestnut gelding, who nervously rolled his eyes and stamped his feet. Riding in the same pallet, her second horse, Lovely Lass grazed peacefully on a bit of hay.

Two hours into the trip, Clay excused himself to go to the bathroom. The plane dipped unexpectedly, and Ellie's stomach rolled. Julius Caesar whinnied loudly and began to kick the board slats holding him in. He jerked at his rope with a snapping pop that rang through the cabin, and a dark-haired groom Ellie didn't recognize unbuckled his seat belt and moved toward the horse at the same time Ellie did.

Standing next to Caesar, now Lass was beginning to get nervous. She kicked the back of the crate and whinnied, and Caesar tore his rope free.

"You sonofabitch," the groom said. "You'll have them all stirred up if you don't settle down." He took the loose end of the rope and whacked Caesar hard across the nose. The horse reared up on his back legs, hitting his head on the top of the pallet.

"Stop that!" Ellie cried. "Leave him alone. He's just scared."

"Stay out of this. It's my job to see these animals arrive safely. The way he's acting, he'll have them all going nuts."

Thwack, the rope came down on Caesar's nose. He flattened his ears and tried to bite. Teeth bared, he snorted and pawed and fought, rolled his eyes back to expose the whites. Thwack, thwack, thwack.

Ellie's chest tightened. "Please don't do that."

"Leave the horse alone." Clay's deep voice cut like a knife. "You know better than to treat an animal like that. If you don't, you don't belong here."

The groom took a step backward. "Look, Whitfield. We're forty-two thousand feet up. The sonofabitch will have them all trying to break out. God knows what they could do to the plane. What do you suggest we do?"

"I suggest we try to figure out what the hell is wrong with him."

"Obviously, he doesn't like to fly."

"Obviously." The sarcasm went unnoticed by the groom. "Snub him down, and I'll take a look."

The groom did as he was told, putting a loop on the end of a stick around Caesar's nose and twisting until his head was immobile. Caesar braced himself on all four feet, trembling all over, but he didn't move. Through the slats of the crate, Clay checked the animal's feet, checked the horse's haunches and flanks. Nothing.

Then Caesar's dark pupils caught Clay's attention. They were dilated abnormally.

"I hate to say this, but I think he's been drugged."

"What?" Ellie moved close. "Why would anyone want to drug him?"

"Apparently to make him hyperactive. If nobody had been back here, God knows how much trouble he might have caused. Maybe whoever did this didn't count on our being here. Or maybe they were just creating malicious mischief. My guess is there was something added to his grain or water. We'll have the buckets checked when we get to Paris."

"Will he be all right?"

"We'll have to keep an eye on him. He's going to make this trip a living hell."

"Let's get a rope over his head and around behind him," Willie Jenkins, the second groom suggested. "That ought to keep him fairly immobile."

In fifteen minutes, they had him tied as securely as possible. Caesar snorted and whinnied, stomped and strained against the ropes, but it looked as though he would be all right.

"As soon as we land, we'll let Jake and the others know." Clay followed Ellie back to their seats. "It's possible whoever did this is a member of the tour."

She paused as she strapped herself back in. "You can't believe it's one of our own people."

"I'm sure it isn't, but you never know."

The trip passed with agonizing slowness, the cold creeping into everyone's bones, Caesar's shrill neighing keeping all of them on edge. Being the farthest away, Jube seemed unconcerned. Off and on, Clay soothed Max, speaking to him quietly, rubbing his nose and his sleek, powerful neck. Surprisingly, each time the horse quieted almost instantly, and eventually settled down to grazing in his pallet.

Returning to his seat, Clay stretched his long legs out in front of him, trying to make himself comfortable.

Ellie flashed Clay a smile. "I just...I want to say how great you were with Caesar. If you hadn't been here, I don't know what we would have done."

"You'd have done just fine." He returned her smile. "Why don't you put your head on my shoulder and try to get some sleep?"

She hesitated. But considering the cold and the grueling hours in the air, it was probably a good idea. Resting her head against Clay's thick shoulder, she let herself relax. He felt solid and warm, and her eyelids began to droop. She closed them for a while, but she never completely fell asleep.

When the plane landed in Paris, she found herself hoping Clay would ask her out as he had before. Against her better judgment, she would accept.

Clay didn't ask.

He helped her descend the steel stairs to the runway and began a conversation with Flex and Shep. When he spotted Jake, he went over to relay the details of what had happened to Caesar. Even from a distance, Jake's expression said he was worried. He nodded at something Clay said, and they walked off together.

Exhausted, Ellie made her way through customs with the rest of the team. The dressage and three-day eventing teams were headed for shows in other parts of Europe but wouldn't depart for a couple of days.

Thanks to Maggie Delaine's skillful maneuvering, they were staying at the Concorde Hotel for a very nominal rate. The horses were taken on to their stalls at the show grounds while the riders would be arriving at the hotel by bus.

Engrossed in the fascinating sights of the city, she didn't notice Clay taking the seat beside her until his deep voice startled her out of her thoughts.

"I'm guessing you've never been to Paris."

She smiled. "Actually, I was here for the horseshow last year. I love Paris. I think it's the most beautiful city in the world. But I've never been anyplace I didn't think was beautiful in one way or another."

Clay said nothing, just kept watching her as if he tried to figure her out.

"You intrigue me, Ellie Fletcher. You seem to have a boundless love of life, yet you enjoy very little of it."

Ellie just shook her head. "You don't have to be a jetsetter to enjoy life, Clay. I find pleasure in the small things, that's all. You overlook them for the bigger things."

She glanced out the window to a row of buildings in the old

section of the city. The structures were three stories high with graceful arches and tiny dormer windows that peeked through mansard roofs.

"For instance, when you look at those buildings, you see the cracks in the plaster, the peeling paint, and the sagging doorframes. I see them as they once were. I wonder who built them, who lived in the rooms upstairs. I wonder what kind of lives the people led. Did they have children? Were they in love? I can almost see them walking through the doorways, the ladies in their bustled skirts, men in top hats and frock coats. There's so much more to seeing things than just looking on the surface."

Clay gazed out at the buildings disappearing in the distance. Now they passed newer, taller buildings. "There are things I could show you, Ellie, things you've never seen." His dark eyes slid down to her lips and for a moment she thought he might kiss her. "Things I could make you feel."

Her heart was throbbing, her breathing a little ragged. She could feel those hot brown eyes like a warm caress and her nipples tightened beneath her blouse. She prayed Clay wouldn't notice.

"What did...umm...Jake say about Caesar?"

Clay leaned back in his seat, apparently resigned to her change of subject. "As soon as the horses arrive at the stables, he'll have the vet take blood and saliva samples. They'll do a complete physical to be sure Caesar's all right, but on the surface, he appears to be okay."

"Thank God."

"I tried to get Jake to report the incident to the Paris police, but he said he'd rather handle the matter through our own security people." Clay shook his head. "I don't know if I agree with him, but—"

"Jake knows what he's doing," Ellie defended

Clay's expression turned dark. "You and Jake aren't... involved...are you?"

"Involved? Good Lord, no!"

At least not yet, Clay thought. *And not if I have anything to say about it.* But he wouldn't press her to go out with him tonight, since she was bound to be exhausted. Besides she'd say no, and he wasn't ready to face another rejection. He had just as much pride as she did. He'd wait for her to come to him this time.

But he wouldn't wait too damned long.

CHAPTER TEN

Jake Sullivan dreamed of Maggie Delaine.

Except Jake wasn't asleep. Jet lag always left him wired-up and edgy. He prayed there was no connection between Popov and what had happened to Caesar on the plane, but his common sense warned him there was.

Just as Clay suspected, Lee Montalvo, the team veterinarian, had found a trace of stimulant in the horse's grain bucket. The question was who put it there?

Dozens of people had access. There was just no way to tell. He needed to call Daniel and let him know about the incident.

Lying on top of the covers, Jake stretched full length on the bed, crossed his long legs at the ankle, and tried to push his troubles out of his head. It didn't take long before his mind drifted to Maggie.

Just before their departure, Evelyn Rothwell, the USET Director, had unexpectedly gone in for back surgery, so Maggie would be coming to Paris. Though he couldn't chance talking to her except on a business level, he found himself anticipating her arrival.

For the first time in weeks, he allowed himself the pleasure of remembering the night he'd seen her at the Helmsley Palace in Manhattan. The loveliest woman in the room, he'd thought that night.

All his life, Jake had avoided attachments, chosen women who wanted nothing more than a comfortable relationship with a man who could satisfy their sexual needs and keep his mouth shut about it. Women who didn't want marriage any more than he did.

His years in the Soviet Union had left him wary and distrustful, afraid to let his guard down. Better to be a loner, rely on himself, avoid attachments of any kind.

After he'd bought Pleasant Oaks, he'd thought about finding a wife, but until he met Maggie, there was never anyone he considered special enough to share his life.

He wanted a woman he could trust and rely on. Someone who shared the same goals. At forty-six, he'd been ready to take some chances, let go of his well-guarded feelings and reach out for something more.

From the moment he'd spoken to Maggie, Jake knew his life would never be the same.

Though he'd seen her once before, at Les Delaine's funeral, it wasn't until a night three years later that he began making inquiries about her. Friends mentioned her daughter, Sarah, and told him Maggie had made charitable contributions and done hours of work in her husband's name for the U.S. Equestrian Team.

"Beautiful evening," he'd said as he walked up beside her on the terrace. "I'm Jake Sullivan. I don't know if you remember me. We met once before."

She turned away from the view of St. Patrick's Cathedral in the distance, toward the lights twinkling in the courtyard below. In profile she had a patrician nose and a delicately sculpted chin. A shaft of moonlight cut through the branches of a potted cypress and touched her honey-blond hair.

"I know who you are," she said with a hint of amusement, as if the whole world knew him by name. "We met at Les' funeral." He caught a flash of pain. "That was a long time ago. I'm glad tonight's circumstances are more pleasant."

"Yes." Jake's gaze followed hers across the courtyard below the terrace. "I made some inquiries about you. It seems we have a lot in common."

"Really?"

"That's right. You like to walk in the moonlight, so do I. You like horses, so do I. You like to dance, so do I."

She arched a golden eyebrow. "How do you know I like to dance?"

"Because all beautiful women like to dance."

She laughed at that and smiled.

"Why don't we go someplace quiet for a drink?" he asked.

Maggie's easy smile faded. "No. No, I couldn't do that."

"Why not?"

"It wouldn't be right."

"Are you involved with someone? I know you've haven't remarried."

Maggie glanced away. "I'm not involved with anyone, but.... In a lot of ways, I suppose I still feel obligated to Les."

Jake caught her chin, turning her to face him, not certain why he felt so sure of her. "It's been three years, Maggie."

She didn't move away. "It has been, hasn't it?"

"How about that drink?"

Uncertainly shone in her pale blue eyes. "I don't know, I..."

"You have nothing to fear from me," he said softly.

Maggie's smile slowly returned, and she nodded. "All right. I'll get my wrap."

It was the beginning he had hoped for. After a few short weeks, Jake never wanted it to end.

Having spent all day Friday with the horses, Ellie had fallen asleep at seven p.m. At five the next morning, she awoke rested and ready to work.

Her roommate in the other twin bed, Prissy Knowles stirred beneath the covers. "God, don't tell me you're up already. I feel like I just closed my eyes."

"Go back to sleep. I'm used to getting up early."

Prissy groaned and pulled the pillow over her head.

Ellie hurried through her morning routine, showered, plaited her hair into a single thick braid, pulled on her breeches and boots, and headed out the door. Since she was too early for the team bus, she'd take a taxi out to the show grounds, work with Jube for a while, then come back and take some free time to go to the Louvre, which was just across the street.

Ellie was headed down the hall toward the elevators, her mind on her morning workout at the show grounds, when the door in front of her opened and a girl she recognized as one of the team grooms stepped through the opening. Her dark hair was mussed, her clothes wrinkled, but the smile on Linda Gibbon's face said she didn't give a whit.

"Bye, lover." She blew a kiss to the person behind the door. Even before Ellie heard his deep voice, she knew it was Clay.

"Wait a minute," he called out. "You forgot your bag."

Ellie tried to force her feet to keep moving, but they wouldn't obey. Clay stood in the opening, holding out the girl's purse, naked to the waist, a towel wrapped casually around his hips. He looked tanned and muscled and perfect. His eyes swept past the girl to Ellie, and he frowned at her stunned expression.

"Isn't that Ellie Fletcher?" Linda said to him as Ellie forced her feet to move on down the hall. "She may be untouchable, but I bet you could give her a run for her money." Linda laughed.

"Go on," Clay said gruffly. "I'll see you out at the stable."

Ellie kept on walking. It took several deep breaths to calm her racing heart. The elevator door opened, and she stepped inside. Linda was hurrying to catch the elevator.

"Wait!"

Ellie gave a grateful sigh when the doors closed in the woman's face.

Dressed in a pair of beige gabardine slacks, a white shirt, and dark brown Italian loafers, Clay left the hotel. He'd decided to take the day off. He wasn't ready to face Ellie Fletcher.

If he closed his eyes, he could still see her shocked expression. Not just surprise, but hurt and betrayal, like a woman who'd just caught her man in bed with a lover. Good God, they hadn't even been out on a date!

Worst of all, Clay felt exactly the same.

What in the hell was the matter with him? He'd been seeing Linda Gibbons off and on for months. She had a lusty appetite and very little conscience. She made no demands on him, just seemed happy when he paid her the slightest attention. Last night she'd cornered him. Feeling edgy after the long plane flight and his bout with Caesar, Clay had taken her up to his suite.

He hadn't really wanted Linda, caught himself more than once pretending she was Ellie. But he'd been determined he wouldn't let the little redhead turn him down again. He'd made a promise to himself. He wasn't about to chase after her any more than he had already!

Besides, there was Jake to consider. Maybe he had serious intentions toward Ellie. Then Clay recalled Jake's affair with Maggie Delaine. Clay didn't know what had happened, but he believed Jake had hurt Maggie badly.

Apparently, Jake Sullivan was no Prince Charming, himself.

Walking across the plush carpet in the lobby beneath crystal chandeliers, Clay shoved open the double glass doors and stepped out onto the sidewalk. It was still early, but he needed some air and a chance to think.

Was Ellie interested in Jake? He tried to recall the times he'd seen them together, tried to remember the look in her eyes. No, Ellie looked at Jake the way a woman looked at a friend.

He grunted. Ellie was old enough to know what she wanted. She was not that many years younger than he. Still, he could tell she was inexperienced. Damn sexy, but nothing like the women he dated.

As he crossed the Rue de Rivoli and headed toward the Tuileries gardens for a breath of fresh air, Ellie's pretty face rose in his mind again. Damn her! The last thing he needed was a Pollyanna like Ellie Fletcher.

Damn her to hell for making him feel so bad.

Two days past. She'd been busy with the horses, getting them accustomed to the time change, working with Gerry and Jake. Tonight, there was a team dinner hosted by Avery Whitfield, who'd apparently taken time from his hunting trip in Scotland to fly in for an evening in Paris.

He was taking them to one of the best restaurants in the city, L'Archestrate.

Ellie found herself dreading the event.

God only knew who the man would be bringing, or for that matter, who Clay would bring as his date. It hurt to realize she cared who Clay entertained.

Glum since the incident in the hallway, she decided to cheer herself up. She would take the day off and go to the Louvre, as she had planned.

It wasn't far from the hotel and though she had been there once, there was so much to see she had hardly made a dent. For the next few hours, Ellie walked the massive rooms beneath carved and gilded ceilings. When her feet began to ache, she went in search of a bench, finding one in an echoing corridor lined on both sides with huge Renaissance oil paintings. There were scenes of the Crucifixion, Gainsborough's Pinky, a Rubens with its cherubic, pink-fleshed women, and across the way in a glass-enclosed box, the Mona Lisa.

Ignoring the sign on the wall that forbid taking pictures, Japanese tourists flashed cameras at the centuries' old canvas.

"So now I discover you like fine art." Whitfield's deep voice sent an unwelcome thrill up her spine.

She stood up from the bench, wishing she were anywhere but there. "What are you doing here? You don't seem the art-lover type."

He smiled. "The Whitfield Collection houses some of the world's greatest masterpieces. But I came to see the Egyptian Antiquities. It's always been an interest of mine. Have you seen the exhibit?"

"No. I've been walking around for hours, but there's just so much to see."

"Why don't you come along?"

She thought of Clay with the female groom. "I'm still a little tired."

"I promise you it'll be worth it."

She read the challenge in his expression. *Why the hell not?* Every other woman in the world seemed to find time for Clay. "All right. Let's go."

They headed down the wide staircase past the Winged Venus of Samothrace that stood on the landing. When they entered the massive Egyptian Antiquities chamber, Ellie was surprised to see huge Egyptian sphinxes, twenty-foot statues of gods and pharaohs, and whole tombs reconstructed, their painted walls completely intact.

"Clay, this is magnificent." She glanced around, forgetting everything but her surroundings. "It's like going back in time."

"It is, isn't it? I come here whenever I'm in Paris. There's always something new to see." They walked through the maze of towering sculptures, the chamber surprisingly void of people.

"Is it always this quiet in here? It's kind of eerie."

"Every time I've been here it has been. It gives the place a tomb-like quality that seems exactly right."

"I wonder what people were like back then."

"Probably a lot like we are now. Some happy, some sad, some indifferent."

"Which are you?"

Clay looked at her as if debating how much of himself to reveal.

"Probably the last."

"I'd rather be sad than indifferent. I'd rather feel anything than nothing at all."

They meandered through the gigantic pieces. "I take it that means you consider yourself happy," Clay said.

"Of course. Why shouldn't I be? Every time I look around, I'm grateful to be alive."

He scoffed. "I'm afraid I'm more than a little jaded."

"Maybe you just don't want to admit your feelings." She smiled. "I read a little of your poetry, remember?"

He grimaced. "Don't remind me."

Clay looked into Ellie's wide green eyes. There was an ocean of feeling in those eyes. Whenever he talked to her, life seemed different somehow. Fuller, richer, immensely worth living.

She brushed past him toward a gray granite wall notched with intricate hieroglyphics. His eyes strayed to her sexy little ass, which he always found fascinating. He wanted to take her to bed, to capture that aliveness, soak up the warmth she carried inside.

"Let me take you to supper," he said, regretting the words as soon as they were spoken.

"Tonight's the team dinner," she reminded him. "Your father's the sponsor. Don't you have a date already?"

In fact, he did. With Gabriella Marchbanks, a model from New York who was on location in Paris for *Harper's Bazaar*.

"I forgot about that. How about tomorrow?"

"What about Linda?"

"Linda and I are friends."

"Clay, I won't deny going out with you is tempting, but I don't want to get involved with a man like you. We just don't want the same things out of life."

"How do you know what I want out of life?"

Ellie didn't answer. She walked around him and ducked into the low opening of a reconstructed tomb. Clay ducked in behind her. It was dark and cool inside.

"I know you feel something for me," Clay said, pressing her up against the rough stone wall. "I can see it in your eyes."

"You're wrong."

"Go out with me." He braced a hand on each side of her,

blocking her escape.

"No."

"You want to. I know you do." Using his weight to keep her in place, he caught her chin, leaned down and kissed her. Ellie tried to turn away, but when he deepened the kiss. Her lips parted with a soft purr of pleasure and her rigid posture relaxed. Ellie slid her arms around his neck and kissed him back, and God, she tasted good, tasted like honey in spring.

His body responded, making him hard, aching to have her. He couldn't remember wanting a woman so badly.

When Clay deepened the kiss, Ellie didn't care if she ever moved away from exactly where she stood. Clay felt big and solid against her, his lips soft, yet firm and insistent. Her limbs felt weak and shaky, and desire curled low in her belly.

When Clay's hands moved to caress her breasts through her white cotton blouse, heat spiraled out through her body. She wanted more, wanted to see where the heat would take her.

If they were someplace else, she would go to bed with him and hang the consequences. She was tired of being untouchable, tired of waiting for God only knew what.

Clay trailed kisses along the side of her neck, then returned to her mouth, softly coaxing, then kissing her deeply again. His hand moved down her body to cup her bottom, pulling her more solidly against him, and she could feel his erection.

What would it be like to make love with him? Linda Gibbons enjoyed it, that much was plain. Thinking of Linda and Clay together the night before hit her like a bucket of cold water.

Ellie pushed hard on his chest, ending the kiss. "I shouldn't have done that. I'm...I'm sorry I let things go so far." She ducked through the opening before he could stop her, but he caught her just outside.

"How can you be sorry?" He seemed incredulous, then his features turned dark. "There was nothing wrong with what we did. It was what we both wanted."

"It's not what I want."

"Damn it, what do you want? Do you want to go on aching for sexual release, as it's obvious you are?"

Ellie flushed. "I get all the sexual release I need," she lied. "Now go away and leave me alone."

"I don't believe you. It's obvious you haven't been laid in weeks. Come back with me to the hotel."

"Are you out of your mind? Two days ago, you were in bed with Linda!"

"Don't you understand? It isn't Linda I want—it's you! And even if you won't admit it, you want me, too."

"Go away! Why can't you just leave me alone?" Turning away, she dashed for the stairs, brushing a tear from her cheek. The man was incorrigible. He was making her *happy* life miserable.

If he weren't such a womanizer, she'd just have sex with him and get it over with. She was twenty-four years old. There was no such thing as a twenty-four-year-old virgin. If Clay found out, he'd laugh in her face.

As soon as the Paris show was over, she was going to find a lover. It was time she grew up. There was bound to be someone out there who would initiate her gently.

Someone who didn't sleep with a different woman every other night!

CHAPTER ELEVEN

Maggie arrived in Paris late in the afternoon. She was traveling with her daughter, Sarah, and Sarah's nanny, Flora Pedigrew, more of a member of the household than an employee.

After the long flight from the East Coast, they'd all slept late that morning, Flora in an adjoining room, Maggie in the room with Sarah.

When the phone rang, Maggie was the first to awaken. She snatched the receiver up and glanced over to find her daughter still fast asleep.

"This is Maggie."

"Thought an old trooper like you would be up and at 'em by now." She recognized Avery Whitfield's too-loud voice.

"Good morning, Avery. I thought you were in Scotland."

"Was till this morning. Only a hop, Shep, and a jump, you know."

Yes, in your Gulfstream, she thought.

"Called to invite you to the little party I'm throwing in honor of the show jumping team. Dinner at L'Archestrate, a little drinking, dancing at Le Palace—all on me, of course."

"I have a date. Can I bring him along?"

"Sure! The more the merrier, I always say."

"Yes, so you do." Maggie was already sorry she'd agreed to go, ashamed of herself for her perverse desire to flaunt her handsome escort in front of Jake Sullivan.

"Go back to your beauty rest," Avery said. "See you tonight at eight."

The day slipped past. As evening approached, Maggie dressed for dinner with more care than she had in months, pouring through her traveling wardrobe three times before deciding what to wear. She settled on a yellow chiffon dress that accented her hair, which she wore loose around her shoulders the way Jake liked it.

She hoped he ate his heart out.

"Will Jake be there tonight, Mama?"

Maggie looked down at Sarah and felt a rush of guilt for allowing him back into her thoughts. "I suppose so, honey. Shall I tell him you said hello?"

Sarah started to say yes, then shook her head. "I don't think he cares."

Maggie managed to smile. "Jake's just been busy." Every time she saw that forlorn expression on Sarah's face, she wanted to murder Jake Sullivan. It was one thing for him to break Maggie's heart, quite another to hurt a nine-year-old child.

"Sometimes I still miss him. Do you miss him, too?"

Maggie touched her daughter's cheek, the face a miniature replica of her own except that Sarah's shoulder-length blond hair was nearly platinum.

"Yes, honey, sometimes I do. But Jake has the team to think about...and running Pleasant Oaks. He just didn't have time for us, that's all."

At least that's what he'd told her. Maggie hadn't believed him for a minute.

"He doesn't love us anymore," Sarah said.

"He sent Ransom down, didn't he?" And Maggie hadn't the heart to return Jake's beautiful horse. Sarah had been hurt enough already.

Maggie had introduced Jake to Sarah when he'd first visited them in Tampa. Sarah had adored him from the start, the first person she had responded to after her father's death. She'd been isolated and withdrawn, as if she didn't want to risk loving someone then losing him again. With Jake she'd been different from the beginning.

Then Jake had called Maggie to say something had come up and he wouldn't be able to see her that weekend. The same thing happened the following week. He made none of his usual calls in between.

When he finally phoned again, he sounded remote and guarded.

"Maggie, I might as well do this now," he'd said. "There's just no way around it. We're going to have to stop seeing each other for a while."

"I-I don't understand."

"Things are just too tough right now. All this traveling back and forth, trying to match our schedules...it just isn't fair to the team."

"But I thought...thought we..." *Might get married.* She had been sure he was going to propose.

"Maybe eventually things will calm down."

Maggie's throat constricted, the hard lump threatening to choke her. "I see." She held the receiver away for a moment, fighting for control. "Thanks for letting me know."

Maggie hung up the phone. Now she knew the truth, that Jake didn't want her anymore. It happened to women all the time.

She also knew Jake Sullivan had broken her heart.

Maggie walked out of the hotel elevator to find her escort waiting.

"You look gorgeous, Maggie. But then you always do." In his expensive Italian suit, Dr. Benjamin Jaffe looked pretty gorgeous himself. "How old did you say you were?" he teased, "twenty-five?"

"I'm thirty-eight, and you know it."

"Well, you look twenty-five." He extended his arm and Maggie took it. They swept through the lobby, turning heads as they passed. Ben Jaffe was tall and blond, Riviera-tanned and handsome. A plastic surgeon from Florida, Ben was in France on a sabbatical. He'd been lounging on the beach in St. Tropez.

"I've missed you, Maggie."

She'd been dating Ben for almost a month before he'd left for France. They'd discussed meeting in Paris, and Ben had phoned last week to confirm the date of her arrival. She had yet to sleep with him. She should have accepted his invitation for a weekend in the Bahamas. But Jake was the only man she'd ever been with besides her husband. She simply wasn't ready yet.

And there was Sarah to consider.

Now Ben was in Paris. He'd been patient so far, but she knew he intended to press his suit.

Smiling down at her, he shoved open the glass door leading out to the sidewalk in front of the hotel. With the long line of people pursuing a night on the town, getting a cab was always a problem. Ben had a private car waiting at the curb.

"Always efficient," Maggie said.

"Just like you." He smiled, his gaze approving as it moved over her yellow chiffon dress. He helped her into the car, and they set off.

A doorman waited in front of the expensive restaurant on the Rue de Varenne. As he opened her door and helped her out, Maggie felt her nerves beginning to build. She hadn't seen Jake since the party at the Burbages in North Salem, and only then for a few brief moments. Afterward, she hadn't been able to eat for three days.

But she hadn't had a handsome escort then. "Thanks for coming, Ben."

"My pleasure," he said.

Inside L'Archestrate, Maggie caught the sound of Avery Whitfield's raucous laughter before they rounded the first corner toward the dining room. The restaurant was crowded, but the plush brown carpeting and textured beige wallpaper kept the noise subdued. They passed huge sprays of orange gladiolas, and the tables were set with fine china and crystal. The waiters all wore black.

Entering the main dining salon, Maggie spotted Avery seated at the head of a single long table next to a sleek-looking blonde. Avery always preferred blondes, she recalled.

Clay sat on his right next to one of the most stunningly beautiful women Maggie had ever seen. She was nearly as tall as Clay, thin, but not skinny, with a bone structure any artist would love. She had thick black hair coiled in a tight chignon but was surprisingly fair complexioned. Her high-necked black silk sheath with its stark white collar and cuffs reeked of expensive good taste. The entire package was stunning. There was simply no other word for it.

Shep Singleton sat on her left, elegant with his silver hair and black gabardine suit. Ellie Fletcher sat across from Clay next to Flex McGrath, who sat beside Prissy Knowles. Jake Sullivan sat near the two vacant chairs at the end.

Dear God, either she or Ben would have to sit beside him.

Sensing her plight, Ben took control, pulling out the velvet chair next to Shep. Grateful for his thoughtfulness, Maggie stepped in front of the chair but didn't sit down.

"I'd like you all to meet a friend of mine, Dr. Benjamin Jaffe." She introduced him to each person seated and surprised herself by introducing Jake with no noticeable inflection. At least he wasn't with a date.

"This is Gabriella Marchbanks," Clay said. "She's here for a photo layout for *Harper's.*"

"And this is Chauncey Reed," Avery added with a leer at the blonde.

They took their seats and Maggie ordered a vodka martini, which she rarely drank. Tonight, she needed all the courage she could get.

Avery had arranged the meal. An appetizer of *Mousse de brouchet,* pike mousse with lobster sauce served with a delicate Riesling Cuvee Frederic Emile. Maggie just picked at her plate.

"Relax," Ben whispered in her ear. "You're doing great."

She was glad Ben thought so. Her stomach was tied in knots and every time she glanced to her left, she found Jake's eyes on her, the vivid blue unreadable.

"Are you pleased with the way the team's shaping up?" Ben asked Jake as the waiters served the soup, *crème de legumes.*

"They're some of the best riders in the world. They'll be competing together for the first time on Tuesday, which will help their confidence and give the horses a chance to get back on their feet."

Jake flicked another glance at Maggie.

"How's Caesar?" Flex asked, worried about Prissy's horse and the trouble he'd had on the plane.

"He looked fine this morning," Jake said. "Whatever they gave him wasn't meant to do permanent damage."

"And Zodiak?" One of Clay's horses, a big Hanoverian, had cut himself deplaning.

"The wound was minor. He'll be able to compete on Thursday." The European horse shows usually lasted from Thursday through Sunday, a little less grueling than the American shows, but no less demanding.

The conversation continued and Maggie forced herself to eat.

Dear Lord, she'd be glad when the evening was over.

"Zodiak's a great horse," Ellie said to Flex. "Clay's done a great job of bringing him along." The minute she said the words, Ellie wished she hadn't spoken. She'd caught Clay's attention, the last thing she wanted to do.

Even in her new two-piece cocktail dress, a pale sea green silk bought hastily that afternoon, she felt shabby in comparison to the woman on Clay's left.

God, was there no end to his list of beautiful women? Every time Ellie looked at the beautiful New York model she felt like throwing up.

"Thanks for the compliment." Clay cast her a grin that dimpled his cheeks. "I believe it's a first."

"Don't be silly, darling," said Gabriella. "There are *dozens* of things you do well." There was no mistaking her meaning, or the seductive look she cast Clay.

Stifling the reply Ellie wished she had the courage to make, she was relieved when the waiters arrived with the main course, *Grenadine de Veau Normande,* sautéed veal medallions with mushrooms and crème fraiche glazed with Calvados and slices of apple. With it, Avery had chosen a Chateau Beychevelle '76.

Ellie took a courage-boosting sip of the rich red wine, and over the rim of the glass, she watched Clay. Dressed in a black suit with a crisp white shirt that showed off his tan, he looked every bit the sophisticated playboy, his date the epitome of elegant chic.

Thank God, she'd had enough courage to ask Flex to escort her. The man was a gem.

"I don't want Clay to think I can't get a date," she said. "Do you think you could pretend to be interested in me? Just for tonight?"

Flex grinned from ear to ear. "This is rich. I'd love nothing better than to see Clay Whitfield get his comeuppance. I'll have him convinced we're red-hot lovers, if that's what you want."

"I thought you two were friends."

"We're good friends. But we've been rat f-ing each other for years. If he thinks I've gotten you in bed and he couldn't, it'll drive him crazy."

Ellie hadn't really intended to carry things that far, but the more she thought about it, the better is sounded.

"That's *exactly* what I want." Even with his red hair and freckles, Flex was a good-looking man. He never lacked for female companionship, and his taste in women was impeccable. She'd heard Clay say so more than once.

"This'll be a gas," Flex said.

"He probably won't even notice."

"Don't sell yourself short, Ellie. You're one sexy lady. Clay's got the hots for you, and he'll damn well notice." Flex grinned and chucked her under the chin. "It'll do him good to stew."

Now, sitting here looking at Clay, she didn't think their plan had the slightest effect. Not when Clay had walked into the room with the most beautiful woman Ellie had ever seen.

Thank goodness for Flex, who'd been charming and attentive all evening. Clay had looked surprised, then skeptical, but Flex had ignored him, holding her hand, whispering in her ear, tickling the back of her knee beneath the table until she giggled.

When the waiter brought dessert, a light Grand Marnier soufflé accompanied by bottles of '76 Dom Perignon, he kept her glass filled and she downed the champagne until she was dizzy.

"Take it easy," Flex whispered. "You're doing great. I never thought I'd say this, but I think he's really jealous."

"You're crazy. Look at the girl he's with. She's gorgeous. Why would he care about me?"

"I'm telling you, I've known Clay for years, and I've never seen him like this. Here, I'll show you what I mean."

Before she could move, Flex bent down and kissed her. Just a soft, quick kiss. Not enough to draw attention, but enough to make Clay's eyes darken. Ellie saw it and her heart leaped. Until he turned to the beautiful brunette and kissed her full on the mouth.

Flex chuckled softly. "What'd I tell you?"

"I'm leaving," Ellie said.

Flex tightened his hold on her arm, keeping her firmly in her chair. "No, you aren't. We're going to see this through. Something's going on here, and I'm going to help you find out what it is."

Ellie sighed. *Why the hell not?* She took a deep breath, a drink of champagne, and smiled up at Flex, the most seductive smile she could manage.

Flex squeezed her hand and flashed her a grin.

"Everybody having fun?" Avery asked.

Shep Singleton lifted his glass. "To our host, Avery Whitfield, for a marvelous evening."

"To winning the gold in Seoul," Avery countered, "and to my son, Clay, who makes me so proud."

Clay's scowl faded at his father's praise, and everyone drank heartily. Glasses were refilled, and by the end of the meal almost everyone was drunk.

"I say it's time we head to Le Palace," Avery said. "Time to work off some of these calories. Wouldn't want you all to break training any worse than you already have!"

Ellie managed not to roll her eyes. They all left in taxis, Ellie trying to convince Flex to let her go back to the hotel, Flex staunchly refusing.

"We're seeing this thing through." He laughed. "I can't wait to see how it all turns out."

"I can tell you how it'll turn out. Clay will take Ms. Marchbanks back to the hotel and screw her all night. I'll go home alone. And you...? Well, I don't know exactly what you'll do."

"Probably the same as you. I'm thinking about getting serious with someone."

"No!"

"Yes."

"Who is she? Do I know her?"

"Nobody knows her. We met at the Tucson show early this year. We've been seeing each other off and on ever since. Her name's Carrie Schweitzer. She's not a rider. She was there with a friend."

"Flex, that's wonderful."

"I'm thinking of flying her over for Seoul."

"That's great. I really wish you the best."

"I know you do, Ellie. That's one of the things I like about you. You want the best for everyone. Even Clay."

"I want the worst for Clay." She glanced down, her gaze catching a spring poking through the cab's worn seat. The taxi driver honked his horn, shook his fist out the window, and cursed at another driver.

"You don't want the worst for Clay," Flex said. "I bet if you thought he'd be happy with that model, you'd be glad for him."

"Probably. I never was very smart."

"You're plenty smart. I think that's one reason Clay's so attracted to you."

"He isn't attracted to me."

"Bullshit. He's been watching you all evening. He's hardly

110

looked at the gorgeous brunette."

"Did you have to bring her up?"

"I'm telling you something's up. Clay never acts like this."

"He just wants to sleep with me. I'm just another challenge to him."

"I bet a hundred French francs, you're wrong. But with Clay, you never know what he's thinking."

"He's thinking about getting laid. That's all he ever thinks about."

"He might surprise you."

"Oh, he's done that several times already."

Flex just laughed. The cab screeched to a halt, slinging them against the seat. Flex got out, then helped Ellie. "Can you dance?"

She smiled. "It's a little-known secret, but I'm a terrific dancer. I use dance routines for aerobics. I don't usually strut my stuff unless I'm drunk."

Flex grinned. "Perfect."

CHAPTER TWELVE

"I've taken a suite at Le Crillon," Ben said to Maggie as the car roared through the crowded Paris streets. Though the words went unsaid, each knew they would not be going to Le Palace. "Why don't we stop by for a nightcap?"

The offer was for more than a drink, and Maggie knew it. Until tonight, it was exactly what she'd planned. There was nothing she wanted more than to forget Jake Sullivan. An affair with the handsome doctor might be just the remedy she needed.

Unfortunately, she wasn't in love with Ben. A fact that an evening with Jake had made all too clear.

"I don't know. It's been a long night, Ben, and I have a tough day tomorrow."

"That isn't it and we both know it. It's because of Jake."

"It isn't." She glanced away. "Well, maybe in a way it is. My guard is up and I'm having an awful time letting it down again."

"How long has it been since you slept with a man?"

Maggie's shoulders straightened. She might not have answered if it hadn't been for his look of concern. "After Les died, there's only been Jake."

Ben smiled indulgently and patted her hand. "You're a mature woman, Maggie. With a woman's wants and needs. You don't have to be in love with me—at least not yet. Let me make love to you. Let me soothe your troubles and give you a little release."

"You make it all sound so clinical."

Ben's smile widened. "I promise it won't feel that way."

"I don't know, Ben."

"Tell you what. We'll start with the drink and see where we wind up. Fair enough?"

"I guess so."

"Driver, *conduisez-nous a Le Crillon, s'il vous plait,*" Ben said. Apparently content with her answer, he leaned back against the seat.

It's only a drink, Maggie told herself. *You don't have to do anything you don't want to.* Streetlights flashed as the car rolled along, braking again and again to avoid the bumper-to-bumper traffic. Maggie's nerves returned as they neared the hotel, making her more and more uncertain.

And something else was bothering her. Something Jake had said to her just as she and Ben were leaving. They'd all been clustered in the doorway, Ben holding her hand while they waited for the car to arrive. When he left for a moment, Jake walked up beside her.

"Maggie, I know I've caused you nothing but grief. You'll never know how sorry I am." His eyes held hers, their old familiar power stirring unwanted emotions. "Sometimes things aren't what they seem." He glanced at Ben, who stood chatting with the doorman. "Be sure of your feelings, Maggie."

As Ben returned, Jake stepped back inside the doorway out of sight.

What had his words meant? Was he just apologizing for the hurt he'd caused, or was he trying to tell her something? *Sometimes things aren't what they seem.* Was Jake in some kind of trouble? She couldn't believe it, yet the plea in his voice sounded real.

Her woman's intuition said she couldn't have been that wrong about the man she loved.

Her common sense said Jake was just covering his bets.

The car pulled up in front of the gray stone exterior of the exclusive Crillon, once a seventeenth century palace. Maggie let Ben help her out. She smoothed her yellow chiffon dress, and headed for the revolving door, a warm breeze ruffled her hair as she walked next to Ben. Though the hour was late, by Parisian standards the evening was still early.

She would make her decision when the time came. Until then, she intended to enjoy herself. Jake Sullivan could just go to hell.

Jake instructed the cab to let him out on the Champs-Elysees. He needed to walk, breathe in some fresh night air, settle his emotions.

He shouldn't have spoken to Maggie. He had given up that

privilege when he'd ended their affair eight months ago. Even then, he'd wanted to tell her, explain, ask her to wait. He hadn't for only one reason—

He might be forced to do what Nikolai Popov demanded.

He hadn't mentioned that possibility to Daniel, and he wouldn't. But Jake would do whatever was necessary to protect his mother and sister. The consequences would be his alone. He wouldn't allow Maggie and Sarah to get involved. He loved them both too much.

Jake walked along the crowded sidewalk, passing couples strolling arm-in-arm, tourists, and old men walking their dogs. The impressive Arc de Triomphe rose ahead, its usually glowing lights shrouded by canvas and a honey-comb maze of scaffolding where workers cleaned and repaired the structure.

As he skirted the Place de la Concorde with its beautiful lighted fountain, he thought of the hours he would spend in his room tonight, trying in vain to sleep. Instead of going back to the hotel, he headed down a side street. It was one o'clock in Paris, but only eight a.m. in Washington. Maybe Daniel would have news of Popov.

Checking behind him, he noticed his usual watchdog following some distance away. Three quick turns, a darting move through traffic, an exit through the side door of a café, and Jake lost him to the teeming Paris throng.

He ducked into a small, crowded bistro and headed toward a pay phone in the rear. Pulling the heavy glass door closed to shut out the raucous laughter and conversation, he dialed Daniel's home number.

"About time you checked in," Daniel said after the first ring.

"Have you come up with anything yet?"

"So far the news is not encouraging. Our people in Moscow have confirmed at least one of Popov's superiors is aware of his moves. We believe it may go all the way to the top."

Jake felt sick to his stomach. If the government was backing Popov, he'd had to do whatever they asked. "How soon will you know for sure?"

"This whole mess is tricky. We don't want to give our people away, so we have to move slowly. We're trying to do what's best for you and your family, but there are other considerations, as well."

Like the safety and welfare of the team, Jake thought. After the incident on the plane, he worried he'd already put them in danger.

"Anything further on your end?" Daniel asked.

Jake took a moment to answer, weighing how much he should say. "Not so far. Popov hasn't made contact again."

"He's bound to, sooner or later. I'm surprised he hasn't made some offensive gesture to prove his point."

"Nothing yet," Jake lied, making a sudden decision not to report the incident on the plane.

He should have notified the Paris police and those in New York, but he'd suspected it had something to do with the Russian. Hearing Daniel's words, he felt more certain than ever. He had to play for time, get all the facts before he decided what to do.

"Stay in touch," Daniel said. "That means I expect a call every day or two. If anything unusual happens, let me know."

"I will."

"And Jake...? Take care of yourself. Popov's no fool. From what it says in his dossier, he's taken more than a few men out."

His stomach knotted. "Is there anything else in his file I should know?"

"Only that his son died in an assembly line accident about five years after you left the country. Apparently, the boy was extremely bright, and Popov had big plans for him. After what happened in Rome, the son was removed from school and placed in an auto factory. Popov might feel you're in some way responsible for his death."

Jake released a slow breath. "Thanks, Dan."

"Get some sleep. You need all your wits about you. Besides, I expect the American team to win."

Jake smiled. After a gruff, "Good night," he hung up. The phone.

Sliding the booth door open, he moved into the hallway, then found a seat at a small table in a far corner of the bistro. The place smelled faintly of tobacco and perfume. A piano player plunked out some timeless melody Jake vaguely remembered.

Leaning back in his chair, he ordered a cognac, then pulled a thin Cuban cigar Avery Whitfield had given him from his inside coat pocket. Though he'd given up smoking, he allowed himself an occasional lapse. He hoped it would brighten his mood.

But as he inhaled the pungent tobacco and the blue smoke curled around his head, the noise and gaiety swept over him, and his loneliness grew even more intense. He couldn't help thinking of Maggie, remembering their evenings together. They'd discovered they had dozens of things in common: horses, classical music, love of the opera and ballet, an appreciation he owed his Soviet upbringing.

He'd only known her a couple of weeks and he was falling in love with her. He didn't want to rush her. He needed to be patient, give her time to get over the guilt she felt for her husband's death.

They'd been seeing each other steadily for over a month before she admitted Les hadn't been the world's greatest husband.

"We didn't really have what you would call a romantic relationship," she had said. "My parents introduced us. Les's father was the senior partner at a prestigious law firm in Tampa. Marrying him just seemed the right thing to do."

"Were you in love with him?" Jake asked.

"I loved him. He was a good provider and a good father to Sarah. I missed him terribly after he was gone."

"That isn't quite the same thing. Your parents wanted you to marry Les, but that's in the past. The question now is what do you want?"

She smiled wistfully. "Pretty much what every woman wants. Someone who loves me. Someone I can love in return. I'm getting older, but I'd like to have another child."

Jake had never considered having children, but with Maggie, the notion felt right.

"I want the kind of love that two people share," she finished. "This time, I won't settle for less."

Jake took a sip of his cognac and shoved the painful memories aside. He wondered if Maggie was still with the handsome Dr. Jaffe and his grip on the snifter tightened.

Let Daniel and his men find a way to stop Nikolai Popov, he prayed. *And let Maggie Delaine wait for me.*

The nightclub echoed to the beat of hard rock music. Clay sat next to Gabriella across from Ellie and Flex. Shep, Prissy, Avery, and Chauncey rounded out the table.

Le Palace was considered very "in" and outrageously chic. Women in leather mini's, patrons with violet blue-black hair, men bare-chested beneath expensive leather vests. The music was loud, and strobe lights flashed above the dance floor.

"Lots of young pussy," Avery whispered to Clay. It was just the sort of place his father loved. Clay figured being there made his dad feel younger.

Chauncey seemed enthralled. She simpered over Avery and played with his thigh under the table. They danced again and again, guzzling champagne in between songs. Clay danced with Gabriella and with Prissy. Shep had returned from his sojourn around the bar, looking for fun of a different sort than Clay enjoyed, though his friend had become more selective over years.

The waitress brought a fresh round of drinks, Clay another scotch and soda, Avery and Chauncey more champagne. Flex whispered something in Ellie's ear, she giggled and flashed him a smile, and they got up to dance.

Clay's stomach tightened and his ulcer began to gnaw. Ellie had been drinking all evening. It was obviously not a common occurrence, and she was more than a little drunk. Flex seemed delighted. Every time her glass was empty, he refilled it. He'd been nibbling her ear, rubbing her thigh, running his fingers through her hair all evening. It was all Clay could do to keep from pulling him across the table and punching him in the face.

The feeling astonished him. He'd never been jealous a day in his life. He and Flex had sparred off and on over the same women for years. It was a hobby, an amusement, nothing more. Tonight, Clay wasn't amused.

The beat of the music throbbed low and sensuous. On the dance floor, Flex pulled Ellie close and settled his cheek against hers. Clay's fury mounted. When had Ellie taken an interest in Flex? Until tonight, Clay had been certain sooner or later she would be his.

"Dance with me, darling," Gabriella whispered in his ear.

Her throaty voice alone was usually enough to arouse him. Tonight, he couldn't summon enough interest for a kiss. Clay helped her up and drew her onto the dance floor. Nearly as tall as he, Gabby pressed against him, grinding her hips in a sensual rhythm that finally achieved what usually came easy.

"You wouldn't want to embarrass me, would you?" he teased.

"But of course, darling." She laughed in that throaty way that used to drive him crazy. "If you prefer, we can do this back in your suite."

Clay's eyes fastened on Ellie. "Not just yet."

Ellie laughed uproariously at something Flex said while his hand moved lower, curving over her sexy derriere.

Damn him! Clay pulled Gabby closer. He massaged her slim hips, but his mind stayed on Ellie.

What was it about her that attracted him so strongly? She wasn't nearly as beautiful as Gabby, yet she seemed more so. He watched her smile up at Flex, and his stomach turned over. She looked enchanting, so fresh and warm and sweet.

Earlier he'd caught the whiff of White Shoulders, the orange blossom perfume she always wore. It fit her somehow, nothing cloying or heavy, just pure and honest, the way Ellie was herself.

The dance ended and the tempo of the music increased. Clay started back toward the table, preferring music with a slower beat.

"Please, darling?" Gabby pleaded.

Clay glanced at Ellie and his mouth dropped open. She swayed to the music, her legs braced a little apart, her skirt riding up and her head thrown back. Flex danced across from her, grinning from ear to ear.

Clay stayed on the dance floor. Gabby danced wildly in front of him while Clay danced unconsciously, ignoring her and watching Ellie in disbelief.

She was good. He'd give her that. Every movement was fluid, practiced, and flawless. She seemed alive in a way he'd never seen her. He felt a surge of desire like nothing he'd ever known. Sweat broke out on his forehead. He was rock hard and throbbing.

Ellie swayed and circled, using her hips suggestively, running her hands through her thick mahogany hair. It cascaded over her shoulders, and heavy red-brown strands fell over one eye. She looked like a beautiful gypsy.

Clay swallowed hard. It was all he could do to breathe. In his mind she danced for him naked, swirling and turning, displaying her full breasts for him alone.

The music increased its tempo. Flex put his hands on Ellie's waist and lifted her onto a table near the edge of the dance floor. Ellie seemed not to notice. She continued her gyrations in perfect rhythm, swaying to the music, her small feet never nearing the edge of the table.

What in God's name would she be like in bed?

The people on the dance floor stopped dancing and surrounded the table. The riders and even his dad started clapping. Flex just stood there, grinning like a fool.

"Looks as though the little church mouse isn't such a mouse after all," Gabby breathed in his ear.

The beat went faster. Ellie whirled and closed her eyes, slid her hands down her body, and began to unbutton the top of her two-piece dress.

Clay's control snapped. "Go back to the table," he told Gabby, then made his way to the front of the crowd where Flex stood clapping and grinning.

"You stop her, or I will." His hands fisted as he tried to control his fury.

"Be my guest," Flex said.

Ellie tossed the top of her dress into the crowd with a throaty laugh. Standing in her skirt and a lacy white chemise, she shook her shoulders in rhythm to the music. She seemed not to notice the others in the room.

When she moved sideways, bending down provocatively, and shaking her shoulders, Clay's arms snaked out, and with one quick tug, he pulled her over his shoulder, her hair falling down his back like a silky curtain. Ellie didn't fight him, just let him carry her across the dance floor and out onto the street where he propped her up against the wall of the building.

"What in the name of heaven do you think you're doing?"

Ellie smiled up at him, unable to focus. "I love to dance, don't you?"

Clay just growled. "You're drunk, and you're going back to the hotel."

"Is the party over?"

"It's over for you." Turning to the doorman, he motioned for a taxi.

"I don't feel so good." Ellie swayed on her feet. Clay helped her around to the side of the building, but she didn't throw up and eventually some of her color returned.

"I'm all right," she told him with a crooked smile. "Thanks."

"What are friends for?" he said sarcastically. He scooped her into his arms and carried her to a cab that had arrived at the curb. Settling her inside, he instructed the driver to wait until he got back, then went back into the bar.

"I'm taking Ellie back to the hotel," he told Flex, who clutched the top of Ellie's dress like a trophy. "You bring Gabby."

Flex shook his head. "No way. I'll take Ellie back."

"Are we leaving?" Gabby asked, walking up beside Clay, martini in hand.

"Yes." Clay set the glass aside, took her wrist and towed her out to the cab, Flex following in his wake. Settling Gabriella in front, both men climbed in back, one on each side of Ellie.

On the ride to the hotel, Clay snatched the top of the dress away from Flex and helped Ellie put it on. He buttoned up the front, trying not to notice the feel of her soft breasts beneath his fingers. Flex pushed disheveled strands of her hair back out of her face.

Once out of the cab, Ellie clung to Flex's arm, Gabby clutched Clay's, and they moved through the lobby, caught the elevator up to the fifth floor. Flex stopped at the door to his room, his arm around Ellie's waist.

"Oh, no you don't," Clay said.

"Let her get lucky," said Gabby. "I intend to." She nibbled the side of Clay's neck.

Ellie straightened. "I'm going with Flex."

"You're going to your room," Clay said.

"It's her decision." Flex slipped the door key in the lock and turned the knob.

"Come on, darling, I'm horny," Gabby said.

Ellie set her jaw. "I'm a grown woman. I can sleep with anyone I want."

"Bravo," said Gabby.

Clay gritted his teeth, grabbed Gabriella's arm, and headed down the hall. Flex's door closed softly behind them.

"Are you all right?" Flex asked once they got inside.

"No. I'm drunk, thanks to you. I made a complete ass out of myself, and Clay hates my guts."

"You look a little better than you did at the nightclub."

"All that dancing, the cool air, and the cab ride helped." She slumped down on the bed, still dizzy, but a lot less drunk. "Why can't I just be like other girls, Flex? I've wanted Clay since the first time I met him. Why can't I just sleep with him and get it over with?"

Flex sat down beside her. "Sleeping with Clay wouldn't solve your problem. I think you're in love with him."

"I can't be!"

"You probably shouldn't be. I wouldn't wish that on my worst enemy, let alone someone I care about."

Ellie's eyes filled with tears. "I'm such a prude, such a stupid, idiotic prude."

"You're not a prude. You're just particular, that's all. I'm sure the men you've slept with have all meant something to you. They weren't just one-night stands."

Ellie sniffed. "What men?"

Flex's red eyebrows shot up. "What do you mean, *what men?*" He grabbed her shoulders. "You're not telling me you've never had a boyfriend?"

"Don't be silly. I'm twenty-four years old. Of course, I've had boyfriends."

"That's what I thought."

"I've just never went to bed with any of them."

Flex's eyes widened. "You've got to be kidding. You're a virgin? No way. Not in this day and age."

"I need to use your bathroom. I feel rotten."

Keeping an eye on her, Flex led her to the bathroom door. When Ellie came out, she felt a lot more sober and a whole lot sicker, her head throbbing with the force of consecutive hammer blows.

"You're not getting off this easy," Flex said. "I want to hear the story. There has to be one."

Ellie released a soft, resigned sigh. She told Flex about her seeing disorder, the years before her surgery, how hard it was to adjust afterward. She told him about her love of show jumping and how much she'd wanted to compete.

When she finished, Flex just stared. "Wow, that's some story, all right. And of all the people you could have fallen for, you had to pick Clay."

"I told you I wasn't very smart." Ellie fell back on the bed. "My head hurts. God, how will I ever face Prissy and Shep, let alone Clay?"

"They've all done as bad or worse. Come on, I'll walk you to your room."

Outside her door, Ellie looked up at Flex. "Tomorrow I'm going to apologize and tell Clay the truth."

"The hell you are. You've gone this far you're going to see it through. Clay's never once shown an interest in a woman the way he has you. He went crazy when he saw you up on that table. He feels something for you, Ellie. Give him a chance to sort it out. I know him a hell of a lot better than you do. Let me do my part and you do yours."

"What *is* my part?"

"Just be yourself. You're not in love with me. You just wanted a little fun. I felt the same way. Got it?"

"Whatever you say." Ellie opened the door to her room. Prissy Knowles was fast asleep beneath the covers. Ellie said a prayer of thanks. She wasn't ready to face Prissy or anyone else.

"Good night, Flex, and thanks for being a friend."

"No problem. You just get some sleep."

Ellie nodded, walked in and closed the door. Lord, what a fool she'd made of herself. And all because of Clay Whitfield. How would she ever be able to face him?

"How could you do it?" Clay said to Flex the next morning at the show grounds. Dressed in boots and breeches and leading Max toward the practice ring, Clay's temper remained on edge.

Why shouldn't it be? He'd sent Gabriella packing while one of his best friends slept with Ellie Fletcher. Unconsciously, his grip tightened on the horse's reins.

"How could I do what?" Flex asked innocently.

"Get her drunk and take advantage of her."

"And you wouldn't?"

"I'm a bastard. You're supposed to be a nice guy."

"You mean I'm the nice guy who got in her knickers and you're the bastard who didn't."

Clay made a noise in his throat that sounded like a growl.

"You heard her yourself," Flex said. "She's a grown woman."

"She's naïve. Any fool can see that."

"Look, if it'll make you feel any better, she's been sleeping with Gerry Winslow all along."

"Her groom?" Clay stopped short, his expression incredulous.

"Don't look so surprised. You sleep with Linda Gibbons, don't you?"

"Yes, but that's different."

"Seems to me, what's good for the gander is good for the goose. Why is it different for Ellie?"

"Dammit, I don't know." He glanced across the ring at his fellow teammates, who worked their horses over the jumps. "I guess I just thought Ellie was...Ellie was..."

"Special?"

"I guess so."

"She is."

Clay's head came up.

"She's a great girl, Clay. She's a hell of a rider, and everyone on the team likes her. On top of that, she's a terrific lover. Probably even better than Gabby Marchbanks."

Clay stiffened. "If you must know, I sent Gabby back to her hotel. After your little display, I felt more like decking someone that getting laid."

"Can I help it if Ellie's got good taste?"

"So I suppose you two are an item."

"Not at all. Ellie and I are just good friends. Last night was a little diversion. I don't think she meant for it to happen, but..." Flex slapped Clay on the back. "What do you care, anyway? You've got a little black book that resembles the Pac Bell yellow pages."

Clay just grunted.

"You never minded sharing before."

"Mind?" Clay smiled tightly. "I hope you taught her a few new tricks."

"She makes love just like she dances, if you know what I mean." Flex winked and grinned.

Clay clamped his jaw. "She isn't sleeping with Jake, too, is she?"

Flex shook his head. "Nah. Jake thinks of her more like a daughter. He's a little over-protective, that's all."

"Right," Clay said peevishly. "Besides, it appears he'd have to stand in line."

"Just because the lady had enough sense to choose a handsome, debonair guy like me over a heartbreaker like you..." Flex grinned again and nudged Clay in the ribs. "Check you later. I want to work Sparky on the lunge line."

Sparky was Flex's nickname for Sebastian. Flex headed off toward the chestnut gelding's stall, and Clay continued toward the ring to work Max. He noticed Ellie wasn't around. *I hope she's hugging the commode,* he thought. It would serve her right.

CHAPTER THIRTEEN

Ellie slept till noon. When she finally awoke, Prissy was gone, and she was alone. Feeling a little like a slug, her stomach still uncertain, she showered, dressed, and headed out to the show grounds. It was time she faced the music.

At least that's what she told herself all the way there. Once she arrived, she stayed close to her stalls, polishing her equipment or grooming Rose and Jubilee. She'd done every chore she could think of and still hadn't found the courage to go out to the show ring.

"How are you feeling?" Prissy Knowles walked into the tack room.

"Like an absolute fool. I'm so embarrassed I could die."

"Hey, don't worry about it. You were among friends."

"Have you ever done anything that stupid?"

"Only a thousand times. I'm engaged to a great guy, so I'm a little more settled down now. But there was a time when I'd have been up on that table with you."

Ellie grinned, liking Prissy more all the time.

"It's none of my business," Prissy said, "but that little display didn't, by any chance, have anything to do with Clay, did it? He was watching you like a hawk all night. I couldn't believe my eyes when he carried you out of there over his shoulder. He looked like a stallion protecting his mare."

"Flex and I were playing a little joke on Clay, only it got out of hand."

"I see." Prissy picked up Ellie's snaffle bit. "How many times a day do you clean this?"

"I was trying to work up the courage to face everyone."

"Especially Clay?"

"I really don't want to talk about Clay."

"Listen to me, Ellie. Every girl on the circuit's in love with Clay. What you're feeling isn't abnormal, believe me. I just don't want to see you get hurt."

"You seem immune to his charms, how do you do it?"

"Simple. I fell for Clay years ago. Slept with him and got dumped just like the others. Fortunately, I met Phil a little while later. Phil's just the opposite of Clay. He's loving and considerate, a one-woman man. I fell madly in love with him, and now we're getting married."

"You think that's what would happen to me if I slept with Clay? He'd dump me, just like everyone else?"

Prissy paused a moment before answering. "Normally, I'd say yes without even thinking about it. But lately, Clay seems different. Maybe he's finally growing up. Sometimes I think Clay would like to stop chasing, but his father's got him convinced that's unmanly. I don't know. The safer route is definitely to keep your distance."

"Believe me, I'm trying."

"Then again, he treats you differently. He certainly came to your rescue last night."

"He rescued me, all right. Then went to bed with Gabriella."

"What can I say? That sounds like Clay. Listen, I've got to run. Maybe we can grab something to eat back at the hotel tonight."

"That sounds great. Thanks, Prissy."

Prissy left. Ellie saddled Jube and led him toward the practice ring. It was late in the afternoon. Everyone else was gone. What a relief, she thought. At least she wouldn't have to face Clay today.

Not for the next few days either, as it turned out.

When the show started on Thursday, she saw him for the first time since Le Palace.

At the beginning of the competition, it was hard to concentrate with Clay so near. Eventually, her years of dedication took over and her desire to win pulled her through. Out of thirty-seven riders, she placed sixth behind Clay and Flex in the Grand Prix on Sunday.

Jake seemed unimpressed. He'd grown increasingly distant and oddly wary. When she asked his advice on one of the jumps, he just walked away as if he hadn't heard her. She was beginning to worry about him. Maybe she should talk to him.

Then again, their friendship was based on their working relationship and love of the sport. They had never delved into the personal aspects of each other's lives, and Ellie wasn't sure she wanted to.

That night they packed up. Tomorrow they were leaving for Rotterdam. She hadn't talked to Clay more than a time or two since the competition began. It was obvious he was avoiding her. When she'd placed second in the 140-meter class, Clay had railed at her for the four faults that had cost her the first.

They were the only words he'd spoken.

She was going to tell him the truth, she decided that afternoon after the show. Screw Flex and his crazy ideas. Of course, she'd have to wait until they arrived in Holland. Clay was long gone, she was sure.

Her mouth tightened. Probably somewhere with Linda Gibbons, celebrating his win.

Standing in the tack room, Ellie stretched and rubbed the small of her back. She'd sent Gerry to get some dinner. He'd been working since dawn, just as she had, and she needed some time alone.

"Back hurt?" Clay stood in the doorway, wide shoulders filling it, head nearly touching the top.

Embarrassment warmed her cheeks. How would she ever explain to Clay?

Ellie swallowed. "Clay, I owe you an apology. I'm sorry about what happened. I really want to thank you for what you did."

"Don't thank me, Ellie, thank Flex." The bitterness in his voice was unmistakable. "From what I hear, he took care of you just fine."

Ellie's color deepened. "What did he tell you?" It came out as kind of a squeak.

"Suffice it to say he seemed more than pleased with your skills as a lover. Coming from him, that's quite a compliment."

"Clay, I—"

"What I still don't understand is your sudden attraction to Flex. I had the strangest idea you felt something for me."

"You!" She nervously moistened her lips.

"Do that again, and I'll come over there and help you."

She flushed. "The truth is, that night was...was..."

"An accident?"

127

"Yes, I mean, no. I mean it wasn't anything like that."

"Look, Ellie..." Clay moved closer. "I've been thinking things over. We're both mature adults. We live our own lives as we see fit. I don't care what happened between you and Flex." Ellie took a step backwards. Clay followed. "I only know I want you—and I think you want me."

Another step put her shoulders against the wall. She could feel the roughness of the boards pressing into her back. "What have I done to give you that impression?"

Clay's hand brushed her cheek. He stood so close she could smell his cologne.

"What have you done?" he drawled. "Maybe it's that tiny pulse that flutters at the base of your throat, like it is right now. Or maybe it's the sexy way you lick your lips."

He smiled in triumph as her tongue touched the corner of her mouth. Lifting her chin with his finger, he bent his head and kissed her. Ellie felt the light pressure, the heady warmth, and closed her eyes. Her hands pressed against his starched white shirt. She could feel his heartbeat, thudding beneath her palm.

I should stop him, she thought. But she couldn't come up with a single reason why. Her lips parted and Clay's tongue tangled with hers. He probed and tasted and deepened the kiss, sending tiny shivers up her spine. His arms went around her, pulling her close. When she laced her fingers in the soft hair curling above his collar, he pulled her full length against him and she heard him groan.

"God, I want you."

Another heady kiss had her swaying against him, trembling all over. His fingers worked the buttons at the front of her shirt then his hand skimmed over skin and slipped inside her bra. He palmed her breast, lifting and shaping it. His thumb brushing her nipple, and her knees went weak. She tightened her hold on his neck just to stay on her feet.

"I hope I'm not interrupting." Gerry Winslow stood in the doorway, a pitchfork in his hand. He looked furious. It was obvious he didn't intend to leave.

Frowning, Clay pulled his hand from inside her shirt, stepped back a little, but kept an arm around her waist. Flushed with embarrassment, Ellie drew her shirtfront closed.

"I think you had better go, Whitfield," Gerry said.

"I believe Ms. Fletcher should make that decision."

"Clay, please." She threw him a pleading glance. "It's getting late and I... Why don't I see you back at the hotel?"

Clay looked furious. "Send him away, or don't bother."

"Gerry's my friend. He just wants what's best for me."

"Tell your *friend,* you're leaving with me."

Ellie looked from Clay to Gerry and back again. "Give me a chance to talk to him."

Clay set his jaw. He stalked past Ellie, past Gerry, and out of the tack room.

"Clay, wait!" Ellie started after him, but he didn't look back. Gerry's hand on her shoulder turned her around.

"What the hell do you think you're doing?"

"I can make my own decisions, Gerry. I don't need any help from you."

"That's where you're wrong." Gerry took a calming breath, raked a hand through his wavy brown hair. "Look, Ellie, you know what Whitfield's like. The man will take you to bed, brag about his conquest and never look back. He's only interested in one thing."

"I don't care. I'm sick and tired of being a puritan. I want to live a little. Why can't I be like everyone else?"

"Because you're not like everyone else. You're...well, you're different. You deserve someone a whole lot better than Whitfield."

"What's wrong with Clay?"

"Nothing a good punch in the mouth wouldn't cure. He's arrogant, conceited. He's a real prick, Ellie. He's not the man for you."

Ellie felt the wetness on her cheek before she realized she was crying. "Then why do I feel like he is?"

Gerry pulled her against his shoulder and smoothed her hair. "You're infatuated with him, that's all. Clay's a good-looking man. He knows how to handle women, and you're inexperienced. He's playing on your trust, the sonofabitch."

Gerry handed her his handkerchief. "You better stop crying," he teased. "Your mascara's beginning to run."

"It's supposed to be waterproof." She blew her nose. "I'll sue them if it runs."

They both laughed. "Come on." Gerry draped an arm across

her shoulder. "Let's go back to the hotel."

Ellie didn't see Clay until the following day at the airport. The horses were being transported by van while the riders were flying on ahead. Ellie was worried about leaving Jube, but Gerry would be with him, so she knew he'd be okay. On the plane, Clay barely spoke. Ellie took a seat beside Maggie Delaine and her little girl, Sarah. Ignoring Clay's broad back, she spoke to the little blond girl.

"How did you like Paris, Sarah?"

"It was really great. Mama took me to see Notre Dame and the Eiffel Tower. We went all the way to the top."

"I saw it from the ground, but I didn't get to go up."

"You were marvelous on Sunday," Maggie said to her. "Until you started having problems in the jump-off, I thought you were going to beat Clay."

"Sometimes I think that's the impossible dream."

"I heard you beat him at the Gardens."

Ellie grinned. "Oh, I'll beat him again. The way Jube's been taking the fences, it's only a matter of time."

"Maybe Rotterdam's the place."

"I hope so. I intend to give it my best shot."

"Did you ever ride against Jake?" Sarah asked. "I bet he was the best rider in the whole world."

"I wouldn't be surprised," Ellie agreed, seeing the hero worship in the little girl's eyes. "Jake coached me a few years back and then again before we left the States. He's a terrific rider, but I've never competed against him."

Ellie glanced at Maggie. Her relaxed smile had tightened. Everyone knew about the love affair between Jake and Maggie. In the show jumping world, it had been a foregone conclusion the two of them would marry.

Then some months back, the relationship had come to an unexpected end. Neither Maggie nor Jake would discuss it. It was obvious little Sarah hadn't wanted to lose him. Ellie's intuition told her Jake hadn't been happy about it either. Ellie wondered how Maggie felt.

They landed in Rotterdam and headed through the bustling traffic by bus. At everyone's urging, Maggie instructed the driver to take the roundabout route from the airport, circle through town and give them a tour of the city.

"Rotterdam is the largest seaport in the world," the narrow-faced driver told them in his heavy broken English. "It straddles the Rhine River and the Maas. The Germans almost destroyed the city in World War II," he said as they passed the War Memorial in front of the Town Hall. "Today it has been restored to one of the most modern cities in the world."

They passed the Laurenskerk, a splendid Gothic cathedral rebuilt in the nineteen fifties. From the Maas Tunnel, the driver pointed out the Euromast, an observation tower with a terrace three hundred feet off the ground. Just across the Maas, the largest oil refinery in Europe glowed like a beacon over an army of supertankers.

They were staying nearer the show grounds this time, at a small hotel called the Steinberger Rotterdam. After lunching near the harbor, the team and crew checked in. Phil Marshall, Prissy's fiancé, was flying in, so Ellie had a room to herself.

That night she joined Flex and Jake for dinner, but Jake seemed distracted.

"You're not worried about what happened to Caesar on the plane?" Ellie asked him as the waiter at In Den Rustwat served her *Rodekool met Rolpens,* red cabbage and rolled spice meat with slices of apple.

"Just some joker's idea of fun," Flex said. He had ordered *Pannekoeken,* a kind of pancake. He looked dashing in his pink shirt, black pants, and black plaid sack coat, the sleeves pushed up to his elbows.

"I don't like people playing games at our expense," Jake said darkly.

"You aren't expecting more trouble, are you?" Ellie thought about Jube and Rose, and worry filtered through her.

"I've had a guard posted at the stables every day since we landed in Paris. Whoever did it is probably still in New York, but I'd rather play it safe."

Ellie felt a little better. "How do you think the team's shaping up?"

"Everyone's riding well except Shep. But he'll settle down. He always does. Nothing bothers Prissy. Clay's winning as usual, but he's been a real S.O.B. all week."

"Maybe he needs to get laid," Flex teased, then his grin slipped as he caught Ellie's turbulent expression. Jake noticed it too.

"You'd do well to keep your mind on the horses, Ellie," Jake said.

Ellie toyed with her food, no longer hungry. "I know I haven't been winning enough. Maybe I should get in a few more hours of practice a day."

"It isn't your riding I'm talking about. Whitfield's a handful. You've got about all you can handle right now."

Her eyes met his. "Not you, too, Jake. Why do I keep getting lectures about Clay? For God's sake, we've never even been out on a date."

"I don't think Whitfield's interested in a date," Jake warned. "More like a one-night stand."

"It isn't always that easy," Flex defended her. "You better than anyone ought to understand."

Jake's gaze swung to Flex. "What's that supposed to mean?"

"I'm talking about the way you look at Maggie Delaine. What happened between you two, anyway?"

"That isn't any of your business."

Flex grinned good-naturedly. "Never stopped me before."

A corner of Jake's mouth tilted into a smile. "Very little stops you, Flex. But that's probably what makes you such a damn fine rider."

Flex's grin widened. A compliment from Jake Sullivan was a gift.

When they arrived back at the hotel, Flex walked Ellie to her first-floor room.

"Thanks for dinner," she said.

"My pleasure," Flex said. "By the way, Clay's barely speaking to me. I think our little campaign is working."

"Oh, sure. That's why he's out to dinner with Linda Gibbons."

"Is he?" Flex seemed surprised.

"I don't know. Probably."

"Cheer up. Things'll either work out or they won't. For Clay's sake more than yours, I hope they do." He leaned over and bussed her cheek, took her key, and opened her door.

"Good night, Ellie." He handed her the key.

"Good night, Flex."

As she stepped into the room, Ellie flipped on the overhead light. She felt bone tired, though she wasn't quite sure why. The horses had arrived with no problems. They'd had a pleasant evening. At least she and Flex had. She wasn't sure about Jake.

Except for his comments about Clay—out of the norm for Jake—he'd been even quieter than usual. What was he so worried about? Or was it just seeing Maggie again that had him on edge?

Fortunately, Flex had saved the evening by keeping them all entertained. He was becoming a very good friend.

Ellie unbuttoned her blouse and tugged it out of the waistband of her navy blue skirt. On her way to the bathroom, she kicked off her sandals and turned on the small radio that sat beside her bed, tuning it to a channel that played easy-listening music. All the while, she kept thinking of Clay, wishing their last meeting had turned out differently.

There are no accidents, she told herself, espousing a philosophy she'd believed in for years. Choices, yes. Accidents, no. Gerry's interruption had saved her—more from herself than from Clay. It was probably for the best.

In her skirt, bra, and chemise, Ellie washed her face and brushed her teeth. Glancing up at the small window over the tub as she finished, she felt a hint of unease. The window stood open a crack, a faint evening breeze drifting in.

Surely the memory of closing it was just a trick of the mind. Or maybe the maid had come in and left if open to freshen the room. She was just tired, she told herself, but she wished she'd checked the room as she usually did.

An odd noise sent a second thread of alarm sliding through her. Working up her courage, she opened the bathroom door. Better to find out the truth than imagine something worse.

The room was empty, the double bed neatly made, the simple Danish modern chair in the corner undisturbed. She dropped down beside the bed to look underneath, but it was only a few inches off the floor, not enough space for someone to hide. She headed for the closet, the only place big enough to conceal an assailant.

The door made a shrill squeak as it swung open, the sound sliding over her nerves. Peering into the darkness, she tried to see behind the row of jackets, breeches, dresses, and blouses that blocked her view.

Ellie shrieked as an arm shot out of the darkness and grabbed her, jerked her against a man's hard body. She tried to scream, but the sound died behind the hand clamped over her mouth.

Panic hit her. Ellie struggled as he dragged her back into the room. She tried to wrench free, but his arm was a steel band around her waist. Dressed completely in black, he half-carried, half-dragged her toward the bed. Ellie scratched and clawed, tried to kick him, jammed her elbow into his ribs.

The man grunted, spun her around, and slapped her hard across the face. The blow knocked her to the floor and sent the chair crashing against the wall. The room spun and her vision blurred.

Dragging her to her feet, he shoved her down on the bed and used his body to pin her to the mattress. He wasn't a big man, but he was wiry and strong. He was wearing a black knit ski mask, but she could read the hard look in his eyes that warned her not to fight him.

Fear rolled through her, so strong she felt dizzy. Freeing a hand, she shoved the radio against the wall as hard as she could. It crashed, then thudded as it hit the floor, continuing to play soft music from somewhere on the carpet. Her attacker slapped her again.

"Nee," he warned, shaking his head. The word was Dutch, but it was spoken with some sort of accent. He showed her the gleaming blade of a knife before he pressed it against her throat. *"Bweeg je niet."*

She had no idea what the words meant, she but understood the meaning. Fighting a fresh coil of terror, feeling the edge of the blade, Ellie stopped struggling. Breathing heavily, gasping for air, she tried to remain calm, tried to force her mind to work.

Her compliance pleased him. His lips curved in what might have passed for a smile. When his fingers groped her breast, bile rose in her throat. Through the folds of her skirt, she could feel his erection pressing between her legs. Then his hand moved lower, sliding her skirt up along her thigh. When he crushed his thin lips against her mouth and tried to force his tongue inside, she lashed out, trashing and flailing, determined to stop him. Whatever happened, she wasn't going down without a fight.

Tears burned her eyes as she swung at him with all her strength, but her attacker managed to block each blow. *Dear God,* she thought, *please don't let this happen.*

CHAPTER FOURTEEN

Another loud thump on the wall disturbed Clay's reading. Stretched full length on his bed, shirt tugged free and unbuttoned but still wearing his slacks in case he decided to go out, Clay set his book, Turow's *Presumed Innocent,* aside. He'd read the same page three times.

What the hell was Ellie doing in there? She and Flex had gone out to dinner. He'd seen them leaving with Jake. Maybe Ellie and Flex were enjoying another "accident." Or maybe this round was with Gerry Winslow. The thought infuriated him. The thump sounded again, obviously the bed moving against the wall.

Clay ground his teeth. Swinging his legs to the floor, he walked to the dresser, poured himself a shot of the Glenfiddish he always carried, and downed it in a single gulp.

A noise that sounded like a sob bled through the walls, followed by another muffled thud.

Clay's pulse began to speed. What if it wasn't Flex? Rotterdam was a big city. Ellie was a pretty girl staying alone. He strained to hear the next noise and could have sworn it was the sound of rending fabric.

Clay slammed the glass down on the dresser and headed for the door. He was making a fool of himself—he knew it. Ellie had a way of doing that to him. Still...

He paused in the doorway. Damn her, if she was in bed with Flex or Gerry, he'd strangle them both! The sound of breaking glass brushed those thoughts aside. Clay bolted for the door to Ellie's room next to his.

He tried the knob, found it locked, and called her name. Ellie didn't answer. He could hear odd noises and soft music playing in the background. He'd be sorry for this, but he'd be sorrier if she was in trouble, and he didn't help.

Raising a boot, he kicked the flimsy latch, and the door swung wide, the knob crashing against the wall behind it. Ellie sprawled on the bed, naked from the waist up, her lacy chemise in tatters, her skirt hiked up, her eyes wet green pools. Nestled between her trembling legs, a man dressed in black fought to free his erection from his pants. A trickle of blood ran from the corner of Ellie's mouth, and a bruise darkened her cheek.

Clay's control snapped. Growling low in his throat, he reached the man in two angry strides, tore him off Ellie, and smashed a fist into his face. The glint of a knife flashed. Clay kicked the blade away and punched him again. The man swung a powerful right hand. Clay ducked and swung, sending the man crashing into the corner on top of an overturned chair.

In two quick strides, Clay reached him, grabbed the front of his shirt, dragged him up and punched him, breaking his nose and sending a spray of blood against the wall and across the front of Clay's white shirt. The man groaned as Clay hauled him to his feet and hit him again, slamming his head against the floor with a thud that had Ellie gasping in horror.

The assailant struggled to his feet, bent low and charged into Clay's midsection, knocking him to the floor. Clay's head the wall with a thud, and the assailant dashed out through the broken door.

With a groan, Clay staggered to his feet. Shaking his head to clear it, he ran after the intruder, down the hall, out the exit door, and around the corner of the building. A scan of the parking lot and the field beyond revealed no sign of him.

"Damn!" Fist clenched in frustration, Clay hurried back to Ellie. He found her huddled on the bed against the wall, her arms covering her breasts, tears streaming down her cheeks.

Clay sat down on the bed and eased her into his arms. "You're all right, love." With a sob, she turned and started crying against his shoulder, deep racking sounds that tore at his heart.

"Everything's all right," he whispered, stroking her tangled hair. "You're safe now."

"That man.... He tried to... He tried..."

"I know. Hush now, it's over."

Ellie looked up at him. "Oh, Clay..." She hung onto him even tighter. She'd just begun to gentle when Flex burst into the room.

"What the hell...?"

"Ellie had an unwanted visitor." Glancing down, Clay remembered her nakedness and pulled the thin chintz bedspread over her shoulders, covering her from Flex's prying eyes.

Ellie just clung to him. She didn't look at Flex or say a word.

"Call the police," Clay said.

Ellie bolted upright. Clay grabbed the bedspread to keep it from falling off. "No! No, Clay, please." Her green eyes looked huge. "No police. I can't go through that, I can't. I have to ride. I have to win. Please...please don't call them."

Flex knelt in front of her. "Ellie, surely you don't want us to let this man get away. He might do the same thing to someone else."

He mouthed the word *rape* to Clay, who shook his head. "Thank God I got here in time."

"I went out to get some ice," Flex said. "I spotted the broken latch. Scared the hell out of me. Looks like she's still pretty shook up. Maybe we should call a doctor or something."

"No, please..." Ellie hung onto Clay's neck as if he were saving her life. "I'm all right. I just need to...to pull myself together. I'll be...be fine."

But she didn't look fine, and both Flex and Clay knew it. She looked so pale her skin appeared translucent, her eyes so huge they dominated her oval face.

"Let's get you out of those torn clothes and into bed." Clay helped her up, the spread still wrapped around her, while Flex rummaged through the dresser drawers and came up with a short, lace-trimmed, pink nylon nightgown, a little too sheer to suit Clay.

"Can you get undressed?" Clay asked. Ellie nodded but didn't move.

"Get her a glass of water," Clay said. "I'll help her put on the nightgown."

"Oh, no you don't. Ellie would kill me."

Clay looked at Ellie and sighed. "I guess you're right. You've seen more of her than I have." He couldn't keep the bitterness out of his voice.

Flex opened his mouth, then glanced at Ellie. "We'll both do it."

Mechanically, they stripped away what remained of her ripped and tattered skirt. She sat beside them in a pair of white bikini panties.

"Damn, what a body," Flex said softly as they pulled her nightgown over her head. Clay gritted his teeth but didn't say a word.

Ellie just stared straight ahead, shivering every few seconds.

"I still think we should call a doctor," Flex said.

"So do I."

"No! I'm...I'm fine. Really I am."

Clay laid a wet cloth against her split lip and bruised cheek while Flex poured her a glass of water.

"There's some scotch on the dresser in my room."

Flex returned, glass of scotch in hand, to find Ellie tucked securely between the sheets, her head propped up with pillows.

"Drink this," Clay ordered, handing her the glass. "Slowly."

Still holding Clay's hand, she sipped the scotch and grimaced. "I'm sorry to cause so much trouble."

"Believe me, love. You're no trouble at all."

"What if...." She nervously licked her lips. "What if he comes back?"

"If he comes back," Clay said, suddenly angry again, "he'll get another dose of what he got before." Unconsciously he flexed his knuckles, surprised to find them skinned and bleeding. "I'm not leaving, so you don't have to worry."

"Me, either," Flex agreed, and Clay scowled. Flex just grinned. "I'll take the floor. You can have the other half of the bed. But you'd better behave yourself."

"Even I'm not that big a bastard."

Flex grinned even wider. "Get some sleep, Ellie. You'll feel better in the morning. Tomorrow we'll decide what to do." Flex left them long enough to return to his room for a blanket and pillows then made himself a pallet on the floor.

Fully clothed, lying on top of the covers, Clay stretched out full-length beside Ellie. He smoothed her hair away from her cheeks, and she finally drifted to sleep.

Sometime later, he drew a blanket he'd found in the closet over himself and closed his eyes. Flex's gentle snoring was the last thing he remembered.

At three-thirty in the morning, Clay awoke from what started as a nightmare about Ellie being raped and ended with him saving her and Ellie being a willing partner. It left him edgy and hard. Ellie lay curled against him, her thick mahogany hair falling across his arm. He hoped she couldn't feel his arousal.

After the attack, he didn't want her to discover her shepherd was really a wolf in disguise.

When he smoothed her hair, she turned to face him, and he realized she wasn't asleep.

"Hi," she said, easing away from him. She flushed a little, as if sleeping curled against him was something she shouldn't be doing.

"How long have you been awake?" he asked.

"A while. I couldn't sleep."

"Feeling any better?"

"I'll be all right. I just never expected…. I've never been around people like that. I guess I've been pretty sheltered all my life."

"I've been sheltered, but I know lots of rotten people."

"Rapists?" she asked, incredulous.

"Maybe not the same kind, but certainly men and women who rape and plunder what others treasure. Crooked businessmen, scheming executives. They aren't much different from the man who attacked you."

"Why do you think he picked me?"

"Probably been watching several hotels, looking for a woman alone."

When Ellie shuddered, Clay pulled her into the circle of his arms. "Go back to sleep. You need your beauty rest."

Ellie lay quiet for a while. She could feel Clay's even breathing, his heart beating softly. He smelled…*masculine* was the word that came to mind. The evening had been a nightmare of violence and terror, yet she lay next to Clay, feeling safe and protected, as if she were exactly where she belonged.

She'd been awake an hour, pretending to be asleep because it felt so good to lie beside him. What was there about him she found so attractive?

She had always considered herself a good judge of people. She didn't see Clay the way others did, and yet she was surely wrong. The other riders knew him far better than she did.

"You aren't sleeping," said Clay's deep voice.

"I can't. I think I'll get dressed and go downstairs, maybe find a café that's open."

"Are you sure you're up to it?"

"I need to get out of here for a while."

"Fine, I'll go with you."

Ellie shook her head. "I've been too much trouble already. I won't go far."

"I've got a better idea." Clay helped her sit up. His blanket fell away, and she noticed his shirt was open. There was a spatter of blood on the shirt that belonged to the man who'd attacked her, but she was more interested in the vee of dark hair curling over   bands of muscle on his chest.

"I'm not sleepy either," he said. "I've got a rental car in the hotel garage. I know a place you might find interesting."

Clay stood up, flexing the ridges across his flat stomach. How many times had she said no to him when she'd wanted to say yes?

"A drive sounds good." Padding barefoot toward the bathroom, she realized was wearing her pink nightgown instead of her shredded clothes.

A flush rose in her cheeks. "Did you...?"

"Don't worry. Flex kept me honest."

Ellie glanced to where her friend snored softly on the floor. "You mean you both...? Oh, God." Hurriedly, she pulled the bathroom door closed behind her.

Hearing Clay's deep chuckle, it dawned on her that he thought she and Flex knew each other *intimately*. Good grief, how had things gotten so out of control?

It would all work out somehow, she told herself. She was going to spend some time with Clayton Whitfield. She shouldn't go, but she was.

And she didn't give a damn what anyone else had to say.

CHAPTER FIFTEEN

Clay showered and dressed in clean clothes and returned to the room next door for Ellie. Flex still softly snored on the floor.

"Maybe we should wake him up," Ellie said. "Surely he'd sleep better in his own bed."

"I'm not sure you *could* wake him up. Besides, Flex can sleep anywhere."

Clay led her out of the hotel to his rented Mercedes and settled Ellie inside, trying to ignore the bruise on her cheek. Every time he saw it, he got mad all over again.

The events of last night still unsettled him. When he'd seen that bastard on top of Ellie, he'd gone half crazy. His anger had given him an advantage, though he didn't like being so out of control. He probably would have killed the sonofabitch if the bastard hadn't gotten away.

And Ellie. Seeing her hurt and scared, he'd felt a surge of protectiveness like nothing he'd known. What in God's name was it about her? She was only a woman, just like the rest, not even as pretty as some.

Only a woman, he scoffed. A woman who'd beaten him at Madison Square Garden. A woman who liked poetry and art and beauty. A woman who loved life and everything in it.

He thought about Flex and Gerry, men she slept with as easily as he did Linda Gibbons or any other woman he wanted. It seemed completely out of character. Or maybe he just wished it weren't so. Why shouldn't Ellie take lovers as easily as he did? Why was it all right for him and not her?

Because deep down he was old fashioned. He wanted a woman whose body she saved for someone special, someone she cared about. A woman whose relationships meant something to her. Someone with a bit of old-fashioned morality.

With a flash of something close to an epiphany, Clay paused. In all his thirty-one years, he had never felt that way. Or if he had, he'd never admitted it to himself. What was happening to him? All he'd ever wanted out of life was to win, have a good time, and get laid.

His father had lived his whole life that way. Avery Whitfield believed pleasure and indulgence were everything. As long as Clay agreed with him, partied with him, and looked up to him, Avery gave Clay his approval. It meant a lot to Clay.

Everything.

After his mother died, Clay had been desperate for his father's love and approval. For years he'd been ignored, shifted from estate to estate, left alone and lonely.

"Will Papa be home this weekend?" he would ask his current nanny. But the visits were rare. Usually, he was bundled up, packed into the limo, and shipped off to Monte Carlo or Martinique or wherever his father was likely to turn up next.

Summers away from boarding school were the worst. At least he had friends there. On the estate, he only had the household staff to keep him company, though his older half- brother, John, stayed at the residence whenever he was home on leave.

At his father's insistence and to fill the void, Clay had started riding. It was considered the thing to do among his dad's wealthy friends. By the time he was nine years old, he'd discovered he was good at it. By twelve, he was consistently winning.

It wasn't until he reached his teens that Avery began to notice. Clay's good looks coupled with his championship wins had women following him everywhere, women of every age, shape and size. Avery was quick to catch on. More and more, Clay's father traveled with him, lavishing him with attention and praise.

For the first time in his life, Clay felt wanted and loved. It drove him to even higher levels of achievement.

Now he was thirty-one. Was Avery Whitfield's love and approval still so important? Clay tried to ignore the tiny voice that answered, *yes.*

Forcing his hands to relax on the steering wheel of the rented Mercedes, Clay glanced across at Ellie. As he could have guessed, she was staring out the window, smiling, enthralled with whatever she saw.

Dawn was just breaking, lighting the horizon with a soft golden glow.

"Pretty, isn't it?"

She smiled. "Beautiful." They passed vast stretches of yellow flowers, then red, then orange. Farmers worked in the patchwork of color, and water sparkled along the rows like strings of jewels.

"I wonder what happened to the windmills," Ellie said. "I always thought there'd be windmills."

"A few are left, not many. Civilization has a way of swallowing up the past."

"That's true, I guess. But it gives us things, too. Sometimes unbelievably precious gifts."

"Like what?"

"Medical advances. Improvements in technology that can change people's lives."

"I suppose that's true."

"And air travel," she added. "Visiting places in the world we'd never be able to see. And there's the quality of life and—"

"I get the picture. I guess I've just grown so cynical I take those things for granted."

She smiled at him in that warm way that made something expand in his chest. "I believe you have," she said, "and it's time for that to change."

Clay smiled back at her. "You're a treasure, Ellie, an absolute jewel."

They spent the early morning hours touring the flower market. Under a huge metal roof, millions of flowers from all over the world were auctioned off every day. On the wall above the bidding floor, giant gauges showed the price of each block of flowers in different types of currency and the amount of the highest bid. Another showed the quantity.

"It's fascinating. The flowers are so beautiful. Each one almost perfect."

"I thought you'd enjoy this. Besides, what else is there to do at five o'clock in the morning?"

She laughed. They left the market, breakfasted in an intimate Dutch café, then headed back to the hotel. Once they arrived, Clay opened her car door and helped her out of the vehicle.

Ellie looked up at him. "About last night. I want you to know,

I really appreciate what you did. I'm ashamed of the way I handled myself with that man."

"Ashamed? For the love of God, why would you be ashamed?"

"I should have fought harder. I should have hit him with something, done something. I don't know..." She sighed. "Then afterward, I couldn't seem to think straight. I had no idea what to do."

"That's nonsense. You fought as hard as you could. If you hadn't, I wouldn't have heard your struggles, and I wouldn't have known you were in trouble. Afterward, of course you were upset. You went through a terrifying ordeal."

She smiled at him softly. "Thank you for saying that."

Clay reached up and gently touched the bruise on her cheek. "You're welcome," was all he said.

By the time they arrived upstairs at the hotel, the door to Ellie's room had been repaired. A note from Jake said he wanted to see her as soon as she got back.

"Flex must have told him," Ellie said glumly.

"He really had no choice," Clay said. "The team is Jake's responsibility. He needs to know what's going on."

"I   suppose."

Clay tucked her arm into his and towed her along the hall to Jake's room on the second floor. Dressed in black slacks and a white shirt, his thick, silver-touched black hair still damp, Jake answered the door just seconds after Clay's knock.

"Are you alright?" he asked Ellie, motioning them inside. Worry lines creased his forehead.

"I'm fine, thanks to Clay."

"What happened?"

With Clay's help, Ellie explained about the man who'd broken into her room and attacked her.

"Do I have to go to the police?" Ellie asked softly. "I don't want to, Jake. I'd rather forget the whole thing."

Jake seemed to mull the situation over. The skin looked tight over his high cheekbones; his lips formed a narrow line.

"I don't see how we can avoid it," Clay said.

Jake remained uncertain. "Maybe Ellie's right. She has to compete. This could cause considerable stress for her. It might even mean some bad publicity. You never know how something like this will look in print."

Clay shook his head. "I don't know, Jake. The man threatened Ellie's life. I think—

"I don't care what you think!" Jake snapped. "I have to do what's best for the team."

Clay clamped his jaw. "It's your decision. Yours and Ellie's." There was no mistaking the disapproval in his voice.

"I'd really like to forget it," Ellie said. "I'm not even going to tell my parents. They'd only worry, and I don't want that. I need to concentrate on my riding."

"Well, I guess if that's what you want...." Jake sounded relieved.

"I don't like it," Clay said. "But if that's the way you want it, I'll accept your decision."

Ellie flashed him a grateful smile. "Thank you, Clay."

"Why don't you stay at the hotel and rest for the day?" Jake suggested. "You can start riding again tomorrow."

Ellie shook her head. "I need to get back to work. It'd rather be busy, keep my mind off what happened. Besides, I want to spend some time with Jubilee."

"You want to go out there with us?" Clay asked Jake.

Jake nodded. "I've got work to do, as well."

"I'll drive. There's a blue Mercedes in the parking lot. Meet me there in ten minutes."

Ellie returned to her room to change into her riding clothes. Just being there by herself made her nervous. She kept glancing around, waiting for someone to leap out at her. The door was locked, and she'd checked the room, but it wasn't enough.

In her haste to leave, she grabbed a shirt in the closet and knocked several pairs of riding pants off their hangers in the process. Groping the closet floor on her hands and knees, her fingers closed over the pants and something else. She pulled the whole handful out into the light to discover a man's black leather jacket.

Her pulse kicked up. Holding the jacket at arm's length, staring at it as if it were a cobra instead of a coat, she tossed it onto the chair, finished dressing, and raced next door to get Clay.

He spied her pale face as he opened the door. "What's happened?"

"The man who attacked me must have gotten too hot in the closet. He left his jacket behind."

Clay followed her back her to her room and picked the jacket up off the chair. Moderately expensive black leather cut aviator-style. He rummaged through the pockets and pulled a pack of Galloise from inside. Two cigarettes had been smoked. In the left pocket, he found a tissue and part of a crumpled white business card. The name had been partly torn away, but the address was in Charleston, South Carolina.

"That's Jake's address," Ellie whispered.

"Yes, it is."

"Then the man didn't choose me at random. He knew who I was."

"Apparently."

Ellie made a sound in her throat and Clay settled an arm around her shoulders.

"We'd better go show Jake." Grabbing her hand, Clay led her downstairs, out to the parking lot. Jake stood next to the Mercedes, watching someone near the building down the street. He glanced away as they approached.

Clay handed him the torn scrap of paper.

"Where did you get this?" Jake's expression went dark.

"The man who attacked Ellie left his jacket in her room. We found this in the pocket."

A slow breath whispered out, but Jake didn't speak.

"It looks to me like there's a link between what happened on the plane and what happened to Ellie," Clay said.

Jake just nodded.

"I think we'd better notify the authorities."

Something shifted in Jake's expression. "I already have."

"You have?"

"After you left my room, I called the authorities in New York. They said they'd bring in some undercover security people. You probably won't be able to spot them, but they'll be around."

"That's a relief," Clay said.

"They want this whole thing kept quiet. I'd appreciate it if you'd keep it between the three of us."

"Four, but I'll tell Flex not to say anything."

Jake just nodded. "Thanks."

The first shrill ring of the telephone sliced through the silence in the room. Sitting only inches away in his big, overstuffed chair, Nikolai Popov lifted the receiver and held it against his ear. The slick black plastic felt cold and unfriendly. The voice on the other end of the line pronounced his name in a way Popov didn't like.

"I have been waiting for your call," Nikolai said to the man on the other end of the line. "I do not like to be kept waiting."

"I wanted to be certain things went as planned."

"And did they?"

"More or less."

"Meaning?"

"Meaning one of the riders interrupted me before I finished. We fought. He is a strong one."

"Go on."

"It didn't really matter. I accomplished what you wanted."

"And the jacket?"

"Left in the closet, as you asked. She has probably found it by now. If she has not, she will discover it when she packs."

"Have they brought in the police?"

"No."

"Good. I do not think Comrade Straka will allow it, but if it happens..." Popov shrugged absently. "So much the better. If we need you again, we will contact you in the usual manner."

The line went dead, and Popov hung up the phone. Only the soft ticking of the walnut clock on the mantle above the small electric fireplace disturbed the silence in his sparsely furnished, one-bedroom Washington apartment.

With a sigh, Nikolai leaned back in his chair. How he missed the old days, missed Tasha's big feet padding around the house, the smell of sausage and boiled potatoes coming from her kitchen. He missed the children's laughter, the questions about their schoolwork they asked before they toddled off to bed.

Those had been happy years. Now his family was scattered across Russia like seeds in the wind. Tasha was now buried alongside his son, Orloff. Irina and Aksandr, had families of their own.

Getting up from his chair, Popov turned on the portable television in the living room. American TV bored him, except for the

147

educational channel.

Capitalism was disgustingly hedonistic. Unlike the hard work required in the Communist system, the lazy, indulgent lives the Americans lived brought out the worst in a man.

He believed in the Marxist ideal. Nikolai would do everything in his power to help the country he loved attain the greatness it was meant for.

No matter the cost.

Jake paced the floor of his hotel room. It was almost midnight. For the first time in twenty years, he wished he had a cigarette. If the sonofabitch didn't contact him soon, he was going to track him down through the Russian Embassy. He wanted these attacks on his people stopped and stopped now!

Jake paused. Who the hell was he kidding? Aside from telling Daniel about the incidents, there was nothing he could do. If he did, Daniel would be forced to take whatever action he felt necessary to protect the team. Jake's mother and sister would suffer as surely as he breathed.

If he didn't tell Daniel, someone on his team might get killed. Either way, Jake would lose. Unless he could convince Popov to stop.

What did the Russian want? Why the attacks against the team? It was a miracle the police weren't already involved. Popov must have known the risk, yet he didn't seem to care. Why not? Was he that confident of his scheme?

Frustrated and needing a breath of air, Jake grabbed his coat and headed out the door, careful to leave by the stairs instead of the elevator, checking to be sure he wasn't followed. It was seven o'clock in Washington, time to call Daniel. From a pay phone several blocks away, Jake placed the call to his friend. It rang four times before Daniel answered.

"Jake. I was in the shower."

"Hot date?"

"Hardly. I'm going over to see my mother. Not exactly the old me, is it?"

"No girlfriend?"

"To tell you the truth, I haven't been with a woman since Marie died. I'm way overdue."

Jake smiled sadly. "I know the feeling."

"Any news?" Daniel said.

"That's what I called to ask."

"Nothing much. Our people have your sister and mother under surveillance. Your family looks fine. We don't think they're aware of what's going on. Our man in the Kremlin should be checking in sometime tomorrow. Call me this time tomorrow night."

"Will do. Say hello to your mom for me, I always liked her."

"She's still as feisty as ever. Take care, Jake."

Jake rang off wondering about his own mother. Was she old and stooped, or as full of life and vigor as Daniel's mother had always been? And his sister? What of Dana? How had she survived the years?

He returned to his room heavy hearted. The phone rang just seconds after he walked in.

"Ah, Comrade, a man of the evening, I see."

At the sound of the rough voice, Jake steeled himself. "Just out for a late-night snack," he lied.

"Did you get my message?"

Jake's hand balled into a fist. "Are you crazy? Your man tried to rape one of my people. It's only a miracle the police weren't brought in—or is that what you want?"

Popov chuckled, the sound grating on Jake's taut nerves. "What I want, *Tovarich* is for you to do as you are told."

"I've already agreed to that, but if you keep up these attacks on my people, I'll be forced to go to the authorities. Whatever you have planned will die on the vine."

"Always so impatient..."

"I want your word, Popov. As I recall, it used to mean something."

"You remember your past whenever it is convenient."

"Your word," Jake repeated.

"I think not. It is good for you to wonder. At least now you know we mean what we say."

Jake thought of Ellie's battered face. "I never doubted it."

A raspy chuckle. "Of that I am certain." The line went dead.

Jake replaced the receiver with a shaky hand. He could still see the fear in Ellie's eyes. He'd gotten no promises, but Popov had made his point. Surely there was no need for more violence. Though he hated himself for it, he would continue to do as the Russian asked—unless Daniel's people could prove the man was acting on his own authority. At the moment, that looked doubtful.

As far as his team went, Jake would have to wait and watch. If anything else happened, he'd consider telling Daniel the truth.

He'd been forced to lie to Clay and the others, had told them he'd brought in security when he had never made the call.

He made a second decision. As soon as he got the chance, he'd talk to Maggie. See if he could convince her to take Sarah and go home.

CHAPTER SIXTEEN

The hotel room still made her nervous. It was past midnight, yet Ellie couldn't fall asleep.

She should have listened to Jake and moved to a room on the next floor, but she hadn't wanted to be that far from Clay. Of course, she couldn't tell Jake that. Nor could she tell him she'd never forget the way Clay had come to her rescue, how protected she had felt when he'd held her.

Ellie checked the door and windows a second time and climbed back in bed, but every sound, every creak and moan, had her eyes shooting open. She read for a while, *Slow Heat in Heaven*, a steamy romance by that made her think of Clay and did nothing to put her to sleep.

There were no noises coming from his room. Either Clay wasn't at home, or he was sleeping soundly. After her attack last night, he'd been solicitous, saddling Jube for her, riding with her a while to be sure she all right.

Finally, at her insistence, he had left her to finish her morning routine. She'd worked Jube for a couple of hours, lungeing him, doing some work on the flat, taking a couple of fences. While Clay was busy putting Max over some Cavalletti, she and Gerry took off for a quick bite of lunch.

When she returned, Clay was almost hostile.

"Have a nice lunch?" he asked sarcastically as he rode up to where she stood watching him with her elbows propped on the fence rail. Max was so big and Clay so tall, she had to tilt her head back to see the dark forbidding expression on his face.

"You were working Max. I didn't want to disturb you."

"So you disturbed your groom instead."

"We just went down the street. There's a little café—"

"I'm sure you were well-entertained. Now if you'll excuse me, Max is tired and so am I." He nudged the big bay forward with a nearly imperceptible pressure on the heel of his boot. "I'm sure Gerry will see you safely back to the hotel."

Max brushed past her, blowing a little, glad to be finished for the day. She watched Clay and the stallion disappear into the stable, wondering what she had done to displease him. They'd been getting along so well and the trip to the flower market had been lovely.

Surely Clay wasn't jealous of Gerry? She thought about the time Gerry had discovered them in the tack room. Clay had been angry, furious, in fact. Ellie had assumed it was because she hadn't jumped at his command. Now she wasn't so sure.

That night she went to bed early, but still had trouble sleeping. Sprawled on the bed, she kicked off her blankets, lifted her heavy hair away from her neck and thought of Clay. Her heartbeat quickened as the usual fever began to heat her blood. Was Clay sleeping alone next door? Or was he with Linda Gibbons or some other woman?

Ellie touched her lips. She could almost taste Clay's mouth over hers, remember the exact scent of his expensive cologne. What if she knocked on his door and he invited her in? How would it feel if he made love to her? How would she feel the next day?

You're a woman. You can do anything you want.

But she didn't go next door. She didn't go to sleep either. She tossed and turned and thought about Clay and knew if he took her to bed, she'd be glad.

At first light, feeling exhausted and out of sorts, Ellie got up, dressed in her riding clothes, and headed out the door. She stopped in the lobby, asked the desk clerk to call her a cab, then went outside to wait on the curb. She'd almost reached the street when a taxi pulled up at the curb in front of the hotel.

Clay opened the door and got out of the cab, swaying on his feet. Dressed in an expensive blue blazer that hung open and a little askew on his shoulders, his striped tie hanging like a noose around his neck, Clay reached down to help a tall brunette in a backless sundress out of the cab. A giggling blonde in a white leather mini slid out behind her.

Teetering on her high spiked heels, the blonde crossed the

sidewalk and snuggled beneath Clay's arm. Clutching an open bottle of champagne, his other arm draped across the brunette's bare shoulders.

There was no place for Ellie to go, no way to avoid a confrontation. She lifted her chin, trying to ignore the anger and disappointment that bubbled inside her. She could feel the heat in her cheeks and the back of her neck.

I should be used to Clay's indiscretions by now, she thought. But she wasn't. How could she even consider sleeping with a man like Clay?

"Well," he said as he approached, "if it isn't little Ms. Untouchable. Only she isn't really so untouchable, is she?" He tilted up the bottle of champagne and took a long pull. Some of the amber liquid trickled along his jaw. Strands of his thick brown hair slanted across his forehead. He needed a shave, but the night's growth of beard only made him more attractive.

"How was dinner?" he asked, wiping the champagne away with the back of his hand and passing the bottle to the blonde. "As pleasant as lunch?"

Ellie didn't answer, just walked past him.

He released the girls and rounded on her. "Wait a minute!" he called after her. She heard his heavy stride on the concrete behind her. Catching up with her easily, he grabbed her arm and turned her around to face him, his dark eyes mocking as they slid over the curves of her body.

"Why don't you forget your damnable horses and have a little fun for a change? I'm sure the girls wouldn't mind if you joined the party."

"Leave me alone, Clay."

"What's the matter? My friends aren't good enough for you? Or is it just that you don't like to share your men?"

"You're drunk and obnoxious. Go back to your little playmates and leave me alone."

"I've *been* leaving you alone. That's where I made my mistake. I should have come into your room like that bastard the other night. I have a feeling you'd have been a little more cooperative with me riding you instead of him."

Ellie slapped Clay's face. His eyes turned even darker, and he set his jaw. Ellie started to say the words on her tongue, but Clay pulled her into his arms and kissed her. It was a hard kiss, demanding, almost punishing. Ellie didn't fight him, just held her temper and remained passive, letting her arms dangle loosely at her sides.

Clay kept kissing her, but his anger had died. The kiss turned gentle, the hand at her waist sliding up to caress the nape of her neck. "Ellie..." he said softly, the word spoken with what sounded like longing.

With a sob of defeat, Ellie's hands clutched the front of his coat and for an instant she kissed him back.

"You're driving me crazy," he whispered against her ear. "I need you, Ellie."

Ellie pulled away, fighting to ignore the yearning she heard in his voice. With a glance from Clay to the girls and back again, humiliated by her own behavior, she blinked back tears, but they spilled down her cheeks.

"How can you be so wonderful and so horrible at the same time?" Brushing away the wetness, she waved at the next cab pulling up to the curb and raced in that direction. Without looking back, she opened the door, climbed in, and instructed the driver to pull away.

Clay stared after the taxi until the car rounded the corner out of sight. Feeling suddenly sober, he turned back to the girls, who were giggling, drinking from the bottle of champagne and apparently oblivious to what had just happened. He pulled his alligator wallet from the breast pocket of his blazer and took out several crisp hundred-guilder notes.

"Here." He handed each girl a wad of money. "Go into the lobby and have the desk clerk call you a cab."

"*Niets meer?*" the brunette asked, her eyes big in her porcelain-like face.

"English," Clay reminded her.

"I thought we were going to—"

"No. Goodnight," he said, though by now it was morning. Clay handed the keys to the valet and left the women standing on the curb.

"*Goedenacht,*" the blonde called after him with a wave.

Clay didn't wave back. His head pounded from the liquor he'd consumed, and he was disgusted with himself. *How could he have said those things to Ellie?*

Because in a way he meant them. Ellie wanted him. He knew

women. Yet every time the two of them got close to having some sort of relationship, Ellie went off with Gerry Winslow, or Flex McGrath. Maybe even Jake.

She'd slept with them when he felt certain he was the man she wanted.

Clay cursed himself for a fool. He should have taken her out to dinner tonight, brought her back to his room, and taken her to bed, would have, if she hadn't had such a bad experience the night before.

When he'd seen her at the show grounds with her groom, he'd gone off half-cocked, gotten drunk, and picked up the girls in the bar on Rochussenstraat. By the time they headed back to the hotel it was almost morning. Now he'd driven another wedge between him and Ellie. Was Ellie Fletcher worth all the trouble?

The voice inside him continued to answer, *yes*.

Jake spent the next two days trying to think of a way to convince Maggie to take Sarah and go home. None of his rehearsed speeches sounded convincing. In the end, he decided to say whatever seemed right at the time.

By Thursday, he realized Maggie was doing everything in her power to avoid him. She didn't go to any team dinners, went to the show grounds as rarely as possible, and generally stayed out of his way. Maggie was doing the same things to him that Jake had been doing to her ever since she arrived in Europe.

It was only by chance he spotted her through his hotel room window, standing on the curb out in front, helping Sarah and her nanny into a cab. The little girl must have been looking up at his room. Through the rear window, Sarah waved good-bye as the cab drove away.

Jake's stomach tightened. He glanced at his Rolex. Seven p.m. The sun was still shining, but copper tinged the evening sky. As Maggie walked back into the hotel, Jake stepped away from the window.

He'd just showered and changed after a long day of competition at the Rotterdam show, during which most of the team had done well. Ellie had taken a first and second. Flex had won a first and a third. Shep had done passably well, winning a third. And Clay hadn't shown up.

Typical Clay. When he wanted to be, he was brilliant. When he wanted to be, he was an ass.

Jake glanced at his reflection in the mirror above the dresser.

His eyes were lined with worry, his skin less swarthy than usual. After Ellie's attack, he'd made a point of finding out where Maggie and Sarah were staying. Since then, every evening before he went to bed, he quietly checked that wing for anyone who looked suspicious.

Long strides carried him down the hall. He turned left into an empty corridor and stopped outside Maggie's room. With a steadying breath, he rapped lightly on the door. There was movement inside the room, the scrape of a chair being pushed back, soft footfalls, then the door opened a crack.

Gentle blue eyes widened as she spotted him on the other side of the door.

"I need to talk to you, Maggie," Jake said.

She hesitated a moment then slid back the chain to let him in. The room, a duplicate of his own, was orderly, a Danish modern chair next to the table, clothes all put away. Only Sarah's *Peanuts* comic book, strewn carelessly on one of the twin beds, betrayed the child's presence.

Maggie's gaze followed Jake's. "Sarah went to dinner with Flora."

"I know. I was looking out my window when they left." His gaze drifted over her. She looked beautiful in an elegant dove gray skirt that fell softly over her slender hips. Her embroidered silk blouse outlined the peaks of her delicate, upturned breasts, and Jake felt a tightening in his groin.

She'd kicked off her shoes, but still wore her stockings, showing off her long, shapely legs. He wanted to pull her into his arms, bury his face in her hair, and never let her go.

"Thanks for letting me in," he said a little gruffly. "Why don't we sit down?"

Her blond brows drew slightly together. "Maybe we should go downstairs to the café."

Jake ignored the suggestion. "How's Sarah?" he asked, trying to ease into the conversation.

"She's fine." Maggie flashed him a nervous look that said she wanted to know why he was there, but politeness won out. "She loves traveling, wants to see everything everywhere we go. Thank heaven Flora is here. I'd never be able to keep up with her."

"She's got plenty of energy, all right." Jake forced a smile he didn't feel. "What about you, Maggie, how are you getting along?"

Maggie's shoulders tightened. "Work keeps me busy. There's plenty to do. More than I would have dreamed. In the morning I join the dressage team in Belgium for a couple of days."

"I wasn't asking about work."

"What are you asking, Jake? Is this a personal visit, or a professional one? Because if it's personal, I think you'd better leave." To make her point she started for the door.

"Please sit down, Maggie. This is difficult enough as it is."

Casting him an uncertain glance, Maggie walked back and sat down in the chair. Jake sat down on the edge of the bed.

"I know you have every reason to distrust me. I led you on, led you to believe we had a future. At the time I thought we did."

"I see. Then somehow you discovered you were wrong."

"I can only tell you that I had no choice. There were...other considerations. The team, Pleasant Oaks," he added lamely. "But you and Sarah mean a lot to me. That's why I'm here."

"It seems to me Sarah and I mean very little to you. Your coaching job and your precious stable are what you care about most. Or was I just another conquest?"

"It wasn't that way."

"It wasn't? Maybe I wasn't good enough in bed. Or maybe you're the kind of man who needs a different woman every few months to keep his...interest...from lagging."

"Dammit, Maggie!" Jake surged to his feet. "You know that wasn't the way it was! I had reasons—things I can't discuss. I wanted to tell you. I still want to, but I can't."

"Can't Jake? Or won't?"

He released a slow breath, trying to stay calm. "I never meant to hurt you."

"Then tell me the truth. What happened to us, Jake?"

"I did what had to. That's all I can say."

"Then why are you here?"

Jake clamped down on his emotions and sat back down on the bed. "There have been some problems."

Maggie sat up straighter in the chair. "Has something happened to the team?"

"That's just it. I'm afraid something might." He ran his fingers through his hair, determined to remain in control. "There have been a couple of incidents...so far nobody's been seriously injured, but—"

"What kind of incidents?"

"One of the horses was drugged. Someone broke into Ellie's room and attacked her."

Maggie eyes went wide. "Oh, my God, is she all right?"

"The guy roughed her up pretty good. Clay Whitfield played knight in shining armor and came to her rescue."

"I think Clay's more chivalrous than he suspects."

"Maybe. But things could have turned out differently. She could have been hurt very badly, maybe even killed. That's why I came. I want you to take Sarah and go home."

"You can't be serious."

"Dammit, Maggie, you know as well as I do, the international climate isn't good. That airbus the Navy accidentally shot down last week could be the fuse that sets off the dynamite. I'd feel a whole lot better if you and Sarah were somewhere safe."

Maggie just shook her head. "You must be out of your mind. I have a job to do—an important job. The team needs me. I'm not about to go home. I can't believe you're even suggesting it."

"What about Sarah? It isn't safe for her here. She's just a child. She'd be better off at home."

Maggie's gaze fixed on his face. "What's this about, Jake? Something's going on. Tell me what it is."

"I just told you. Surely, for Sarah's sake you'll consider what I'm saying."

Maggie watched him closely. His face looked drawn and tired, the skin taut over his high cheekbones. "This isn't about the international climate, is it?"

"Of course, it is."

"This is about you, Jake. Something's wrong and you're involved."

"Don't be ridiculous. It's just that things are heating up, and I think you'd be better off back in the States. You shouldn't be here by yourself in the first place. Evelyn was supposed to come with you."

"Evelyn is in the hospital having back surgery. I'm her assistant. The fact that she isn't here only makes my job more important. This isn't like you, Jake. I want to know what's going on." His anxiety was almost tangible, his fists clenched as tightly as his jaw.

He took a deep breath and let it out slowly. "Listen to me, Maggie. I don't know what's going on. I only know I want you and Sarah safe. I want you to go home."

"Why, Jake?" Maggie whispered, her heart beginning to pound with a strange feeling of hope. "Why should you care?"

Jake reached out and touched her cheek, his hand calloused and as strong as she remembered. "I care, dammit. The *why* doesn't matter."

"It does to me."

"Maggie, please."

"I've got to know, Jake. You owe me that much." Maggie swallowed past the lump in her throat, but she couldn't stop the tears welling in her eyes. "You lied to me, didn't you? You said you didn't have time for us, but it wasn't the truth. There was some other reason, something you're afraid to tell me. I wasn't wrong about you—tell me I wasn't."

"I'd better go," Jake said, his voice gruff as he rose and started for the door.

Maggie rose and touched his arm and that single contact stopped him. "Tell me, Jake. Tell me the truth." She raised a trembling hand and cradled it against his cheek. Jake leaned into the warmth and closed his eyes.

"Maggie, don't," he whispered. "It isn't safe for me to be with you. You've got to forget about us and go back home."

Tears spilled down her cheeks. "I want to know why you left us. I want to know if you loved me."

"Maggie..." For a moment he just stood there, his beautiful blue eyes filled with despair. Then he reached out and pulled her into his arms. "I loved you then, I love you now. I'll always love you, Maggie. That's never going to change."

Jake..." Longing speared through her. Maggie kissed his mouth, his cheeks, his eyes. She wanted to say the same words to him, but the tears clogging her throat made it impossible to speak. Jake pulled her down on the bed and kissed her hungrily, kissed her as if he couldn't get enough. It was a kiss of possession, of longing and love, a kiss that tried to make up for the time they'd been apart.

"I love you," Maggie whispered, and felt his lips on her cheek, kissing away her tears.

Jake unbuttoned her blouse and slipped his hand inside to gently cup her breast. Maggie moaned and tore at the buttons on his shirt. The first two popped free, the next one didn't. Jake grabbed hold of the fabric and tugged so hard the button tore loose and the shirt fell open. Maggie helped him pull it off over his head and he tossed it away. Her fingers played over the familiar lines and sinews, tangled in the curly black hair on his chest.

Jake slipped the blouse off her shoulders, worked the zipper on her skirt. A short, sweet buzz and the skirt joined the clothes on the floor. His mouth moved along her throat as he whispered her name, telling her he loved her, touching and caressing, healing her with his hands and his kisses. She could feel his care in every touch, and love for him blossomed inside her.

"Tell me you aren't just saying the things I want to hear," she said softly.

Jake pressed his lips against her bare shoulder. "I mean every word, Maggie. I love you. We don't have to do this. We can stop now, if that's what you want. Holding you is enough."

He was telling the truth. She could hear it in his voice, see it in his face.

The last of her heartache fell away. "I want you, Jake. I've never stopped wanting you."

Jake kissed her and kissed her, unhooked her simple cotton bra, baring her breasts. His lips skimmed along her throat and shoulders, covered her hard, dusky nipple, sucked the rigid tip until she trembled and arched against him.

Her hands shook as she reached for the buckle on his belt, then unbuttoned and unzipped his pants. Jake stopped kissing her long enough to pull off his boots and remove the rest of his clothes.

Both gloriously naked on the narrow twin bed, Jake covered her body with his, pressing her down in the mattress. She loved the way it felt to have him there, loved the warmth of his mouth moving over her skin as he kissed his way down her body.

He knew just what to do, just how to touch her, exactly what pleased her. Heat rolled through her, and a burst of wild, fiery passion that had her clutching his shoulders, then tipping into climax.

The world spun and she drifted, drifted, finally returned to the world to find Jake watching her.

She reached out to him, touched his cheek. "I need more of you. I need all of you, Jake. I need to know you're really here."

Jake pressed a kiss on the flat spot below her navel. "I'm here, Maggie." Coming up over her, he kissed her hard and slid himself inside. She moaned at the feel his arousal, his hunger as he started to move, slowly at first, letting her absorb the weight of him, then faster, deeper, harder.

She could hear his ragged breathing, feel the pounding of his heart. Jake drove into her, his movements more and more urgent, his control slipping, along with her own. A tight knot hummed inside her. She felt Jake's muscles bunch, knew he was close to release, and the feeling sent her over the edge.

Jake's climax followed, the two of them clinging together as if they were afraid to let go.

"I love you," he whispered. "No matter what happens, I'll never lie to you again."

Tears threatened. "I love you so much."

They lay together for a time, spiraling slowly back to earth, Maggie curled on her side, Jake behind her spoon fashion. His warm breath tickled her shoulder while his arm wrapped protectively around her. Maggie knew a feeling of contentment she had only experienced with Jake.

Then she remembered his words. *No matter what happens....*

Fresh fear slipped through her, which Jake must have sensed. She rolled onto her back to look at him.

"I can't tell you what's going on, Maggie," he said. "I can't tell you it will all work out and things will be the way they were."

"I'll send Sarah home with Flora. Don't ask me to go with them."

Jake kissed her hair. "We can't be together—not for an hour or even a minute. Not until this is over—one way or another. You've got to promise me that."

She managed to nod. "I'll do whatever you say." Now that Jake was there, she could handle whatever lay ahead.

Jake kissed her, slow and deep, and desire rose hot and greedy inside her. Grateful to be back in his arms, Maggie stoked the flames.

CHAPTER SEVENTEEN

Rotterdam was an Official International Competition involving a Nations' Cup. In the two-round event, out of the eight countries represented, the Americans came away with a third-place win. Not bad, considering Clay racked up fourteen faults in the first round, eighteen in the second. One of the poorest rides he'd made all year.

Ellie won the Grand Prix on Sunday. Flex should have.

In the jump-off, Sebastian took the final fence too fast, landed wrong, and Flex came out of the saddle, his chest and shoulders thrown hard against the bottom two rails. Sparky stood over him, the gelding rolling his eyes and trembling, as if ashamed of what he'd done.

Flex spoke to him softly, forgiving him, it seemed. The horse nuzzled his master's head while the medics gave him the once-over. No broken bones, they pronounced. Flex limped off the field with a half–hearted smile.

Clay rode so poorly, taking out half the fences and stacking twenty faults, that Ellie felt little satisfaction in beating him. She collected her silver cup and made a victory lap around the ring. Jube, who had no trouble accepting the accolades, pranced and tossed his head, nickering to Sparky as they left the arena.

"That was fine riding," Jake said when she jumped down from the saddle. He stroked Jube's sleek sorrel neck. "You've come a long way since New York. I couldn't be more pleased."

Jake's words of praise meant more than the trophy she'd won. "Thank you. I just hope I can keep winning."

"You will. The worst part, the nerves and uncertainty, are behind you. Now you know you can win so there's nothing to be afraid of."

They walked to the barn in silence. Jake seemed more relaxed than he had been in the last few weeks, though in some ways he seemed even more guarded. Ellie had noticed him glancing behind him on more than one occasion or jumping at the slightest noise. She was sure it had something to do with the incidents that had plagued the team, though nothing more had happened.

Jake had tremendous responsibility, and he was the kind of man who took that seriously. If anything happened to the team, Jake would blame himself.

At the stables, Maggie Delaine stopped by. "Congratulations. I knew you could do it."

"Thanks, Maggie. Did you get Sarah off all right?"

Maggie flicked a soft glance toward where Jake stood talking to Shep Singleton. Ellie caught the subtle movement and wondered if Maggie had in some way been responsible for the change in Jake.

"She didn't want to leave, but she had fun while she was here."

Ellie smiled inwardly. Maggie's eyes moved over Jake like a caress, a far different look than she'd given him a few days ago. Something must have happened between them. Usually adept at hiding his emotions, when Jake looked at Maggie, he was easy to read.

Ellie hoped the two could work out their differences.

"I miss Sarah already," Maggie said, drawing Ellie's attention back to the conversation. "But it was just too hard to get my work done and watch out for my daughter, too."

"Did she get to ride much while she was here?"

"Flex took her out a couple of times. So did Prissy."

"I would have, if I'd thought of it. I guess I've been a little preoccupied lately."

"I know what you mean," Maggie said. "Well, I just wanted to drop by and tell you how thrilled I am for you. I'd better get back to the hotel." Maggie threw a last glance at Jake, their eyes locked, then each turned away.

"Congratulations." Prissy Knowles approached the barn, leading Julius Caesar. "You and Jube were terrific."

"Thanks." Ellie stood outside her tack room brushing Jube, her mind going over events of the day.

"What's the matter? You're supposed to be excited."

Ellie shrugged. "I wanted to beat Clay."

"But that's what you did."

"Not really. Clay wasn't trying. I've never seen him ride as poorly as he has this week."

"So he's a little down in the dumps. So what? We all have our off days."

"Not Clay. Clay rides his best no matter what mood he's in."

"You've got a point there. He's one tough competitor. It takes a lot to get him down."

Ellie continued stroking Jube, who nickered softly at her gentle touch.

"You don't suppose he's pining away over you?"

Ellie laughed. "Hardly. He's got women two at a time these days."

"Same old Clay. Just be glad you didn't go to bed with him."

"We really never came close."

"Lucky for you."

"I suppose."

"You suppose what?" Clay sauntered into the barn, stopping a few feet from Ellie. He propped a wide shoulder against the wall and crossed his long, booted legs in front of him.

"She supposes you could have ridden better today," Prissy said. "What do you suppose?"

"I suppose the lady is right," he said darkly. Reaching down, he picked up a piece of straw and clamped it between his teeth, but his eyes remained on Ellie.

Prissy glanced from one of them to the other. "I'll see you two back at the hotel," she said, and Ellie felt a moment of panic.

"What's the matter?" Clay growled as Prissy disappeared out of sight. "Afraid I'll carry you into the tack room and make passionate love to you? Or afraid I won't?"

"I see you're in fine form today," Ellie said, beginning to stroke Jube faster.

"I feel like hell, and you, Ms. Fletcher, are the reason. In two long strides, Clay ducked under Jube's lead rope and came up beside her. "Even my riding is beginning to suffer."

She looked up at him incredulously. "Your riding is suffering because of me? Now I've heard everything. I think you're just a sore loser. I beat you, and you can't stand it."

164

"I don't like to lose. I'll grant you that. It won't happen again."

"Oh, really?" Ellie stopped brushing and turned to face him. He was standing so close she could smell his cologne. "I hope you get over whatever is ailing you, Clay, before we get to Hickstead. I hope you ride the best you've ever ridden. And when I beat you, I don't want to hear any excuses. I just want to hear congratulations."

"Congratulations, Ms. Fletcher," he said, his tone suddenly lighter. "How about letting me buy you dinner by way of celebration?"

Ellie released an exasperated sigh. "I don't feel like celebrating. Somehow my victory seems hollow."

Clay tipped her chin up. "You rode brilliantly today. Better than I've ever seen you. I still can't believe you've learned to compete like that in just four years."

Ellie felt a thread of guilt. "That's the way the newspapers see it. Actually, I started riding when I was three. I just didn't compete."

"The truth will out. Now where shall we go for dinner?"

"I'm sorry, Clay. I've got too much to do. We'll be leaving in the morning. I've got to pack. Rose's tack needs mending and—"

"You've got a groom for that, or are his services more valuable elsewhere?"

Ellie pressed her lips together. The hard, fast strokes of her brush gave him his answer.

"Damn it, Ellie, you're driving me crazy. Go out with me."

"No."

"Why the hell not?"

Ellie hurled the brush against the wall where it landed with a clatter. "Why not? You ask me that after the way you acted? You have your women—dozens of them—what do you want with me?"

"I didn't sleep with those two girls. I sent them home."

"I don't believe you."

"I'm a bastard, Ellie, not a liar." Clay didn't flinch or glance away. "I didn't sleep with Gabriella either," he said, suddenly serious. "The truth is, there are far less women than you believe." A grin dimpled his cheeks. "And I know all about safe sex."

Ellie flushed and glanced away.

"I was mad because you left with Gerry," he told her. "I acted abominably, and I apologize. Now how about dinner?"

Barely trusting her voice, Ellie shook her head. "No," she

165

whispered.

Clay cursed so low it sounded like a growl. "I'm tired of taking no for an answer, Ellie. I know you want me as much as I want you. Tomorrow night we'll be in London. I've taken a suite at Claridge's. We'll have supper at Le Caprice, celebrate your win, then go to bed. One way or another, tomorrow night I'm going to make love to you. It's what I want, it's what you want—and we both know it!"

Ignoring her stunned expression, Clay slid an arm around her waist, hauled her against him, and kissed her, long and deep. When he let her go, she clutched Jube's mane of support.

"You can't just...you can't just..."

"The way you just kissed me says I can!" His lips covered hers again, and he kissed her even more thoroughly, sending little slivers of warmth down her spine. Ellie clutched his neck, praying he wouldn't hear her purr.

"I'm a fool not to take you right here," he whispered against her cheek as he nibbled her ear.

An alarm went off at his words. Ellie broke away and glanced guiltily around to see if anyone could hear.

Clay chuckled softly. "So fiery. So proper. Tomorrow night we'll see which one you really are."

"What makes you think I'll go with you?"

"Because, if I have to, I'll find you and convince you that's what you want."

Ellie moistened her lips. She hated to admit how good that sounded.

"Keep that up, and I won't wait until tomorrow." He flashed her a grin that said he was only half teasing. "Don't worry, love. I want what happens between us to be special."

Lowering his head, he kissed her again, quick and hard, making her insides melt.

"Maybe you're right," she said. "I've been trying to convince myself to stay away from you, but we both know that's not what I really want."

Clay's eyebrows arched in disbelief, then he smiled so brightly his whole face lit up. He looked vulnerable, almost boyish.

"We'll be at Hickstead by ten o'clock tomorrow. We'll see to the horses, then go into London and do a little sightseeing. Have you seen the Tower?"

"I've never been to London," she said, still slightly breathless.

"Then you're in for a treat. We'll go to lunch and prowl around a little afterward." He ran a finger down her cheek. "I've got a meeting with some of my father's business associates tonight. Believe it or not, I work for a living, just like everyone else. The family business usually takes up a lot of my time, but this year, I made an exception." He smiled. "I'll see you in the morning."

Ellie just nodded.

"Get some rest, love. This is all going to work out." With a last quick kiss and a sweeping glance that sent the blood singing in her veins, Clay was gone.

When morning arrived, Ellie felt nervous and jittery yet filled with anticipation. Tonight, she would sleep with Clayton Whitfield, let him make love to her as she'd wanted him to do almost from the start.

The brief flight to Gatwick Airport left at nine o'clock sharp. The horses, traveling by ferry, had left hours earlier and would arrive in Hickstead ahead of them. Clay sat in the seat beside her, smiling, touching her a little more than necessary, his eyes warm, yet she couldn't miss the hunger. He laughed and smiled easily, and Ellie felt herself smiling in return, approaching the inevitability of their lovemaking with an unexpected sense of relief.

She wanted to take the final steps to womanhood, and she wanted to make that journey with Clay. What happened tomorrow didn't matter, she told herself. She'd deal with whatever problems arose when the time came.

"Tell me about your first pony," he teased as he tried to get his wide shoulders comfortable in the far too narrow seat. "How old did you say you were? Three?"

"I was three when I sat my first pony, but I didn't get one of my own until I was five. I'll never forget her. Cuddles. She was a ten-hand Welsh Mountain pony, blaze-faced, the most beautiful dapple gray."

Ellie flashed on a blurry image of her pony, then the photo she had seen after her surgery. The pony was gone by then, but she remembered the feel of the pony's sleek coat beneath her hands. She wished she could see Cuddles as she really was instead of just a picture.

"My father gave her to me on my birthday. I really loved that pony. I rode her every day until I was ten years old. It always makes me sad to think of her." Ellie swallowed and glanced away.

"What happened to her?" Clay asked.

She turned back. "Just before my birthday, one of the stable boys left her stall open. She wandered out and got into the feed bin, gorged herself on hay and oats, then got colic. I sat up with the vet all night, holding her head in my lap. She'd just nuzzle me and whimper as if she were asking for my help. Around midnight, my mother and father brought me a tray of food, but I couldn't eat. By then the vet knew she wasn't going to make it."

Ellie ignored the catch in her throat. "My parents knew I'd want to be with her at the end."

Clay brushed a tear from her cheek. He reached over and caught her hand, brought it to his lips. "You are so damned sweet."

Ellie shook her head. "I didn't mean to do that. Now I feel foolish."

"You shouldn't. I lost a horse I felt that way about, a big chestnut gelding. His name was Nickels and Dimes. I called him Nicky. I was fourteen when it happened, and it was my fault. I put him in a class he wasn't ready for, then put him wrong over a fence too high for him to handle. Nicky went down, me along with him. I got a broken leg out of it, so did Nicky. They put him down right there at the show grounds. I didn't cry. I was afraid if I started, I wouldn't be able to stop, and someone would see me."

Ellie glanced up at him and realized he still felt the pain.

Clay cleared his throat. "It was probably a good lesson. After Nicky died, I never let my ego come between me and my horses."

Ellie smiled up at him. "You never cease to amaze me. You write poetry, you like art and ancient history, now I discover, deep down inside, you even have a heart."

Clay laughed. "Another of my deep dark secrets."

The plane began its descent. Somehow with Clay beside her, the plane ride wasn't so unnerving. They landed at Gatwick and were shepherded quickly through customs. On the bus ride to the hotel, she and Clay sat across from Jake. She didn't miss the scowl of disapproval on his face. Sweet God, she couldn't imagine what he'd say if he knew about their plans for tonight!

It was none of Jake's business. He wasn't her father, for

heaven's sake. Besides, he had his own problems with Maggie to worry about.

Across the aisle, Flex noticed Clay sitting beside her and winked. Prissy looked uncertain.

Ellie glanced at Clay and found him watching her, as he had been off and on all day. His eyes looked dark and hungry. Ellie felt a knot of tension curl in the pit of her stomach but willed herself to relax, certain she was making the right decision.

Who was she kidding? There was no decision to make.

Ellie turned her attention to the lush green English landscape outside her window. All the cars drove on the wrong side of the road, and she loved the narrow, very British black taxis with the tiny white lights on top.

People walked the roads in trench coats and carried umbrellas, though it wasn't raining. It was like watching a color version of an old Basil Rathbone movie.

At the Hickstead stables, Ellie checked on Jubilee and Rose. Clay checked on Max and Zodiak. When he didn't return, Ellie went to find him and bumped into Jake on the way.

"Getting awfully cozy with Whitfield, aren't you?"

"Since when did my love life become your affair?"

Jake seemed surprised by her tone. "Sorry. I guess I deserved that."

Ellie softened. "I appreciate your concern, Jake. I know you mean well, but I have to do what's right for me."

"Believe it or not, I know what it feels like to love someone. When that love is returned, it's the most wonderful thing in the world. When it isn't, well... nothing's more painful."

"You're talking about Maggie."

Jake seemed to collect himself. "I'm talking about you and Clay. I know him better than you do. Clay may not be capable of giving you the kind of love you deserve."

"But you aren't sure."

Jake didn't answer.

"Look, Jake, I don't expect Clay to love me. But I *am* attracted to him, and it's clear he's attracted to me. So far, that's all it is."

"Ellie—"

"Leave it alone, Jake. Please?"

Jake touched her cheek the way her father often did. It was a gesture of affection so foreign Ellie glanced up at him in surprise. The only time he'd let down his guard was when he'd been with Maggie.

"Just be careful," he said.

She smiled. "I will. I promise."

Jake turned to leave, but Ellie stopped him. "I don't mean to interfere in your business either, Jake, but I think Maggie still loves you. She's a great lady. If you two had a fight, maybe you should try and make up."

Jake's smile came easy. "I'll give it some thought."

Ellie watched him walk away, thinking maybe he already had. Continuing down the long line of stalls, past whinnying horses and bustling grooms, Ellie found Clay brushing Max, smiling and speaking to him quietly, as if he were talking to a friend.

"You have a groom for that," she teased, repeating his words.

"Sometimes Max gets nervous in a new place. Or maybe there's been a mare in heat in one of the stalls."

Ellie flushed. It was ridiculous. She'd been around horses all her life. Now the implication seemed more personal.

"I just want to get him settled," Clay finished.

"You think of him the way you did Nicky."

Clay looked surprised. "Yes, I guess I do. He's the finest animal I've ever owned, but he's more than that. When we ride together, we're partners. He knows what I want, even before I ask. Usually, it works both ways."

"But not last week."

"I think my dismal mood rubbed off on him." He grinned, flashing his dimples. "This week, I'll be fine and so will Max." He threw her a look that said making love to her would solve all his problems.

Ellie hoped it wouldn't be the beginning of hers.

170

CHAPTER EIGHTEEN

Since the Hickstead competition didn't start until Thursday, the riders had been offered the chance to spend a night in the city. The excitement of London was contagious and almost everyone went

The bus was nearly full as it reached the small hotel in Knightsbridge, and they checked into their rooms. Clay took over from there, guiding Ellie into a taxi and heading off toward Claridge's where he left his bags with a huge black doorman in a long red coat and black silk top hat, telling him he'd be back later to check in.

Their late lunch at Indigo Jones on Garrick Street in Convent Gardens was glorious. The restaurant was old brick and stained glass, and the food was delicious. Afterward they walked the narrow streets. The sun broke through the overcast, warming the day and brightening their already sunny moods.

"Convent Garden used to be the fruit and vegetable market for London," Clay said as they wandered in and out of a dozen tiny boutiques. When Ellie held up an expensive gray silk, hand-painted scarf, Clay bought it for her.

"I want you to have something to remember the day," he said with a smile that touched her heart. She bought him an old, leather-bound volume of Shakespeare's sonnets, which, though inexpensive, he accepted as if it were the crown jewels.

While Clay excused himself to use the phone, Ellie discovered a quaint little shop that carried French lingerie. On a whim, she bought a very sheer and expensive white lace teddy she'd seen in the window, and a pair of lace-topped, thigh-high stockings.

Back on the street, she flushed just carrying the shopping bag.

From Convent Gardens, Clay took her to the Tower of London. Ellie was awestruck by its enormity, the timeless feel of the place, even before she went inside.

"The oldest part of the Tower was built around ten seventy-eight by William the Conqueror," Clay said. "It's been a fortress and a prison. Of course, it's most famous for its executions."

Ellie shivered. "Yes. Thomas Cromwell, Anne Boleyn, Sir Thomas More."

"And dozens of others. The last executions took place in World War II."

Her eyes widened. "Really?"

Clay nodded. "Nazi spies."

They walked along a stone corridor that crossed a grassy flat that was once a moat and entered the damp, thick-walled interior. The stones felt rough and cold against her palm. Clay led her through room after room filled with ancient weaponry.

"I didn't know there were this many lances left in the world," Ellie said. She studied the terrifying accumulation of axes, hatchets, bows and arrows, spiked clubs, and swords of every lethal shape and size. "It makes me sad to think how much death and destruction all this has wrought over the centuries."

"I guess it's just human nature for people to kill each other."

"I suppose. But wouldn't it be nice if mankind learned from the past and stopped?"

"I wish they'd stopped before Vietnam. If they had, John would still be alive."

Ellie squeezed Clay's hand.

They walked in silence through the oppressive, dank, gray stone rooms, but talk of fighting had turned the conversation in a different direction.

"This may sound crazy, Clay, but I've been thinking about what happened on the plane and that man who attacked me. You don't suppose it's some kind of plot? I mean something to do with the Olympics and international politics, or terrorism, or something?"

"It sounds far-fetched, but it doesn't sound crazy. In fact, I've been wondering if it could be something like that. Nobody else seems too concerned. I've been looking for those security people Jake mentioned, but the only one I've seen is the man he hired to watch the horses. Either they're very good at what they do, or Jake's telling just us that to keep us from worrying."

172

"Jake wouldn't do that," Ellie defended.

Clay's shoulders tightened. "You think a great deal of him, don't you?"

"Yes, I do."

"Enough to sleep with him?"

Anger slipped through her. "We're friends. Jake's been good to me. He's never been anything but a gentleman. And I resent your implying anything else."

Clay's shoulders relaxed. "Take it easy. So I'm a little jealous." He leaned down and brushed a soft kiss ovee her lips. "To tell you the truth, it's a new experience. Forgive me?"

How could she not when he looked so sincere? "I swear you are the most incorrigible man I've ever met." But her anger had faded.

Clay smiled down at her. "I promise to reform at least for the rest of the day." He linked her arm through his and they walked out into the sunshine.

"Believe it or not, I think a lot of Jake, too," he said later. "I just hope he isn't involved in something he can't handle."

"If he is, we'll just have to help him handle it."

Clay took her hand and by silent agreement their talk turned to more pleasant subjects. The day was meant to be special, and both were determined it would be.

Clay hired a cab to tour the city and the afternoon passed in a whirl of colorful sights and sounds. They saw the usual places of interest: Parliament, Big Ben, and Westminster Abbey. She especially loved St. Katharine's dock with its collection of historic ships.

Throughout the day, Clay remained solicitous, playing the gentleman so well Ellie was able to forget the evening ahead and just enjoy herself.

Late in the afternoon, he took her back to the team hotel where she was staying and carefully checked the room for unwanted visitors.

"I'll be back for you at seven," he said at the door.

For the first time, he let his gentleman's façade slip, flashing her a look filled with such lust Ellie's stomach started to churn. Then he pulled her into his arms and kissed her until she was breathless.

"You've got time for a nap," he said. "You'd better get some sleep because you won't get much tonight." Another quick kiss and he was gone.

173

Ellie closed the door behind him. She thought of the night ahead. As Clay's footsteps faded, so did some of her courage.

Ellie paced her room in nervous anticipation.

After a long soak in a pine-scented bath, she washed and curled her hair, then took extra care with her make-up. She'd gone through every garment in her closet trying to decide what to wear over her expensive white lace teddy, finally choosing a simple black cocktail dress with a scooped-neckline and fitted skirt. Even after her lengthy preparations, she was ready twenty minutes early.

Pacing her room, which seemed smaller by the minute, she wished she had a glass of wine to soothe her ragged nerves. Again and again, she checked the time and tried to relax. At least Maggie had chosen comfortable accommodations for the team.

Under normal circumstances, Ellie would have loved the Victorian motif, the dainty rosewood furniture, carved antique armoire, and queen-size bed with its fluffy down comforter

Circumstances were far from normal.

With every step, Ellie remembered what would happen tonight, the sheer white teddy whispering a reminder between her legs. Her lace-topped stockings hummed against each other, setting up a sensual rhythm that heightened her anticipation even more.

At seven o'clock sharp, Clay rapped on her door. Grateful the waiting was over, she answered the knock, forcing herself to smile.

Clay leaned into the doorway, gave her a brief kiss, and returned the smile. "Ready?" He looked elegant and handsome in his tailored camel jacket. Coffee brown slacks matched the color of his eyes, and his white shirt set off his suntanned skin.

"I'm ready," Ellie whispered, and Clay looked at her oddly.

"That nervous?"

"Does it show?"

"I'm afraid so."

Ellie moistened her lips. "I'll be fine."

"I've got a bottle of champagne waiting in the car. As I recall, champagne eases your inhibitions."

Wishing he hadn't reminded her, Ellie managed another weak smile and picked up her black beaded purse. Clay grabbed her tapestry overnight bag and took her arm to lead her out of the room. When they reached the street, a white Bentley limousine waited at the curb.

"I'm impressed," she said, reassured that Clay had meant what he said about making the evening special.

A uniformed chauffer held the door while they slid into the back seat. Ellie forced herself to relax against the soft gray leather while Clay uncorked and poured champagne into two crystal flutes.

"You look lovely," he said, his voice a little husky. Dark eyes studied her face then swept down to the cleavage above the neckline of her simple black dress.

Ellie's heartbeat quickened. "Thank you," was all she could manage.

"To us," Clay said, holding up his glass.

"To us," Ellie repeated, "and to winning." They clinked glasses, then both took a drink.

"Tonight, I promise both of us will win," Clay said.

Ellie took another nervous sip. She felt the light pressure of Clay's fingers as they played over the back of the hand she rested in her lap and saw him studying her, his eyes dark and warm. The glass shook ever so slightly in her hand.

Clay watched the woman next to him. Ellie looked beautiful tonight, her hair loose around her shoulders, all sweet curves and tremulous smiles.

She was nervous, far more than he'd expected, and he wondered why. She never seemed nervous with Gerry, but then according to Flex their affair had been going on for some time. She hadn't been nervous with Flex, but then she'd been drunk that night.

Clay didn't want her drunk. He wanted her breathless and eager. He wanted to forget about dinner, take her straight to the hotel and make love to her.

Her hand shook as she took another long sip of champagne and glanced at him from beneath her dark-fringed lashes. Clay bent down and kissed her, a soft, chaste kiss meant to soothe instead of heat, but her lips felt so lush and sweet he forgot his purpose.

Her response was timid at first, but he didn't stop, just nipped and tugged her bottom lip, ran his tongue over her full bottom lip, then slid inside to taste her.

When Ellie relaxed against him, Clay deepened the kiss and pulled her into his arms. He heard her tiny purr and felt her fingers slide into the hair at the nape of his neck.

She was kissing him back now, making him hard and aching. He wanted to take her right there on the seat. He massaged her breasts through the front of her dress, felt the peaks stiffen against his palm, felt her trembling with desire instead of nerves--and made a decision.

Clay gently ended the kiss and spoke in low tones to the driver. When he finished, he pulled Ellie back into his arms and started kissing her again. Until the car stopped and the door swung open, he was lost in a world of sensuous pleasure, oblivious to his surroundings. He jumped with a guilty start as the hotel doorman blew the whistle outside the car.

"We've arrived, sir," the chauffer said without looking into the dark interior.

"Oh." Ellie glanced at Clay, blushing prettily and trying to rearrange her clothes.

"There's been a change of plans," Clay said to her. He helped her out of the car and the doorman closed the door behind them.

"We're at Claridge's," Ellie said, glancing up at the words on the marquee.

"Trust me." Placing a possessive hand at her waist, he guided her into the lobby.

The interior was elegant, old world, and extravagant, in a style reminiscent of the thirties. They crossed the lobby and walked into the elevator, Ellie looking a little uncertain. When they stepped out on the fourth floor, he guided her down the hallway to his suite.

Inside the sumptuous room, decorated elegantly in coral and cream, he headed straight for the bar, which took up one whole corner. Pulling a bottle of Dom Perignon from the refrigerator under the marble-topped counter, Clay popped the cork, which cracked against the beautiful, molded ceiling. Ellie laughed, but it sounded a little forced. Clay poured two crystal flukes of champagne and handed one to Ellie.

"What about dinner?" she asked, glancing around as if he had lured her into his lair.

"Believe it or not, I had every intention of taking you to Le Caprice." He smiled down at her. "But I didn't think you could survive it, so we came here instead." A look of relief mixed with uncertainty crossed Ellie's face.

Clay almost smiled.

"I was really looking forward to going," she said. "It's just that I kept thinking about...afterward." She glanced away.

"So did I, love." He led her to the plush, cream-colored sofa that rested in front of the marble fireplace. Once she was seated, Clay bent over and slipped off her high-heeled shoes.

"If you're hungry, we can have dinner sent up...or we can wait until later."

"My stomach's a little unsettled. Later would be better, I think."

Clay smiled indulgently. Good God, she seemed innocent. It was endearing, even if it wasn't entirely real. When she emptied her glass of champagne, Clay refilled it. The phone rang just as he finished.

"Damn. I told the desk clerk to hold my calls."

When he picked up the receiver, his father's voice cracked across the line, and Clay knew exactly how the call had gotten through. Few people had the courage to ignore a command from Avery Whitfield.

"Evening, son. Just called to remind you we'll be there bright and early tomorrow morning."

"Tomorrow? What are you talking about?"

"Surely you haven't forgotten. The contessa is expecting us in Monaco."

A sinking feeling settled over him. "Look, Dad, something's come up. I won't be able to make it. You'll have to give the contessa my apologies."

"Nonsense. She's got guests invited who expect to see you...if you know what I mean. I'll be there in the morning."

Without waiting for a reply, Avery rang off. Clay sighed resignedly. He knew his father would win--he always did. Clay glanced at Ellie. He'd rather be spending the next few days with Ellie instead of the contessa and her jet set friends.

Whatever happened, tonight was his and Ellie's. He'd been looking forward to making love to her for weeks. Nothing was going to spoil it. He forced himself to put thoughts of his father aside and concentrate on the young woman on the sofa.

It wasn't difficult to do.

CHAPTER NINETEEN

Ellie sipped her champagne and knew she should be feeling the effects, but she wasn't. Her nerves had returned, squeezing a hard knot in her stomach. She realized Clay had taken the seat beside her and was speaking to her in soft tones, but his words sounded as if they came from somewhere far away.

What are you doing here? Said a voice inside her head. *You're making a mistake.*

"Ellie?" Clay's deep voice finally reached her. "Dammit, Ellie, this isn't supposed to be some sort of punishment."

"I'm sorry, Clay." She moistened her lips. "I guess the champagne isn't working."

Clay cupped his fingers beneath her chin. "I think I know what will." He kissed her then, a soft, seductive kiss that sent shivers all the way to her toes. He nibbled the corners of her mouth and ran his tongue inside to tease and tangle with hers. She thought he would never stop and little by little, she didn't want him to.

You're all right, now, the little voice said. *Clay knows what to do.* Wrapping her arms around his neck, she leaned into him and kissed him back with everything inside her.

Clay felt Ellie's response and a wave of relief washed over him. He wanted this to be as good for her as he knew it would be for him. He was thick and hard, aching to be inside her. Shifting his weight on the sofa, he ignored the throbbing in his groin that had been building all day. He tried to get comfortable, but he didn't stop kissing her. He couldn't bring himself to break away.

He nibbled an earlobe, trailed kisses along her neck and shoulders while his hand teased her breast through the fabric of her dress. He could feel her trembling, not from nerves this time. She clung to him, kissing him back, running her hands down the front of his shirt. Clay unfastened the buttons and guided her fingers beneath the starched white cotton.

"Touch me, Ellie," he whispered. "I need you."

Ellie moaned. Clay's muscles bunched at the feel of her small hands running over his chest, circling a flat copper nipple. With a soft buzz, Clay unzipped her little black dress, pushed it off her shoulders, then caught his breath at the sight of her lacy white teddy with its delicate pink satin bow. The sheer material clung tantalizingly to her ripe, feminine curves, outlined her luscious breasts. He pulled the narrow pink ribbon and they spilled forward, into his hands.

Clay groaned at the picture they made. "Lovely," he whispered, his voice low and husky. Clay cupped them, caressed them, bent his head to take the dusky peaks into his mouth. Ellie arched against him, slid her fingers into his hair.

Ellie helped him out of his shirt, then traced the muscles across his chest. Dipping her head, she pressed her mouth over his heart, ringed his nipple with her tongue, her hand sliding up his thigh until she brushed the hardness straining beneath his zipper. With a gasp, she jerked her hand away and color flooded her cheeks.

Clay chuckled and shook his head. Flex had said she was a terrific lover, better even than Gabriella. She was certainly setting fire to his loins, but not because of her skills. In fact, just the opposite. Her innocence seemed so genuine, so endearing, he found himself struggling to go slow. He wanted to take her, drive into her, possess her, but he wanted to wring every ounce of pleasure out of it for her.

He glanced down at her snowy lingerie. The lacy white teddy and stockings enhanced the image of purity, the fetching sight making his blood pound. If this was a game, it was one of the most intriguing he'd ever played.

He caught her wrist and drew her hand down to his erection. She seemed reluctant at first, then she let him rest it on the bulge in his pants. For a moment, she didn't move. Then, as if her curiosity were stronger than her fear, her fingers roamed over him, feather lightly touching the fabric, exploring, measuring the width and length.

"So big," she whispered, eyes wide in her flushed oval face. A fine sheen of perspiration dampened the reddish hair at her temples.

Strangely pleased by her approval, Clay felt a wave of

astonishment. Good God, he wasn't some preening rooster. He didn't need her approval to know he was a man. Bending his head, he kissed her. He wanted her out of her skimpy clothes, as luscious as they were. He wanted her in his bed.

Shirtless, but still wearing his pants, he came to his feet, scooped her into his arms, and headed for the bedroom. Ellie wrapped her arms around his neck and rested her head on his shoulder. When he reached the bed, he set her down gently, kicked off his kidskin loafers, unbuckled his belt, and took off the rest of his clothes. With obvious fascination, Ellie watched him, her eyes moving down his naked body.

"I hope you aren't disappointed," he teased, though he could see she wasn't.

"You're beautiful."

"So are you, love." Clay kissed her, his tongue gliding over hers, hers entwining with his, making him groan. They were both breathing hard. Her cheeks were flushed, her eyes slightly unfocused. He pulled off her teddy and rolled down her stockings, leaving her naked and lovely.

Wanting to memorize the sight, he let his gaze roam over her. She was luscious and sexy, full-busted, curvy and sweet. Red-brown curls invitingly marked her sex, and it was all Clay could do to keep from tasting her there, bringing her to climax.

"Clay," she whispered, breaking into his thoughts. "Please kiss me. I don't want to get nervous again."

Clay complied, covering her on the mattress and kissing her deeply again.

Ellie had never felt anything like it. Wherever Clay touched came alive. Her skin felt hot and tight. His hands seemed to be everywhere at once, gliding across her sensitive skin, cupping her breasts, teasing her nipples, driving her insane. His touch moved down her body to the flat spot below her navel, then lover, lacing through the triangle of curls beneath.

When he began to stroke her, Ellie couldn't stop a moan. She was wet. So impossibly wet. Clay set up a sensual rhythm that brought her to the edge of frenzy, then he shifted, came up over her, and she felt his erection pressing against the entrance to her core.

Closing her eyes, she arched toward him, wanting him to ease the ache that burned there . Clay eased the tip of his shaft inside. He stopped when he felt her tense.

"Easy, love, I'm not going to hurt you."

"Don't stop, Clay," she said softly.

"I don't want to rush you. Try to relax." He eased forward a little farther, and Ellie bit her lip. He was so big. Much larger than she had expected. She liked the feeling of fullness, but it hurt a little, too.

Clay inched forward, then stopped. "Are you always like this?" When she looked into his face, his worried expression made the decision for her.

"You feel wonderful, Clay, it's just..."

"Just what, love?"

"I've never been with a man before."

"What?"

"I said I've never—"

"I know what you said." Clay's soft look turned dark. "I think this little game has gone far enough. If you have some sort of physical problem I should know about, you'd better tell me now."

Ellie pushed against him, trying to drive him farther inside. "Don't stop, Clay, please. We can talk about this later. I just didn't want you to worry about hurting me."

"Damn you, do you think I'm a fool? I know about Flex and Gerry."

"Gerry?"

"Yes, Gerry. Flex told me about him."

Ellie thought if Flex were there in that moment, she might kill him. "Flex made it up. Please, Clay, can't we talk about this later?"

Clay looked at her hard. "Why in God's name would he do that?"

"It was a joke. Please, Clay—"

"A joke!"

When she felt him begin to withdraw from her body, Ellie clutched his neck. "Don't go. I promise I'll explain later." She tried to kiss him, but he pulled away.

"You'll explain now." Clay rolled away from her. He swung his legs over the edge of the bed and strode immodestly into the bathroom. He returned wearing a thick white terrycloth robe. He tossed a second robe to Ellie, who pulled the huge garment up over her, but didn't put it on.

181

"Now, let's start all over. Are you telling me you're a virgin?"

"Does it make a difference? Surely it doesn't mean you won't make love to me. I mean everyone's a virgin until the first time."

"Let me get this straight. You've never been to bed with Flex, and you've never been to bed with Gerry."

"Flex made it up. He said you'd go crazy if you thought he could get me in bed and you couldn't. And I didn't want you to laugh at me," she added softly.

The words had a ring of truth Clay couldn't deny. He couldn't deny her tight little passage either. "You're a twenty-four-year-old virgin," he repeated, still trying to convince himself. "Am I supposed to expect blood on the sheets?"

Ellie flushed and toyed with the sash on the robe. "I doubt there'll be blood. I've been riding horses for years."

Clay felt the most ridiculous leap of joy.

"It isn't a crime, you know," Ellie said, beginning to get defensive. "Besides there were extenuating circumstances."

"What circumstances?" Clay demanded, but he could barely control the smile that hovered on his lips.

"I don't want to talk about this." Ellie balled her hand into a fist. "I want to make love. I'm sick and tired of being a virgin. It took all my courage to go through with this tonight, and you're determined to spoil it. I wish I'd never told you."

Clay tipped her chin up with his hand. Tears of frustration filled her green eyes. "I'm glad you told me. It doesn't change the way I feel about making love to you. If anything, it makes me want you more. We'll just take our time, that's all. When I get back from Monaco, we'll spend a few days together. Get to know each other so you won't be so nervous. Then when we make love—"

"Are you telling me you won't make love to me tonight?" Her voice rose a notch. Clay reached over and caught her hand.

"Ellie, listen to me. The phone call I got was from my father. He'll be here in the morning. We're flying down to Monaco with the Contessa Pavetti. I don't want to make love to you tonight, then leave you in the morning."

"I don't care what you do tomorrow," Ellie cried, near hysteria. "I can't stand this one minute more. I swear, Clay Whitfield, if you won't make love to me tonight—this second—I'll walk out that door,

182

go back to my hotel, and find someone who will!"

"Don't be absurd."

"I will, I swear it." Clutching the robe, she came to her knees on the bed. "I'll go to Flex. Or maybe I'll find Gerry."

"Surely you don't mean that." But he had seen that determined look before.

"Every word."

"Ellie, be reasonable. I have to leave in the morning. I have to—"

"I'll do it, Clay, I swear it."

She might. He knew her well enough to know how stubborn she could be. "Damn you, Ellie, this isn't some kind of game."

"Isn't it?"

Clay clamped his jaw. "You little witch, you're leaving me no choice—because I'm sure as hell not going to let someone else take you to bed!" With that he reached out, grabbed her robe and jerked it away.

Ellie caught her breath. Clay circled her wrist with his fingers, pulled her into his arms and kissed her, a kiss so hot and demanding Ellie's knees went weak. In moments, his erection pushed against her, and she heard her own little purr. Clay shrugged off his robe and pressed her into the mattress, his hands everywhere, touching her, teasing her, heating her from the inside out.

The ache returned to the place between her legs, and her the peaks of her breasts went hard. He nipped them with his teeth, licked and sucked until her fears receded and all she could think of was Clay. When he began to stroke her, she cried out his name and begged him to take her.

"Soon, love," he promised. "Soon."

Kisses trailed over her stomach while he continued to touch her, tease her. Dear Lord, she felt consumed by desire, ready to burst into flame. Clay seemed to know. By the time he positioned himself above her, spreading her thighs with his knee, he felt even bigger than he had before.

Inch by inch he pushed into her, a little easier this time since she was so ready. She felt no tearing, just a tightness that had her moaning and shifting beneath him.

Clay kissed her endlessly, whispering soft, encouraging words, telling her he didn't want to hurt her. All Ellie could think of was how much she needed the fiery ache to end.

"Please, Clay," she pleaded.

Clay clenched his jaw, fighting to go slow until he filled her completely. When he eased back and slid into her again, heat rushed through her, desire so thick and hot she dug her nails into the muscles across his shoulders.

Out and then in. Out and then in, the rhythm slow at first, then building. She arched her hips to meet each thrust, heightening the pleasure, immersing herself until she was acting on instinct alone.

A momentum built inside her, a feeling so powerful, so intense, she couldn't think of anything but the impact of flesh against flesh, the fiery heat of their bodies joining together. Clay was relentless. She felt his hands beneath her hips, lifting her, driving himself deeper and deeper. He kissed her again, his mouth and tongue as insistent as his body.

With a soft sob, Ellie came apart, pleasure bursting through her in thick, glorious waves. Stars burst behind her eyes; her skin tingled and burned as one spasm followed another, the force of her response sending Clay over the edge. Still driving into her, he came with a shuddering climax so powerful it seemed to surprise even Clay.

Ellie spiraled down, her body limp and sated. For long moments, she lay there, heart pounding, joy filling her. Then the incredible feeling began to recede as Clay gently withdrew. Insanely, she wished she could hold him inside her forever.

When their breathing eased, he rolled to his side and took care of the condom she hadn't realized he had put on. Clay relaxed on the bed and settled her in the curve of his arm.

They lay quietly for a time, Ellie full of wonder and contentment, praying Clay was one-tenth as happy as she. Slowly, his breathing returned to normal, and he propped himself on an elbow.

Clay smiled down at her. "Glad you didn't go back to the hotel and find Gerry?"

Ellie smiled back. "You were wonderful."

"You are, love." He kissed her gently while his eyes remained open in a warm caress. When the kiss deepened, Ellie's eyes drifted closed. Clay's lips felt soft and determined and to her surprise, fresh desire washed over her.

Ellie shifted restlessly on the bed.

"Such a lusty little baggage," Clay teased, nibbling the side of her neck. He was hard again, she realized as he came up over her, careful to keep his weight propped above her. "But then you've always been a quick study."

Ellie gave him an impish grin and welcomed him inside. Clay groaned. Ellie felt no discomfort this time, just a deep hunger that seemed to match Clay's.

Afterward, they slept, only to awaken several hours later and start all over again. Ellie didn't remember sleeping, though she knew they must have. But she remembered every moment of their lovemaking.

Exhausted, she snuggled against him, the sheen of their exertion mingling beneath the crisp white cotton sheets. Clay's breath felt warm against her hair. He smelled male and musky, and they shared the intimate odor of sex.

Her body still tingled, yet Ellie felt strangely complete. *Whole* was the only word she could think of to describe it. As if she'd found the lost half of herself. It was the most wonderful sensation she'd ever known.

And the most terrifying.

Because Clay Whitfield couldn't possibly feel the same.

It doesn't matter, she told herself, ignoring the painful lump that rose in her throat. She'd known what she was getting into, in the end, had forced him to take her to bed.

But she hadn't anticipated the emotions making love to Clay would bring.

It had to happen sometime, she told herself. *Sooner or later, you would have made love to someone. It just happened to be Clay.*

But the hard truth was, she was in love with Clayton Whitfield. Sleeping with him had only made her love him more.

She felt him shift beside her, snuggle her a little closer.

"Tell me about the extenuating circumstances," he said softly, smoothing a lock of her hair between his fingers. Ellie shifted and turned on her side to look at him. A sliver of weak sunlight peeked through an opening in the heavy silk draperies, signaling the dawn and bathing the room in a dim yellow glow.

"I had a vision disorder. A little over four years ago, I had an operation that corrected my eyesight. I'd been riding horses since I was a child, mostly by feel, tuning into the horse's movements. It wasn't until after the surgery that I was able to see well enough to compete."

"You mean you were blind?" Clay looked incredulous.

"Not exactly. I could see colors and shapes and light. I just couldn't focus. Sort of like seeing through wavy frosted glass."

"Good God." Clay pulled her back into his arms and kissed the top of her head.

"I didn't date before my surgery," Ellie said. "I was kind of a loner. People always felt sorry for me, and I hated that, so I just sort of kept to myself."

"What about your schooling? You're obviously well-educated."

"I could see up close. If I held the book just a few inches from my nose, I could read. My parents hired the best tutors money could buy. After the surgery I went on to college. I dated a little then, but most of my time, I was either studying or working with the horses. They were always my passion."

Clay leaned over and kissed her. "How about now?"

Ellie grinned. "Now I have two passions."

Clay hoped she was referring to him and not just the lovemaking he'd taught her. "Why didn't you tell me before?"

"I didn't tell anyone because I wanted to be accepted as an equal. I didn't want to be different. I was always looked at and talked about...pitied. I wanted to make a fresh start."

Ellie gazed up at him. "Flex and Jake know. Maggie Delaine. Nobody else. I'd like to keep it that way."

"I'd never do anything to hurt you, Ellie." But as he said the words, his stomach tightened. The bitter truth was, hurting her was inevitable. He was Clayton Whitfield, dedicated bachelor, womanizer. Bastard. If he had it to do over, he wasn't sure he'd take her to bed.

Who was he kidding? He'd do it again in a heartbeat. He'd wanted Ellie Fletcher since the first time he'd seen her. And he was the kind of man who took what he wanted.

Still...when she looked at him with those trusting green eyes, he couldn't help wondering if things could be different. If he could be different.

Clay blew out a breath. With time a little short, he rolled out of bed, climbed into the shower, then got dressed for the day. While Ellie showered, he ordered breakfast: eggs, bacon sausage, potatoes, juice, toast, and coffee.

The food arrived before she had time to put on her clothes so she joined him wearing the big terrycloth bathrobe, her hair damp and curling down her back. Having Shepped dinner the night before, they ate ravenously.

Clay found himself watching her, enjoying the way she smiled at him, the playful laughter in her voice. He was more fascinated with Ellie than before, wanting her and wishing he could make love to her again. He didn't because it would only be a short time before he left for Monaco with his father and the contessa, expected to play his usual role of playboy.

Ellie leaned over and gave him a quick kiss on the mouth. "I'd better get dressed." Holding half a slice of toast, she got up from the table. Clay grabbed her waist and pulled her down on his lap, kissed her so thoroughly he went hard. She tasted like marmalade and orange blossoms.

"I wish we had more time," he whispered against her ear.

Ellie cupped his face with her hand. "So do I. How long will you be gone?"

"Too long." He wished he didn't have to leave at all. "I'm not exactly sure."

Ellie just nodded and turned to leave.

Clay smacked her playfully on the behind. "Will you miss me?"

"I don't think I'll tell you." With a saucy grin, she darted into the bedroom they had shared and made her way back to the huge master bath.

With so much to do, Ellie dressed in slacks and a pink knit top. She'd just finished combing her hair and putting on her make-up when she heard the doorbell ring. Ready to leave, she headed back into the bedroom and pulled open the door to the living room.

Clay stood in the foyer, an attractive, dark-haired woman, slender build, late-thirties, clinging to his neck. The woman's expensive blue silk blouse outlined her small, cone-shaped breasts. She was kissing him, her tongue in his mouth. Avery Whitfield stood beside them, grinning.

Ellie swayed against the doorjamb, watching Clay with the morbid fascination of a cobra studying its victim and feeling her stomach roll. Clay extracted himself from the woman's arms and turned in Ellie's direction. His face paled when he spotted her, a reflection of her own.

Staring at the woman whose lips still looked wet from Clay's kiss, Ellie felt a surge of revulsion. Fighting a wave of nausea, she closed the bedroom door and raced for the big marble bathroom, turned the lock, and emptied the contents of her breakfast into the commode.

"Ellie?" Clay pounded on the bathroom door.

She didn't answer.

"Ellie, please come out so we can talk about this."

"I'm not feeling well," she said, her face bloodless and numb. Beads of perspiration gathered on her forehead and dampened the hair at her temples. "Go with your father. I'll take a taxi back to the hotel."

"Ellie, please let me in."

"No. I'm fine, really I am."

"I can't leave you like this."

"Come on, son," Avery called out. "The plane is waiting. We've got one more stop to make, and I don't want to be late."

"Come on, Clay, darling," the woman said.

Ellie bent over and wretched again.

"Damn it, Ellie, let me in."

"Come on, son," Avery said impatiently. "Pack a bag and let's go."

"I'll leave some money for the cab on the dresser," Clay said softly.

"Don't you dare!" Ellie called through the door.

Clay cursed and stalked away. She could hear him opening and closing drawers, snapping the latch on his suitcase, then slamming the door behind him.

Ellie leaned her head against the cold marble wall of the bathroom. Tears gathered and slipped down her cheeks. Clay had warned her. She had no one to blame but herself. It didn't stop the hurting, the sheer, bone-aching grief.

She slid down the wall and rested her head on her knees, wrapped her arms around them. Tears rolled down her cheeks.

She'd gotten what she wanted, hadn't she?

A sob escaped. At least she'd gotten what she deserved.

CHAPTER TWENTY

Sitting alone in her hotel room, Maggie Delaine stared at the silent telephone. For the fourth time in the last half hour, she reached for it. This time she lifted the receiver, gripping it a little too hard.

She made the call methodically, as if it were nothing more than business. After going through the director's private secretary and the live-in nurse, her boss, Evelyn Rothwell, came on the line.

"Maggie, it's good to hear from you." They exchanged the usual pleasantries, Evelyn assuring Maggie that she was recovering better than expected, Maggie filling her in on team business.

"I'm sorry to bother you at home, Evelyn," she said, working to keep her tone nonchalant, "but the press has been all over me. They want to do an article about Jake Sullivan. They want to approach it from a whole new angle. Since Jake's so tough to interview, they've asked me to help. I thought you might give me some background, something I don't already know."

Evelyn chuckled. "You know how Jake is. He hates for anyone to interfere in his private life."

"I know, Evelyn, but surely there's something you can give me. How about his early years, where he was born, something about his family, that sort of thing?"

"That's the last thing Jake would want to see in print."

"Why is that?"

"Surely you know he's from Hungary."

"I know his father was Hungarian. I assumed Jake was born in the States."

"I'm sorry, Maggie, I thought you knew. All the members of the selection committee were informed of Jake's background before his appointment. Since you came onboard later, I guess it was an oversight.

Jake was born in the Soviet Union. His real name is Janus Straka. He defected to this country during the 1960 Olympics in Rome. Maybe you remember reading about it."

"No," Maggie whispered, fighting for control. "I would have been pretty young. I guess I was more interested in boys than current affairs."

"He was only nineteen at the time. Jake—I mean Janus—was a top competitor. He had a strong chance of winning the gold medal that year. After he came to this country, he wanted to stay out of the limelight so he changed his name and started a new life." Evelyn chuckled. "Jake wouldn't be happy to find that story in print."

Maggie could barely speak. *Why hadn't he told her?* "No, of course not. Thank you, Evelyn. I'll think of something."

"Keep me posted, will you? It's a definite pain the neck being laid up like this. I'm itching to get back to work."

"Just get well. I'll stay in touch." Maggie hung up the phone, her mind racing. Jake's problems were even more serious than she'd imagined, and she'd imagined the worst. What did the Soviets want with Jake?

He'd been gone from their country for...? Twenty- eight years, she calculated. She tried to tell herself it was just a coincidence, but she knew in her heart it wasn't.

She checked her watch. It was one o'clock in the afternoon. Jake would probably have gone on to Hickstead as Maggie planned to do as soon as she checked out of the hotel. She'd promised not to talk to him, but the stakes were just too high. She'd be careful, but she had to know the truth.

Jake owed it to both of them.

I shouldn't have left her like that, Clay thought for the ten thousandth time. *I should have kicked the fucking door down if I had to.* He knew why he hadn't. Because when he'd seen her standing in the doorway, looking so utterly betrayed, she'd aroused feelings so foreign to him—so completely overwhelming—he just couldn't deal with them.

He'd wanted to go to her, explain that Adrianna had kissed *him,* not the other way around. He'd wanted to tell her he didn't even want to go with the contessa and his father. But his dad expected it, and Clay hadn't wanted to disappoint him.

What about Ellie? How much did you disappoint her? It didn't matter, he argued with himself. It would have happened sooner or later. She didn't fit into his lifestyle. He couldn't afford to get any more involved with her than he was already.

"Why don't you take a little toot and join the party?" His father's voice broke into Clay's thoughts. "We'll be landing in Monaco in just a few minutes."

Clay shook his head and leaned back against the leather sofa that ran along one wall of the Whitfield Corporation's plush Gulfstream III.

"No thanks, I'm in training." The jet was custom designed, with a thirty-foot cabin and a bedroom in the rear, all in shades of burgundy and gray.

"You aren't thinking about that little redhead you left behind, are you? She's the last woman you need to get involved with. Don't delude yourself, boy. You'll never be a one-woman man. You're too much like your father." He flashed Clay his I'm-proud-of-you-son grin.

"Come on," Avery coaxed, sprinkling more of the white powder onto the mirror on the chrome coffee table in front of the sofa. With a razor blade, he carefully minced any lumps, then straightened the powder into rows. "You're too uptight. It'll do you good to forget your troubles for a while."

His father rarely pressed him on the issue of drugs. It was one Clay felt strongly about. Booze and women were usually enough of a high for Clay, but he couldn't even feel the Glenfiddish he'd been guzzling. Apparently, his black mood was obvious to his father, who seemed determined to end it.

"Come on, son," he coaxed.

Clay smiled grimly. "Why the hell not?" he said. "You only live once."

"Good boy!" Avery clapped him on the back and Adrianna ran her hand along the inside of his thigh.

Clay accepted the rolled up hundred-dollar bill from his father, covered one nostril, leaned forward and inhaled a single white line. He did the same with the other nostril, then passed the bill to Adrianna.

"That's my darling," she cooed and nibbled the side of his neck.

Clay could barely feel it. He felt warm from the drugs and best of all, numb, exactly what he wanted.

"Clay, honey," a second female voice put in. "You aren't ignoring me, are you?"

It was Gina Pavetti, Adrianna's niece, a younger version of her attractive aunt. Gina had the same flawless olive complexion and thick-lashed, black eyes. The last time Clay had seen her, she'd just turned sixteen.

"How could any red-blooded man ignore you, Gina?" Clay hadn't forgotten the way the girl had come into his room in the middle of the night and climbed naked into bed with him. Clay had smacked her bottom and sent her packing.

He looked at her now, a grown woman whose sexual appetites appeared to have blossomed along with the rest of her. She scooted up beside him and slid her arms around his neck.

"Isn't this better?" Her black hair touched his cheek as she dipped her head and kissed him. Her lips felt soft and warm, but he thought of another pair, lush and smiling, and eyes so trusting he felt a crushing weight on his chest.

His father passed him the rolled-up bill, and Clay lowered his head to the beckoning white powder.

The pilot announced their imminent arrival in Nice, and they all fastened their seat belts. Though the cocaine had numbed him, Clay rested his head against the back of the sofa and closed his eyes, hoping to block his thoughts. He didn't stir until the plane touched down and taxied to the executive terminal.

Every summer the Contessa Pavetti rented a villa on either the French or Italian Riviera. This summer the sprawling mansion she had chosen overlooked the blue waters of Monaco. Clay's room was huge and elegant: ceilings with painted frescos, marble floors, a massive four-poster draped with expensive velvet tapestries, a marble bath with golden cherub fixtures.

The valet had unpacked for him. Clay had come to the room to change into his swimsuit for a few hours out by the pool. He threw off his clothes and pulled on his suit. He'd been drinking steadily, and the cocaine was doing its insidious best to keep his mind in a state of numbness.

Grabbing a towel, he returned poolside to find his father, Adrianna, and Gina splashing gaily, stark naked in the water.

"Come on, Clay," Gina pouted. "Don't be a spoil sport. Take off your suit and join us. The water feels wonderful."

Clay looked at the lush curves of her body. She was built more voluptuously than her aunt, an almost Grecian appearance. Her sexuality seemed in character with those overindulgent times.

It was what he had come here for, wasn't it? He pulled off his suit and dove into the pool. Gina was beside him the instant his head broke the water. Giggling, she wrapped her arms around his neck.

"I've been waiting to do this for years," she teased, kissing the corner of his mouth.

Clay looked down at the sculpted lines of her face. Water beaded on the swells of her breasts, the tips just cresting the surface. "I should have whacked you harder," he said, only half teasing.

"Anytime, lover, a little pain just enhances the pleasure." She giggled, one hand traveling down his body, determined to arouse him. Clay felt strangely unmoved. He pulled her arm from around his neck and dove beneath the water. Craving the exertion, he swam several laps, trying to understand why none of this appealed to him as it had in the past.

"Let's go inside," Adrianna suggested after they'd all climbed out of the pool.

"I think I'll stay out here and catch some sun," Clay said.

"Come on, Clay, you've been drag-assing all day." Impatience was back in Avery's voice. "What the hell's the matter with you?"

"I guess I'm just worried about the competition," he lied. "I hate to break training."

"That's a lot of horseshit. The contessa's been planning this for weeks. We can't disappoint her, can we?" There was no mistaking his father's annoyance. "Come on inside, we'll have a little more blow, party, and then relax."

The tight expression Avery wore was one Clay had hated since childhood. One of disapproval and disappointment. Avery Whitfield's son was supposed to be the consummate ladies' man. Clay was letting him down.

"All right, let's go," he said. No one bothered with towels, just walked naked into the salon. Avery mixed drinks and handed them around, then picked up the tiny vial that rested on the bar and tapped out eight more lines of cocaine.

Everyone took a turn. Finishing last, Clay glanced across the room to see Adrianna on her knees in front of his father, gearing up for a round of oral sex. Gina slid to the floor in front of Clay.

"Relax and enjoy, son," Avery called out. "You deserve it."

Clay had been with dozens of women, but always in private. He'd never been into group sex, which seemed even more debauched when one of the participants was his father.

Seeing Gina on the floor in front of him, Clay caught Avery's smile of approval. Instead of desire, Clay felt a surge of fury and a knot of disgust in the pit of his stomach.

He grabbed Gina and pulled her to her feet, grabbed a condom and dragged her behind him into the bedroom.

"You want to play games, we'll play games," he growled. Hard from the drugs, he tossed her on the bed, covered her and drove deep, giving no thought to her pleasure, pounding into her until he reached a climax. Gina came, too.

Clay rolled away and rose to his feet, saw Gina's satisfied smile. Clearly, she had enjoyed herself, and the knowledge filled him with even more self-disgust.

Regret overwhelmed him. As he stalked out of the drawing room, he felt sick inside. Sick and dead. And so empty he wondered if he'd ever be able to feel anything again.

In his room, he showered, spent extra time scrubbing his skin until it turned an angry red, trying to remove the feeling of self-loathing.

How could he have done it? How could he have let his father goad him into doing something he hated himself for? Something he couldn't forget or forgive. How could he have betrayed Ellie's trust so vilely?

He remembered the look on her face as she stood in the doorway, watching him with Adrianna. At the time, he hadn't deserved that look.

Now he did.

No one was around when he reached the bottom of the marble staircase. Carrying an overnight bag, he headed straight for the servant's quarters in the rear.

"I need you to take me somewhere," he told the chauffeur.

A few minutes later, the driver brought the limo around to the front of the house. Clay got in and the car pulled away.

There was a small chateau in the hills above Nice called St.

194

Martin. There were only twenty guest rooms, but the owner was a friend, and he always found a place for Clay.

This time, Jean Paul put him up in one of the small, private villas that surrounded the main chateau. The wizened little Frenchman spoke to him only briefly, just led him to his rooms away from the rest of the house and left him alone.

Clay wondered if the grief he felt inside was evident on his face.

As soon as she arrived in the village of Hickstead, Maggie checked into the Crown and Rose Hotel. She had been waiting for Jake to arrive all afternoon. The moment she spotted his rental car pulling into the parking lot, Maggie hurried down to the lobby.

"I need to speak to you, Jake."

He stopped as she approached, worry lines digging into his forehead. "What's happened? Are you alright?"

"Nothing's happened. I'm fine, but we need to talk."

"I told you we couldn't do that, Maggie. You promised me."

"I know, but I can't keep that promise any longer. I spoke to Evelyn today. I asked her to fill me in on your background."

Jake's expression grew grim. He took her arm and led her over to the sofa in the hotel lobby. Several tourists, cameras hanging from their shoulders and laughter in their voices, walked past, heading for the dining room.

"Dammit, Maggie, you've got to stay out of this," Jake hissed. "You're putting your life in danger."

"Why didn't you tell me, Jake?"

Piercing blue eyes bored into her. He sighed. "I was planning to. I just wanted the time to be right. I wanted to tell you about my past, then I was going to ask you to marry me."

"Oh, Jake." Maggie touched his face. His skin was warm, but the muscles were taut over his cheekbones.

Jake pulled her hand away and glanced around to be sure no one was watching. "Go back to your room, Maggie. Stay away from me until this is over."

"No. I want to know what's going on."

"Dammit, Maggie."

"I   want   to   know,   Jake."

"All right. I'll meet you tonight. There's a little pub just north of

195

here called Geoffrey's. I'll be there at ten o'clock. And for God's sake be careful no one follows you."

Maggie nodded. With a last glance at Jake, she stood up and headed for the door.

At nine thirty that night, Maggie left her room, hailed a cab, had the driver haul her around for fifteen minutes, then let her off four blocks from Geoffrey's Tavern.

Inside the smoky, low-ceilinged pub, she spotted Jake sitting in the far corner, his back against the wall. A fan drifted in lazy circles above his head and smoke hung in dense blue patches over the nearby tables.

The patrons looked like locales. None wore the weary smile or the I-don't-dare-miss-anything look of a tourist.

Jake glanced furtively around the tap room, then fixed his gaze on Maggie. A corner of his mouth curved up in what seemed an appreciative smile, and Maggie's heart beat faster. She'd missed him so much these past few days. He looked so handsome and dear it was all she could do to keep from rushing into his arms.

Instead, she continued at a steady pace across the room until she reached his side. "Hello, Jake."

Jake stood and pulled out her chair. "Hello, Maggie."

She let him help her with her lightweight coat. "But then your real name is Janus, isn't it?" The words sounded harsher than she had intended. He should have told her long ago. He should have trusted her.

"I haven't been Janus Straka for twenty-eight years," Jake said. "Not since the day I arrived in America."

They both sat down. Jake took her hand, leaned forward and kissed her cheek. Maggie forced herself to ignore the warmth of his touch, determined Jake wouldn't charm her out of the answers she deserved.

"What do they want with you, Jake?"

"Maggie, I agreed to meet you because I love you and because I owe it to you. But I don't want you involved in this. Whatever it is—and I don't really know myself—it's something that's dangerous to you and Sarah. Let's enjoy our time together. Then you've got to go back to the hotel. You've got to stay out of this. If you won't think of yourself, think of Sarah."

"Sarah loves you as much as I do. She would want to help you and so do I. I won't stand by and watch you get hurt. You've got to tell me what's going on."

Jake leaned back in his chair. He studied her face, taking in the tiny furrows at the corners of her eyes, the dark smudges that noted her worry. She wasn't a woman who took no for an answer. It was one of the things he admired about her. She deserved to know the truth.

"As I said, they haven't told me what they're after, but whatever it is, they'll do anything to get it. They've threatened my mother and sister, Maggie. If they find out about you, they'll use you against me, too. Your life and Sarah's could also be in danger."

A waiter arrived, a youth about eighteen. "Take your order, sir?"

"We just want coffee," Jake said. The boy brought it quickly, then busied himself with other patrons. A burst of raucous laughter rose in one corner and died away.

"Does anyone else know what's going on?" Maggie asked.

"An old friend of mine in the CIA. A man named Daniel Gage. He helped me when I first came to America. He's doing everything he can to find out."

Maggie's shoulders relaxed. "Thank God. I was afraid you hadn't told anyone."

"I haven't told him everything. I haven't told him about the attack on Ellie or the incident on the plane."

"Why not?"

"Because the government has to be concerned about the safety of the team. They'll step in. The Soviets will know I've told them, and my mother and sister will suffer the consequences."

Jake reached over and caught her trembling hand. "Maggie, I've got to ride this out. I've got to find out what they want."

"How much longer do you think before they tell you?"

"Not long. Whatever they're planning has something to do with the Olympics. Or possibly this European tour. It won't be long now."

"Oh, Jake, I'm so frightened for you."

"We've got to stay strong, Maggie. We've got to hope Daniel can find a way to stop them."

Maggie nodded and blinked back tears.

More pain, Jake thought. *All I've ever brought her is pain.*

Maggie absently stirred her coffee, which had to be cold by now.

He could see how worried she was.

"You'd better go back," he said. "Before someone sees us together."

"I don't want to go back. Isn't there someplace we'd be safe? Someplace we could go?"

Jake hesitated. The loneliness in her eyes matched the ache in his heart. He wasn't sure how many more chances they'd have to be together.

"There's a small hotel just down the street. If we're lucky, maybe they'll have a room."

Maggie smiled so brightly his chest clamped down.

"Let's go," she said.

Leaving money for the coffee, Jake grabbed her coat and settled it across her shoulders, then guided her toward the door. It felt good just to be close to her.

Outside the tavern, the streets were wet, reflecting the lights of passing cars. The damp seemed to sink into his bones. Jake guided Maggie down the sidewalk to the hotel, and she waited in the tiny hotel lobby while he signed the registry Mrs. and Mrs. Stevens.

The minute the door to their small upstairs room closed behind them, she turned into his arms, and he felt the coldness of her cheek against his.

"I love you so damned much," he whispered. "I can't stand to think of losing you again."

"Jake...." Maggie kissed him with such yearning his chest clamped down. He ran his fingers through her silky blond hair and kissed her mouth, her eyes, her nose.

"I love you," she whispered. With trembling hands, they helped each other undress and made love on the lumpy double bed. It didn't matter where they were. They were always so right for each other.

He shouldn't have brought her here, but he didn't regret it.

Jake had never regretted a moment he'd spent with Maggie Delaine.

198

CHAPTER TWENTY-ONE

Since the Hickstead competition started on Thursday, a team dinner was scheduled for Wednesday night. Busy with team problems, Maggie couldn't go, which suited Jake fine. The less they saw each other, the safer they'd be.

Wanting to keep things simple, Jake chose a moderately priced country inn called The Wellington, only a short distance from the hotel. The service and the quality of food were better than he expected: roast beef, roasted potatoes, horseradish, and Yorkshire pudding. There were scones, crumpets, and a form of gingerbread called parkins, which was served for dessert.

Everyone ate heartily except Ellie, who seemed unusually reserved. Flex and Shep were in rare form, Flex laughing and telling off-color jokes and Shep adding his usual droll humor. The only rider who didn't attend was Clay. Jake had no idea where he was and figured he probably didn't want to know.

"How do you size up the competition?" Flex asked him as the conversation turned serious. They were seated at a long narrow table, an old iron chandelier overhead.

"The British team will probably be the toughest to beat," Jake said. "The French will give us a good run as well."

Hickstead was another international competition, the rules simple. Each country selected four riders to represent them in a two-round competition. After each round, the worst score was thrown out. The team with the least total faults was the winner.

Jake wondered if Clay would show up, or if he'd have to substitute Ellie in for him. He didn't really care. The way she had been riding, she'd been giving Clay some tough competition.

His jaw tightened. If the bastard would stop panting after her, keeping her emotions stirred up, she'd ride even better.

Jake sighed. Who the hell was he to criticize? His own emotions were constantly in turmoil over Maggie.

"Most of you have ridden Hickstead before," Jake said, capturing the riders' attention. "Is there anyone here besides Ellie who hasn't?" No hands went up. "I'd appreciate some input, anything any of you might remember that could help her get a feel for the course. We can talk about it over drinks in the bar."

Rumbles of agreement rolled around. As the waiters began clearing the dishes, Ellie rose and so did Prissy, who'd been sitting beside her.

"Somehow I get the impression your mind's not on the competition," Prissy said as they headed for the bar.

"No, I guess it isn't."

"Thinking about Clay?"

She felt a wave of sadness. "I thought he might call. I guess I'm kidding myself. Clay left town with a beautiful woman. Why would he be thinking about me?"

"You saw them together? Where?"

"Claridge's," Ellie said softly.

"Claridge's? What were you doing at Claridge's?" Prissy's eyes widened. "Clay had a suite there. Surely you didn't let him lure you up to his room?"

Ellie blinked back tears. "Please, Prissy, I'd rather not talk about it—especially not here." When Ellie glanced away, Prissy caught her arm.

"That sonofabitch," Prissy said furiously.

"It wasn't his fault. Please, let's not talk about it now."

With dinner over, everyone gathered in the pub, a dark-paneled room with an old, carved mahogany bar. Very staid and very British.

When Jake spotted Ellie getting ready to leave, he pulled her aside.

"You need to stay a little longer," he said. "Spend some time with the team. They can give you some help with the course."

Ellie headed into the bar to join the rest of the group, and Jake stayed behind to pay the bill. Leafing through the wad of twenty-pound notes he carried, he paused at the sound of footsteps coming up behind him.

"Good evening, Comrade Straka."

Jake's hand froze on his wallet. He turned to see a wiry, dark-haired man with an angular face and eyes so brown they appeared black. He wore black slacks and a gray knit pullover whose short sleeves revealed sinewy arms and not an ounce of fat.

A second man, blond and boyishly handsome, stood beside him dressed in a very British tweed coat over a shirt with initials on the cuff. A pair of expensive gabardine slacks flared over dark brown kidskin loafers.

They seemed a bizarre twosome.

"What do you want?"

"I just wanted to say hello," the first man said. "We have several mutual friends. Comrade Popov...and your Ms. Fletcher. Ms. Fletcher and I know each other...rather ...intimately."

Jake's whole body tightened. He forced himself to stay calm but the hand at his side balled into a fist.

"Unfortunately, Ms. Fletcher and I did not have the chance to develop our...friendship...as fully as I intended."

"Listen to me," Jake warned, fighting to control the fury burning through him. "Ellen Fletcher has nothing to do with this. You want something from me? Well, you won't get it if you hurt my people. You understand me?"

The dark eyes seemed to glisten. "Like you, Comrade, I will do whatever it is I am asked to do. That is how I earn my living." He smiled thinly. "I just hope my next assignment is as pleasant as the last."

Jake took an unconscious step forward, his jaw clenched so hard it hurt. It was too late for Ellie. But if the bastard came near Maggie, Jake would kill him.

"The way I heard it," Jake said, thinking of the beating Clay had given the man. "Your last assignment wasn't as pleasant as you'd like me to believe."

He grunted. "No, I suppose not. One of your overzealous riders interrupted our...conversation. I would enjoy paying him back for the bruises I still carry." His eyes looked hard, but the smile stayed frozen on his too-thin lips. "Enjoy your evening, Comrade." With a nod to his partner, the pair slipped quietly out of the room.

Jake glanced up to see several waiters and the owner of the

restaurant staring in his direction. They had witnessed the hostile exchange, even if they hadn't heard the conversation.

Popov wants me connected to his scheme, Jake suddenly realized.

That was the reason the Russian had risked police intervention by attacking Ellie. Jake's business card in the pocket of the assailant's jacket connected the two of them. The men's presence in England, in the bar tonight, linked him again.

Jake felt the web of lies and deceit enveloping him, pulling him closer and closer to disaster.

And there seemed no way to stop it.

Jake didn't tell Maggie about the two men. She was already worried enough. Last night he had checked to be sure she was safely inside her room before he'd gone to bed, but he hadn't fallen asleep until almost dawn. Once he'd dropped off, he'd slept so hard the phone rang six times before he awoke.

Fumbling with the receiver, he sat up on the side of the bed and pressed the cold black plastic against his ear.

It was Shep Singleton—calling from his hospital bed.

"Shep. What the hell happened?" Jake ran a hand through his hair, trying to unscramble his sleep-muddled brain. "How bad are you hurt?"

"It could have been worse," Shep said. "As it is, I've got a couple of bruised ribs, two black eyes, and a face that looks like it's been run over by a good-sized lorry."

"How did it happen?"

Shep laughed dryly. "I'm going to give it to you straight, old man. I invited the wrong English gentleman up to my room for a toddy. I rarely get my signals crossed, but I certainly muddled them up last night. He and another chap gave me a lesson in English protocol and left me in the alley behind the pub."

"At The Wellington?"

"Afraid so."

Jake's pulse was racing, his stomach tied in a knot. "What did they look like?"

"I didn't see the second man." Jake could tell by the muffled sound of Shep's voice that his lips were swollen. "The one I was interested in was blond and gloriously handsome. If I'd gotten him in bed, the beating might have been worth it."

"Dammit, Shep."

"As I said, I didn't see it coming. Richard was friendly at first, a gentleman, and so very British I couldn't resist."

Jake gripped the receiver. "Did you call the police?"

"Somebody did. I was unconscious when they brought me in."

It was the men in the bar. Had to be. *The web tightens.* "How long will you be in the hospital?"

"I'll be out in the morning. Unfortunately, the doctor says I won't be able to ride until Dublin."

"Don't worry about it, Shep. Just take care of yourself. What time do they allow visitors?"

"From four to six then from seven to nine."

"Everybody will want to stop by."

"Jake?"

"Yes?"

"I'd appreciate it if you told them someone tried to rob me."

"You got it."

"Thanks, Jake."

"Take care." Jake rang off and rolled out of bed. While he showered and changed into slacks and a fresh white shirt, he tried to decide what to do. In the end, he didn't have to do anything. By mid-afternoon, he had a visitor.

"Hello, Jake. It's good to see you."

Standing at the fence outside one of the show rings, Jake's head snapped up. He would have known that rich baritone anywhere. "Hello, Daniel." He glanced around. "Taking a bit of a chance, aren't you?"

"Not really. I haven't been in the field for years. I'm Tom Rutledge, here to buy horses. With the papers I'm carrying, they'd have a helluva time making me as anything other than a breeder."

"It's a relief to see you," Jake said.

Daniel Gage smiled, his freckled face looking younger, more the way Jake remembered him. At fifty-five, Daniel was a little thicker around the middle, a few more lines around his eyes, a bit of gray in his light brown hair, but still imposing.

"I heard about the incident outside the pub last night, the beating, one of your riders winding up in the hospital. You were seen talking to

203

the two gentlemen in question."

Jake nodded.

"Popov's men?"

"Yes."

"First time you've seen them?"

"Yes."

"The police will want to question you. Just tell them the truth—you've never seen the men before last night. Give them a general description and let it go at that. Have there been other incidents?"

There was no point in lying now. "Unfortunately, there have." Jake filled Daniel in as quickly and precisely as possible, telling him about the incident on the plane and the attack on Ellie.

"They want you to know they'll carry out their threats," Daniel said. "They want you convinced they're serious."

"Believe me, I'm convinced."

Daniel looked past him into the show ring, where a big gray horse and rider moved along the fence. "Our inside man thinks it goes all the way to the top, Jake."

His stomach tightened painfully. "Is he absolutely sure?"

"He's identified one very high official. Everyone's keeping quiet. It's only by accident he's discovered as much as he has."

"What do we do now?"

"Try to catch the bastards and stop them from doing whatever they have planned—without them knowing you gave them up."

Jake rubbed his forehead, where a headache had started to build. "Sounds like a pretty tough order."

"It'll be tough, but with your help, maybe not impossible. We've already beefed-up security. You just play along with them—and this time keep us informed."

Jake smiled at the authority in his friend's voice as Daniel handed him a slip of paper with a Hickstead phone number on it. But his mind kept darting ahead to the what the consequences of his actions would be for his mother and sister.

"I know what you're thinking," Daniel said, "and I don't blame you." His eyes remained on Jake. "Just don't do anything you'll regret." Daniel drifted off with the crowd and Jake was left alone with his troubled thoughts.

What the hell did the Russians want him to do?

Jake looked up to see Ellie riding up beside him on Rose of Killarney and forced his mind back to the job he was there to do. The riders on the team were depending on him.

"You were behind Rose all the way through the course," he said. "Your mind isn't on the fences, Ellie, and it's beginning to show. You'd better get your priorities straight. You're here to ride for the United States, not moon over Clayton Whitfield. You're expected to win."

Her eyes glistened. "I'm sorry."

"You don't have another class until tomorrow. If you need the rest of the day off, take it, if not, try watching the competition. Maybe you'll learn something."

Ellie blinked back tears. "You're right, or course. You always are. I'll ride better tomorrow, I promise."

She reined Rose away, and Jake stared after her, already sorry he'd been so harsh.

"Weren't you a little tough on her?" Flex asked as he walked up beside him.

Jake sighed. "Whitfield's got her all balled up."

"Whitfield's a little balled up himself."

"Where the hell is he?"

"I don't know."

"Well, he damned well better get back here soon. This team isn't going to revolve around Clayton Whitfield's whims." He glanced over to where Ellie was climbing down from Rose, handing Gerry Winslow the horse's reins.

"Go talk to her, will you?" Jake said, suddenly tired.

Recalling the expression on Ellie's face when he'd mentioned Clay, Jake figured had one more problem to add to his list.

Ellie spotted Flex walking toward her, red hair gleaming beneath his hunt cap.

"Jake's got a lot on his mind," Flex said.

"I know." Ellie forced a smile she didn't feel. She should be worrying about the team. Instead, all she could think of was Clay.

"It isn't Jake's fault, it's mine," she said. "I'm making a fool of myself, Flex. Everyone knows how I feel about Clay. They look at me like I've finally gone over the edge. God, I hate it."

"Try to forget Clay and concentrate of your riding. Give him some time, maybe things will work out."

Her lips trembled. She'd given Clay enough time already. A one-night stand was all Clay wanted. But Ellie wanted more.

"Has something happened between you two?" Flex asked, his posture suddenly stiff. "I mean, the two of you haven't...?"

"Of course not." It was none of Flex's business, and the last thing she needed was sympathy.

"Just keep it that way and you'll be fine."

Ellie managed to smile. "I'll do my best."

The afternoon dragged on. Ellie tried to concentrate on the riders, tried to assess the course designer's style, how the footing would affect the jumps on Sunday, but her thoughts kept returning to Clay.

Where was he? Who was he with? Had he thought about her at all? He had left with his father. He'd probably had no choice.

She tried to convince herself the woman who had kissed him in the foyer meant nothing. She'd made more out of it than she should have. Clay would call and straighten things out.

She wished she could believe it. Clay had tried to warn her. Now she was paying the price.

After the show, the team bus took them all over to the hospital to see Shep. The nurses let them into his tiny Spartan room two at a time. There was another patient on the bed next to Shep's, but the curtain was drawn. Only an occasional cough came from that side of the room.

Shep sat propped up in bed, his eyes black-and-blue and puffed almost closed. His lips were cut and swollen.

"You look terrible," Prissy said.

Shep tried to smile. "Thanks. Believe me, I don't need to be reminded. My face looks like the rest of my body feels."

Prissy squeezed his hand. "The doctor says the damage looks worse than it is."

"I don't think they meant it to be any worse. They knew what they were doing. I think they could have killed me if they'd wanted."

"Oh, Shep."

Ellie's attention went on alert. Was the beating Shep had taken connected to what had happened on the plane and the attack in her hotel room?

"How's Lass?" Shep asked, concerned for his horse.

"Lass is fine," Elle said, helping him take a sip of water through a straw. "I knew you'd be worried so I checked on her myself."

"I should have known I could count on you. Any new gossip?"

Prissy grinned. "I heard one of the American riders got mugged and wound up in the hospital. The British team is highly disappointed. They expect us all to be able to handle ourselves like Dirty Harry."

Shep winced as his split lips curved into an unwanted smile. "Please, Prissy, have mercy. The last thing I need is a laugh."

"How long will you be laid up?" Ellie asked.

"I'll be able to ride by the time we get to Dublin. I expect you to hold up my end on Sunday."

With Shep unable to compete, she'd be taking his place in the Nations' Cup. Though she had been competing all along, this would be the first time she was representing the United States. "I promise to do my best."

"You'd better."

"And we'd better get going," Prissy said as the door opened, emitting a stiff-backed nurse dressed in a stark white uniform that seemed to fade into the backdrop of the sterile white walls.

Ellie and Shep both wrinkled their noses at the hospital smells traveling in her wake.

"I get out of this hellhole in the morning," Shep told them. "Make sure Jake doesn't forget to send someone to pick me up."

"I'll remind him, but I'm sure he won't forget." Ellie turned to go but stopped at the door and turned back. "The man who mugged you.... You're certain he was just after your wallet. I mean it wasn't anything to do with the team or anything?"

"No. I'm sure it was nothing like that."

Ellie sighed in relief. "Feel better, Shep."

CHAPTER TWENTY-TWO

As Shep was getting released from the hospital early the following morning, Ellie was heading for the stables. She was determined to ride the best she knew how. She wanted Jake and the others to be proud of her.

The sky was an azure blue, the day short-sleeve warm. Distant clouds puffed on the horizon, hinting at a possible change in the weather. Ellie worked Rose, worked Jube, and readied herself for the day's competition.

When she won her first class, her spirits lifted. Then she spotted Clay.

He was working Max in the practice ring, his form just as perfect as she remembered. Ellie watched unnoticed as horse and rider took the fences, remembering the night they had spent together. She remembered the way he had touched her, the things he had made her feel. She thought of the way his powerful body had pressed her into the mattress, the way her body had responded, the connection they had shared.

Without him, she had felt lost these past days.

Clay took another fence, and she got a good look at his face. He was all concentrated effort, he and Max working in perfect unison. He wasn't looking for her, that much was clear. Ellie's heart squeezed.

Flex walked up beside her. "I see he made it."

"Yes," she said softly. "I guess he just got in."

"He got in last night. He called about ten o'clock to ask about Max."

"Last night?" Ellie could barely choke out the words. "He called you last night?"

"Yes." Flex glanced down at her.

She could feel the blood draining out of her face. Her hand trembled where it rested on the arena fence.

"Are you all right?"

She shook her head. "I'm afraid I'm not feeling very well." Flex put an arm around her shoulders and guided her toward her tack room, shielding her from the horses and riders they passed along the way.

"You lied to me, didn't you?" he said. "You went to bed with him."

"I couldn't help it. I wanted him so much. I just didn't know how rotten I'd feel afterwards." They reached the tack room, and Flex led her inside. Wearily, she sank down on a bale of straw. "I knew he didn't love me, but I thought he cared a little."

"That bastard. He just couldn't leave you alone. He had to score, no matter how much he hurt you. He hasn't got a decent bone in his body."

Ellie willed herself not to cry, but her eyes burned, and the room seemed suddenly too warm. "I have a mind of my own," she whispered. "I could have said no."

Flex took a last look at her tortured expression and stormed out of the room. He headed straight to where Clay now stood beside Max. The big blood bay stallion stomped a hoof and swished his glossy black tail while Clay adjusted the length of a stirrup.

Clay glanced up as Flex approached, but his expression remained inscrutable.

"You rotten, no-good bastard. I didn't think even you could sink so low."

Clay ignored him, just kept working on his stirrup. Max pawed nervously, anxious for him to finish.

"Don't you have anything to say for yourself?"

"Since when did I start answering to you?"

"Since right now." Flex grabbed Clay's shoulder and spun him around. "You couldn't leave her alone, could you? You even had me fooled into thinking you cared for her, but all you wanted was another piece of ass." Flex doubled up his fist and punched Clay in the jaw so hard he sprawled in the dirt a few feet away between Julius Caesar's legs. The horse twisted his head to look down at him, but otherwise didn't move.

"Get up."

"I won't fight you, Flex."

"Why not? Afraid I might give you the beating you deserve?"

"This is none of your business." Clay climbed to his feet, brushing himself off. Flex stepped forward and hit him again. Clay went down hard, his hat rolling off into the dirt. By now Prissy had returned and a circle of riders begun to gather to watch the fray.

"Get up and fight." Flex stood over him, breathing hard, his mouth a thin, grim line.

"No."

Flex reached down and grabbed the front of Clay's shirt, jerked him up and punched him again. Blood trickled from the corner of Clay's mouth.

"Stop it!" Ellie rushed toward them, her voice high and strained. "Leave him alone!" She stood at the edge of the circle, ashen faced.

"Stay out of this, Ellie, this is between Clay and me."

"Don't you understand? It wasn't his fault! I wanted him to make love to me. I practically forced myself on him. He didn't do anything I didn't want him to. It wasn't his fault—it was mine!" The wind whipped strands of her hair while tears slid down her cheeks. "I'm not sorry about what happened. I cherish that night, even if he doesn't."

Flex glanced from Ellie to Clay. Not a flicker of emotion crossed his face. "You're a fool, Whitfield." Flex stepped across the circle to Ellie.

"All right, the show's over," he said to the crowd of riders, who began to disperse.

Slicing Clay a last hard glance, he put an arm around Ellie's shoulders and led her away.

Clay watched them go. Climbing to his feet, he wiped the blood from his mouth with the back of his hand and combed his fingers through his hair. He picked up his riding cap and settled it back on his head. His stomach was knotted into a hard tight ball, his ulcer eating at his insides.

Through the whole ordeal he'd kept his expression carefully blank. He hadn't once looked at Ellie. He didn't dare.

"I hope you're proud of yourself."

For the first time Clay noticed Prissy, who leaned against the rail, knee bent, a booted foot propped on the fence behind her. He hated the condemnation in her voice.

"Why shouldn't I be? I scored, didn't I? Let her say what she wants if it'll soothe her ego. The truth is, I set out to seduce her. I lied to her and lured her into my bed. I'm the same bastard I've always been."

Prissy came away from the fence to stand beside him. "You could have let her down easy. You've got a knack for keeping ex-lovers as friends. Why not Ellie?"

Clay shrugged his shoulders. "Too much trouble," he said, but a nerve twitched in his cheek.

Prissy eyed him strangely. "Why am I not convinced?"

"That's your problem. I seduced her. When I had my fill, I dumped her. If you want to blame someone, blame me." Clay turned away.

"I don't get it. She's trying to protect you after all the shit you've given her. You're staying away from her, making her hate you on purpose. Why?"

"Leave it alone, Prissy." He pulled Max's reins loose from the top rail of the fence and slipped them over the animal's head. Max nickered softly, and Clay stroked the horse's thick neck.

"Why, Clay?" Prissy asked softly. "Why would you treat Ellie so badly? It isn't like you to be cruel to someone on purpose." She reached out to him then, saw him stiffen even before her fingers touched his cheek. Gently, she turned his face with her hand, forcing him to look at her. Prissy sucked in a breath at the pain, the crushing despair that went beyond sadness to the outer limits of grief.

Her expression changed to pity. "Oh, dear God, Clay, you're in love with her."

Clay closed his eyes. The lump in his throat closed so tight he couldn't speak. His chest felt leaden. His stomach gnawed without pity. He could hear Ellie's voice echoing in his mind. *It was my fault—not his!*

What had he done to her? He'd seen the pity on their faces, known how much she hated that, but he could do nothing. Nothing could ease the hurt he had caused.

"Don't you understand? I'm no good for her. Ellie isn't like the rest of us. She's special. She deserves someone who can make her happy. She certainly doesn't need a man like me."

"She doesn't want someone else, Clay," Prissy said softly. "She wants you."

Clay looked out across the practice ring, watching the riders and seeing only Ellie's stricken face as he'd left her that day in London. His gaze dropped to the leather reins he gripped too tightly in his hands.

"I betrayed her trust. I did something she could never forgive, something even *I* can't forgive."

"It can't be that bad."

"I left her that morning. I went off with my father with no regard for her feelings. All I cared about was my male ego and my father's approval. I behaved like an animal. There were drugs involved, other women. I feel sick inside, Prissy. Sick and disgusted. What I did, I can't undo. Not ever." The words felt wrenched from his soul. Each rang with sadness, each was a condemnation, a death knell.

Prissy touched his cheek. Her hand felt warm and comforting and he thought of Ellie, the way she'd touched him that morning at breakfast. *How long will you be gone?*

Too long, he'd said. Too long had become an eternity. He could never go back. Never repair the damage he'd done. He would never again feel the happiness he'd known when he was with her.

"We all make mistakes, Clay. Even Ellie."

"It's better this way. I could never be a one-woman man. I'm too much like my father."

"You're nothing like Avery. Haven't you figured that out?"

Clay released a bitter sigh. "I suppose that's the one thing I have learned from all of this."

Prissy pulled a tissue from the pocket of her breeches and dabbed it against the fresh trickle of blood in the corner of Clay's mouth. "Then it isn't too late."

"That's where you're wrong, Prissy."

"Don't throw away this chance, Clay."

His chest tightened with a fresh rush of self-loathing. His face felt so bloodless he knew he looked more pallid than tan. "You don't understand—I threw everything away when I left her in that hotel room."

His stomach gnawed in pain. He almost relished it. The pain was the only thing that felt real. Until these past few moments, he'd left his emotions in Monaco. He'd destroyed himself for a woman he cared nothing about. A woman he would remember as the one who encouraged his destruction.

Clay took a breath, masking the misery he felt inside. He'd spent the week turning his feelings into a carefully guarded void. Prissy had opened the wound, but soon he'd be able to close it, block thoughts of Ellie as if she'd never existed. He'd taught himself well.

As a child it had been a necessity. As a man, he was even more adept. Soon there'd be no outward signs of the emptiness that ate at him like the ulcer he fed.

"I'd appreciate it if you didn't say anything to Ellie. What's past is past."

"Clay, don't do this."

"I want your promise."

Prissy sighed. "All right. I won't tell her. But promise me you'll think this through again."

"I've done nothing but think since it happened. I have no choice." He turned his back on her, swung up into the saddle and nudged Max forward.

His mind was made up. Whatever he and Ellie had found was over. As dead as he felt inside. He would put all his energy into winning. Nothing else mattered now.

His insides tightened. Just days ago, his life had seemed full and rich, filled with endless possibilities.

But days ago, he'd been dreaming of Ellie Fletcher, holding her, kissing her, making love to her. She had filled him with the joy of life and living.

Now he had to let her go.

CHAPTER TWENTY-THREE

Jake finished drying off, then casually wrapped the towel around his waist, preparing to shave. He'd heard about the fight between Flex and Clay just minutes after it happened. Dammit, he'd hoped Ellie would have more sense that to get involved with Clay.

Three days had passed since then. Jake hadn't mentioned it and neither had Ellie. But Ellie wasn't good at hiding her emotions and the hurt was clear in her face.

Aside from the protective, almost fatherly feelings he held for her, Jake hated the dissension between the team members that had blossomed overnight. Part of him felt Clay deserved exactly what he'd gotten. But another, larger part kept telling him things weren't what they seemed.

Clay Whitfield was acting out of character. Or maybe, he thought, acting too much *in* character, even for Clay.

In the days following his return from Monaco, Clay had become the epitome of his own legend. He was riding beautifully, drinking hard, laughing and carousing, acting every bit the infamous celebrity playboy—except for the women. Clay had yet to be seen with a woman.

Even Linda Gibbons' advances had been politely refused, much to Linda's chagrin. Jake had seen them talking after the competition on Saturday. Linda had bluntly asked Clay to take her to bed. Clay had gently refused. Linda had stormed off, calling him a bastard, among several other choice descriptions. Clay had smiled indulgently and returned to his work with Max.

Jake wanted to talk to each of the team members in private, especially Ellie, Flex, and Clay. He needed to repair the rift between them before the team competition. Since it wasn't his nature to intrude on problems of a personal nature, the task would not be an easy one.

Jake was considering what approach to use when the phone rang. Praying nothing else had gone wrong, he crossed the floor of his hotel room toward the nightstand and picked up the receiver.

"Good morning, *Tovarich*." The raspy sound of Popov's voice set his nerves on edge. It was an eerie gift the man used to perfection.

"Perhaps it's good for you," Jake said.

"Do I hear a touch of bitterness, Comrade? Surely, I am mistaken."

Jake quelled the sudden urge to laugh. Popov was destroying his life, yet he spoke as casually as if they were friends.

Jake's hand tightened on the phone. "I need to know what you want. Just tell me—and leave my people alone."

He heard Popov's irritating chuckle. "On Tuesday you will be in Dublin. At two o'clock you will go to the Bit O' Dublin Tobacconist Shop on Molesworth Street near Dawson. There you will receive instructions—precise instructions as to what we wish you to do. You are to follow those instructions to the letter. You will receive your final directions the following week. When you have completed your assignment, your obligation to us will have been fulfilled."

"That's it?"

"Does it not sound easy?"

"Too easy."

"Oh, and *Tovarich,* one more thing. Should you decide to amend those instructions or divulge them in any way, your Mrs. Delaine and her daughter will pay, along with your mother and sister."

Jake closed his eyes against a rush of despair. This was his fault. He should have kept Maggie out of it, found a way to keep her and Sarah safe. "I barely know them."

"Do you take me for a fool? We knew of your affair with the woman. Until your small...indiscretion...the other night, we assumed the relationship was nothing of importance. We were wrong, it seems. But you needn't worry. I am certain you plan to cooperate."

"Yes," Jake said softly. "I'll cooperate."

"I was certain you would. The tobacconist shop on Tuesday." The line went dead.

Jake hung up the phone, his mind racing, his pulse thundering. If he hadn't gone to meet Maggie, her life wouldn't be in danger.

If he hadn't slept with her.

If he hadn't loved her.

He took a deep breath and walked into the bathroom to finish getting ready.

There was nothing for it now. Nothing left to do but lie to Daniel—and do exactly what the Soviets asked.

Ellie moved through her Sunday morning routine by rote, as she had done all week.

She left the hotel at dawn, arriving at the stables early enough to help Gerry complete his morning routine with the horses. Like everyone else, Gerry had heard about the fight between Clay and Flex McGrath. He had guessed what had caused it but refrained from mentioning it.

Instead, he'd been supportive, insisting he needed a little extra help to get the horses ready for the Nations' Cup and the Dublin competition the following week.

Ellie knew it was a ruse but appreciated Gerry's concern. And the extra work helped keep her mind off Clay, a subject she kept carefully buried in the deepest part of her heart.

As far as Ellie was concerned, her time with Clay was a momentary lapse now relegated to the past. Maybe someday she'd allow herself to remember the night they had shared, the love she had felt for him, but not now.

Too much was at stake.

Immersing herself in her riding and care of the horses, she planned her strategy, using every means available to assure a win. She told herself the extra effort wasn't a desire to thwart Clay and regain some of her injured pride. If it was, so what?

She had come to Europe to win. She intended to do just that.

"What number did the team draw?" Gerry asked, referring to the competition about to begin and breaking into her thoughts. They stood in front of Jubilee's stall, Gerry giving the stallion a second going over. Earlier, the horse had been carefully groomed, his tack cleaned and polished to a brilliant sheen.

"Number six. I ride last." One team member from each country took the course, then the sequence was repeated until all the riders had finished.

"Great, that should give you a chance to look over the course and correct for any problems. Did Whitfield bother to show up?"

Just saying Clay's name seemed to chill the air around them. "He's here," Ellie said, trying to keep her voice even. "Max looked strong going over the practice fences."

Gerry nodded but his expression said he was surprised Clay had the nerve to show up. "I'll bring Jube over to the arena as soon as I'm finished. You go ahead."

With a last stroke of the sorrel's soft muzzle, Ellie headed for the ring.

The All-England Jumping Course, Hickstead, Sussex, in the Southern English countryside, was a permanent show-jumping arena, turf-covered, and surrounded to overflowing by cheering fans. British television had made the event second in popularity to soccer and generated thousands of enthusiastic followers.

As Ellie neared the arena, the excitement became contagious. She felt a growing smile of anticipation, the first she'd experienced in far too long. Jube was working his best, and Ellie was as mentally prepared as possible, given her current circumstance. Only the sight of Clay in his immaculate, blue-trimmed red team jacket and tight cream breeches as he stood talking to Jake, gave her a moment's pause.

To hell with him! She thought. *I'm a winner—with or without Clay Whitfield.* She flicked her crop against the side of her boot and realized just how much she wanted to win. This was the first time she'd officially represented the United States as a member of the Equestrian Team. It was a moment she'd dreamed of for years. Not even Clayton Whitfield could spoil it for her.

Skirting the two men, she headed to where Flex stood beside Sparky and one of the grooms.

"Time to walk the course," Ellie said, flashing Flex a smile. "Come on." She tugged his arm, and he grinned down at her.

"That eager, are you?"

"I've got a good feeling about this." She flicked him a second quick smile, and they started through the gates. Once she got on the course, some of her enthusiasm fled. The fences looked huge, the biggest by far since they'd come to Europe. Some were close together while others seemed too many strides apart. How in the world would Jube be able to handle such a difficult course?

"Who designed this?" Flex grumbled. "One of the 217herpas from Mount Everest?"

They stepped off the paces between a Liverpool water jump and a big triple oxer. Ellie groaned. "I think my good feeling just turned to worms."

"I know what you mean."

All in all, there were fourteen jumps, some of them doubles and triples, making a total of seventeen fences. A taxing course, to say the least. Ellie was thankful the weather was cooperating. Wispy white clouds drifted overhead while a gentle breeze rippled the red-and-gold ribbons hanging on the arena fence.

Ellie fiddled nervously with the piece of string that tied her number to the back of her red team jacket. From the corner of her eye, she spotted Clay pacing off the distance between the first and second fences. Squaring her shoulders, she hurried to keep up with Flex.

Once more outside the arena, she spotted Prissy, who had already finished. "Looks awful, doesn't it?" Prissy said.

"Worse than awful. Poor Jube."

"Poor Jube?" Prissy teased. "I think Jubilee will rise to the challenge. That horse seems to jump a little higher every week. He's eating the whole thing up. Poor little Caesar will be frightened out of his wits."

Ellie laughed. "We're all going to do just fine."

Prissy glanced up and Ellie followed the line of her gaze. Clay strode by without a glance, his mind apparently lost in thoughts of the competition. Ellie watched his broad back, the lean hips and muscular thighs outlined by his tight cream riding breeches.

Thinking how handsome he looked, she smiled and felt a tug at her heart. She missed him, she realized, the thought coming swift and hard and completely unwanted. Damn it to hell, she wished they could have at least remained friends.

She watched him till he rounded the corner of the timer's box out of sight.

"That bad, is it?"

"I'm just another casualty, Prissy. I'll get over it. Right now, the most important thing I have to think about is my riding."

Prissy opened her mouth as if she wanted to say something but didn't.

"Look, the first rider's coming on," Ellie said, pointing toward the ring.

The British rider on a horse named Admiral Horatio circled the arena at a posting trot. The tone sounded. Nearing the eye of the timer, the rider touched the brim of his cap and started the round, his big dun horse, a Hanoverian, approaching the first fence, a vertical five feet high, sailing over it with ease. Unfortunately, the gelding landed a little too far ahead, throwing off his stride for the next jump, a red and white oxer bordered by white chrysanthemums.

Admiral Horatio knocked down the top rail with his forelegs and the crowd groaned, Ellie and Prissy along with them. Things went downhill from there.

At the third jump, a tricky combination difficult for both horse or rider to judge, the animal downed all three fences. He refused the fourth jump twice, but finally made it over. With a defeated expression, the British rider finished his round.

"Looks like this is going to be just as tough as we thought," Prissy said.

"Think positive, lady. We're here to win."

Prissy nodded but didn't seem convinced.

Rider after rider approached the awesome course and left it with double digit faults. Flex was the first American rider to enter the ring. He did better than Ellie expected, clearing the course with just two rails down and one time fault, which put them in the lead.

Now the riders knew the course was at least manageable. Ellie and Prissy studied each jump, trying to find the best approach. Prissy's turn came up.

"Good luck," Ellie said.

Disheartened by the twelve faults she stacked up, Prissy returned a few minutes later, all of them hoping the other team members would do better and her low score could be thrown out.

Gerry brought Jube around before the next rider took the course. Ellie wanted to make some practice jumps before she rode the course. While she worked with Jube in a different arena, Gerry would carefully watch the competition for any tips he might discover.

Excited by the crowd, Jube was feeling high, responding to her every command. Ellie returned to the main arena just before Clay took the course. He entered the ring looking relaxed and confident, Max prancing beneath him. A medieval knight in a jousting competition— or at least some Hollywood version of one.

Despite her attempts to wish him the worst, Ellie found herself rooting for him. *Only in the interest of the team,* she told herself. As she watched him clear jump after difficult jump, his movements so in tune with Max they seemed one creature instead of two, she thought he had never ridden better.

The crowd was on its feet by the time he approached the last two fences: a Liverpool water jump that had dampened its share of victims in the pond and a vertical that deluded the horses into believing it was easy when it wasn't.

Ellie held her breath. "Come on, Clay," she whispered, "you can do it." And he did, clearing the jumps as if they weren't there.

Max was blowing and prancing, Clay smiling triumphantly as he headed out of the show ring. For a brief instant, their eyes locked. He seemed surprised by her smile. For an instant, his gaze softened— or maybe she imagined it—then they both turned away.

Forget about Clay, she told herself. *This is your chance. Take it.*

The next two riders both went clear, as often happened. Once a rider saw that it could be done, they seemed to relax. The next four riders weren't so lucky, and the odds evened-out a little.

Tensely awaiting the sound of her name, Ellie checked her position in the saddle, stirrups beneath the balls of her feet, her weight evenly distributed above her hips and legs. As Jube's name was called over the loudspeaker, followed by her own, she nudged the big stallion forward.

She wanted this moment. She needed it as never before in her life.

Focusing on her ride, she let her body relax, let herself feel the stride of the animal beneath her as she'd taught herself since childhood. As she increased Jube's speed, the noise of the crowd receded. She was ready for this. More than ready.

Feeling more relaxed than she ever had, Ellie took the first fence at an easy gallop, Jube's body moving with subtle assurance. Four long strides to the red and white oxer, which the big horse took with confidence.

She smiled. Dog leg left, easy breezy, to the big triple combination Jube made look small. Over the next vertical, the pace a little faster, Jube's concentration as powerful as her own.

Next came a big wide oxer, six long strides, Jube stretching out, then collecting himself just as she commanded—over with just the merest click of a hoof.

The crowd held its breath as the bar shimmied in the cup but didn't fall. Dog leg right to a green and white vertical, then a brick wall jump. Clearing the wall, she started the next series of fences, which passed beneath her as if they weren't there.

The crowd was on its feet cheering, and Jube seemed to lap up the sound. The big horse was taking the fences with ease, making them look like the pros they'd trained to be.

They approached the water jump, Ellie's heart pounding but filled with pride. No matter what happened now, they'd ridden like champions. Over the water jump—the crowd still on its feet. Over the last vertical.

They made it! They'd gone clear and within the time allotted! Ellie felt the sting of tears and a swell of pride in her heart.

Jake was applauding above his head, grinning from ear to ear. Flex and Prissy stood beside him looking radiant. She glanced to the announcer's stand where Shep sat with his back propped up with pillows giving her a thumbs-up.

Gerry rushed up to meet her. Jumping down triumphantly, she handed him Jube's reins, and gave him a hug. "We did it!"

"You were wonderful. That's by far the best ride you've ever given the old boy."

She couldn't stop grinning. "It was, wasn't it?"

"I'm proud of you, lady."

"Thank you, Gerry."

"Me, too," Prissy added, walking up beside her.

"Don't get too cocky, young lady," Jake said. "I expect to see more of the same in the second round." But his eyes glowed with pride.

Only two other riders went clear, the contest far from over. Ellie found herself searching for Clay, hoping he'd say something to her, but he didn't. She wondered why sleeping with him had changed his attitude towards her so completely. Linda Gibbons had slept with him, and God knew how many other women. He didn't seem to hold them in contempt.

Maybe it was something she'd done. Not telling him she was a virgin then demanding he take her to bed. *Something.* All she knew was that whatever it was, she'd undo it if she could.

At the end of the first round, the others had done well enough they'd been able to throw out Prissy's low score, leaving them in fourth position. In the second round, both Prissy and Flex put in good rides, Flex with eight faults, Prissy with four. When Clay's turn came up, he seemed a little less sure of himself this time, Max a little tired. The first round had been grueling, this one no less so.

Clay rode beautifully, but Max caught a hoof on the last big vertical and the rail went down. Four faults in the time allotted. A good score and one that moved them up to third position. The next two riders each had two rails down. A French team member finished with sixteen faults and an Italian with twelve. At last, it was Ellie's turn.

Willing herself to ride clear, she entered the arena, took her time getting into position. The first jump, the vertical, Jube took with ease, but Ellie could sense his fatigue. As with Max, the first round had taken more out of him than she'd suspected.

The second jump, the oxer, they cleared, but Jube landed out of stride, and she put him wrong at the combination. He righted himself and went over all three fences. Silently, she thanked him for saving them and continued over the next set of fences, working their way toward the water jump.

They cleared the jump, but Ellie feared they might have touched the fault line. She wouldn't know until they finished the round.

Over the next set of fences, Jube tapped a hoof on the rail, which wobbled in the cup but remained in place. The crowd was cheering as she cleared the last big vertical and finished the course. She rode up to Jake still uncertain how she had done until the announcer called her score.

No faults within the time allotted. The crowd roared to its feet, applauding until her ears rang.

The last rider, a Frenchman, chalked up twelve faults. When the scores were tallied, the U.S. team had moved from third position to first—and most of the credit went to her.

It was the proudest moment of her life.

The team made a victory lap then rode to the judge's stand to receive their trophy. Clay sat beside her on Max, Flex and Prissy on her right. The British had finished second by the narrow margin of only four faults. The French team placed third.

As Jake accepted the trophy, the band played the National Anthem and a tight lump swelled in Ellie's throat. She forced herself not to look at Clay but weakened and took one quick glance. He sat tall and proud, but she couldn't read his expression. When the song ended, they made another lap and left the ring. Clay rode up beside her as she dismounted.

"You said you'd beat me," he said evenly. "And you did."

"I didn't beat you. We're on the same team."

"If it hadn't been for you, we wouldn't have won. You rode brilliantly."

"Thank you." It was all she could manage. With the sun at his back and Max prancing beneath him, Clay looked ten feet tall. His face was in shadow, but it wouldn't have mattered. She could tell by his words and the tone of his voice, his expression would reveal nothing.

"Congratulations," he said, then turned to go.

"Clay?" she called after him.

A light touch of the rein and Max stopped and turned. Clay looked down at her but wouldn't quite meet her eyes.

"For whatever I've done, I'm sorry. I hope that we might still be friends."

"My God," he whispered, looking thunderstruck. "You've done nothing. Nothing." He whirled Max and dug his heels a little too hard into the horse's flanks. Max leaped forward at the unusually active command. Clay slowed him and they moved away.

Ellie closed her eyes. Why did it hurt so much to love someone? Why couldn't he have loved her in return?

CHAPTER TWENTY-FOUR

The team dinner that night was a celebration of sorts, though Clay didn't show up and much of the conversation seemed stilted, the laughter a little too brittle. Clay's absence seemed a reminder of the ill feelings among the team members that hadn't been resolved.

The party broke up early, the riders tired from the grueling competition, and there they needed to be ready to leave for Dublin on Tuesday.

Jake remined in the hotel pub, warming a snifter of brandy between his palms. He sat in the corner of the nearly deserted room, thinking about the instructions he would receive in Dublin.

"May I join you?"

Jake glanced up to see Maggie standing in front of him, her tone carefully business-like. His brooding mood lightened, and he smiled warmly. "There's nothing in this world I'd like better." Since the Soviets knew about the two of them, staying away from her would do nothing to protect her. On the other hand, if he was forced to do something criminal, he didn't want Maggie associated with the deed.

But a brief conversation, a bit of her warmth now and then, he'd allow himself.

"You look beautiful tonight," he said as she sat down beside him.

Maggie smiled. "Thank you." Thick overhead beams and a fireplace at one end gave the pub the charm of the English countryside surrounding them.

"Everything lined up for Dublin?" Jake asked.

"Everything's ready except the team. That's what I came to talk to you about."

"I'm worried about them, too. They rode well today, but Ellie and Clay are barely speaking. Flex and Clay aren't speaking at all. Sooner or later the strain is bound to cause problems."

"This is all Clay's fault," Maggie said. "Ellie is too trusting, and Clay took advantage. I really didn't think he was that kind of man, no matter his reputation."

"I'm not completely convinced he is. He hasn't been himself since he came back from Monaco. Oh, he's riding well. Too well. He has little interest in anything else. The solitude isn't like him."

"I noticed. And Flex feels guilty. He and Clay have been friends for years."

"At least Ellie's kept this from destroying her momentum. She's riding better than ever. I knew she had guts."

"She's competing in the Grand Prix in Dublin. I hope she's up to it. Working so close to Clay is bound to be tough on her."

Jake just nodded. "I wish there was a way to draw the team together again. Maybe I could convince Clay to talk to Ellie. Explain why things didn't work out. Maybe even apologize."

"How do you apologize for breaking someone's heart?"

Jake's gaze ran over her beautiful face. "I love you, Maggie," he said softly.

Maggie touched his cheek and Jake leaned into her hand. "I love you, too."

Jake straightened away from her. "You'd better go now." He gave her a last warm smile. "I'll see you back at the hotel."

Maggie rose from her chair, feeling a trickle of alarm. Why Jake's sudden change of mood? More and more uneasy, she headed for the door. All the way up to her room, she wondered what had changed. The warm smiles, no glancing over his shoulder, no entreaties for her to leave. The worry lines on his forehead seemed a little less evident tonight. His voice betrayed a note of resignation that hadn't been there before.

Her alarm blossomed into full-fledged fear. There was only one reason Jake would behave as he had. He had made up his mind to do what the Soviets asked.

They must have found out about her, threatened to hurt her, maybe threatened both her and Sarah. Jake was doing whatever he had to in order to protect them.

225

And Maggie Delaine had to stop him.

After the team supper, Ellie left the restaurant, went up to her room and straight to bed. The hotel was old and quaint, the bathroom not completely modern, but the bed was comfortable, the cracks in the ceiling now familiar.

She'd spent hours just lying there, tracing those lines, counting them, imagining the patterns they formed, trying to sort through her thoughts about Clay. Mostly trying to bury them.

So far, her efforts had been futile.

Ellie sighed and closed her eyes, but sleep wouldn't come. Not for hours, not even after all the champagne she'd drunk at dinner. Clay hadn't shown up, as she could have predicted.

She had tried not to watch for him, but the effort was exhausting. She would have been miserable if he'd come to the dinner and ignored her or arrived with another woman. But she'd been just as miserable without him.

Ellie listened to the rhythmic tick of the old-fashioned alarm clock on the bedside table and forced her thoughts in another direction equally disturbing.

She kept seeing Shep Singleton's battered face, his swollen lips and black eyes. Was the assault just coincidence? Just another tourist mugging? Or was there a connection to the other mishaps that had occurred?

When she'd mentioned her concern to Jake, he'd brushed her worry aside.

"These things happen, Ellie. We're traveling through foreign counties. Shep should have been more careful."

"You don't think it could be connected to what happened to me?"

"It seems highly unlikely." But he wouldn't meet her eyes.

It wasn't like Jake to be so evasive. Though he'd always been a private person, he was usually forthright to a fault.

Thank heavens, they'd be leaving for the States right after the Dublin show. She'd be going home, putting all this behind her, returning to her familiar apartment above the garage of her parent's house.

They'd had a few brief conversations, but she was busy and so were they, and it was hard to keep secrets from them. She wasn't ready to talk about Clay, and she'd promised Jake she wouldn't discuss the mishaps that had befallen the team.

Ellie heard a light rap at her door and came to her feet. Dressed in a yellow nylon nightgown, she grabbed a robe and slipped her arms into the sleeves, lifting her heavy mass of hair away at the same time.

"Who is it?" she asked, suddenly nervous as she thought of the man who had attacked her.

"It's Prissy. I saw your light beneath the door. Can I come in for a minute?"

Ellie slid the chain off with the grating sound of metal against metal and unlocked the bolt. "Hi."

Prissy came in, also wearing a robe, hers a thick blue terry. "I guess you couldn't sleep, either."

Ellie smiled wanly. "I've had a tough time all week."

"I kind of figured that." They both sat down on the bed.

"Is something wrong?" Ellie asked, noticing Prissy's troubled expression.

"Wrong? Yeah, something's wrong, but not with me. That's what I came to talk to you about. There's something wrong with Clay."

"Clay?" Ellie's fingers bit into the folds of her robe.

Prissy released a slow breath. "This is hard for me, Ellie. Clay made me promise not to tell you, so what I'm doing now is breaking my word." She sighed. "I guess I'm just a hopeless romantic..."

"What is it? What's wrong with Clay?"

Prissy fiddled with the sash on her robe. "You'll have to talk to Clay about this in person. I shouldn't be telling you at all but.... All I'm going to say is that Clay feels he betrayed you. When he left you that morning at Claridge's...well, apparently, he did some things he's ashamed of. He mentioned something about drugs and...I won't lie to you, Ellie, there were other women involved."

"More than one?"

"I don't know. He just said women."

She bit back the sound that tried to escape her throat.

"Clay can't forgive himself. He believes you deserve someone better. That's why he hasn't called you. He can't face you. More than that, he's trying to protect you."

"Protect me? Protect me from what?"

227

"From himself. From the kind of person he believes he is."

Ellie just stared, trying to digest the things Prissy was saying. The image of Clay in the arms of the woman at Claridge's flashed through her mind. Her eyes closed against a wave of remembered pain. Everything she had imagined was true. Everything and more.

"How could he?" Her voice whispered out, little more than a breath of air in the quiet room. "When we were together, it seemed so beautiful...so special. I felt cherished. I thought he cared about me. How could I have been so wrong?"

"I'm not sure you are. That's why I came to talk to you."

Ellie looked up at Prissy, beginning to get angry. "How could he do it? How could he do a thing like that?"

"That's the question Clay keeps asking himself. He's sick about it, Ellie. Sick inside. I've never seen a man sorrier about what's happened than Clay."

"I don't believe it. He isn't sorry at all. He did just what he told me he would do. There's no reason for him to be sorry."

"Ellie, please try to think this through."

"I've already thought it through. I've thought about nothing but Clayton Whitfield for hours. Days. Every time I think of him, I see him in the arms of that...that...woman! He's just as big a bastard as everyone says he is." She jumped up from the bed and started pacing. "And to think I apologized to *him!*"

Prissy stood up, blocking the path Ellie was carving into the carpet. "I didn't come here to upset you. I thought there might be a chance you'd understand. All I can tell you is that Clay regrets everything that's happened. He won't tell you because he thinks you're better off without him. I believe he cares for you very much and that he's learned something from what he's done. Whatever happens from here on out is up to you."

"I hate him." Her face felt hot, her shoulders tense.

Prissy moved toward the door. "I guess he knew you better than I thought," she said softly.

Ellie glanced up at her. "What do you mean?"

"Clay said you could never forgive him." With a last glance at Ellie, Prissy walked out and closed the door.

The trip to Dublin on Tuesday went smoothly. The horses were taken to the stables and settled in their stalls while Jake and the riders were driven to their hotel, the Lansdowne on Pembroke Road in Ballsbridge, not far from the show grounds.

All except Clay, who had taken a suite at the Shelbourne on St. Stephen's Green.

Renovated to its former elegance, the Shelbourne was the finest hotel in Dublin. Jake wasn't surprised at Clay's decision to stay there but he'd hoped to dissuade him, end the feuding between the riders, and make them once more a team.

"You know I don't approve of what went on between you and Ellie," Jake said to Clay as he worked to settle Max and Zodiak into their new stalls. "Given her lack of experience, I think it was a lousy thing to do. But Ellie's a grown woman, and I've got no business interfering in her personal life."

Clay didn't answer.

"On the other hand, the team *is* my business, and I'm worried about what's happening. Why don't you take a room with the rest of us over at the Lansdowne? Give things a chance to get back to normal."

"I always go first class," Clay said. "You ought to know that by now."

"That isn't the reason and we both know it. It's because of Ellie and Flex. I've never known you to run from a problem, Clay. Won't you talk to them, at least try to work things out?"

"Flex and I have agreed to disagree. Ellie is riding better than she ever has. I don't see the problem."

Jake just sighed and shook his head. "Well, if you can't see it, far be it from me to point it out. You do what you have to, Clay. But remember, these are the same riders you'll be traveling with to Seoul. You need to settle things before the Olympics."

Clay scratched Max between the ears and the stallion nickered softly. "I'll give it some thought, Jake."

"I'd appreciate that." Jake started to leave, then turned back. "And, Clay, remember one thing. These people are your friends."

Absently, Clay ran his fingers along his jaw. The bruise from Flex's punch had faded, but apparently not the memory. "I know," he said.

Jake nodded.

"By the way, what do you think about what happened to Shep?"

229

"I think he ought to be more careful who he tries to pick up," Jake said.

"You're saying his beating had no connection to what happened to Ellie? Nothing to do with the team?"

"I don't see how playing cat and mouse with the wrong sex partners could possibly be interpreted as a threat to the team."

"What do the authorities say? Those undercover security people you called from Paris?"

Jake's insides tightened. "They said the same thing. Shep got in over his head."

"You wouldn't mind if I had a talk with them, would you?"

Jake's worry kicked up. "Look, Whitfield, if you've got something to say, just say it."

"All right, Jake, I will. I don't think you ever notified the authorities and I want to know why?"

What could he say? How much of the truth could he afford to tell? Jake suddenly felt a hundred years old.

"There are considerations I'm not at liberty to discuss with you, Clay. But I give you my word I've spoken to people of the highest authority." It was the truth. Daniel knew most of what was going on. Most, but not all. "I really don't think there's anything for you to worry about."

Clay watched him closely.

"I'm asking you to trust me, Clay. Let me handle this my way."

Clay took a deep breath. "All right, Jake. For now, I'll agree. But if anything else happens—anything at all—I'm going to the police."

It was more than he'd hoped for. "Fair enough," Jake said and prayed nothing else would go wrong.

CHAPTER TWENTY-FIVE

Upstairs in his room, Jake unpacked and put away his clothes. Since the competition didn't start until the following Tuesday, they'd be staying in Dublin for almost two weeks. Jake had been looking forward to seeing a little of the country. Now he just wanted whatever was going to happen to be over with and done.

Sliding back the sleeve of his coat, he checked his watch. Almost one o'clock. He was due at the tobacconist shop at two. Picking up his money clip and the wad of Irish bills called *punt* he'd exchanged from English pounds at the airport, he headed out the door.

The cab ride to Molesworth Street normally didn't take long, but Jake decided to take a roundabout route, change cabs a couple of times, just in case he was being followed by Daniel's men.

At two o'clock sharp he got out of the taxi in front of the Bit O' Dublin Tobacconist Shop, a small store wedged between two antique dealers. The window was filled with a multitude of pipes, cigars, cigar clippers, cartons of cigarettes, anything and everything that had to do with smoking.

Jake pushed open the glass-paned door, making the bell ring, and inhaled the aroma of tobacco, so pungent it made his mouth water, though he'd never take up smoking again.

The store was narrow but deeper than he'd imagined when he'd seen it from the street. A wizened, gray-haired man wearing spectacles stood behind a counter at the far end.

"I believe you have something for me," Jake said.

"If your name is Straka, I do indeed."

"It *was* Straka," Jake said pointedly, but his meaning was lost on the little man.

"You're taller in person," the man said. Jake wondered what

231

pictures the man had seen.

The shopkeeper wiped his hands on the canvas apron he wore over his shirt and pants, reached beneath the counter and pulled out a small, sealed manila envelope. He handed it to Jake.

With a curt nod, Jake stuffed it into the inside breast pocket of his jacket, turned and left the shop. Outside, he glanced around, but saw no one suspicious. The streets were crowded with tourists, an unusually large group since Dublin was celebrating its Millennium, as well as the Dublin Horse Show, the biggest event of the year, starting next week.

Jostling his way along the bustling sidewalk, Jake rounded the corner and walked a few blocks. The green lawns of Trinity College beckoned, a quiet respite where he could sit undisturbed and open the package that seemed to burn a hole in his chest.

Finding a shady bench, he pulled out the envelope and carefully broke the seal. Inside he found a small round plastic vial contained a pair of contact lenses, two hotel keys—one to the Lansdowne, one to the Shelbourne—and a bottle of chalky white liquid. The instructions were simple:

> On the morning of the Nations' Cup competition, you will substitute the enclosed contact lenses for those worn by Felix McGrath. The night before, you will exchange the enclosed prescription for the one used by Clayton Whitfield. Your final instructions will be given on Friday morning at ten o'clock.

At the bottom, a diagram showed the location of the Friday morning rendezvous, the day of the Nations' Cup. Saturday was the final day of competition.

Jake looked at the brown plastic bottle of chalky liquid. It had a typed label on the front showing Clay's name and the name of his doctor. It looked exactly like the bottle Clay always carried.

He studied the contact lenses floating in the tiny vial, certain they would be identical to Flex's. What the consequences would be for Flex and Clay? What if the substances were deadly? What if Jake was supposed to murder Flex and Clay?

Jake's stomach rebelled at the thought. Could he actually commit murder? His conscience screamed *no!* But his mind warned he had to think carefully, stay open to every possibility if he was going to save Maggie and Sarah and his mother and sister.

But about Clay and Flex?

His fears increased. Jake walked a few more blocks then went into a small, crowded restaurant. Heading straight for the men's room, he found it empty and ducked out through a low window that overlooked an alley. He couldn't chance being traced to the chemist's shop he intended to visit.

He needed answers. Maybe he could get them there.

Late in the afternoon, Jake returned to the hotel. The telephone was ringing when he walked into his room.

"Jake, thank heavens you're back." Maggie's voice rang with alarm. "I've been worried sick."

"I'm back. Everything's okay."

"Where have you been?"

Jake hesitated. "Why don't you meet me in the bar? We can talk about it over a drink."

"That's...that's fine. I'll be down in five minutes."

Jake hung up wearily. *She knows me too well,* he thought. Maggie had sensed something was wrong, but Jake couldn't tell her what it was.

He walked over and stared out the window, thinking of the last few hours. All he'd discovered was that Clay's prescription contained a mild amount of chloral hydrate. Not enough to kill him even if he drank the whole bottle, but enough to make him violently ill. Knowing Clay, he might still try to ride, but the odds of his winning would be almost nil.

Flex's contacts remained a mystery. The chemist could find nothing unusual in the solution that housed the lenses, which appeared to be of the standard plastic material. Tomorrow he'd work on the puzzle again.

In the meantime, it didn't look like they expected him to commit murder—at least not yet. Maybe things could still work out.

Then he asked himself the question he'd been avoiding all day: *Why would the Soviets go to this much trouble just to ensure that the American team lost the Dublin competition?*

There had to be more to it. Forcing aside his fears, Jake headed downstairs.

Maggie waited in the pub, a popular spot called the Pirate's Den, sipping a glass of white wine. A whiskey and water sat in front of the empty chair across from her, ready and waiting for Jake. She glanced across the room to the staircase just as he reached the bottom step and started toward her. Maggie forced herself to smile, though after worrying about him all day, it was an effort.

Jake sat down and picked up the drink she'd ordered for him. "Thanks."

"Is everything all right? Has something happened?"

"Everything's fine."

"Where did you go? I've been worried sick."

"I just went sightseeing. I wish I could have taken you along, but you know I can't."

"Why not?" she asked peevishly. "It's obvious the Soviets know about us so there's no need to keep our relationship secret."

Jake stiffened. "What makes you think they know?"

Maggie reached for his hand and Jake linked his fingers with hers. "Because you've suddenly become so congenial." She glanced pointedly at their interlocking fingers. "Last week you'd hardly speak to me, let alone hold my hand. Tell me the truth, Jake."

He released a slow breath. "They don't know any more than they did before. I just did some thinking and decided I was overacting. I don't think they'd threaten an American citizen."

"You're an American citizen," she reminded him. "And they're darned well threatening you."

Jake smiled indulgently. "The circumstances are different, and you know it."

"What about Ellie?"

"They were trying to make their point." He managed another smile, but it looked strained.

"And Shep?"

"What happened to Shep had nothing to do with this." He leaned forward in his chair. "Everything's going to be all right, Maggie, but we don't want to take any chances. As long as we remain discreet, there shouldn't be a problem."

Maggie watched him closely. She'd spent enough time with Jake to know he wasn't telling the truth. She would have to keep an eye on him.

Inwardly she smiled. Leaning back in his chair, his white shirt open at the throat, he was one of the most attractive men she'd ever seen. His vivid blue eyes looked at her hungrily, and she knew what he was thinking.

"I suppose you're far too prudent a man to be seen with me at dinner," she said, just to see how he'd react.

"Far too prudent," he agreed with a lazy half smile.

"And far too prudent to Shep dinner altogether and join me in my room?"

His smile faded and his eyes darkened. "Don't tempt me, Maggie. It's all I can do to keep from hauling you up those stairs and into my bed. But I can't afford to involve you in this."

Maggie swallowed. She'd forgotten what a formidable opponent Jake could be.

"I'm sorry," she said, not really sorry at all.

Across the table, Jake relaxed and smiled. "I don't know how I'm going to stay away from you for the next ten days."

You aren't, Maggie thought. "I'm sure you'll find a way. You've always had a will of iron." Moving her foot until her calf rested lightly against his leg, she could feel the lean muscles through the fabric of his trousers.

She *accidently* brushed his leg again and pretended to be unaware of the pleasant sensations.

Jake cleared his throat and moved his leg away. "You probably ought to go," he said, but she heard his half-hearted tone and seized on it.

"I suppose so. I thought I'd prowl around a little, maybe take a taxi ride through the city." She studied him through lowered lashes.

"Oh, no, you don't. It's getting dark. I don't want you going off by yourself. Get Ellie or Prissy to go with you."

"They've already left. I'm tired of staying here alone." Maggie stood up. "I'll be careful, Jake. Besides, you said there was no real danger." She picked up her purse and headed for the door.

Jake caught up with her in two long strides. "I don't want you going out alone."

"I'll be fine."

Jake muttered something beneath his breath. "Damn you,

Maggie, you've got a knack for getting your way."

"Do I?"

"Leave your door unlocked. And get out of those clothes. I'll be up in five minutes."

"But Jake..." Her eyes widened, all innocence.

"Don't push your luck," he said gruffly, but there was amusement in his expression and when his gaze swept down her body, she couldn't mistake the warmth.

"I love you, Jake," she said softly, and then she was gone.

Ellie spent her days in Dublin working with Rose and Jubilee, sightseeing with Flex, or shopping for woolens and crystal with Prissy or Maggie. Shep took her to see the Radio Telefis Eirean Symphony Orchestra in the National Concert Hall. He was still a little battered, his face still bruised and slightly swollen, but his attitude was back to normal.

He grinned as he looked up at the old women on stage of the Concert Hall. "How can such wrinkled faces make such beautiful music? Those old girls look like they're already half dead and the other half is leaving right after the show."

Ellie laughed. "Not all of them are that old. Look at the boy playing the cello. He can't be more than nineteen."

Shep's gaze scanned the singers. "Ah, yes, delicious. You're right, my dear, if one looks hard enough, one can always find a light in the darkness."

Along with Flex, Prissy, Gerry, and several other grooms, she made a trip to the singing pub, the Brazen Head on Bridge St. The lovely Irish ballads turned her a little melancholy, but overall, it was a memorable evening.

As the week slid past, Ellie kept her days and nights so full she had little time to think of Clay. Still, she wondered what he was doing with *his* days and nights. She hated him, she told herself for the ten thousandth time. He was a bastard. It was easier to think of him with anger than the love she had once believed she'd felt for him.

It was just infatuation, she told herself.

Friday night, they all went out to dinner. There'd been no more incidents with the team, and her worry was beginning to fade. Then, just as the meal was ending, Clay walked in. Ellie saw him striding through the door and suddenly couldn't swallow another bite of food.

"Hello, everyone," he said, his tone even.

"Hello, Clay." Prissy cast him a warm smile.

"I don't want to interrupt your dinner. Gerry Winslow told me where to find you. I just dropped by to extend an invitation. My father has taken a place in the country for the weekend. He's having a few friends over, and he'd like to invite you all to come. The house is quite large, so there's plenty of room." He glanced at Jake and then at Prissy. Both of them smiled at him.

Shep fairly beamed. "Personally, I could do with a little bit of hobnobbing. You haven't lived until you've been a guest of Avery Whitfield."

Flex looked uncertain. Ellie knew he was battling his conscience, trying to decide whether, for the sake of the team, to end his feud with Clay.

"I'd like that," he finally said, and Clay looked relieved.

"How about the rest of you?" Clay asked.

"I think it would be good for all of us," Jake said.

Ellie could see he was determined to pull the team together before the competitions in Seoul. *I'm not about to join your little party,* she thought, lifting her chin.

"I'd love to see the Irish countryside," Prissy said.

"So would I," Maggie agreed.

"Ellie?" Jake asked with a pointed glance that warned her to say yes.

She looked at Clay. His expression had tightened. He seemed to be looking at a spot somewhere above her head. *Bastard,* she thought. *I won't let you win.* "I'd like nothing better," she said.

Clay just nodded. "The limousines will be here tomorrow at noon. They'll bring you back Monday morning."

"Sounds wonderful," Prissy said.

"Delicious," Shep added.

"Then I'll see you all tomorrow."

CHAPTER TWENTY-SIX

Now that her decision had been made, Ellie looked forward with relish to the coming confrontation. Two could play this game.

She'd had it up to her ears with Clayton Whitfield. Whitfield had used, humiliated, and shunned her in front of the entire show jumping world. Jake hadn't said anything, but he'd looked at her as if he wanted to. Ellie knew what he was thinking—*you were a fool, Ellie. Don't let it happen again.*

Clay had won every round so far, but he wouldn't win this one. It was Ellie's turn to win.

Up at first light, she packed a traveling bag. Not her usual easy-to-carry suitcase, but a big piece of luggage she packed with infinite care. Choosing an expensive, embroidered, peach-colored sweater and matching linen slacks, she dressed carefully.

She and Prissy had selected the outfit and several others on their shopping excursion last week. The clothes were all elegant. At Prissy's insistence, less conservative and a little more forward in fashion that the usual clothes she wore.

She already had most of what she needed, and when the stores opened this morning, she intended to be the first customer through the door.

Two hours later, a shiny little black taxi dropped her off at Michael Moretti in the Westbury Center off Grafton Street. She'd never used the gold American Express card she carried for emergencies. Today she intended to.

It was extremely short notice to find and fit the perfect evening gown for the black-tie dinner Avery Whitfield was certain to host but find one she would. If the first shop couldn't help her, Richard Allan was nearby, as well as Westbury Designs.

Though she rarely indulged in expensive fashions, she wasn't ignorant of where to find them. After a phone call to her mother, she could find them in Dublin.

"May I be of assistance, madam?" It was the reedy voice of a thin, dark-featured man. There wasn't a trace of an Irish accent, only clipped, no-nonsense British.

"I'm in a hurry. I need an evening gown, fitted and ready to go before I leave here in an hour. Can it be done?"

He smiled, a feral gleam that said for the right price anything could be accomplished.

"Something simple," he said, turning her around for his inspection. "No ruffles, no fuss. Black maybe. No. A luscious emerald green to enhance the color of your eyes."

"That sounds perfect." She flashed him a smile that said she had complete faith in him.

"My name is Mabry Carstairs. I believe we had better get to work."

Ellie nodded and followed him through the heavy silk draperies into the elegant fitting salon.

By twelve o'clock sharp she was back at the hotel, standing next to Prissy and the others, watching as a string of Daimler limousines pulled up to the curb.

"You're looking good," Prissy said, noticing Ellie's polished appearance and satisfied smile.

"I guess I'm looking forward to this after all."

"So I see." Prissy grinned at Ellie's battle stance. "One thing Clay should understand by now—you're a tough competitor, Ellie. I'm glad to see you back in the game."

Ellie smiled. "Thanks, Prissy."

Chauffeurs dressed in black opened the car doors and Ellie saw Clay step out of the first limousine. His eyes flicked over her briefly, then moved on to the others waiting on the curb.

"Good morning," Clay said to them. "I'm glad to see you all could make it. If you haven't had a chance to see the countryside, I think you'll enjoy the ride out to the house."

Everyone voiced their excitement, and the drivers loaded the bags as team members filled each car. Clay had already climbed back inside.

"Why don't we ride with Clay?" Ellie said to Prissy. Her friend's mouth dropped open.

Ellie didn't wait, just ducked through the open car door and sat down on the seat next to Clay. His eyebrows shot up in surprise, then drew together in a frown as Prissy slid into the seat beside them and the driver closed the door.

She wondered if the warmth of his thigh against hers bothered him as much as it did her, then forced herself to ignore the tingling that crept over her skin.

"I'm really looking forward to this," she said. "It was very thoughtful of your father—and you, of course—to invite us."

"Thank you," Clay said, but his voice sounded dry. He glanced out the dark-tinted windows and smoothed an imaginary crease from his immaculate navy blue slacks. His nervousness was the first real emotion he'd shown since the night they'd spent together. A thrill of satisfaction shot through her.

Let *him* sweat for a change. *The bastard.* She was ready for him, ready even for Gabriella Marchbanks, or the contessa, or any of the other bits of fluff he might be bringing along.

"You look lovely," he said to her, his eyes going over her more sophisticated appearance. "Both of you," he quickly amended. Prissy had worn a simple beige silk dress. "I almost didn't recognize you, Ellie."

Ellie flashed him a carefully controlled smile. With her hair slicked into a stylish chignon at the nape of her neck, expensive high heels, and a little more makeup than she usually wore, she looked older, more remote. It was exactly the look she wanted.

"It's time I changed my look, begun to dress a little more mature. This makes me appear more cosmopolitan, don't you think?"

Clay couldn't quite meet her eyes. "I rather liked you the way you were," he said gruffly.

"Well, I love it," Prissy put in before Ellie could reply. "It gives her an aura of sophistication, a certain presence. If your father throws his usual gala affair, we'll be able to see if the effect is as dazzling as I think it is."

Clay just grumbled and looked out the window.

"When I get back to the States," Ellie said, "I'm going to throw out my entire wardrobe, make a trip to Saks and start all over. Then I think I'll get a new car. Somehow I don't think my little Toyota will be right for my new image."

"What kind of car so you want?" Clay asked, brows pulled together in disapproval.

"Oh, I don't know, maybe a Porsche. That might be fun."

Prissy smiled at Clay. "You know the difference between a Porsche and a cactus, don't you?" She flashed Clay a grin. "The pricks are on the outside of a cactus."

Ellie laughed. "What's the difference between a woman and a car? A car doesn't get excited when you shove a hose into its—"

"Don't," Clay said, his frown even deeper. "It doesn't become you. Or is that part of your new image as well?"

Prissy sliced him a glance. "When did you turn into a prude?"

"I'm not a prude. I just don't think what happened between Ellie and me should turn her into something she's not."

Ellie just smiled. "I think that's a rather conceited statement, Clay. What makes you think a little romance could have that much effect on me?"

"A little romance! Is that what you call it?" Clay's face turned red, and Ellie felt a rush of satisfaction.

"I'd rather we didn't discuss this in front of Prissy," she said. "Maybe we can find a moment or two this weekend, if you really feel there's something that needs to be said. In the meantime, you were right about the scenery. It's quite spectacular."

As the caravan of limousines headed out of Dublin, Clay clamped his jaw and leaned back against the deep red leather seat.

"What's that?" Prissy asked, leaning across Ellie to get a better look at some sort of battlements atop Mount Pelier.

"That's the Hellfire Club," Clay said with studied nonchalance. "Or what's left of it. The ruins can be seen for miles. It was a club for eighteen century rakes, people who wished to take part in immoral acts."

Ellie lifted an eyebrow. "Really? I suppose you would know more about that than I."

Clay glanced away. Ellie didn't miss the lines of tension around his mouth.

They drove on through the lush green landscape, along roads lined with bright yellow gorse, past ancient churches, weathered cottages, and centuries-old monuments. The drive took them past

Glencullen, Kilteman, and the Scalp, into Enniskerry, one of the prettiest villages in Ireland.

"It's lovely," Ellie said softly, for a moment forgetting her newly acquired role of sophisticate. "Like something out of a storybook."

Clay flashed her a questioning glance, reminding her of her new, woman-of-the-world role, so Ellie added, "Of course there's probably so little to do, one would find oneself bored in a fortnight."

Clay started scowling, and Prissy pressed Ellie's thigh in a sort of female code for a high-five. It was all Ellie could do to stifle a triumphant grin. Clay obviously preferred the ingénue to the sophisticate. Someone naïve enough to fall for his phony charm instead a woman who would laugh at his practiced lines.

Well, Ellie—no Ellen Elizabeth Fletcher—had only just begun!

Clay glanced out the window, trying to fathom the sudden turn of events. Things weren't going at all as he'd planned. In fact, far from it. For the sake of the team, he'd hoped to speak to Ellie in private, tell her he was sorry, explain how ill-suited they were, tell her how much better off she was without him.

It appeared all his arrangements had been for naught. Ellie seemed to be handling their estrangement just fine. *Too fine,* he thought, and realized how much it rankled him.

He wanted her to be upset, he grudgingly admitted. Wanted her despondent at his leaving.

He hated this new woman Ellie seemed bound and determined to become. He hadn't seen much of her lately, purposely staying away. Had their single night of lovemaking changed her so completely?

It was possible, he knew. What had happed in Monaco had certainly changed him.

He glanced at Ellie, sitting regally beside him. When she felt his eyes on her, she tilted her chin at precisely the angle to display her features to their best advantage. It was a gesture he might have expected from Gabriella, or Angela, but never from Ellie. Where was the warm, vibrant woman who had captured his heart?

Clay looked back out the window. Outside the car, the wild splendor of the Wicklow Mountains passed by. The road wound its way through some of the most beautiful country in the world.

They drove through Glendalough, a secluded, wooded valley

between two lakes, arriving at their destination, Castle Glenmorra, not a moment too soon for Clay.

"Good heavens," Ellie said. "This is what your father calls a house? It looks more like a palace." Her face lit up with childish delight, that *joie de vive* Clay had come to love.

His heart began to pound. He felt her leg pressing against his, smelled her subtle perfume, and his blood began to pound.

Damn! He'd come up with the idea for this weekend in order to put things right between the members of the team, not to set himself up for more problems with Ellie. He'd have to stay away from her, steel himself as he had before. He could do it, he knew. He'd kept his emotions controlled for most of his life. He was even better at it now.

Waiting as the car slowed to a stop, Ellie's excited look faded, replaced by her newly acquired veneer. She was making it easy, Clay thought. Becoming the kind of person he'd come to hate almost as much as he'd hated ending their ill-fated affair.

"Actually, this is the ancestral estate of the Baron of Lahinch," he said dryly. "My father has expensive taste." Then the chauffer opened the door.

"Have you ever seen anything like this?" Ellie whispered to Prissy as they climbed the massive marble staircase, the sound of their voices echoing off the stone walls. The huge, vaulted entry was magnificently paneled in walnut, exquisitely carved, and lit with ornate gilded sconces. Original oil paintings hung above ancient suits of armor.

Prissy's gaze followed hers. "The Whitfields sure know how to live."

Ellie was shown to a huge sleeping chamber, Prissy to one across the hall. From the frescoed ceilings to the tapestry-draped four-poster bed, the castle spoke of an elegance long forgotten. Even though she had to put up with Clay, Ellie was glad she'd gotten a glimpse of an era and a way of life few people ever discovered.

A black-suited servant brought up her bags, which were unpacked by a uniformed maid.

"You ready?" Prissy stuck her head through the door. Avery had invited the guests to what he termed "a light repast" by the pool. Ellie had changed into a mauve silk jumpsuit, very chic, and drawn her hair into a long ponytail that started at the top of her head.

"Ready as I'll ever be."

Dressed in a two-piece navy linen pant suit piped in white, Prissy flashed her an approving glance. "Didn't take you long to catch onto the high society look."

"My mother has a passion for clothes. For years she's been dying to get me to dress like this. Up until now, it wasn't my style."

"Times do change," Prissy teased.

Ellie grinned. "Clay said I was a quick study."

"I think he's eating his heart out."

That was a sobering thought. "I doubt it. But I can't help hoping you're right."

They headed downstairs to join the rest of the team members as well as the dozens of other guests Avery had invited. Ellie's armor was holding up and she felt good about herself for the first time in days. She'd show Clayton Whitfield.

Or damn well die trying.

Though he tried to remain immune, Clay found himself watching Ellie throughout the day. The poolside party, overflowing with guests invited in honor of the team, provided her an endless stream of admirers. The laughter, flirtatious smiles, and teasing expressions she bestowed on the men around her aroused feelings in Clay more powerful than anything he'd been prepared for.

His emotions ran the gauntlet—anger, jealousy disappointment, humiliation, and heartache.

The wealthy young men lavished Ellie with compliments, fetched her drinks, and vied with each other for her attention. Ellie toyed with them, flirted, bantered, did all the things a charming, utterly sophisticated female knew how to do.

Then he discovered—to his utter amazement and profound relief—that when Ellie thought he wasn't watching, her sophisticated façade disappeared, her shoulders drooped, and she sagged as if she'd been delivered from the tortures of hell.

She's acting, he realized with an astonished grin as he watched her performance from his vantage point on the terrace above her. *She's been acting from the start.*

Thank God his cruel treatment hadn't truly destroyed her.

Feeling as if a weight had been lifted off his shoulders, Clay sank down on a gray marble bench and looked out across the manicured lawns, past the formal gardens, to the lake. Dusk was beginning to fall. The guests were retreating to their rooms to change for dinner.

His mind returned to Ellie. *She's amazing,* he thought with an inward smile. As usual, he'd been underestimating her. Maybe this time he'd learn his lesson.

Glancing back to where Franklin Marston, one of his father's friends, had spotted her and begun a conversation, Clay felt a rush of admiration—grudging, he admitted, since he was the butt of her joke.

Jake said she had balls—and heart. Clay had discovered those qualities some time ago but mistakenly believed they applied only to the sport she loved. Now he realized just how much strength she had.

On the grounds below, Ellie had moved away from Marston and was heading into the castle on the arm of Darren McKittrick, a fortyish playboy who owned a large block of stock in Whitfield International, one of the family's trading companies. Olive-skinned and handsome, McKittrick was an even more notorious ladies' man than Clay.

His chest tightened. Damn, he had to stop reacting this way.

At the sound of a soft knock, Maggie turned toward the French-paned doors that led onto a secluded terrace outside her room. Hurriedly, she pinned her hair back with a rhinestone comb and headed for the door. Parting the heavy silk draperies, she unlocked the door and turned the knob to find Jake standing outside. With a rakish smile, he stepped over the threshold, and Maggie went into his arms.

"Our rooms share the same private terrace," he said against her ear, tightening his hold. "Apparently Clay has his suspicions about us."

When Maggie pulled back to look at him, Jake bent his head and kissed her, a tender kiss, but one that made his passion clear. He looked magnificent in his black tuxedo, his shoes so shiny they reflected the amber glow of the gilded wall sconces.

"I knew Clay was a romantic at heart," Maggie said when Jake pulled away.

"I can't say I'm sorry. Though I probably should be. This is damned dangerous, and we both know it."

"I don't care. God only knows what could happen next week."

Jake kissed her again, this time more deeply, and heat slid out

245

through her limbs. Maggie could feel the warmth of his hands on her body as he pulled her closer, letting her feel his arousal. He kissed her a moment more, then, with a heavy sigh, set her away.

"If we keep this up, we'll never make it downstairs," he said.

"I suppose it would be rude not to at least make an appearance."

Jake smiled. "Have I told you how beautiful you look tonight?" His gaze swept over her bare shoulders, down the snug-fitting bodice of her pale peach, watered-silk gown, over the gently belled skirt. Beneath his hot gaze, her breasts pebbled beneath the fabric.

Maggie smiled. "It isn't something a woman can hear too often."

"Well, you look lovely. And thanks to Whitfield, I suddenly find myself looking forward to the evening. I suppose I'll have to forgive him for all the trouble he's caused."

"He's doing this to set things right."

"I know." Jake ran a finger down Maggie's cheek. "I'd better go. I'll see you downstairs, but now that I've discovered your terrace door, I hope you aren't planning a lengthy evening."

Maggie smiled. "Dinner and a dance or two with you, the handsome *Chef d' Equipe,* and I'm certain to develop a headache."

"Just make sure it disappears by the time you get undressed."

Violins played softly as Clay greeted guests in satins and silks, sequins and tuxedos. His father stood across the way, shaking hands and smiling, a buxom blonde named Marian clinging to his arm. Some of the guests Clay knew, some were unfamiliar, friends of his father's or members of the Irish show jumping community.

Clay's glance flicked to the doorway where he continued to search for Ellie. It was Prissy who walked into the room.

"Hi, Clay," she said. "You sure know how to throw a shindig."

"Thank you." He glanced back at the door.

"She'll be here any minute." Prissy smiled, and Clay felt the heat at the back of his neck.

"I was looking for Flex."

"Sure, you were. Why don't you just admit it? For once in your life, you're hooked."

"Don't be ridiculous, Prissy. Ellie and I are about as well-suited as a maiden aunt and a pimp."

246

"Have it your way. Looks to me like she's getting over you just fine. She certainly doesn't seem to be hurting for attention."

Shep strolled up beside them. "Who's hurting for attention?" Champagne glass in hand, silver hair gleaming above his tailored black evening clothes, Shep glanced around the room. "I'm the only one hurting around here. And I never did get the attention I deserved."

Prissy laughed. Turning Shep's face with her hand, she inspected the fading bruises, now a purplish gray. "Poor Shep."

"Poor Shep is right." Then he spotted Martin Saperstein, one of Avery's entourage, talking to a handsome black-haired man in his late twenties. When the young man caught Shep's interested look, he smiled back so warmly there was no mistaking the invitation. Shep grinned. "Maybe poor Shep will have a change of luck."

Shep excused himself and so did Prissy.

Then Flex walked in.

"I'm glad you came," Clay said, extending a hand.

Flex accepted it with a smile. "I'm glad you invited me. Nice party. Your father's idea or yours?"

"Mine."

"Listen, Clay, I'm sorry about what happened. I shouldn't have hit you, but you have to admit you deserved it."

Clay grinned. "More than you'll ever know."

"She seems to be picking up the pieces."

"She'll be fine."

"You could have let her down a little easier."

"If I could have, I would have."

"Which means?"

"Which means it wasn't easy for me, either."

Flex's eyes widened and opened his mouth to speak. Clay stopped him with a warning glance.

"Sorry," Flex said. He glanced around. "I wonder where she is?"

As if on cue, Ellie swept through the door on Darren McKittrick's arm. He was smiling at her, totally entranced, and Ellie was smiling back. This time it didn't appear to be an act, and Clay was suddenly furious.

"Like I said, she seems to be on the mend."

"So I see." Without a farewell, Clay left Flex and followed

247

McKittrick and Ellie into the main salon. Heading for the bar, he ordered a Glenfiddich on the rocks, but his eyes never left Ellie.

"Great party, eh, son?" Avery walked up beside him, the blonde still clinging to his arm. Though his father was twenty-six years Clay's senior, dressed in a black tuxedo, as Clay was, the resemblance between them was striking.

"I think they're all enjoying themselves."

"There's your little redhead." His dad pointed rudely in Ellie's direction. "For once in my life, I was wrong. Get her all decked out, she's a real looker."

It figured his father would change his opinion as soon as Ellie began to fit in with the rest of the social elite. Tonight, she wore a floor-length designer gown of emerald crepe de chine. There was little trim, just two narrow rhinestone straps that went over her bare shoulders, and a small self-bow in front that subtly emphasized the soft white mounds of her breasts.

The lines of the garment were simple and elegant, showing off her figure to perfection, accenting the gentle curves Clay remembered only too well. Her hair was swept up in back, but left undisciplined around her face, giving her a very stylish, almost pagan appearance. Desire slipped through him, and his body stirred to life.

"Since you aren't seeing her anymore," Avery added, "I guess she wasn't much good in bed."

Clay bristled. "Ellie and I were ill-suited on a far different level, I assure you. Now, if you'll excuse me, I believe we're being summoned to dinner."

CHAPTER TWENTY-SEVEN

Throughout the meal, which was as sumptuous as only Avery Whitfield and a kitchen full of chefs could make it, Ellie fought not to look at Clay.

To her surprise, Darren McKittrick had been seated beside her. She had a feeling he'd pressed Avery to accommodate him. Clay obviously disapproved, though she didn't really understand why since he wasn't interested himself. And since he had chosen not to invite one of his women friends—for the good of the team, she supposed—Ellie was feeling quite proud of herself.

After dinner, she danced with an endless number of handsome, available men and was pleased to find Clay scowling even harder. By midnight she was tiring, and Darren was back at her side.

"Why don't we go for a walk?" he suggested. "You look a little weary."

"I am. Thank you, Darren, that would be nice."

When they reached the massive carved wooden doors that led onto the lower terrace, Ellie was surprised to see Clay appear in front of them.

"Going for a midnight stroll?"

"Ms. Fletcher would like a little air. Any objections?"

"As a matter of fact, I do."

Ellie's eyebrows shot up.

"I see." Darren's lips tightened and his arm settled at her waist. "And what about you, Ms. Fletcher? Do you also object?"

She straightened. "This is none of your business, Clay. I'd appreciate it if you'd take your belated concern someplace else."

"Ellie, listen to me. You don't know him. He's a philanderer.

He's—"

"Like you?" she interrupted. "Excuse us." She urged Darren through the door. Clay frowned but didn't follow.

"What the hell's the matter with him?" Darren grumbled.

"He's just being Clay."

Darren laughed at that, and they crossed the terrace, onto the sweeping lawns. Ellie took off her shoes and left them on an old stone bench as they strolled along the lake, getting farther and farther from the castle. The wet grass soaked her stockings but relieved the ache in her feet. There was a boathouse down by the water, a small sailboat bobbing at the end of a rope that moored it to a little wooden dock.

"Why don't we go aboard?" Darren asked. "Avery said it comes with the castle."

Ellie glanced back toward the house, now looking like a brightly jeweled toy in the distance. "I don't think so. We'd better be getting back."

"Relax," Darren said, rubbing a hand along her arm and pulling her through the trees toward the boat. "It's early. We could go for a sail if you want."

"Maybe tomorrow." They were standing at the water's edge among a thicket of fir and spruce.

Ellie turned away from him, but he pressed her back against the trunk of a tree and moved closer. Before she realized his intentions, he had lowered his head and kissed her. She could taste the licorice cordial he'd been drinking. He smelled of some musky cologne. Warm fingers caressed her shoulders, but to her disappointment, Ellie felt nothing.

"Don't, Darren." She pressed her hands against his chest, unhappy that Clay still loomed so strongly in her thoughts. "You've been very nice all evening, but I really must be getting back."

His voice turned cold. "Don't play coy with me. I know you wanted me to kiss you." Leaning closer, he trapped her against the tree, captured her face between his hands, and kissed her so hard she tasted blood.

Though she tried to break away, he held her easily. One hand cupped her breast while his thumb rubbed back and forth across her nipple. More angry than afraid and hoping her dress wouldn't get in the way, Ellie kicked him in the shin.

"Get away from me!"

"Ouch! That hurt. What the hell do you think you're doing?" He said something foul beneath his breath but didn't let her go. "Don't try to play innocent with me. Everybody knows you put out for Whitfield. Now that he's through with you, how about giving me a chance?"

"Go to hell!" Though she fought to kick him again, Darren only laughed and began trailing kisses along her shoulder.

She was furious but his cruel words burned deeper than his touch. She was about to twist free when she felt him lifted away, a look of surprise on his face. Clay had a hand on the nape of his neck and another on the seat of his pants. With a quick turn and heave, Clay tossed him into the lake.

Ellie just stood there gaping. Darren came up sputtering, water running down his face, bits of leaves and twigs in his hair, his evening clothes plastered against his body. Shouting obscenities and shaking his fists, he sloshed ashore.

"I'll get you for this, Whitfield!" But he headed for the castle, wanting no more of Clay.

When Ellie turned, she found Clay grinning, his cheeks dimpled in the moonlight. The sight had her grinning in return. In seconds they were laughing together the way that had what seemed eons ago.

"It's good to hear you laugh," Clay said softly as they began to regain their composure.

"It's been a while."

He walked to where she stood beside the tree.

"Thank you, Clay. I guess I should have listened to your warning."

"You couldn't have known." Clay reached a hand to the ponytail that had slid haphazardly to the side and pulled the band, freeing her hair. He spread the heavy curls around her shoulders. "That's better."

It had been so long since he'd touched her, so long since he'd looked at her with such tenderness. A lump formed in her throat.

"I never meant to hurt you," he said.

She read the sincerity in his face. "I know." She'd known all along, she realized. She just hadn't been ready to accept it.

"At first it was just a game...a challenge. Then later...." He released a slow breath. "Later it became something more." He glanced

251

back toward the castle. "I heard what he said. I'm sorry for the grief I've caused you."

She only nodded, afraid to trust her voice. He looked so dear, and she had missed him so much.

"We'd better be getting back," he said.

Ellie shook her head. "I'm not ready yet. I'll be all right out here for a while. Darren won't be back."

Clay smiled, a bit sadly, she thought. "No, I don't suppose he will." He watched her a moment. "I'll see you back at the house." Turning, he started toward the castle.

"Clay?"

He stopped and turned, his black satin lapel gleaming in the moonlight, lighting the sun streaks in his dark hair. "Yes?"

"Prissy told me what happened in Monaco. About the drugs— and the women."

His expression tightened, turned grim, as if he were reliving a painful memory. "She gave me her word."

"It was hard for her. She said something about being a romantic."

"If she told you what happened, then you know what kind of man I am."

Ellie's throat closed-up. "I know exactly what kind of man you are," she said softly. "It's you who isn't sure."

She wondered if he understood how much he had to offer, how intelligent he was, how sensitive he could be.

"I'd better be going." With a last soft glance, he started striding away.

Ellie's eyes filled. She couldn't stop the words from spilling out. "Would you do it again?"

Clay stopped and turned. "Again?"

"What happened in Monaco. If we could replay that morning, would you do it again?"

His incredulous gaze went to hers, the lines of his face so drawn and tight he seemed a character from the pages of a tragedy.

"My, God, I'd die before I'd hurt you again. I never meant to...I shouldn't have left you...I love you...I'd never do anything to—" Clay broke off, realizing what he had said. His stricken look said he wished he could call back the words.

Ellie's heart twisted. The tears in her eyes spilled onto her cheeks. Those times they were together, the way he had looked at her. The way he had made love to her that night. *Clay loved her.* He would never lie about something like that. She hadn't imagined it.

With a soft sob, she gathered her emerald gown and raced toward him across the grass. When she reached the little knoll where he stood, he caught her up in his arms and held her hard against him.

"I've missed you so much," he said. She could feel him shaking, feel the pounding of his heart.

"I love you, Clay," she whispered as she clung to him. "I love you so much."

He kissed her then, a wild, hot, needy kiss, and yet it was the sweetest, most tender kiss she had ever known. She kissed him back, her heart swelling with love for him.

"Are you sure?" Clay asked, his beautiful brown eyes searching her face.

"I love you. I know the man you are inside. That's the man I fell in love with."

Clay kissed her softly. "Marry me," he whispered, and Ellie's heart broke for this man she loved so much.

"It doesn't have to be right away," he said. "If you aren't ready, you can take whatever time you need to be sure."

She had to ask. "Could you...could you be happy with only one woman? Could you spend a lifetime with only me? I could never share you, Clay. I love you too much."

His hands framed her face. "I don't need a throng of women to make me feel like a man anymore. I've learned things about myself, about who I really am. You're what I want. What I've wanted for a long time. If you need me to prove it, we'll wait. I'd wait for you forever, Ellie."

Fresh tears rolled down her cheeks. "Oh, Clay. I'll marry you. I'd marry you tomorrow, if that's what you wanted."

Clay kissed her again. His hand cupped her cheek. "When I saw you leaving with McKittrick something just snapped. I couldn't let him touch you. Not when I love you so damned much."

Ellie smiled at him softly. "Tell me again."

Clay's big hand rested against her cheek. "I love you more than life."

"Oh, Clay." She thought that he would kiss her, but he just stood there, waiting for her to decide whether she would forgive him. "I want you, Clay. It's been so long since we were together."

"I want you, too. There's been no one else. I haven't wanted anyone else. Only you."

"I've thought of that night so many times. I remember every moment, every touch." She glanced over at the little sailboat bobbing against the dock. "Make love to me, Clay."

Clay leaned down and kissed her. "Yes," he said. "I won't hurt you this time. I'll never do anything to hurt you again." Sweeping her up in his powerful arms, he carried her down to the wooden dock and set her on her feet on the deck of the sailboat, the teak cold beneath her stockinged feet. Clay stepped aboard and kissed her again. When the fiery kiss ended, his gaze searched her face. Then he took her hand and led her below. In seconds, he had a small gas lamp burning. A wide berth upholstered in sturdy brown tweed filled the bow of the boat. Water lapped softly against the hull.

Ellie felt the heat of his hands as they skimmed over body, slipping off the narrow rhinestone straps of her gown, sliding down the hidden zipper. Feverishly, she pushed his jacket off his broad shoulders, worked the buttons on this white tuxedo shirt, the button at the waist of his slacks, then his zipper.

Clay gently kissed her. "I tried to forget you, but you were all I could think about. There's no one else for me, Ellie. Not ever. Only you."

Her throat ached. She hadn't been wrong about Clay. She had followed her heart and it had been true. She kissed him full on the mouth. They took off the rest of their clothes and Clay lifted her up on the berth in the tiny cabin, then joined her.

"I'll make you happy, Ellie. I promise, you won't be sorry. I won't ever let you be sorry."

"I'll never be sorry, Clay."

He kissed her deeply while he settled himself between her legs. He trailed kisses over her shoulders, down to her breasts where he captured the peak and tugged it gently into his mouth. Ellie laced her fingers in his hair as Clay moved lower, his tongue darting into her navel, his lips sliding over the flat spot below. When he started moving lower, Ellie jerked upright in surprise.

"It's all right, love." Clay eased her back on the berth. "Let me do this for you. Let me pleasure you."

Ellie started to protest, but the heat of his mouth moving over her washed any thought of protest away. Ellie cried his name as she reached the pinnacle, and deep saturating pleasure spilled through her. The moment went on and on. Tiny ripples still pulsed through her body as Clay came up over her, braced himself on his elbows and slid himself inside.

"Ellie," he whispered, kissing her again. "I love you so much." The heavy hard feel of him rekindled her passion, and she arched against him, lifting her hips to meet each of his thrusts.

Digging her fingers into the bands of muscle across his shoulders, she heard him whisper her name and tightened her hold on his neck. Her body clenched around him as she reached another shattering release. Seconds later, Clay groaned, shuddered, and gave himself up to his own powerful 255elease.

Together they spiraled down. Easing her into his arms, Clay settled himself on the bunk beside her.

"Everything's going to be all right now," he said, more to himself than to her.

"Yes..." she said softly.

Clay was her lover, her friend, and he had found his way home to her.

He was hers as it seemed he was meant to be. But Ellie wondered what would happen when Clay's father found out.

And she worried that Avery might find a way to ruin what they both seemed to want so badly.

CHAPTER TWENTY-EIGHT

An eleven o'clock poolside brunch had been scheduled for the following morning, late enough to allow the revelers to recover from last night's party.

Ellie arrived to find Clay already there, along with Avery and just about everyone else. She and Clay had returned to the castle a little before dawn, she to her room, he to his. From the moment they parted, she'd been assailed by doubts.

Her mind kept remembering the way they had parted before. Clay had left her alone in a London hotel room and gone off with another woman. She remembered the betrayal she had felt, the seemingly endless pain. Last night, in an emotion-filled moment, Clay had asked her to marry him, but he hadn't mentioned it again.

They'd spent the night making love, passionately yet tenderly, stirring emotions even more intense than before. But what would happen now?

In a white linen pants suit, her hair in loose curls, the way Clay liked it, she headed outside, her heart beating a little too fast. What would he say when he saw her? How would he treat her?

Spotting him on the pool deck, she summoned a tentative smile. Clay saw her, and his return smile she was so bright and so full of pleasure it made emotion twisted her heart. In beige gabardine slacks, alligator shoes, and a white shirt with the sleeves rolled up, he looked impossibly handsome.

Clay picked up a crystal flute filled with orange juice and champagne and tapped it lightly with a silver spoon. In seconds, the ringing began to quiet the crowd.

Clay's deep voice did the rest. "Excuse me, everyone. Could I please have your attention?" All eyes turned in his direction as Clay strode across the terrace to her side. She felt the warmth of his hand at her waist and the reassuring sweetness of his smile, and some of her nervousness faded.

"First, I'd like to thank my friends, those of you who are fool enough to admit it, for putting up with me for all these years. In one way or another, when I really needed you, each of you has been there for me. But I especially want to thank Prissy—for having the courage of her convictions—and a lot more sense than I have."

A slight chuckle went through the crowd, though no one completely understood the comment. Prissy hoisted her glass in mock salute and smiled.

Clay put an arm around Ellie's shoulders and her eyes filled with tears. "Last night I asked Ellen Fletcher to marry me. She has done me the great honor of accepting. Today I feel like the luckiest man in the world."

After a moment of stunned silence, everyone cheered. Flex was on his feet in an instant, engulfing Clay in a warm man-hug. Prissy was crying and hugging Ellie, Shep was smiling. Jake looked surprised and pleased, and Maggie discreetly dabbed at her eyes.

Only Avery didn't seem happy. With a scowl that made his opinion clear, he signaled the waiter to refill his glass then drained it in a single long swallow.

"Congratulations, son," he said, approaching Clay at last. The smile on his face looked tight. "I said she was a looker, didn't I?" He laughed a little, the sound forced, and turned in Ellie's direction. "You're a brave girl, Ellie. A woman willing to take on a man like Clay. A man of his appetites, I mean." He winked. "She's either got a lotta grit—or she's downright crazy!" Avery laughed.

Ellie tensed. "I love him, Avery." Instinctively, she knew she'd never call him father. A man like Avery Whitfield hated to be reminded of his age.

"Of course, my dear. He's my son, isn't he?" He turned to the circle of people surrounding them. "A toast." He lifted his glass. "To the bride and groom. May they both come to their senses before it's too late!"

There was a round of nervous laughter, but nobody drank.

"To the future bride and groom," Flex put in smoothly. "May they continue to enjoy the happiness they've found in each other. It took them long enough!" Everyone laughed, lifted their glass, and drank to Clay and Ellie. More champagne flowed, corks popping while the guests drank freely, each excited by the news.

From across the terrace, Maggie watched Jake congratulate the happy couple as she had done a few minutes earlier. He seemed genuinely pleased for them.

They were a good match, Maggie thought. In an opposite way, maybe as good as she and Jake. Ellie brought out Clay's more sensitive nature while Clay generated a certain strength in Ellie.

Maggie sighed and took a sip of champagne. Seeing the glow on Ellie's face and the happiness and pride in Clay's only made her own situation more heartbreaking.

She and Jake had spent every clandestine moment they could together, the time more precious because of the uncertainty ahead. Jake had told her, albeit grudgingly, that whatever the Soviets were planning seemed likely to happen this week.

The show would end on Saturday, the team leaving for home on Sunday. Would she and Jake be together this time next month? Or would something happen so terrible it would keep them apart forever?

After a last glance at Jake, Maggie quietly left the terrace. The beautiful Irish countryside was alive with colorful red and yellow blossoms, their sweet scent filling the air. The grass was a vibrant green, the air so crisp and clear the surrounding mountains seemed only a few short meters away.

Maggie plucked a delicate pink rose, the petals soft beneath her fingers, and sank down on an old stone bench in the garden. She still didn't know what the Soviets wanted Jake to do, but she was determined to find out. And equally determined to stop him.

After this weekend, she was more convinced than ever that Jake had decided to comply. He was too resigned, too determined to enjoy what little time they had left.

"I wish we were the ones announcing our engagement," Jake said softly as he walked up beside her.

Maggie looked up at him and managed a tremulous smile. "So do I. But I'm glad for them. It's obvious they love each other very much."

Jake nodded. "It's a side of Clay I've rarely seen. But I had a hunch he was far more complicated than he appeared."

"I had a feeling Clay cared more for Ellie than he was willing to admit," Maggie said.

"Thanks to his father, Clay's always kept his emotions locked away."

Jake glanced back toward the pool where Clay had an arm wrapped protectively around Ellie. "I'm not really surprised he fell in love with her. Ellie has a lot to offer a man.

Maggie followed his gaze. "Avery's going to give them fits."

"Unless Clay puts a stop to it."

"He's never confronted his father before. I'm not sure he'll be willing to do it this time."

Jake's hard look settled on Avery. "Neither am I."

The Dublin Horse Show, held at the Ballsbridge Show Grounds, began on Tuesday. The setting, with fields of lush green grass and beautiful flowers, was alive with pageantry. Fifteen hundred horses had been brought together for events that included international show jumping, the Dublin Show Chase, and Irish National jumping competitions. Pony jumping, hunter jumping, driving horses, dressage, and countless other events were scheduled.

On Friday, the prestigious Aga Khan Trophy would go to the winner of the Nations' Cup. On Saturday the individual international stars would compete in the Grand Prix of Ireland.

Jake had prowled the show grounds, checking the horses incessantly and reviewing the team's equipment, but he couldn't get his mind off the final demand the Soviets planned to make on Friday. His anxiety and constant fear of surveillance were keeping him on edge.

"Have a good weekend?"

Jake jumped at the sound of Daniel's low voice. "Damn, you scared the hell out of me." They stood at the back of the arena watching a group of thoroughbred and Irish draught stallions being judged.

"Sorry." Daniel took a long, appraising look at him. The man had always been good at reading people. Jake did his best to appear nonchalant.

"Why do I get the feeling you've heard from the Soviets and haven't told me?" Daniel said.

Jake held his gaze. "What makes you think that?"

"Because you're jumpy as hell, and the way you're acting,

259

something's coming down and it's coming down soon."

Jake fought the impulse to lie. Daniel was an astute observer and a very good friend. "You could be wrong," he said, buying time. "It isn't much fun having someone watching your every move. I could just be worried about the team."

"And Maggie Delaine?"

Jake bit back a curse. "What's she got to do with this?"

"We've been friends too long, Jake. Why don't you just level with me?"

So far there wasn't that much to tell. Jake released a slow, resigned breath. "You're right. They did make contact. But what they're asking isn't life threatening. I want your word as my friend you won't interfere."

"You know I can't do that. You'll have to tell me what's going on and let me make the decision."

"Sorry. Too risky."

Daniel laid a hand on Jake's shoulder. "I only want to help, Jake. There are a million things the agency could do to stop you. We could have you taken in for questioning or flown home on some sort of phony emergency. But that's not what we want. We want to help you solve this problem so no one else gets hurt."

Jake thought of the years he and Daniel had been friends. He hadn't forgotten the hours of conversation, the dinners they'd shared in Washington during those first trying months when Jake had first arrived and hadn't known a soul.

Then later in Charleston. Jake had become a successful businessman by then, and Daniel was pleased and proud of his accomplishments.

"All right, I'll tell you." With a calmness he didn't feel, Jake related the most recent happenings, including the threats against Maggie and Sarah, and the package he'd picked up in the tobacconist's shop.

He relayed every detail but one—the demand the Soviets would be making on Friday.

"Something's not right," Daniel said. "I'll have our people look at the package they gave you, have the contents re-analyzed. If they're as you've described, you can do as they ask. It's a shame McGrath and Whitfield have to suffer, but under the circumstances we have no choice."

Daniel rested a thick hand on the arena fence. "Are their people following you?"

"They must be. Back home, they made no bones about it. Here, I haven't been able to spot their tail, but they damned well know my every move."

Daniel shook his head. "I wish I knew what the hell this is about."

"So do I."

"You're sure there's nothing more?" Daniel pinned him with a last hard stare.

"That's it so far. Maybe they'll expect more from me in Seoul." He glanced at the huge draught stallions in the arena. Anything to avoid his friend's perceptive gaze. "Anything new on your end?" he asked.

"Nothing good. We know there are some high-ranking officials involved, which is why their demands seem so out of proportion to the effort they've expended."

Daniel's gaze followed Jake's into the arena. "Whatever happens, I think this should be the last direct contact you and I make— at least until we get back home. I don't want to take any chances."

Jake just nodded.

"If something new develops or you need anything..." Daniel handed him a folded slip of paper with a local phone number on it. "Be sure you call from a pay phone."

"What about the package?"

"Bring the items down to the stable in the morning. One of our undercover people will pick it up and return it as soon as we're through testing."

"All right."

"Good luck, Jake." Smiling at a passerby, Daniel moved away, blending easily into the throng of horse people watching the competition.

The next few days progressed uneventfully, except that early in the evening on Wednesday the water line that serviced the team barn broke, leaving grooms from the Canadian, British, and American teams hauling water from quite some distance away. The problem was rectified early the following morning.

That day Julius Caesar pulled a muscle in his foreleg going over a water jump.

"He'll be all right." Lee Montalvo, the team vet, spoke to Prissy and Damien Gould of the Greenbriar Stables, the horse's owner. "But he won't be competing again until Seoul."

Lee was a top-notch veterinarian who specialized in horses. His family had emigrated from the Philippines just after the war.

"You're sure the horse will be all right?" Gould asked, thick gray eyebrows drawn together in a frown.

"The injury isn't that serious, but we don't want to take any chances."

With Caesar out, Jake wanted Ellie to ride Jubilee in the Nations' Cup. The way she'd been competing, combined with Jube's shining performance at Hickstead, Ellie would be an asset to the team.

Daniel's people were working to verify the contents of the package, but Jake didn't have time to wait. Since the medicine would probably make Clay too sick to ride, Prissy would wind up riding her alternate horse, Deuteronomy.

Through it all, Maggie had been sticking to Jake like fly paper, sure something was going to happen and determined to help in some way. Jake had indulged her at first but when she showed up at the stable the third morning in a row, he lost his temper.

"Damn it, Maggie, if you don't take your sweet little ass back to wherever it belongs, I'm going to haul it there for you. How's that going to look to your associates back home?"

Maggie just smiled. "I only wanted to see how you were doing. I missed you."

"Well, I haven't had time to miss you. You've been underfoot for days."

She smiled as if the remark meant nothing, but he couldn't miss the hurt in her eyes. He wanted to hold her, tell her everything would be okay, but he couldn't afford the luxury. Still, it was impossible for him to stay mad at her.

"Listen to me, Maggie. You've got Sarah to think of. In a little while this will all be over—one way or another. Until then, I don't want anything to go wrong—and I don't want you involved."

She brightened at his concern. "All right, you win. I've got some paperwork to do anyway." She threw him a last warm glance and left, only to return two hours later, pretending to need his help.

Jake sighed in frustration but resigned himself that she wasn't going to let him get too far away.

On Thursday, he sponsored a team dinner in the small restaurant off the hotel lobby. Using the Nations' Cup competition as an excuse for the get-together, the dinner created the perfect opportunity to fulfill Popov's demands.

"Hey, Clay," he said, approaching him at the bar. "My stomach's killing me. You wouldn't happen to have any of that medicine you use, would you?"

"I'm afraid it's practically a fixture." Clay pulled the plastic bottle from his inside coat pocket. Jake excused himself, went into the bathroom, dumped out the liquid in the bottle, poured in the mixture from the second bottle, and returned the bottle to Clay. It didn't matter whether Clay got sick tonight or in the morning. Either way, he'd be out of the competition.

Flex was a more difficult proposition. Since he was wearing his hard contact lenses, Jake would have to get into Flex's room in the morning and make the substitution before he dressed.

Depressed at the thought, he ordered a drink and sat down at a table after the others had gone up to their rooms. Then Maggie walked in, looking tired and strained, and so damned beautiful his chest ached.

"I caught a late flight back from Germany." A problem had arisen with the dressage team, and she'd made a quick trip over to straighten things out. "Anything new?"

"Not a thing," Jake said as she sat down beside him.

Maggie noticed the way his eyes slid away and knew he was lying. Something had happened—or was going to.

"How was your flight?" Jake asked, giving her a brittle smile.

"Tiring, but it gave me time to think."

One of Jake's black eyebrows went up. "About?"

"About what you're planning to do."

"I told you, Maggie, Daniel's working on the problem. You don't have to worry."

"Stop it, Jake. I'm not a fool. You're going to do exactly what the Soviets tell you to do."

Jake's gaze fixed on the drink in front of him.

"You're an American now, Jake," Maggie said. "How can you even consider doing what the Soviets want?"

He turned toward her. "I have to do what's best for my family.

263

When I went over that fence in Rome, I left my responsibilities behind. It's time to pay the price." He covered her hand with his. "You're part of my family, you and Sarah. I won't let anything happen to you."

"What about the others? I don't know what the Soviets want, but the team is part of your family, too."

"Maggie, please try to understand."

Maggie fought to hold onto her temper. "Hasn't living in this country taught you anything? If you do what they tell you, you'll never be truly free."

Jake's expression hardened. "Can't you see I have no choice? Unless Daniel finds an alternative, there's nothing else I can do."

Willing him to understand, Maggie's voice softened. "When I told you about the car accident in Florida, about what happened to Les, you said it wasn't my fault—that God makes those decisions. You can't play God, Jake. Not with other people's lives."

Jake shook his head. "I don't expect you to approve."

"If you go through with this, what will it do to *us?* I love you. Nothing can change that. But how will you feel about yourself? Even if you get away with it, what will it do to our relationship?"

Jake didn't answer, just stared down at his drink. When he picked it up, his hand shook, making the ice cubes clink against the side of the glass.

"You'd better get some sleep," he told her, his voice hollow and flat. "We've got a big day tomorrow."

"Think about it, Jake. Please." Ignoring the ache in her throat, Maggie came up out of her chair. With a last glance at Jake, she headed up to her room.

At the sound of the buzzer on the alarm clock, Jake jerked awake. Five-thirty. He'd barely slept. Knowing Flex usually slept later than the other team members, Jake figured he had time to shower and dress and still get into Flex's room with time to spare.

It took six raps on the door before Flex's unkempt, red-haired head appeared in the narrow crack he opened.

"Yeah?" His voice was thick with sleep.

"Sorry to wake you. Thought you'd be up already. Mind if I come in?"

Flex slid the chain off, and Jake pushed through the door.

"What time is it?" Flex asked, yawning.

"About six. Figured you'd want an early start."

"Six o'clock?" Flex's eyebrows went up. "In the morning?"

"Yeah. Mind if I use your john?"

Flex ruffled his hair with his hands. "Help yourself."

"Thanks." Jake stepped through the door, found the contacts in their tiny plastic vial, put the container in his pocket, and substituted the lenses in the vial the Soviets had supplied. At least Daniel and his staff had discovered Popov's intent—the prescription had been changed, a subtle difference that would alter Flex's vision enough to throw off his riding, but not enough for him to notice the change.

Jake's lips thinned as he thought of the Soviets' scheme. *Glasnost,* they preached today. New freedoms, a new westernization of thought. Jake had almost begun to believe it. Obviously, things in his homeland hadn't really changed.

Flushing the toilet for effect, he stepped back into the room. "Listen, Flex. I'm sorry I woke you. I just wanted to come by and tell you I know you'll do well."

Flex stretched and yawned. "Thanks, Jake."

"I'll see you down at the stables."

Flex nodded. Jake walked back into the hall and the door closed behind him. He'd done what they asked, though his conscience nagged him.

In an hour, he'd know what they really wanted him to do.

CHAPTER TWENTY-NINE

After sending Maggie into Ballsbridge on an errand, Jake headed for the stables, going straight to the appointed meeting place, a vacant tack room at the end of the farthest barn.

Around him, riders hurried past and curious spectators came and went, everyone engrossed in the excitement around them. With an eerie creak, the door swung wide, and he stepped into the darkness.

The flare of a match, the acrid smell of sulfur, and the room brightened to a dull glow, lit by a single white candle on a dusty table, the only furniture in the otherwise empty room.

"Good morning, *Tovarich*." Jake stiffened at the sound of Popov's grating voice.

"So the keeper of the hounds arrives in person to direct the hunt," Jake said.

Popov chuckled, the sound brittle. "Surely you didn't believe I would miss it?"

"I wasn't sure you'd take the risk."

"What risk? Surely you can see that it is you who takes the risk."

Unconsciously, Jake's hands fisted. "You're right. Still, you're a long way from home."

"As are you, my friend."

When Jake didn't answer, Popov sighed. "Tired of jousting so soon?" He shook his balding head, the thin strands across the top unmoving, a fine coat of hair oil keeping them in place. "A shame. I have always enjoyed this part of the game."

"You would."

"*Da*. Well, now it is time for our final request."

Jake tensed, trying to prepare himself. Outside the tack room, a horse nickered and blew. There was laughter, then voices that faded along with the clatter of hooves as the horse walked away.

Jake's eyes met Popov's. A knot tied in his stomach as he awaited the words that would decide his fate.

Instead of speaking, the Russian struck a second match and lit a cigarette. As Popov blew the heavy Russian tobacco smoke into the tiny room, Jake forced himself to stay silent.

"I see your patience has improved, Comrade Straka. It seems one is never too old to learn."

"You're enjoying this, aren't you?"

"But of course, *Tovarich*." He shrugged his shoulders, his ill-fitting, Russian-made coat rustling with the movement. "It is always a pleasure to bring an opponent to his knees. I assume you have completed the tasks we assigned."

"Yes."

"Good. One more should not be a problem." He blew a stream of smoke, the pungent smell stirring memories of a people and a time long past. "I presume your Ms. Fletcher will be riding?"

Ellie was riding. He would put Prissy back in for Clay if he was too sick to ride. "Yes."

"Then it is her tack you'll alter. You will make an incision in the girth. You must be certain the saddle will hold together long enough for her to enter the ring, but not long enough for the ride to be completed."

Anger mixed with fear trickled through him. Sabotaging Ellie's equipment could result in serious injury. And yet he'd expected them to ask far more. "That's it?"

"Did you think there would be something else?"

"What are you after, Popov? We both know there is more to this than causing the team to lose the competition."

"There is the added benefit of making you look bad."

"That's not enough."

"The rest is none of your concern." Popov's expression remained inscrutable, the lines across his forehead carefully schooled to reveal nothing.

"If I do as you ask, my mother and sister will come to no harm?"

Popov inhaled deeply, blew out a stream of smoke. "Or your Mrs. Delaine and her daughter."

"There'll be no more demands, nothing else you'll ask me to

267

do?"

"That is correct. However, I will require a word with you after the show."

"What for?"

"A final good-bye, perhaps?"

"Where?"

"Here, should suffice."

Jake nodded, more uncertain than ever. "Fine." He surveyed Popov's features, looking for some clue as to the Russian's plans. Not the flicker of an eyelid. The Russian was good at his job. The best.

The more things change, the more they stay the same.

Jake turned and pulled open the rough wooden door. The air had turned chill, the day blustery and overcast. Flat-bottomed clouds grew thicker by the moment, blocking the sun.

"Have a good day, *Tovarich.*"

Jake didn't answer, just rolled up his collar against the wind and walked out the door. All the way back to the barn, he grew more and more uneasy.

The demands the Soviets had made would destroy any possible U.S. win of the Irish Nations' Cup, but Ireland was just one country among dozens that held the event each year. The United States hosted two.

What was the significance of this particular event? Why had they gone to such lengths?

By the time Jake reached the area where the horses were being groomed, he was more worried than ever. What were they after? What in God's name were they using him to accomplish?

"There you are." Maggie walked toward him. He didn't miss the accusation in her tone. "I've been looking all over."

"I'm sure you have," he said brusquely, then felt guilty when she touched his cheek.

"I know you're still upset with me, but—"

Jake pulled her around the corner of the barn out of sight. For a moment he just looked at her. He hadn't held her since their last night in the country. He wished this whole thing was over.

"I spoke to Popov this morning," he said. "Whatever they're planning, they aren't going to tell me. That means anything could happen. Now, or even in Seoul."

"Oh, dear Lord, what do they expect you to do?"

"I'm still not sure where I fit in."

"Remember what I said, Jake. You're a free man now. Do what they say, and you'll never be free again."

Jake didn't answer. "Daniel's here. I'm going to contact him, tell him the rest of what's happened. In the meantime, you've got to be careful, Maggie. I wish you'd go back to the States."

She only shook her head. "Not without you."

Jake released an exasperated breath. "I love you, dammit. But sometimes, lady, you're a genuine pain in the ass."

She smiled up at him. "You be careful, too, Jake."

"I will. And if you notice anything suspicious, anything that doesn't look right, let me know."

She nodded and walked away.

Jake watched her meld into the crowd of people coming and going, turned and walked back to the grooming area. His head came up in surprise when he spotted Clay, obviously feeling fine, smiling and talking to Ellie. Why hadn't he taken the medication?

"You two are looking chipper this morning," Jake said with forced lightness, shaking off a feeling of doom. *You've done your part,* he told himself firmly. *What happens now rests in the hands of fate.*

Clay winked at Ellie. "It's probably getting such a good night's sleep."

Ellie blushed.

"Ulcer not bothering you?" Jake asked.

"Funny thing. I haven't had a moment's discomfort since the night Ellie agreed to marry me."

Despite the circumstances, Jake laughed. Amazing, the way Fate had a will of its own. "Another advantage to finding a good woman."

"Exactly," Clay agreed.

Shaking his head, Jake wondered how this would affect the Soviets' plan. He headed over to where Flex stood next to Sparky while the groom brushed the horse's shiny chestnut coat.

"You about ready?" Jake asked.

"I'm ready."

Jake didn't press the issue. "Clay and Ellie both seem up for this."

Flex smiled, a bit wanly it seemed. "Clay oughta be happy. He's marrying Ellie. That makes him one lucky S.O.B."

Jake smiled back. "Clay wins again. But the changes I've seen in him...I think Ellie's a winner, too."

Flex nodded and began rubbing his temples with his forefingers.

"You alright?" Jake asked.

"I've got a headache. No big deal. I took a couple of aspirins. I'll be fine."

Feeling a rush of guilt, Jake said a quick "good luck" and headed toward the pay phone at the end of the barn. In a grassy area on his left, Gerry Winslow worked Jubilee on a lunge line. It would be easy to slip into Ellie's tack room and weaken her saddle. Her equipment had been checked and rechecked. Odds were, she wouldn't go over her gear again.

But it was equally possible either she or Gerry would discover the damage before she entered the arena. It would be better to make the cut after the saddle was in place.

Jake's hands balled into fists as an image arose of Ellie lying injured and broken beside one of the jumps. Flex, too, could come to harm.

Jake struggled with his conscience and continued toward the phone.

"Well, if it isn't the happy couple." Avery approached Ellie and Clay where they stood at the arena fence. A gust of air tugged at her red hunt jacket and Ellie shivered, uncertain if she were reacting to the chilly air or Avery's chilling presence.

"'Morning, Dad," Clay said, but his voice sounded harder than it had just moments ago. He straightened, standing a few inches taller than his father.

"Good morning, Avery," Ellie added dutifully.

Since Clay had announced their marriage plans, Avery had been cold and sarcastic. His disapproval had been obvious, yet for the most part, Clay seemed not to notice. Since he hadn't mentioned the problem, Ellie hadn't either. But the more Clay ignored the situation, the more nervous Ellie became.

Avery's approval meant everything to Clay. Ellie was certain he would want his father to support his choice of bride. By withholding his support, Avery might be able to change Clay's mind. Another shiver slipped down Ellie's spine.

"Are you cold?" Clay asked.

"No...no, I'm fine."

He looked skeptical.

"Really," she added.

"Ready for the competition, son?" Avery asked.

"More ready than I've ever been in my life, thanks to Ellie."

"Yes.... You know, son, you've been so busy all week, we haven't had much chance to talk."

"Then why don't the three of us go out for dinner tonight?" Clay suggested. "Celebrate a little. It'll give you and Ellie a chance to get better acquainted."

Avery cast a hard look in her direction but spoke to Clay. "There are things you and I need to discuss in private."

A muscle bunched in Clay's jaw. "If the things we need to discuss include why I shouldn't get married, you needn't bother."

"If you two will excuse me," Ellie cut in, pulling away from Clay. "I think I'll go check on Jube."

Clay slid an arm around her waist and drew her back against him. "I don't want you to go. I want you to hear what I have to say."

"But if you and your father need to talk—"

"When it comes to you and me, to our marriage and our life together, my father has nothing to say." He looked pointedly at Avery, who looked equally annoyed. With obvious effort, Clay reined himself in. Ellie could feel the tension in his body, how desperately he wanted his father to understand.

Clay squared his shoulders, purpose in his stance. "You and I have been through a lot together," he said to Avery. "You're my father and I love you. I always have and I always will. Nothing can change that. When I was young, I rarely saw you. You had little time for me, but still I loved you. Now there's someone else I love, and I want you to be happy for me. For us. If you aren't, that's your business. It isn't going to change the way I feel about Ellie or what we intend to do."

Avery's face was beginning to redden but Clay didn't stop. "You can be happy for us or not. It's up to you," he finished.

"I didn't want to say this in front of the girl, but you're leaving me no choice. You think you want to get married. You think you're in love. I understand because I felt that way once, when I married your mother. But I can tell you from experience, you're not only hurting yourself you're hurting her. You'll be a good husband, all right. For a few weeks, a month or two at most."

Ellie went cold.

"Then you'll be off chasing skirts just like I was. You're just like me, Clay. Just like your old man."

Ellie's stomach rolled. Tears burned behind her eyes. She felt Clay's arm tighten around her.

"That's where you're wrong, Dad. For years I've worked hard at being like you. I wanted you to be proud of me. Wanted it bad enough to bury the person I really am. Oh, I won't deny I've enjoyed myself. I've traveled all over the world, been with some of the world's most beautiful women. But I always felt hollow inside—like something was missing. These last few years, it's been harder and harder for me to keep up the pretense."

"That's all nonsense. You're just a little tired, that's all."

"It isn't nonsense. You don't really know me. You never have. Did you know I write poetry? That I enjoy reading the classics? That I collect fine art? And not because it's a good investment, the way I told you, but because I love it?"

Avery looked stunned.

"I want a home, Dad. A wife. Children to play in the yard." He smiled down at Ellie, a wistful, yearning smile that touched her heart. "A Labrador retriever in front of the fireplace." Clay grinned.

Avery started to speak, his mouth moved, but no words came out.

"I love her," Clay said. "She isn't like any other woman I've known. I'm happy when I'm with her. Happier than I've ever been in my life."

Avery glanced from Clay to Ellie and back. He swallowed and cleared his throat. "I don't know what to say."

"Say you'll be happy for us."

Avery looked down at his feet, kicked at the soft, damp grass with the toe of his Italian leather shoe. "I really do want what's best for you, son. It's just...well...it's my nature to be selfish. It's too late for me to change. I've enjoyed the times we've shared."

"There'll be other times, just different, that's all."

272

Avery nodded, still looking dazed. "I suppose you're right. If it isn't too late, good luck, son." He extended his hand and Clay shook it, then enveloped him in a hug.

A little unsettled, Avery flicked Ellie a tentative smile, started to walk away, then turned back. "Welcome to the family, Ellie."

She smiled. "Thank you."

Avery's eyebrows suddenly lifted, and he grinned, dimpling cheeks very much like Clay's. "When this gets out, you two will make headlines around the world. We'll throw a huge engagement party, make the formal announcement there. Maybe in Paris—the Ritz. Or the Plaza in New York."

Both Ellie and Clay started laughing. "He'll never change," Clay said to her. "Definitely New York," he said to his father. "I'm damned well ready to go home."

"New York, then. You two can move into Far Hills. You'll like it there, Ellie. I'll take the apartment in Manhattan."

"That sounds fine," Clay said, and Ellie read his relief. He'd wanted his father's blessing and in Avery's way, he'd given it. The last of Ellie's doubts faded. Clay was his own man now. Ellie loved him more than ever.

As Avery disappeared into the crowd, Clay smiled down at her. "You know it's crazy. I'm about to get married, give up my freedom, my dad would say." He tipped her chin up to look at him. "The truth is this is the first time in my life I've ever felt really free."

"Oh, Clay." Ellie threw her arms around his neck and hugged him.

Clay leaned down brushed a kiss over her lips. "Brave enough to call your parents now?"

Wanting to be sure, Ellie had put off the phone call. She'd said she wanted to tell them in person. It wasn't the truth as Clay must have known.

"We'll call them right after the show." She smiled up at him. "You're going to love them, Clay. And once they get to know you, they're going to love you, too."

"Your father may be somewhat skeptical."

"Dad's a fair man. Once he knows I love you and you love me, he'll be happy for us. Besides, he knows enough about you to understand getting married is no small step. You wouldn't take it lightly."

Clay grinned. "That, my love, is probably the understatement of the year. I'm just glad you were crazy enough to say yes." Clay kissed her and nothing had ever felt so right.

CHAPTER THIRTY

Jake's phone conversation with Daniel went about the way he figured. Daniel was emphatic. "In no way will you do anything that might harm Ellen Fletcher."

"Odds are, she'll just take a fall," Jake argued. "It's happened dozens of times. She's used to it." It was the truth, but any fall was dangerous, and Jake knew it. He forced himself to go on. "If I don't do what they want, you know what will happen."

"It's a risk we'll have to take."

"It's too damned big a risk. There's no way you can protect my family." *Or Maggie and Sarah.* "I know these people better than you do. They mean what they say."

"Jake," Daniel said softly. "You can't take the chance of getting the Fletcher girl hurt, maybe killed. They're obviously using you as some sort of diversion. You're the least of their worries."

"I might agree with you if it weren't for Popov. For him this is personal. He'll use any excuse to get to me. I think he's hoping I won't do what they say."

"I doubt it. Somebody has gone to great lengths to put this scheme in motion."

Jake's fingers tightened on the phone. "I'd better be getting back."

"I repeat," Daniel warned. "You will not comply with the final Soviet demand. Have you got that, Jake?"

"I've got it, Dan." Jake managed to sound convincing.

"Keep in touch and keep your eyes open."

"I will." He hung up knowing Daniel had done what he had to do. Now Jake would do the same.

By the time Jake had finished his phone call, the riders were walking the course. Ellie and Clay were in the ring with Flex. Shep was riding Lovely Lass over to the gate.

"I must have missed you this morning," Shep said as he dismounted, handing the reins to his groom.

"Sorry," Jake said. "How's Lass?"

"She feels good. A little stiff, but I think if she takes a couple more fences, she'll lengthen and soften a little." He glanced at the course. "I'll be the first of us to go."

"Just take it easy. Don't worry about time faults; just get her over the fences. They look pretty imposing. Why don't we go ahead and walk the course?"

The two of them made the rounds, noting the height of the fences and deciding the number of strides Lass should take, then Shep took the horse over a couple more practice fences before the competition began.

"What did your friend Daniel have to say?" Maggie asked, spotting Jake and walking up beside him as Shep led Lass away.

"Not much. He just told me to keep my eyes open and believe me, I intend to. I want you to do the same. At the first sign of trouble, I want you back at the barn. I'll look for you there."

"Can't I stay with you?"

It wasn't a bad idea. He could keep an eye on her, be there to protect her if trouble started. "All right. But first I need a few words with the team." He smiled and touched her cheek. "I still have a job to do."

He urged her toward a spot near the arena fence. "I'll be back as soon as I can." With a last glance at Maggie, he headed to where Ellie stood next to Jubilee.

On the way, he unsheathed the heavy folding knife he'd picked up in the equipment room after his conversation with Daniel. The knife was small enough to conceal in the palm of his hand, but sturdy enough for the job he needed to do. The trick would be to get Ellie's attention diverted until he could accomplish his task.

"What number did the team draw?" he asked her as he approached.

"Number five. Shep is first, then me, Clay, then Flex."

Jake glanced into the arena. Shep was taking the course. Lass had a rail down at the third fence but seemed to be smoothing out. Shep was riding well, taking the course just as they'd planned. He still carried the remnants of his beating and, Jake suspected, a few aches and pains.

276

He seemed certain to wind up with time faults and had another rail down at the triple.

A glance at Ellie told Jake she was tensely involved in watching Shep's round. Behind them, Clay was taking Max over some practice fences. The heavy little folding knife seemed to burn into Jake's palm. He opened the blade and moved toward Jube. On the pretense of checking the animal's cinch, Jake lifted the stirrup flap.

You can't play God, Jake. If you do what the Soviets ask, you'll never be free again.

Jake swore beneath his breath and glanced around to see if anyone was watching. He had to do this, didn't he? He had Maggie and Sarah to consider, his mother and sister.

Flashing red lights drew his attention. Shep had completed his round, but a British rider was down at the first fence. Several attendants stood over him looking worried. The lights on the top of an ambulance flashed their warning as the vehicle entered the ring.

How would you feel if that was Ellie? How would he face himself? She'd come so far, accomplished so much. He thought of her years of near blindness, how much of life she had missed. Now life was out there waiting for her—all she had to do was take it.

What right did he have to risk destroying what Ellie had worked so hard for? Jake's hand fell away from the girth. He tried to raise the knife, but it felt as heavy as lead. No matter the outcome, he couldn't go through with it.

With a last glance at Ellie and a sigh of resignation, Jake turned to walk away and found Daniel blocking his path.

"Give me the knife, Jake." The sharpness in his friend's deep voice was unmistakable.

Jake held out his hand, dropping the blade into Daniel's waiting palm. "It's all right, Dan. I couldn't do it anyway."

Daniel seemed relieved. "It may not matter. We've had some news. The Soviets seem to be having a problem. There's a rift in the party. A split of some kind. Whoever is behind this, it isn't the government—at least not the leaders we know. We've informed the proper authorities, and they've already begun to take action."

"I'm not quite following."

"We don't have all the facts yet. So far, all we know is that some of the higher-ups in the KGB and in the government, itself, disagree with current Soviet policies toward the West. They feel the policies are too lenient, that they're risking the very existence of the Communist Party. Apparently, they've taken matters into their own hands."

Jake's pulse was speeding.

"Whatever's happening," Daniel continued, "the action isn't sanctioned by the government. Gorbachev has personally assured us the Soviets will take whatever steps necessary to protect your mother and sister."

Hope flared in his chest. "What about Maggie and Sarah?"

"Our people in Florida have already been notified. They'll keep Sarah under constant surveillance until this is over. Our men here will be watching you and Maggie."

Jake felt a wave of relief that drained some of the tension from his shoulders. "Thank God."

"Come on. You look like you could use a drink." Daniel led Jake to a spot beneath a shade tree where they could watch events in the ring. Reaching into his coat pocket, he pulled out a silver flask and handed it over.

"Thanks." Jake gratefully accepted the brandy Daniel had carried for as long as Jake could recall. Though his friend never drank on duty, Daniel claimed the flask had come in handy on numerous occasions. At the moment, Jake agreed. Tilting the flask, he took a long, nerve-steadying swallow.

"Better?"

"Much." Feeling the biting warmth of the liquid sliding into his stomach, Jake handed back the flask. "Listen Dan, I'm sorry about all of this. Please believe I was doing what I thought was right."

"I know that. In your position, I might have done the same." Daniel grinned. "That's why I've had you watched so closely."

Jake grunted. "I should have known."

"By the way, what changed your mind?"

"Something Maggie said about never being free. As usual, she was right. A man's got to follow his conscience. That's what freedom is all about."

Daniel smiled. "I guess we're never too old to learn."

"Funny, that's what Popov said."

The two stood quietly for a while, Daniel giving Jake time to calm his ragged nerves and assess the information he'd been given.

"So where does all this leave us?" Jake finally asked. "What game are they playing?"

Daniel's broad features turned grim. "Unfortunately, that's a question I can't answer. Our men are everywhere. The Irish security people are top rate, but no one's turned up anything. Everything appears to be running smoothly. Nothing unusual, nothing out of sync."

"I don't like this, Dan. Whoever's behind this has something planned and we both know it."

Daniel's dark gaze surveyed their surroundings. "I wish you were wrong, but I don't think so. We'll just have to wait and see. Stay close to Maggie."

"You know I will."

Daniel dug his hands into the pockets of his coat and wandered away. The wind at his back ruffled his light brown hair.

Jake watched his friend go, wondering why he hadn't mentioned his final upcoming meeting with Popov. But down deep he knew. He'd ride this round on his own, make the best of the number he'd drawn.

He hadn't complied with their final demand and soon they would know it. But if he met Popov this last time, maybe he could garner information that would tell him what the Russians had planned. It was risky, but a risk he had to take.

Moving toward the arena, Jake saw Ellie mount Jubilee and ride into the arena. As he watched her canter around the fences, he breathed a sigh of relief. Whatever happened out there now was up to Ellie.

With that thought, Jake sobered. Making an abrupt turn, he strode over to Flex.

"Headache gone?" he asked.

Standing next to Sebastian, Flex pulled off his hunt cap and ran a hand through his carrot red hair. "Unfortunately, it's worse than ever."

"I think I know what'll help." Reaching into his pocket, Jake dug out the tiny vial that held Flex's contact lenses. "Take out the ones you're wearing."

"What? Are you crazy? I've got to ride in less than ten minutes."

"Then you'd better hurry."

"What's this about, Jake?"

"No time now. I'll explain later."

Hurriedly, Flex popped out the lenses he was wearing, washed the ones in the vial in his mouth, and used the tip of his finger to insert them into his eyes.

"Any better?" Jake asked.

"Yes, but I don't know why."

"The prescription is a little bit off in the other pair."

"I don't get it."

"Later," Jake said. "Right now, the important thing to think about is the course. How's Sebastian?"

"He's a little bit full of himself but I think he'll settle down. He's really enjoying this."

"Good. Just watch the pace. You'll have to make some neat turns to finish in the time allowed. The line with the triple combination looks the most difficult."

"I plan to override the triple and steady immediately so I can ride forward to that first wide oxer."

Jake nodded his approval. "Good luck."

Jake moved off toward Clay, who was keenly watching Ellie take the fences. Leaning against the rail, Clay rubbed Max's ears, smiling and talking to him softly. Jake came up beside him. In silence they watched Ellie's faultless round.

When she cleared the last fence, Clay grinned. "She's really something."

"Something very special. You're a very lucky man."

"Believe me, I know it."

An Irish rider took the course on a big black Irish thoroughbred.

"Max looks ready. How about you?" Jake asked.

Clay smiled. "We're both ready. Max has been taking the jumps as if he has wings."

"You carrying that medicine of yours?"

Clay nodded. "Security blanket, I guess. Why? Your stomach bothering you again?" Clay pulled the plastic bottle out of his inside coat pocket.

Jake took the bottle and stuffed it into his own coat pocket. "Not exactly. We'll talk about it after the show."

"Anything wrong, Jake?"

"Nothing for you to worry about. You just take care of those fences."

"Listen, Jake...if you're in some kind of trouble...if there's anything I can do..."

"Thanks, Clay. I appreciate that, but I think we've finally got things under control."

The Irish rider finished, knocking down the last two fences, riding glumly out of the ring. Clay threw Jake a last glance and swung up into the saddle. As he moved toward the arena, he passed Ellie, who leaned over and kissed him as he rode past.

Another rider completed the course, then the Irish announcer's voice came over the speakers. "From the United States. Maximum Effort. Clayton Whitfield, the rider."

Jake glanced around the arena. Some distance away, Maggie stood watching the competition. A man Jake recognized as one of Daniel's stood just a few feet away. Since Maggie was well-protected, Jake decided he'd take a last look around.

When the competition was over, he'd have his final meeting with Popov. Then he'd talk to the members of the team, explain what had been happening. He'd resign his position, of course. There was nothing else to do. He just hoped they'd understand his actions, try not to judge him too harshly.

Deciding to make a pass through the stables and around behind the grandstands, Jake headed off. He still felt tense and uncertain, but his role in the drama was coming to an end. In the meantime, he would watch the outcome of the competition.

For the first time in days, he allowed himself to pull for the American team.

CHAPTER THIRTY-ONE

A brisk wind whipped Maggie's hair and tugged at the bottoms of her pale gray slacks. She wondered why Jake hadn't returned but consoled herself knowing he'd spoken to Daniel, someone in authority, and that as team coach, he had a job to do.

Maggie propped her arms on the rail and looked out across the grassy arena. Dublin fans filled the grandstand to overflowing. The event had begun with marching bands and honor guards. Teams of sleek-coated draught horses pulled wagons filled with flowers. Shep had ridden well, under the circumstances. Ellie had ridden brilliantly.

Clay had just passed through the beam of the timer, signaling the start of his round.

Maggie smiled as she watched him. He seemed to sit taller, ride with even more confidence than usual. He smiled easily as he took the first three fences: a red and gold vertical, a wide blue oxer, and a five-foot jump at the end of the arena.

The crowd applauded enthusiastically, warming to the beauty of his ride. There was something about him today. Something undefeatable. He rode like the champion he was, and Max made the course look easy. They made the round in the time allotted and with no fences down. Only a few people had ridden as well; Ellie, a German rider; and a member of the Irish team.

Maggie glanced around, still looking for Jake. No sign of him but Prissy stood at the rail in her riding clothes, in case of any last-minute changes.

"Wasn't Clay something?" she said as Maggie walked up. "He and Ellie both rode beautifully. I think being in love agrees with them."

"No doubt about it."

Several more riders took the course and finally Flex's turn came up. He and Sebastian got off to a shaky start. Sparky settled down at the third fence, clearing it with room to spare, but Flex put him wrong at the water jump. Flex completed the course with no more fences down but had several time faults.

"I think I'll go console him," Prissy said.

"Good idea." While Flex rode out of the arena, Maggie spotted Jake striding toward her. He was carefully surveying the people around her, but she noticed a subtle relaxation in his posture.

As he walked up, he surprised her by sliding an arm around her waist and kissing the top of her head. "Miss me?"

"Enormously."

"It's almost over, Maggie." He relayed his latest conversation with Daniel, and that the Soviet government was not behind the threats to his family.

"As hard as it is to believe," he said, "the Russians seem to be doing everything possible to prevent whatever Popov and his minions have planned."

Maggie felt a surge of relief so strong her knees wobbled. "Thank God." She could feel the burn of tears behind her eyes.

"Everything's going to be all right." He caught he shoulders. "We can be married—if you'll have me."

"Oh, Jake." Maggie buried her face in the hollow of his neck and Jake smoothed a hand over her hair.

"Is that a yes?" he asked softly.

Maggie looked up at him. "Of course, it's a yes." Unmindful of the milling crowd, the members of the team who stood a few feet away, Maggie kissed him.

"Just two more days and we'll be home," he whispered against her cheek. "All this will be behind us, and we can get on with our lives."

She pulled a tissue out of her purse and dabbed her eyes. "In the end, you did what was right. I never really doubted you. Just another reason I love you."

Jake leaned down and kissed her.

"What happens now?" Maggie asked.

Jake studied the overcrowded stands. "We wait. We watch. And we hope like hell Daniel's people stop Popov from doing whatever evil he's got planned. If it doesn't happen today or tomorrow, chances are their own people will stop them."

Maggie squeezed Jake's hand. She wished they could be alone for a while, spend some time discussing their future. Instead, she searched the stands and the people around them just as Jake was doing, looking for some clue as to what might happen.

In the arena, they were beginning the second round of jumping. The final team scores would decide the winner of the Nations' Cup.

The second time through, the difficult course took its toll on the horses. From the beginning, the faults were higher; none of the first eight riders went clear. Shep and Lass had time faults and three rails down. Ellie had one rail down and Clay had one. It was Flex who saved the day, going clear and within the time allotted. His grin was so broad it almost touched his ears.

As the final horse and rider, a small dark Irishman on a big white gelding, took the course, the crowd came surging to its feet, their applause thunderous. The Irishman rode beautifully, clearing the last fence well within the time allotted. The crowd fell silent while the tabulations were made.

"We've won!" Clay roared when the announcement came over the loudspeaker. Flex released a high-pitched whoop of joy. Jake hugged Maggie. Clay hugged Ellie and Prissy, while Flex and Shep hugged two female riders who just happened to be walking by.

The team members took a victory lap around the ring. Jake accepted the prestigious Aga Khan Trophy while the National Anthem played.

Afterwards, the showgrounds still in turmoil as the horses were put away, he slipped off for his final confrontation with Popov.

Before he reached the tack room, he spotted Clay. "Congratulations," Jake said.

Clay grinned. "Thanks."

"I need a favor."

"Of course."

"If I'm not back in twenty minutes, tell Maggie I had a meeting with Popov in the most easterly tack room in the farthest barn. Tell her to contact Daniel Gage." Reaching into his pocket, he pulled out the slip of paper with Daniel's phone number on it and handed it to Clay. "There's always someone there."

"What's this about, Jake? Not more trouble, I hope."

"I'll explain everything as soon as I get back. Twenty minutes," he repeated. "It's important, Clay."

"I'll see she gets the message."

With long strides, Jake moved off through the crowd, making several detours to be sure he wasn't followed. When he reached the tack room and pushed open the door, a harsh white bulb had replaced the glow of the candle.

Popov wasn't there.

Jake turned to go outside and wait, preferring fresh air to the musty odor of the tack room. Then he spotted the white sheet of paper lying on the wooden table.

Jake's pulse began to pound as he read the note.

In 1960 I defected to the United States of America, believing it a land of freedom and opportunity. Over the years, I have discovered the United States is a land of decadence and privilege for the few.

I betrayed my homeland. Now, I wish the world to know the truth. Events of this day will not be forgotten. My Soviet countrymen, remember what I've done as a lesson to you all.

The letter was signed Janus Straka, then Jake Sullivan. The writing looked identical to Jake's.

At the sound of the door creaking open, he dropped the paper on the table with a trembling hand.

"Good afternoon, *Tovarich*." The gravelly voice betrayed nothing, the tone so mild they might have been passing on the street.

"My handwriting...how did you...?" But he didn't finish. They had ways, he knew. Forged passports, documents. It was no trick at all once a sample of the person's writing had been obtained.

The more important question was, "What have you done?"

"I see your impatience has returned. I'm afraid it is a characteristic you will carry to your grave."

Jake stiffened.

"You disobeyed your instructions." Popov smiled thinly. "Which came as no surprise. You, my friend, are far too predictable." .

"I intended to comply, but fate intervened."

Popov grunted. "Fate takes second place when events are well-planned, well-executed. You, for example. Your actions in this mattered little. There was nothing you could have done except divulge our involvement to the authorities. To avoid that, we counted on your unwavering loyalty to your family and friends."

Jake said nothing. *He doesn't know about Daniel.*

"As to your compliance—it was merely a diversion. Of course, each incident will ultimately be connected to you. Revenge will be sweet, my friend."

Popov pulled a package of cigarettes from his inside coat pocket. A match flared as he lit up and the acrid smell of sulfur filled the tack room.

"I presume you are here to plead for the lives of your family and friends," the Russian said.

Jake seized on the words. "They're innocent in this. I'm the one who didn't comply with your wishes."

Popov released a raspy chuckle. "You may ease your mind. None of them will be harmed. You were the pawn, they merely the device to obtain your cooperation."

Popov's smug, satisfied expression sent a chill down Jake's spine.

"I see by your look," the Russian continued, "you wish to know why we have gone to so much trouble. It is simple really. *Glasnost.* Among those of us loyal to our cause, it is a vile word. A filthy word that corrupts the people of our country.

"New freedoms," he said sarcastically. *"A new Westernism.* Bah! Adopting bourgeois capitalist beliefs! Turning us into a nation of drug users, despoilers, and decadents. Already it has caused unrest among the people. Surely you have read what is happening in Armenia—the rioting and protests? If it should continue, there is no telling where it might end. The very walls of Communism could be felled."

Wouldn't that be something, Jake thought.

"What is happening today," Popov continued. "What we are doing in Dublin, is just one incident among many we have engineered to weaken the bonds between East and West. The missile that *accidentally* destroyed the Korean jet liner, for example...or that airbus over the Persian Gulf your own Navy shot down. Each event is designed to breech those ties, cause rifts and descent. In layman's terms, we do not want peace with you. We are committed to doing whatever it takes to enforce and spread our beliefs."

"Whatever it takes," Jake repeated, the room feeling suddenly airless. "What are you planning to do in Dublin?"

"Since you will not live to see it, I suppose telling you can do no harm." He blew a thick stream of smoke into the air. "You remember the inconvenience your people suffered here on Wednesday evening?"

Jake searched his memory. "Sorry, I don't recall."

"Nothing much, nothing to be concerned about. A broken waterline. It could happen anywhere. Except in this case...*our* people made the repairs. While they were working, they installed an interesting little device. A pressure valve set with a timer."

Jake's pulse began to hammer as Popov slid back the sleeve of his dark brown overcoat and checked his watch.

"It started working some time ago. The valve was set to begin release at four o'clock this afternoon and continue, intermittently releasing small quantities of strychnine into the waterline that leads to your barn. With each subsequent watering, your horses, along with those of the British and Canadian teams, will be ingesting lethal amounts of poison. By midnight they will be dead—along with any persons unlucky enough to be thirsty. With the Olympic Games just a few weeks away, the impact should be extremely far-reaching. In fact—"

Jake lunged, knocking Popov out of the way and bolting for the door. He jerked the latch and the door swung wide, but a hard grip on his shoulder and the feel of a cold steel barrel against his temple stopped him.

"Close it," Popov hissed.

Jake didn't move.

"Now." The barrel of the gun slid lower, into the flesh under Jake's jaw.

One bullet and the madman's plan would succeed. Jake needed time. Time for Clay to tell Maggie where he'd gone. Time for Maggie to reach Daniel. But there was no time. Not for the horses. Not for the people who might be dying right now.

The copper taste of fear filled his mouth. Stepping back inside, he heard the door creak closed behind him. The harsh white bulb reflected off the cylindrical object Jake recognized as a silencer on the barrel of the automatic pistol in Popov's hand. He used it to motion Jake away from the door.

His expression hard, Popov carefully positioned himself

between Jake and escape.

"A wise decision, Comrade. A few more moments of life, no matter how brief." He smiled ruthlessly. "One must always take what precious little time one has been given."

Clay looked down at the paper he held in his hand. He'd been trying to find Maggie for the past ten minutes. He had gone to look for her as soon as he'd left Jake. Still no sign of her.

Worry building, Clay shoved against the tide of people leaving the show grounds. He scanned the practice field as he moved toward the stables, rounded a corner, and slammed headlong into her.

"Maggie! I've been looking all over." He pressed the slip of paper into her hand. "Jake said to tell you he had a meeting with someone named Popov in the most easterly tack room in the farthest barn. He said if he wasn't back in twenty minutes, you were to call Daniel Gage at that number."

"How long ago did you see him?" Maggie asked, feeling the blood drain from her face.

"About ten minutes. He's in trouble, isn't he?"

Maggie didn't answer, just brushed past him in the direction Jake had gone.

Clay grabbed her arm. "Tell me what's wrong."

"I'm not sure. Something to do with the Russians." She glanced down at the paper she clutched in her hand. She had to stay calm, try to think. She handed the paper to Clay. "Get to a phone. Call Daniel Gage. Tell him exactly what Jake said."

"Let me go with you."

"You've got to make the call."

Clay hesitated only a moment, turned and rushed off toward the phone booth. Maggie ran in the opposite direction, her heart thundering.

Dear Lord, she had to reach Jake.

CHAPTER THIRTY-TWO

The silence in the tack room was stifling, yet Popov looked relaxed.

Adrenaline pumped through Jake's veins. He had to find a way out. When a horse whinnied outside the door, Popov glance away, and Jake dove toward him, slamming into him and knocking him backward.

At that instant, Maggie opened the door, ramming into the Russian from behind. The gun went off, a whizzing sound as the bullet thudded into the rough wooden wall.

"Jake!" Maggie shouted.

Still on their feet, the two men grappled for control of the weapon. Clutching the Russian's wrist, Jake twisted the gun barrel upward. He heard Maggie's gasp as the second muffled gunshot rained a shower of splinters down from the ceiling.

Maggie threw herself at the Russian, raking her nails across the side of his face. Swearing, he slapped her viciously, knocking her into the corner. Popov came after Jake. Jake drove an elbow under the Russian's chin and kicked Popov's feet out from under him. Both men crashed to the floor, fighting for control of the weapon.

Popov rolled on top, his free hands curling around Jake's throat, biting into his flesh and cutting off his air supply. He could hear Maggie's movements as she struggled to her knees and began frantically searching for a weapon.

The smell of Russian tobacco drifted up from Popov's clothes as Jake pried the man's fingers from around his throat, and his hand locked around Popov's wrist. The pistol moved between them, discharged, once, twice, both men jerking with the shock, the dull thuds muffled by the body the bullets smashed into. The smell of gunpowder filled the room.

Maggie stood transfixed, an expression of horror on her face. A warm, oozing wetness soaked the front of Jake's once-white shirt. A growing pool of crimson spread on the cold wooden floor.

"Jake," Maggie whispered, rushing to his side.

"It's all right, it's Popov's blood, not mine." Jake shoved the Russian's body away and surged to his feet. "They've poisoned the water. We've got to stop them!"

Jake charged for the door, but when it swung open, the black-haired man Jake had met at the tavern stood in the opening. The man responsible for the attacks on Ellie and Shep.

"So, Comrade Straka, we meet again." The pistol in his black-gloved hand pointed directly at Jake. Easing Maggie behind him, Jake could feel her trembling.

"You won't get out of here alive," Jake said.

"Neither will you." Running footsteps sounded outside the door an instant before the door burst open, hurling the man forward as Clay crashed into him and the two men rolled in a jumble of arms and legs at Jake's feet.

"Bloody bastard!" Recognizing him as the man who'd attacked Ellie, Clay grabbed him by the shirtfront and punched him hard in the face. Clay kept hitting him until his eyes rolled back and his jaw hung slack. Clay's arm went back to hit him again, but Jake caught his shoulder.

"They've poisoned the water! We've got to get to the horses!"

"Good Christ!" Clay turned and ran back out the door, Jake and Maggie right behind him. Shoving riders and grooms aside, they raced toward the barn where the horses were stabled. Just ahead of them, Jake spotted Ellie and Daniel, running toward them.

"Popov's dead. They've poisoned the waterline that leads into the barns. We've got to get the horses out!"

"Oh, God!" Ellie started running toward Jube. Clay ran toward Max.

"Split up," Daniel ordered Jake and Maggie. "Cover as much ground as you can. Get everyone to help."

But when they reached the barn, they found the horror had already begun.

In the Canadian team stalls, two of the horses were down. Others were snorting, pawing, and nickering wildly, their eyes rolled back until only the whites appeared.

Two horses in the British section, excited by the pandemonium around them, tried to climb over the top of the open stall doors. On a bench outside, his neck stiff and his eyes bulging, one of the grooms thrashed against the building, his muscles twitching spasmodically.

The British *chef d 'equipe* stood over him, calling out orders while one of the female riders knelt beside him trying to restrain the young man's rigid, flailing body.

Don't let them die, Jake thought. *Don't let it be too late.* In minutes, word was spread that water had been poisoned. Like the grooms and riders around him, Jake began jerking open stall doors, leading the horses to safety. One after another, they were led out and away from the death in the usually life-giving liquid.

Some of the animals hadn't been watered since the first release of the deadly poison, so they were not at risk. Others were reacting so violently to the excitement it was difficult to tell if they had been affected. So far, none of the people or horses were dead.

An ambulance, its siren wailing in a high-low, sing-song manner, roared up in a cloud of dust. Another siren rang out. In seconds, white-coated attendants were directed to the groom who had drunk some of the water. They set to work on him immediately, shoving a needle into his arm.

Others were being checked out, but it looked as if the only other victims were the horses.

Making a sweep of the barn, Jake approached Daniel, who'd been speaking in low tones to the ambulance attendants who worked over the groom. "How is he?"

"They're administering sodium pentobarbital intravenously. They give him a good chance of recovery. Our people are testing the water now, but as near as we can tell, the poison was being released in small doses. Probably because the horses are watered at different times. They didn't want to alert anyone before they'd gotten to them all."

"There was a note," Jake said. "It was signed by me, claiming I was the one responsible. There's a man in the tack room—"

Daniel's palm settled gently on his shoulder. He reached into his pocket, pulled out a haphazardly folded sheet of white paper and handed it to Jake. It was the note Popov had forged.

"Our people have taken care of the body and arrested the man they found in the tack room. You take care of the note."

Jake's shoulders sagged in relief. "Thank you, Daniel." Leaving the British and Canadians, he returned to the American section.

"The horses are all out of the stalls," Ellie told Jake as they approached. "Most of them seem all right, but some of them...we can't be sure. Jube's all right. So is Rose. The vet's with Lass. She doesn't look good. Maggie's helping Shep."

"What about Max?" Jake asked.

Ellie's eyes filled. "Max is down in his stall." Her voice broke. "Clay needs help."

"I'll get Lee there as fast as I can."

"Gerry went to get him." Wiping her eyes, she turned and raced back to Clay. He was sitting on a mat of fresh straw on the floor of the stall, holding Max's head in his lap, talking to him softly. The stallion's eyes were dilated, his muscles rigid then twitching, his teeth bared, his jaw clamped shut.

"Be careful," Clay cautioned. "He may start convulsing again." Outside, people rushed past, horses whinnied, and grooms busied themselves carting the deadly water away. "Where the hell is Lee?"

"Gerry went to get him." Kneeling next to Clay, Ellie touched his icy hand. At the contact, the muscles in his forearm tensed. With a slow breath, he forced himself to relax.

"He'll be all right," Ellie said, fighting back fresh tears. "He's got to be."

The vet ran up just then, Jake and Maggie right behind him.

"We've got to get an I.V. started," Lee said. "Jake, get the oxygen."

Another paroxysm struck, set off by the touch of the doctor's hand as he slid in the needle. Max went rigid, his eyeballs rolling up until only the whites appeared. His body twitched spasmodically, hooves thrashing, head jerking, a terrible keening sound coming from deep inside.

A sob came from Ellie's throat.

"He needs darkness and quiet," the vet said softly. "As you just saw, even a touch can set off a spasm." Jake reappeared with the oxygen and as soon as the paroxysm had ended, Max's soft dark muzzle was covered and the oxygen turned on.

"His pulse is extremely weak," Lee said. "I'd say he's taken the largest dose by far."

A shudder rippled through Clay. Ellie rested her cheek against his shoulder. She could feel the fearful pounding of his heart.

"Will he make it?" Clay asked while the vet checked the dosage and the short-acting barbiturate continued to flow.

"Too soon to tell."

"I'll be right outside if you need me." Jake climbed to his feet and silently left them, joining Maggie outside the stall door. He closed it behind him, throwing the stall into shadow.

Ellie swallowed past the thick lump in her throat. "Is there anything else we can do?"

Lee released a sorrowful sigh and shook his head. "At this point, I'm afraid not. I've got to be truthful. It doesn't look good." Coming to his feet, he moved toward the door. "I need to check on Lass. I'll be back as soon as I can."

Clay nodded. Lee left them and the stall fell into semi-darkness. Faint light slanted in through an air vent above the door. Max whimpered and tried to lift his head, but the stallion was just too weak. His chest moved in short shallow pants.

"It's all right, boy, you're going to make it," Clay said softly, and refit the oxygen mask. His hands shook where he held it over Max's nose.

A shuddering breath whispered out. "I can't stand to see him like this," Clay said.

Ellie reached for his hand. "Just keep talking to him, Clay, the way you always do. I'm sure Max can hear you. He'll know you're here."

"Talk to him," Clay said, his voice turning gruff. "Stupid for a grown man to talk to a horse. He's just an animal after all. Just a dumb animal. If he dies, he dies. There are dozens of others who could take his place. He's just a horse."

Ellie laid her palm against Clay's cheek. It felt as cold as his hand. His jaw was clamped, his muscles rigid, as if he shared his friend's pain. He turned his head away, but not before she felt the wetness on his cheeks that dampened her fingers.

"It's all right, Clay. I know you love him."

"He's just a horse," he repeated, but his voice cracked, making the words come out low and strained.

"Not to you," Ellie said softly. "He's Max. And he's your friend." Max's shallow breathing filled the room. The musky smell of straw mingled with the sweet smell of alfalfa and the stallion's familiar scent. He shuddered, grew rigid, then released a last, final, noiseless breath.

Clay closed his eyes, fighting the burning sting of tears and the terrible ache in his chest. When he looked down at Max, a shaft of sunlight touched the stallion's red-brown ears. *So much heart,* he thought. And wondered how he'd ever be able to replace him.

He felt like that same little boy who'd taken the jump wrong and broken his horse's leg. This time it wasn't his fault but that didn't stop the pain he felt inside. They'd been a team, he and Max. One of the best in the world. In Seoul, they might have proven it beyond a doubt. Without Max, Clay wasn't certain he wanted to go.

He swallowed hard, his eyes still locked on the animal's beautiful ears. Just hours ago, Clay had been rubbing them as Max so loved.

They'd ridden well today, one of their best performances ever. How much further might they have gone? What greatness could have been theirs? Together, they might have won the gold.

Lock it away, Clay told himself. *Forget the pain.* He had done it before. He could do it again. He had Ellie to think of now.

Still, as hard as he tried, he couldn't quite shut down his emotions.

In a last, small gesture of affection, Clay ran his hand along Max's sleek neck as he had so many times before. *Such a beautiful animal,* he thought.

Max managed a faint whiffle, and Clay started, realizing the stallion wasn't yet dead.

"He's a fighter, Clay," Ellie said softly.

With a steadying breath, Clay turned and buried his face in her hair. Ellie's arms went around his neck, and Clay just held her.

"Thank you," he said. *For understanding* were his unspoken words.

"I love you," she said.

In minutes that seemed hours, Lee returned. "He's still breathing. He hasn't given up yet. If the spasms stop completely, we'll administer a gastric lavage using a potassium permanganate solution.

This isn't over until it's over."

Clay felt a surge of hope. He felt Ellie's hand in his and laced their fingers together.

Later, during the long hours of the evening, Jake called the team together and explained what had happened. He left out nothing, including the part he had played. He didn't ask for forgiveness, only that they try to understand.

His resignation, he promised—over their extremely vocal protests—would be tendered as soon as they reached the States. In the end, he agreed to accompany the team to Seoul in an unofficial capacity.

Daniel asked that he explain the Soviet Government's cooperation in the incident, the steps they were taking to apprehend the individuals responsible. The Russians wanted it made clear that they were in no way sanctioning what appeared to be acts of violence by a small group of influential men bent on destroying U.S./Soviet relations.

Good will with the United States would continue, they promised. *Glasnost* would succeed.

Jake prayed their words were true and wondered what earth-shattering changes might take place in the world if they were.

Ellie and Clay sat with Max throughout the night. By morning it was obvious the big blood bay stallion was going to live. Max nuzzled Clay awake where he lay sleeping next to Ellie on the straw.

Clay sat up. Reaching out, he ran a hand along the animal's powerful neck. "So, you wouldn't let them win." Max nickered as if he understood. "You never did like to lose."

Ellie came to her knees beside Clay. "He's all right?"

"Looks like he's going to make it. He'll need some special pampering for a while, but he deserves it."

Ellie slipped her arms around Clay's waist. "I knew he could do it."

"I see Max is up before the two of you," Jake said as he opened the top half of the stall door, standing arm-in-arm with Maggie.

"Clay, I'm so glad for you," Maggie said.

"What about the others—Lass and the British groom?" Clay asked.

"We got to them in time," Jake told him. "The plan failed. Everyone's going to be okay."

Ellie sagged with relief. "That's wonderful news."

"I don't want to think what would have happened if the plan had succeeded," Clay said.

Maggie leaned into Jake, who wrapped an arm around her.

"Everyone's all right," Clay said. "And it appears the two of you are going to be fine, as well." He smiled, dimpling his cheeks.

"We're getting married." Jake looked at Maggie. "We'd like you both to be there."

Ellie grinned. "We wouldn't miss it." Max tossed his beautiful head and nickered. "Apparently, Max approves."

Everyone laughed.

"When?" Clay asked.

"As soon as we get home. You?"

"The same. Unfortunately, if I know my father, we'll have to endure the whole damned ritual twice. He'll want some huge social affair, and I'm not about to wait that long."

"Well, one thing's certain," Jake said. "There'll be an error on the programs in Seoul. There'll be a new *Chef d' Equipe* for the U.S. team. And the assistant director and one of the riders will both have new last names."

Ellie looked at Clay. "In that case...." She flashed him a challenging grin. "One way or another—a Whitfield is bound to win the gold!"

AUTHOR'S NOTE

The Berlin Wall was completed August 13, 1961, closing off the final portion of West Berlin from Soviet controlled East Germany.

Glasnost was a policy introduced by Mikhail Gorbachev in the mid 1980s that called for increased openness and transparency in the Soviet Union. It contributed to the fall of the Berlin Wall on November 9, 1989, just a little over a year after the conclusion of this story.

I hope you enjoyed LETHAL JOURNEY, a tale of the U.S. Equestrian Show Jumping Team and its amazing horses and riders. If you get the opportunity to see a Grand Prix event, I promise you won't be disappointed.

This book was my first Romantic Suspense, written more than twenty-five years ago. Since then, I've written dozens of others. If you enjoyed this one, I hope you'll look for some of those.

Until next time, very best wishes and happy reading, Kat

Made in the USA
Middletown, DE
28 January 2025

70461647R00166